P9-AOX-598

The Textures of Silence

THE TEXTURES OF SILENCE

Gordon Vorster

WILLIAM MORROW AND COMPANY, INC.
NEW YORK • 1984

First published in 1982 in South Africa by Howard Timmins (Pty) Ltd.

Library of Congress Cataloging in Publication Data

Vorster, Gordon.
The textures of silence.

Originally published: Cape Town, S.A. : H. Timmins, 1982
I. Title.
PR9369.3.V67T4 1984 823 83-25064
ISBN: 0-688-03494-2

Printed in the United States of America

First U.S. Edition

1 2 3 4 5 6 7 8 9 10

BOOK DESIGN BY VICTORIA HARTMAN

In memory of
my mother
Nancy Christina Vorster.

Acknowledgments

My sincerest thanks to the many physicians, surgeons and specialists in several fields, who cannot be named individually, for ethical reasons, as well as the social workers, therapists, and nurses who gave me so much of their time and patience during the research phase of this work.

All surgical procedures described in this novel have been performed in South Africa.

G.V. 1976
Crocodile River Valley
Broederstroom
Republic of South Africa.

Contents

Not for these I raise
The song of thanks and praise;
    But for those obstinate questionings
    Of sense and outward things,
    Fallings from us, vanishings;
    Blank misgivings of a creature
Moving about in worlds not realised,
High instincts before which our mortal nature
Did tremble like a guilty thing surprised:
But for those first affections,
Those shadowy recollections,
Which, be they what they may,
Are yet the fountain-light of all our day,
Are yet the master-light of all our seeing.

Thou, whose exterior semblance doth belie
Thy soul's immensity.

    Thou eye among the blind,
That, deaf and silent, read'st the eternal deep
Haunted forever by the eternal mind.

William Wordsworth
extracts from: Ode. Intimations of Immortality

Silent silver lights and darks undreamed of
Where I hush and bless myself with silence.

Robert Browning
from: One Word More

The Textures of Silence

1

DANIEL CILLIERS

I have only recently begun to use words, but my tuition has been such that, while I make perhaps too much use of the first thousand selected by the wise ones at Oxford who compiled "Basic English," as being adequate for communication, my teacher has been a person given not only to Victorianisms but also to a robust manner. If I should appear therefore to lapse occasionally into a rather coarse way of speech it is because of this teacher, whom I will adore until the second darkness, and in whose silken hands I place everything I have.

This is probably the first time in your experience that you have been spoken to by a person who has been, for many years, nearly a lifetime in fact, blind, deaf, dumb, and worse, with very little control over his muscles and limbs. This has been my condition, brought about because of an accident when I was a baby only a few weeks old. This accident left me a spastic child, blind and with bi-lateral deafness. The late great lady, Helen Keller, was a similar case to mine; with these two exceptions: She could make full use of her body. The other exception was that she was incurable from a medical point of view.

For the first fifty years of my life I experienced only the vaguest of sensations. I knew, for instance, a form of light. They tell me that this must have happened when I was moved from the sunlit garden to the cool darkness of the nursery. There were, also, certain audio experiences, caused by my ability to feel vibrations. And it was at the age of fifty that I was first brought out into the open, having known only vaguenesses, not even my name, which I was later told was Daniel Cilliers, or Daan.

Today I often hear people using words like "interesting" and "fascinating." They are words I find most difficult to understand. What is interesting? What is fascinating, and what is beautiful? Everything, surely.

A certain number of years have passed since the day I was taken in hand by Maria and Maryna van der Kolff, the district nurse and social welfare officer of the village of Skeerpoort in the Transvaal, and her sister. I think that the best way to make a record of what I remember, for the purpose of medical and sociological study, is to attempt to start at the beginning. Obviously I can only report what I heard later about the first fifty years of my life, about which I have very little to say anyway, not even having been aware that I existed as a personality, or as a problem, or that time was passing. I shall attempt just to get the facts into some sort of order because Maria has insisted that I tell it myself. As she says: "Anyone else can only make a balls-up of it, and you were screwed anyway, so you may as well tell it as it was, a total balls-up of a life." I agreed, on condition that when it came to her part in the description of events, she would do the same. I must say that I do not agree with her about its being a balls-up in any way; that, in fact, I find it to have been singularly satisfying, but the reasons for my gardenia attitudes will no doubt reveal themselves dawnlike as my tale progresses from the darkness of my vault life.

I must confess to you that Maria is an outspoken person in every way, and that she is scorned by the so-called proper people of the village. But when I use her frank form of speech it is not to titillate those who may be reading these words, but merely to tell about her, the way she is, without trying to turn her into some sort of angel of mercy or grace. She is that anyway, but such words make her puke, which, my Roget tells me, is a synonym for throwing-up, originating in Britain, but beloved of the Americans.

My mother, Bettina, had died at the age of seventy-one, and on the day of her death I was fifty years of age.

In the village, for those fifty years, everybody had known that the Cilliers family had an idiot son, deaf, dumb, blind, and without much in the way of a useful body. His sense of touch must have been, they thought, pretty retarded as well, because he had to be forced to move in the first years of his life. Today, my conversations with doctors seem to confirm that the tragic accident, so far-reaching in its consequences, had not only caused me to lose my sense of hearing, but that a certain amount of shock had also been present during my early years. Traumatic, psychological withdrawal which, thank God, had not been permanent, had also been a part of my childhood personality. I had not experienced enough of life as a three-week-old infant to withdraw completely from it. So, what was at first thought to be under-developed tactile senses, or even injured nerves, which would have been incurable, turned out to be a condition which healed itself, from within over a period of some years. At least I didn't seem to mind the winter or the summer. Not knowing whether I was mad, or simpleton, they did not know what to do with me. The family physician, a Doctor Cloete, had seen me very many times, and had assured my parents that these things sometimes have a way of coming right, and that his advice was that they should exercise not only patience, but also my little limbs so that they would not "waste" away.

There was another solution to the problem of caring for me. It was to place me in an institution, where I could be attended to. But this was in 1921, when the only institutions were asylums, where lunatics were kept, and my parents had very good reasons for not wanting me to be placed there, although there was one nearby in the town of Krugersdorp, some thirty miles to the east: Very few people survived in those places. They were more like prisons than hospitals. Also, lunacy was in those days popularly thought to be a hereditary disease. As it was, the problem never arose, as my parents did not again have children.

Lunatics had to be committed to an asylum by at least a minister of the church, the family, a justice of the peace, or a magistrate, as these institutions were not strictly considered to be places of rehabilitation, but rather vaults of incarceration where the madmen and women could create their own Bedlams out of sight, and just as often out of the minds of their neighbours and relatives. Doors, they were, behind which to hide family embarrassments. I was fortunate that my parents Dawid and Bettina Cilliers, had been talked into some sort of idiotic hope by our family doctor, Anton Cloete. Had I, with my nearly total disabilities been placed in an asylum, there can be very little doubt that I would not have survived. The expert and devoted care that was needed in my case could not have been provided in the under-staffed and badly equipped mental hospitals of that time.

But this is no place for an examination of the Bedlams of 1921. They existed and I was lucky not to be in one of them. Doctor Cloete had told my parents that there was hope that my illnesses would pass, for I had bright blue eyes, pink ears like little shells, ten toes and a pair of testicles, a penis and a navel and a mop of fair white hair. My proportions were perfect and I sucked at the black breast of my nanny with proper greed. My mother, Bettina, was a lady of quality, and in those days ladies of quality kept their figures for the demands of fashion, their husbands, or their lovers. The glorious breasts of the daguerreotypes, in the family photo-albums, illustrating ladies of wasp-waisted beauty, bursting from their bodices, were not meant for turning into razor strops by a succession of greedy mouths in those far-off pill-less days, when even the vaginal douche was considered risque.

I must once again apologise for a certain knowledge of females, their insides, and their mores, morals, manners and mannerisms. It would not seem proper that a person, unable to speak or hear anything only a relatively few years ago would now be able to write about these things with a certain superficial knowledge, and I must assure you that the Mesdames Maryna and Maria van der Kolff are excellent teachers, if a bit on the frank side when it comes to medical or anatomical facts.

My tactile senses returned slowly and over a period of some years with the self-healing of my shock-withdrawal. I have no knowledge of it, but Mina, my black nurse, has been able to describe quite a lot of it to me. People, as a rule, do not remember anything about their infant days. Usually only a few major incidents are fixed in the conscious memory from about the age of three onwards, so I am told. They don't remember a thing about the years of early infancy. Now, if that is the case with persons who are normal in every way, with all their senses intact, there can be little wonder at the fact that I remember nothing at all of the things that may have happened to me during my young years.

I don't really remember anything at all, only a shadowy, vague tunnel, with occasional spasms of pain as landmarks, stretching far back into what I now know to be the past. I have, even now, very little sense of time. It is, to me, too much of an abstract concept. I never grew into time like other people, never experienced it as an important fact or factor in life, so its existence is something that has very little meaning for me. When people speak of it they say things like, "what a shame, all those wasted years." I have no such feelings because I don't really know, yet, what a year is. In this case, although I've tried, I am still a six-year-old with the time-perception of a child of that age.

My capacity for reason had never been impaired, the thinking part of my brain had been intact, uninjured. There just had not been any facilities for communication with the world outside my tunnel. When it had finally become a possibility I took to it with great enthusiasm. In this respect I am not a boy of six but a normal, gregarious, talkative adult, only too happy to be able to use words.

Which brings me to a point that I may as well get out of the way right now, because it is an embarrassment for me to speak of it, but I have to.

I knew when my bowels needed evacuation, and I knew when it was necessary to pass water. So, although I was a semi-Zombie in all other respects, I was at least a house-trained one. I felt pain, such as abdominal spasms, but I had no idea what they were, and I remember only that when such things happened I felt a grating texture in what I now know to be my throat. This must have been some primitive urge on my part to cry, or at least to whimper. I don't know. I've been told that I made certain noises, which meant only that I had vocal chords. But I wasn't conscious of any of these things. It was just greyness, darker or lighter as my surroundings were changed while they moved me about.

Being a family of fair means, in fact, wealthy for those depression years, it had been no problem for my father to make a boarded and bricked encampment abutting onto the main house, just off the kitchen wing where the dogs, geese, chickens and I were kept. Not that we all lived together, you understand; my father had been a kindly man, and he had loved me as my mother did. Had they not loved me it would have been easily done, my death I mean, for in those days children did die of neglect, often. In fact, I know now, having with Maria's aid investigated as much as possible of my family background, that a certain niece Anna had died of neglect in the village of Christiana when I was about fourteen years of age. She had been left in the yard after her illegitimate birth, and the dogs and black servants had tried to keep her alive, as dogs and blacks will do, but she became part of a statistic of infant mortality, which was terrifyingly high in those days. They are all statistics now, that family of mine. I am the only one left.

But I have a lot of other evidence of the love that my parents must have had for me. My accommodations, true, were in the yard, but they were very special. There was a room that had a door that swung open both ways. It is still there, and I often go to look at it, because I inherited the place and I live here now. It was so constructed that it was virtually impossible for me to hurt myself as I moved from place to place, with the halting, painful, jerky movements of the spastic.

There must have been times when I was considered potentially violent, because a callus on my wrist reveals that I had been chained for most of my life, a length of blue galvanised wire stretched the thirty yards of what I refer to as my "run," but not bitterly. Please do not think that any of the things I have to tell you is black or gall or bitter. I am content with my very bruised gardenias, and last year's carnations have a perfume of heaven.

And, oh my God, how I love the weeds of the fields and the flies. Can you, in your total knowledge of your life, love a maggot? Can you understand how I am able to love that little brother who will one day consume me in my coffin? It is because I *know* of him, I *know* that he *exists*, whereas before I had no such knowledge, only the vague darkness of the groping mind, not knowing that it is groping, not knowing that it is a mind, without even the understanding of the eternal earthworm. A nothingness with, somewhere, far beneath the murky surface, a somethingness. Not realisation, not the beginnings of understanding, only just a texture of feeling, on surfaces like the feel of marble or the sense of the coarse sandiness of carborundum, a far-away distant sense of non-feeling. To attempt to describe it, now that I know the world, and I know things to which we can relate, you and I, I would say that what I was able to feel, to experience, to live, in those first fifty years would be, in ordinary terms, say, a remembrance of a perfume that had never existed in your life, that you had never smelt, and in remembering, forgetting what you are trying to feel, and in forgetting, remembering that it never was. Perfumes are important to me, because of the things my mother did with them.

I was loved. Of course, I didn't know it. I didn't know that my diapers were being changed. I had been conscious only of the fact that my bowels had moved or that I had urinated. After that there was no feeling, no discomfort, the internal problems had been solved. And yet I was loved.

Do you realise how moving it can be when you research your own life, go back fifty years, and with the doggedness of a detective you discover what the relationships of your life must have been? Having done that research, can you imagine what it means when you come up with the undeniable and ungainsayable fact that, for those fifty years, you were loved, although fate had never made you aware of it? It would have been so easy for my parents to desert me to the tender mercies of the many servants on the farm. And I know that they did, but only to a certain extent. Many of the days of my life were spent being looked after by servants, and, as I have said, I know that I was suckled by a black woman called Mina, but, although I was at first offended by this, what seemed to me to be a lack of motherly love, I found later that it was the generally done thing, a mark of quality common among the best people. And, what is more, the medical opinions of that time fluctuated greatly between what was best for the baby, the mother's milk of the effete European strain, or the strong milk of the African, goatlike in its richness. There are several papers in the archives of the medical schools of the southern states of America, written in that period and before, in which this point is strongly debated by what were respected authorities of the time. Today, I am grateful that I lay at the breast of an African woman as well, because it gives my identity a further dimension. Afterwards, my researches took me to the Biblical countries, via Rome and Athens, and I learnt a great deal about the systems of wet-nursing that had been in use through the ages, a subject that fascinated me so much that I was almost on the point of going into it in great detail here, thinking that whatever fascinates me must be of interest to you also. It is my way of thinking that could be important, because the thoughts of a hastily educated mature man of fifty, who is in reality only seven years of age, are perhaps unique. People say that my knowledge of words is remarkable for the very few years of my education, but it must be remembered that my brain had never been damaged, and it was mature when it first started absorbing external knowledge, a far cry from the undeveloped and rebellious brain of the seven-year-old. Much of my education came from the Bible, and I have spent many of my most interesting hours listening to the voices of the great readers of our time quoting the lovely words. I like its abstractions, I understand them, and they are very appealing to one whose life has been a series of abstractions. But, as for the eternal life, I have my own thoughts on that subject, having already experienced quite a bit of it myself; but, this is no time for such speculations.

The point remains, I was loved. My mother could easily have thought that my olfactory senses were totally nullified by a nerve block, which is about the simplest way of describing a medical condition that has an enormously long and complicated definition in which you can have no possible interest. There was every possibility that the accident could have hurt or even severed the hair-fine strands of the nerves that carried the messages of perfume or of corruption to the brain. Once damaged, these little telegraph lines are too delicate to repair, and there had always been a ninety per cent chance that I could not smell anything no matter how delicate, no matter how sharp.

In my "run" of thirty yards, the blue wire to which my chain was attached ran through a carefully considered, fantastically grouped, series of plants, shrubs, bushes and flowers that created olfactory experiences, wild thyme, rosemary, basil and other herbs, roses and gardenias, carnations. A thirty-yard-long corridor of scents that my mother had planted just in case I could smell, just in case there was something for me, beyond the besnotted nose, the drooling corners of the mouth, the wet eyes and the strange noise I was able to make, like a puppy missing its master, but suffering from the voice of a goat.

I should like to make a point of my voice and the noises I was able to indulge in, because, when I used my vocal chords for the grunts, the vibrations did penetrate my severely damaged hearing mechanism in the form of vibrations. I was able to at least communicate with myself in an extremely limited manner, just a faint awareness, perhaps, but I am very proud of the fact that I have vocal chords, not always a good thing in a human being. How wonderful to be able to use those words "human being" and to know that I am one of them. How magnificent to be among the communicating gods, those with minds, voices, and pens, no matter how much anguish there is in my heart even now as I write, for I do assure you that there is a great anguish here because of something that I have found out, about the reasons for my accident; nevertheless, how godly to be able to feel anguish, pain, joy and even to know that the worm waits for you, not far away.

But poor mother did not plant her aromatic herbs and perfumed flowers in vain, because they made their impression of joy on my nostrils. And I know also, from what Mina and the other servants tell me, that the kitchen prepared my dishes of food even more carefully than anything that was served at the table in the main dining-room. The flavourings and the seasonings had to be more right and more subtle than they had been for my parents and their occasional guests.

I know that I received all the love that a child of those years could expect from fairly busy parents who had to run a farm of great size, and that my welfare was exceedingly well cared for by devoted servants, particularly Mina, who loved and nursed me even more carefully than if she had been my own mother. You must remember that I was regarded not as a cripple, a spastic, or any of the identifiabilities of medicine today. Being without most of the recognised senses I was regarded as pretty senseless, which was another word for lunatic. And among certain African tribes the lunatic is a holy thing in a house. That is why Mina, my wet-nurse, having come from such a tribe, regarded me not just as a job but as a sacred charge, although she denies thinking of her work in such terms.

What a shame I find it now that I never felt the tenderness of my motley collection of parents, so that I could just for once, perhaps, in my fifty years, have clasped one of them closely to me. I would have liked them to know that there was absolutely no necessity for them to keep me chained, that I would not have harmed them, that I would have loved them also. It's such a waste, to know that all those years eyes looked at me with tears and sometimes with fear, and that never once could I look back at them and smile, and make them feel good. And what a horrible waste for them, day in and out, every week, month and year that passed, trying to make life in some way bearable for me. I wish I had known that there had been people about me who had felt concern for me, for my comfort, for my happiness.

As for my father, the evidences of care that he had left all over my "run" are even more profuse than mother's perfumes were. He had been a skilled carpenter, and he had made my room a model of all that is practical in the care of a patient with my singular needs. There were no sharp points or places where

I could be hurt. Once I was inside the wire relaxed, but never to the extent where it could become tangled or dangerous to me, and, although I have mentioned a callus about my wrist, it was rubbed there by the softest of tooled leather sheaths, with an almost gossamer chamois touching the skin.

Mina was the one who cared for me during all the years of childhood and puberty, when I had to be bathed and clothed twice a day. And Mina was the one who house-trained me, so that I could go to the toilet myself. Of post-toilet hygiene I of course knew nothing, and there was no way to train me to cleanse myself, because I just was not there, I wasn't anywhere, not even in limbo, not even waiting. But father had built a number of contraptions to assure that I rose, walked about, and exercised without knowing what I was doing. He had made various things, he may have thought of them as toys, that I could, if I wished, touch and handle without hurting myself. He and Hans Arp would have been good friends, he knew what a rounded or an egg-shape was, he knew what to do with a corner, and where to lay a stress.

The lessons of his shapes have been invaluable. Today they are in my room, glories of purity, that I frequently handle with amazement.

Of all the things that were done during those early years to bring life to my lifelessness, nothing was done with more intelligence than the making of those large shapes of perfectly polished wood, the toys of my incomprehension, my years of shadow.

Of the nursery of my childhood I remember nothing. I can now see that it was a space enclosed by four walls, three doors, and a window. The doors led to Mina's room on the porch outside, the corridor, and my mother's bedroom. When I had become old enough to occupy the outside room, with the perfumed avenue, which my parents had constructed for me, the nursery had been turned into a little library and study. I don't think that it was ever used because my father's office, from which he administered the estate, was in one of the front reception rooms, and my mother's little gilt desk was at a window in her bedroom. It was in this desk that she kept her doubly-locked journal.

I had been born and I grew up in the years between the two world wars, which, fortunately for me, was the golden age of physiotherapy, with new machines and methods being discovered almost daily. My father was an avid reader of papers and books about the subject, and he kept in touch with all the major manufacturers throughout the world, often ordering a machine which he thought would help exercise my limbs, because he was determined that my body should not waste away through the usual inactivity of the cerebrally palsied.

I do not know just how much of his time my father gave to me, but it must have been a great deal. He was, like many a gentleman of his day, a woodworker of great skill. There was a sort of pride in carpentry that lifted it above the normal accomplishments of trade, and a man lost no face at all in making a perfect cabinet for a friend, or a window-frame for the rectory, or even a table for his own house. My father's particular hobby was the making of pulpits, and what is strange about this is that he was not a very religious man in the orthodox sense. I know that he had made the pulpits for the Dutch Reformed church and the Methodist hall of Skeerpoort in the days when the Methodist community was still strong enough to hold weekly services in its own church. The church at Skeerpoort is now used by our coloured community and is, I believe, interdenominational. It belongs to our family, actually to me personally, and I often go to service there because the coloured people don't mind, and I certainly don't care which God I worship because I like them all.

The pulpit still stands, and I have employed someone to make sure that the silken sheen of the wood is polished at least once a week. It was very important to me that the little church, which had fallen almost into decay, was restored to look exactly as it must have been in my parents' lifetime on the day of its inauguration, with my father modestly sitting halfway down the aisle, in his usual place, and the Reverend Doctor George Webb, mounting the steps, as the little pipe organ, with its foot pedals creaking away quietly, sang out a shaky Bach, played by the slightly trembling hands of the red-nosed Mrs. Winters; the choir singing and my mother lightly touching my father's arm, in pride, with a lace-gloved hand that had been wrist-perfumed with the most delicate of lavenders. At least, that is how I think of that day, and of my parents, and it gives me great pleasure to do so. These pictures of peace live softly in my mind, visions of the days before the troubles.

As our family name is Cilliers, which is of French origin, my forefathers must have come to Southern Africa at the time of the persecution and fleeing of the Huguenots, but, as the centuries passed, we became a part of the Boer community, which simply means a settler group of farmers, later to become part of the South African nation. Then, at the time of the emancipation of the slaves and other ill-advised moves by the British, who always did the right things in Africa, but, it seems to me, invariably at the wrong time, the family must have joined the great trek and ended up in the Transvaal. They were to find that you do not get away from an Englishman that easily.

I think that that is about as much history as is necessary here, because it has all been told, and, if you are interested, read those who write interestingly about Africa, like Stuart Cloete and Robert Ardrey, two authors who appear to have a lot of respect for both fact and its re-telling in interesting ways. I like people who know what they are doing. I suppose I must have inherited my father's respect for craftsmanship.

What I was trying to explain was why we, the Cilliers family, were not members of the Dutch Reformed Church, but of the Methodist Church. You see, my mother Bettina's maiden name was Paulson. I know that the family was English-speaking although I believe that its origins must have been Scandinavian, and the Paulsons were Methodists. She had met Dawid Cilliers when they were both only seventeen years of age, and at that time my father had not yet undergone the catechism necessary for a youth of that time to be a member of the august DRC. This catechism entailed giving up two nights a week to Bible Study, as well as certain attendances on Sundays, at least twice at the almost continuous-performance services, and, as Maria would put it, he found all this religion a huge pain in the arse, as most children do when God is shoved down their throats in huge threatening doses. I believe that one should grow into God, and He into you. I may be wrong, but I think that one's relationship with God should be a partnership.

Now, the Methodists required little more than a knowledge of the Lord's Prayer and the Ten Commandments for full membership of their church so my father, always one for doing things differently, informed my paternal grandparents of his intention of becoming a Methodist. They survived the horrible shock admirably, and it must have been dreadful for them if what I have heard of those bigoted days is true. This ghastly business was followed in quick succession by another equally awful announcement on the part of the prodigal: Now that he was a fully-fledged Methodist, he was going to take, as his bride, one, Bettina Paulson, spinster, of Skeerpoort, an English-speaking girl. The shock must have been somewhat alleviated by the fact that both the Paulsons and the Cilliers were among the wealthiest families in the area, and that my maternal and paternal grandfathers had, if not a friendship going for them, at least a respectful acquaintance, both having been seen at one time in the billiard saloon of the Greater Magaliesburg Hotel. Although my grandparents spoke different languages, and held differing political views, they were as close to being friends as circumstances would permit in those days, and at least they enjoyed similar pleasures. Soon after my parents had been married, both sets of grandparents had gone to attend a function in Pretoria and, on the way there, all four had been killed in a level crossing accident near Broederstroom.

I have gone into my antecedents in some detail because I am told that the medical people are interested in hereditary factors. Something to do with certain things called genes that appear to be responsible for a lot of our behaviour. I should hate to blame my faults on my parents, and the genes I got from them are most welcome to reside in me, in spite of the troubles.

I had felt violence when my person was most vulnerable, so I have been told, although I can't remember the incident of my twenty-first day on this earth, that caused me to withdraw into a boyhood existence in my mind, for some years. The injuries of that day made me a spastic for most of my life, certainly all of my youth and middle age, returning me to the world when I was already past fifty. My sense of time being somewhat lacking, I can be unimpassioned, and dispassionate, about this, but the violence that had occurred on the day they had found out that I had been going blind from the moment of my birth has, by my learning of it, stirred some kind of memory at the end of the tunnel. It isn't anything definite, just a vague knowledge, or an atmosphere, a shivering fear, a slight sensation of gruesome violence, as you would remember a now-faded nightmare.

What is the difference, after all, between a massive and a little violence? Some few years ago a young lady decided to do away with her lover's wife, so she stabbed her, or caused her to be stabbed with a pair of scissors. This became a cause célèbre.

What is so strange is that we kill each other, all over the world, with red-hot bullets and pieces of shrapnel, and we burn our children with fires and spray them with inextinguishable napalm, and that's all right.

Why is a pair of scissors so dreadful a weapon that newspapers will, for months, hang onto every word of prosecution and defence, while a new weapon that will destroy millions is old hat, not even good for two inches in the middle pages, where the boring stories are?

I believe that a little violence is as massive as a massacre, and my violence, which was committed upon me, was only a small, momentary, uncontrolled violence, and yet it was a massacre.

I will not have my violence made small, underplayed, relegated to the back pages. I want it to stand out for a long time, to remain in the memories of people, because I believe that it was terrible, and that anyone in this world who comes up against the values, and the lack of them, that caused my parents to commit my violence, must try to understand that we are all in the same boat, so that we can go forward as brothers, having committed our crimes, for which no court can ever find us guilty.

The problem is that we can be found to be legally insane, and this is the thought that is driving me a little mad now. A magistrate, upon application by a next of kin, can have had the power, and the glory to commit me to an institution for lunatics. After they had done their violence, and had settled down with its awesome result, that had been the one thing that my parents had spent fifty years at preventing, hiding me from those who said it would be best for me, for them, for everybody. And now it is staring me in the face. Now that I know what the words "staring" and "me" and "in" and "the" and "face" mean. These are the little terrors that come with delving too deeply into the past, and uncovering things that should have been allowed to sink away into the earth or into the fading memories of the old people. I think I will stop my delving, and let other people do the remembering, and the digging up, for other eyes to read. I have other appointments to keep.

2

MARYNA VAN DER KOLFF

My name is Maryna van der Kolff. It was I who told Daan of the events of the day when his mother's death was discovered, because I believe that those circumstances were gentle. Bettina Cilliers had lived as a recluse for a number of years. Her husband, Dawid, had died in his sixty-first year but she, although frailer in appearance, had survived for another decade. I believe she was a completely inactive person for most of that time, and had begun faltering in the exercising of her familial duties. She had withdrawn herself from virtually all of the social life of the village. The aged Reverend Doctor George Webb had called on her frequently, as the little church in which he had preached all his life had by that time, in 1971, fallen on low times. The Methodist population had dwindled to less than a quorum for a congregation, and the church had been given to the coloured people, who found solace in many different religions, so that it had become interdenominational. And a good thing too, because they gave life to the old building, being happy in their many ways of giving praise. Their singing, especially, was always lovely as it floated across the rich farmlands like an almost tangible mist.

I have been the district nurse and social worker here since 1942 and my duties were loosely defined and only half of them were official. I was supposed to visit all the schools, black and white, and see that the official programmes of anti T.B. X-rays, and the several compulsory inoculations were carried out and administered. Smallpox, yellow-fever, diphtheria, all that sort of thing; and I was also supposed to make sure that everybody was at least reasonably well fed. Among the white children this was no problem at all, although a number of very poor people lived in our area, but the black and coloured children were more difficult to help. It was not very easy to solve because it wasn't just a matter of providing food and clothes to the children. There were a number of charitable and semi-official organisations able to cope reasonably well with those troubles, but their efforts were hampered by a few discouraging local habits. There was, at that time, for instance, a district-wide drinking problem among both the poorer blacks and the whites, and often the new shoes and shirts, as well as the school books, would be sold and the money used for buying liquor. Once again, the problem was easily solved among the whites, as a call from the police sergeant and a few nights in the cells up on Thornhill would drive the fear of hell into the malefactors, especially as I would lash at them with my sharpest forms of speech. I could use curse-words like a sailor, and my vocabulary, as well as the volume of my voice, ensured that a stream of abuse, audible to the entire village, followed the wrongdoers all the way up the hill. But with the blacks it was more difficult, insuperable really, and although my 1½ ton Ford truck could be seen and heard from miles off as I chased the fear of God and Sergeant Hendricks into anyone who maltreated a child, mine was a battle that took a long time to fight before it was won. The whites capitulated easily, but some of the blacks were difficult. In those days there was just too much to be done and too few hands to do it. Today, things have changed, and I can have as many assistants as I need.

I had not often called on the Cilliers family, for personal reasons. They gave generously to the good causes anyway, and I worked in close collaboration with the ministers of the church and the missionary societies. The Cilliers family had been active in church affairs, because, as leaders of the community, it had been expected of them. They were wealthy, and I know that Dawid Cilliers, especially, had given much to the village. I believe that he had been responsible for the survival of its economy during the depression years of the twenties and thirties, before my arrival.

My early life there more than thirty years ago now, had been made up of dusty drives through the Magalies hills almost every day, always with some medical problem that my inexperience found difficult to solve. My 1½ ton Ford was the ambulance of the area, and very often the hearse also, and I frequently painted white the little boxwood coffins of my early failures, before the miracle drugs. Those were the days before the general distribution of the sulfa drugs and the antibiotics, and anything from laryngitis to a thorn in one's foot could be fatal, and very often was.

One day about five years ago, just on the brink of 1971, when I was a woman of fifty-six summers, I was doing my rounds in a little Landrover pick-up truck, something I had acquired because of the need for a four-wheel-drive vehicle during the rainy season. I was stopped at the gate of the Cilliers's Estate by one of Mina's grandchildren, who had been told to stop any car of any sort that happened to be passing by and to bring the people to what they called the Great House. Mina was the nursemaid who had looked after the retarded son, Daan, since his birth.

Mina had reached the age of sixty-seven years and had cared for Daan for almost all of the years of her life, although she did have a large three-generation family of her own, who were then, as is their custom, attempting to care for her. But she had at that time refused to retire, as she still felt responsible for her charge. She had been waiting on the front porch as I drew up, sitting patiently with her bare feet on the almost white-polished planks of the wide verandah that shaded three sides of the house.

"Yes Mina," I asked, "why are you stopping people at the gate?"

"The telephone lines went in the storm last night," she answered.

"All right Mina, I'll report it." I made as if to leave.

"That is not all, there is another thing."

I knew then, that there was something serious, because a light thing like a cold or a broken arm would have been spoken of differently, in another tone of voice, using other phrases, with a different droop to the shoulders and a firmer attitude of the toes on the porch-wood. Also, the wood had been freshly polished, and the stoep looked as it did on Sundays, when company sometimes came to tea in the afternoons, a habit of the district that had not really been approved of by Dawid Cilliers, although he had tolerated it in his good-natured way. But I had been in the district for too many years to break the protocol-manners of Skeerpoort.

"You say," I said, "that there is another thing?"

Mina stood up, almost ritually. "A heavy thing," she said.

"It must be a heavy thing, let me help."

"It is so heavy," said Mina, "that there can be no help."

"I'm sorry," I said. I knew that this meant that there had been a death in the house, but I had to hear her out before doing anything.

"She was as our mother, and our grandmother, and the spirit of the good fields was always in her. Now who will be our mother? Who will sit at the great yellow-wood table, and who will drink the little wines of the Magalies mountains?"

This was all nonsense, of course. Bettina had been a stranger in her own house for fifty years. But, she had occupied the position as wife of the master, officially, and had sat at the opposite end of the table from him, so there were certain ritual things that had to be said, as Mina was of the Balobedu tribe.

"Take me to her," I said.

"You will find her ready. She has been washed and her arms have been crossed on her breast, and she is wearing the things she made for this time, because she had been expecting it for some years now, and the coffin is ready as it has been ready ever since the Oubaas Dawid died, when she asked for two, and kept one in the store-room."

"You have done your work well, Mina. I'm sure her spirit is pleased with you. When did it happen?"

"Some time in the night, not too late, and she knew that it was happening. I was with her, to help her go. You must ride to town, to the magistrates and the dominees and the lawyers, Miss Maryna, and you must tell them to come, and we will dig the grave next to Oubaas Dawid's grave, and we will make ready a song that we will sing at the funeral."

It hurt me, deeply, that Bettina should be buried in the cattle kraal, but I could do nothing about it.

"And what will you do," I asked, "when it is over? When there are no people left here. You have been a long time here, Mina. What will you do now that your work is over?"

"My work," said Mina, "will only be over when Baas Daan has been finally taken care of."

Then I remembered, yes of course, there was that other, hidden one, the idiot child who had grown up in the backyard. But the subject had been so sensitive and had not been spoken of for so many years, it had been indelicate to do so. I had not forgotten him, because there had been a time when he had been an important person in my life, but that had been ten years ago, in 1961.

In 1942, I had called on Bettina during my first week in the village, but she had refused to mention their son. Later, I had helped with certain physiotherapeutic advice, when asked to do so by Dawid Cilliers, the boy's father. Daan, the spastic son, was the silent one, and he was so little trouble that there had never been any necessity to speak of him at all. And in the village people stayed silent about him. It was one of those things that the entire community seemed to agree about, and it was very rare to hear any conversation concerning the Cilliers's son. I suppose it must have been a built-in courtesy. Dawid Cilliers wasn't one to give himself airs, but people respected him because of his own dignity and the actions that caused him to be the most esteemed citizen of the area.

I had, in my capacity as social worker and district nurse, left Daan alone, as I knew that nothing could be done for him other than the exercises that he was already receiving daily. I had often discussed these matters with his father, but never with anyone else. And, since Dawid Cilliers had been dead for ten years, I had had very little contact with the Great House, having heard of Daan's condition only through the occasional very slight amount of talk still about in the village. His case had been of such long duration that he had become forgotten to all but the most hardened of gossips. Personally, I checked occasionally, and surreptitiously, but he had been in good hands throughout his life. There was nothing more I could do, except arrange for an occasional new therapeutic apparatus. I never discussed these matters with Bettina, all business being conducted through Andries Burger, the farm manager.

Daan's parents had never invited discussion of his condition with the people of the village, and only the minister, the doctor, and I had ever felt free to advise and help his father where it was possible. His mother had never allowed reference to Daan in her presence, and ignored any attempt at conversation of that kind, from whatever quarter it may have come. And now, for the first time in all those years, he had been referred to. His file was open again. He was alive and officially back in the world. His existence came as a shock to many people, because you do not talk about a potato or a carrot or a turnip year after year.

He did not even have the useful qualities of a vegetable, or the endearing ones of a pet pig, dog or donkey. So can you wonder that the silence about him was broken only by a mention, in passing, to a newcomer, with an admonishment that this was something not ever spoken about, and can you wonder at my shock, when I realised that Daan was still alive, and, somewhere in my quasi-medical field of activity, he was now a very real responsibility?

Grief had made me forgetful, and memories that had been treasured passively became active again as a door that had been closed for ten winters creaked open.

I was taken to the great bedroom of the house, and there, all laid out on the bed, was Bettina, whom Daan had never seen, or heard, or felt, or kissed, except as he would one day describe her, as an abstract combination of warmths and vibrations.

There was something in the situation that made me realise that this was the last opportunity that Daan would ever have to make a kind of contact with his mother. I looked at the lovely death-clothes, the draperies, the discreetly revealed lace underwear at the ankles, shown only by a half-inch turn in the silk dress, heavily decorated, and the sash of embroidered angels, all intricately made by Bettina early in her life, before she had lost all interest in living. I saw the face, so waxen, in death, because it was before the undertakers would arrive with their grotesque array of cosmetics (and sent away before they could use them), and my heart was heavy and sad with a knowledge that something was happening here between Mina, Bettina and Daan that I could not be expected to share. I would do what I could, but there could be no hypocrisy here, and my actions were not loving.

"Baas Daan," I said to Mina, "do you think we should let him into . . . ?"

"See her?" said Mina. "To what purpose, when he has no eyes, and no ears?"

"Just because she was his mother, and perhaps it is right."

"Yes," said Mina, "and I know a way to bring tears to his eyes, if you want me to do that, I will, and then he will have cried also for his mother. Do you want me to bring tears to his eyes?"

"How do you bring tears to his eyes?" I asked.

"I tried once, when his father died, the Oubaas. That was many years ago, and I felt that a man should cry when his father dies, so I made tears for his eyes, and I let them roll down his cheeks.

And, if you like, now that his mother is dead, I will once again make tears for his eyes, and let them roll down his cheeks. Although, Miss Nurse van der Kolff, you must remember that he is now a man of fifty, and when they get to that age it is very seldom that you see a white man cry. Black men do, all their lives, for their mothers and fathers and children and friends, but white men, after a certain time, do not cry any longer, and I think Baas Daan is past that age."

"But how do you bring tears to his eyes?" I asked, because I was more than just curious about that time, ten years ago, when she had made Daan cry.

"It is easy," said Mina, "I make him very tired. I keep him up when he wants to sleep, and he staggers about with that funny way he has of walking, and when he gets very tired he starts stumbling. After an hour of that he starts to open his mouth in great yawns, because he is so tired, and I light an electric torch, one of the great ones with the six batteries that they use to hunt jackals with at night. I shine this great light in his eyes, right close up, and he yawns, and after a while his eyes become wet and red-rimmed like he has been drinking, and, as he yawns his biggest yawn, some tears come out of his eyes, and it looks as if he is crying."

"And when his father died, all those years ago, that was what you did?"

"Yes," said Mina, "because I felt it right that he, who had never shown anything, and who still has not shown anything, should cry on the day they buried his father."

"You were right," I said. "If the Oubaas Dawid had known of it, he would have thought that you were right. But now, before I go to get all the other people, and the lawyers and the dominees, I think let us just bring him into this room, let us just put his hands on her forehead, or let his fingertips touch hers, and let us then put him back, and we will tell no-one of what we have done to let him say a kind of farewell to his mother."

"But," said Mina, "they say that he must not be unchained."

"Who says so?"

"It is the law. When a man is not right in the head, and they are frightened of him, he must be locked by his wrist to a chain, and that chain must never be taken off, because he can be dangerous and hurt someone, or himself, and the law will be angry."

"Then I must speak to the law about it, and bring a stop to it, because Baas Daan is not dangerous, and that chain is supposed to be for balance, so that he does not fall. I want this thing done before the others arrive. I will go to the new sergeant, and I will speak to him about it, and let him supervise it, because I think that it is a necessary thing that must be done and without chains, or you and I will always feel that there was a good thing to be done, but that we never did it, and that is one of the worst things in the world to know about yourself."

So that day I drove up to the police station at Thornhill, only about five miles away, and reported the death of Bettina Cilliers, née Paulson, to Sergeant Karner, who was in charge of the establishment, which consisted of himself, two privates, a corporal, and a Black constable. I had to be courteous while I spoke to Mina in the almost elegiac manner of the ritualistic Balobedu, which is typical of the courtesy of the languages of Africa, especially when matters of life or death are discussed. But when it came to talking to Sergeant Karner my style changed. I wonder why I had never yet been locked up for public indecency. Karner was a young German whose father was the chef of the Greater Magaliesburg Hotel, which is one of the scruffiest little joints imaginable. The word "Greater" was added to the name when the new billiard saloon had been added, but it soon also faded into the general seediness of the rest of the place. Sergeant Karner was an immaculate person, in his late twenties, and ran what he liked to call a "tight ship" although he had never been at sea. You could eat your breakfast off any surface both inside and outside of the police station, but the only problem there was that the food itself was not worth eating. Karner did not like layabouts to enjoy their stay in his cells.

"Get out a death certificate for Auntie Bettina," I announced, when I entered the charge office. "Cause of death, oh, put in anything you like."

"I'll have to have a proper cause of death," said Karner.

"Listen, you big Kraut crap, when you're seventy-one you don't have one cause of death, you take your pick of anything from eight to twelve different kinds. But call it heart failure if you like, that's about what it was, I suppose her heart just stopped in her sleep."

"What about her people, her next of kin, advertising, all that stuff?"

"There aren't any, only Daan, so get off your backside and get the parson and all the other people over to the church. She's already been laid out but we still have to get her in the coffin. They're digging the grave now, and it's a hot summer so let's get it done by this afternoon, at sunset, if you can get it organised by the Reverend Webb. She was the last of the Paulsons, I know there was a sister called Magda or Magdalena, but she buggered off from the district about forty or fifty years ago and there's been no further news, no letters, nothing. And then of course there's Daan, that's trouble for you."

"Oh," said Karner, "I suppose he'll just get shoved into the asylum at Krugersdorp. Nothing more you can do for him."

"Asylum shit," I said, "you can be bloody sure that's out. Better get hold of old Bertie Theron and have a reading of the will before you get yourself in the crap. Daan's harmless, isn't he?"

"He must be," said Karner, "I've never heard of him giving any trouble, nobody has. He must be forty or fifty years old by now, still just a vegetable, no brain, nothing. They should just put him away quietly, that would be best. Murder though, so I don't know."

"I want you to come with me for a few minutes," I said, "we need you down there at the house. There's something we must do, and we won't keep you long."

We drove down to the house and I asked Karner to witness Daan's farewell to his mother. I had already explained to the sergeant that Daan was harmless, and the chain was for balance only. We led him into the room where his dead mother lay. Karner thought it was a lot of bullshit, and he said so, in the presence of the dead woman, but Daan did not feel bad when I told him about it some years later. There are moving moments that embarrass people, so they are inclined to use bad language. I didn't feel bad about it either, because the sergeant had used one of my more frequent words, and Mina had long since steeled herself to the shockingly bad manners of policemen, drunkards, and white people generally.

I led in Daan by his chain, like some sort of docile dog, which of course he resembled. Mina had wiped the goo out of his eyes, the snot from his nose, and the drool from the corners of his mouth. She had dressed him in a fresh khaki shirt and pants, and had put socks on his feet, as well as sandshoes. She had combed his hair and shaved him, and he looked quite presentable as I led him in to view the remains with his sightless eyes, and to pay his last respects with that shuttered, unknowing brain.

Now, as I look back on the scene as it must have been, trying to remember an occurrence at which I was both totally present as well as absent, I try to think if it was a good thing that we did there that day, and I have finally decided that it was right. It was a tender scene, and his father would have approved. I knew that Bettina had withdrawn a long time ago, but she *was* his mother, and he had a right to say goodbye. So many people, over so many years, did things for him, not knowing to what extent he experienced the bits and pieces of life that they had organised just in case they could be used in his mind's hidden places, even if they were only subliminal. I strongly believe in the realness of intangible things.

I took Daan's free right hand, the one without the chain, and guided it to his mother's forehead, and there I allowed his fingers to lie for a while, quietly among the furrows of his birthflesh, the lines of his fifty years, the ruins of the saddest of all the long-faded gardenias, whose fragrance had never been his, like the wraith of a lost time in his impenetrable consciousness.

Just lately, Daan has told me that he has no memory of that event at all, but that it had become so sharp in his mind since he had been told of it, so well-etched with acids of love and longing, that it seems one of the greatest things that has ever happened to him. "If I had had a memory of it I would have used a word like memorable, or unforgettable," he says.

When we had completed our little ceremony of allowing him to touch his mother's forehead in farewell, he was led back to his accommodation in the backyard, where the dogs and the chickens and the pigs were. Although let me stress that his father had been a fine woodworker and designer, and the place where Daan lived had been made with love.

I realised even more strongly that Daan had become a problem. Before that his care had been a matter of a set of instructions to Mina and her underlings. Now, suddenly, there was no one to instruct Mina, no one to make the big decisions.

So I did what I thought was the right thing. I drove into town with Sergeant Karner, and while he was gathering all the dignitaries of Skeerpoort together, I went to the office of the little town's attorney, old Bertie Theron, a septuagenarian of uncertain habits, who had for many years seen to the few legal problems experienced by the inhabitants of the little Victorian town. And, as I had expected, there was a will that lifted a lot of the responsibility from my shoulders, and, in the process, solved a problem that had been lying heavily on my shoulders for some years.

Karner the policeman, and the new young Doctor Anton Cloete, as well as the Reverend George Webb, senile and willing, congregated over sherry in the lounge of the Great House at sunset that day, and old Bertie Theron, in his shaky voice, read what Bettina and Dawid had had in mind for the disposal of the estate, and the care of their retarded son. It was a joint will that had been drawn up fifteen years previously, and there was no reason to contest any of it. The estate was to be used to obtain the funds that were required for the care of their son, and that was that.

After Daan's care had been completed, should he be unable to draft a will, the estate would become the property of the Cripple Care Association. No mention had been made of his missing Aunt Magdalena, and it was assumed that there would be no difficulty from that quarter, as she had been five years older than Bettina. Later, Daan tried for some years to trace her, as she was the only relative that he knew of. He wanted to know if she needed anything, if he could be of help, whether she had married; if there had been children. He had traced her as far as Christiana, to the diamond diggings there. There had been a family, but they had either died or disappeared. He was greedy for relatives, but could never find any. Both families, the Paulsons and the Cilliers, ended with him, a seemingly moronic idiot, an unseeing cul-de-sac. That is how things must have seemed to his parents, as they took their turns at dying.

A going-over of the books of the estate, admirably kept by old Bertie Theron, showed that the whole operation was a viable one. There was plenty of money in the bank, and the estate manager, who had conducted the farming activities for a number of years, had done an excellent job. He was away at the time of Bettina's death, it being December and the land fallow for the January planting, but he would be returning sunburned and peeling from the Natal coast early in the new year to continue his work, making sure that the crops that Dawid Cilliers had inaugurated in his lifetime would continue to be planted, harvested, sold, and the profits wisely invested by old Bertie.

There was one stipulation in the will that made life a lot easier for me. Upon the death of the surviving spouse a trained nurse, who would be empowered to hire such help as she needed, was to take up residence in the Great House in order to be near to Daan at all times, so that, if he needed help, it would always be at hand. This caused the others a little concern, as the house was some miles from the nearest neighbour's, and it would be impossible for a nurse to stay there all by herself, as very few women live alone in Southern Africa, for fear of whatever it is they fear. I knew of a nurse who would do the job, and who wasn't afraid, so that clause in the will was to be solved that very afternoon. I had arrived after the reading of the will, because of the amount of work that I had had to do. Because of its being December and extraordinarily hot and humid, I had applied for and been granted a permit by Karner to inter the deceased's remains promptly, as there were no next of kin, except Daan, to worry about, and he certainly didn't count in this connection. The Reverend Doctor Webb was despatched to get his book of Common Prayer, Henderson the lay preacher was asked to get the ladies' choir to church as soon as possible, and Calitz the storekeeper and Karner the policeman were to get the hearse from the Indian storekeeper Moosa's yard, polished and ready for action by sunset. One further point in Bettina's personal addendum to the will moved some of the people, but no one contested it or thought it wrong. She had asked to be buried from the little church, once Methodist, for which her late husband had constructed the pulpit, and not the chapel on the farm. The church was no longer in use by White people, but Dawid, and after him the farm manager Andries Burger, had always seen to it that it was clean and not disgraceful to God.

Her coffin was transported there by sunset, to the singing of the coloured folk, who had come from far and wide as if by magic command, and they and the dead woman's few acquaintances made up a reasonable congregation. Mina had not allowed any cosmetic other than a little lipstick, a touch of rouge, and a sprinkling of the lightest lavender water.

They do not allow coffins in churches any longer, and I really don't know why, because in the years gone by, when you went to a funeral, the open coffin was in the church, and you could go and pay your respects, but all that (and it is a bloody disgrace), is changed now. The hearse with the coffin is left outside in the hot sun while all the people who have come to the funeral go into the cool house of God and have themselves a ball singing and weeping, while the poor old dear departed lies outside in a bloody big juke box of a second-hand Cadillac, rotting his poor guts out in the heat or going blue in the cold. I am very pleased that I was able to tell Daan that that was not at all the case with Bettina's funeral. She was first in the church, open coffin, proper screws, the lot, a real burial for someone who had taken a long time over dying. I don't suppose I can be blamed for being a little cold about it all, but I am happy that I was there, so that one day I could tell Daan about it, in a kind and decent way, so that he would be able to dream the lavenders of Bettina's perfumed departure in the splendid style of gleaming wood, laces, and candlelight filtering softly into the eddies left by the great and sonorous songs of death so richly sung by black voices and the vibrations of the organ, deep into the time of tears. This was to be her final sadness, and for it she had been brought back to the silken yellow-wood pulpit that Dawid had made for her in their first year. It was inlaid with ebony wood and mother-of-pearl, their reflected sparkle singing out, as the sun caught them, like the shining soprano-tones of the child-voices singing of the roll being called up yonder. The horse-drawn hearse had been polished, the horses combed and brushed, and their tails plaited. Her coffin was carried from the church by a number of the men who had known her.

Something moving happened. The coloured men would not allow her coffin to be placed in the hearse, splendid though it was. They would allow the flowers to be put into the hearse, and they allowed the hearse to follow, but they all took turns at carrying the *ounooi* to her grave, only a few hundred yards away, right at the side of the cattle kraal where Dawid had decided to rest. In the farmyard, where he could count his sheep and oxen at night, and see that the cows had been properly milked. Bettina had not protested at the fact that she would rest next to him, there, by the rough stone wall that was the kraal for the cattle. The only monument that Dawid had allowed was that a stonemason should come out to the farm, bringing his letter-cutting tools; and, on a huge block of granite, rough and weather-beaten, he had asked that their names be cut, reasonably deeply but not deep enough to be ostentatious, in a little polished section, above their heads. Nothing else. At evening it is lovely to hear Mina tell Daan as the cattle are brought home: "The night that the Oumiesies was buried, the cattle and the sheep were just coming to the cribs for their water and corn, and all the coloured and black boys were taking turns carrying her coffin. They arrived here, at sunset, with the calves and the lambs, and they laid her to rest. Not with that horrible machine that lets coffins down. They had dug the grave wide so that the side of your father's coffin could also be seen, and they let her down gently, by hand, and wedged the two coffins side by side, touching. They all took turns along with the white men to fill the holes and pat them smooth. After the lambs and sheep, the bulls, cows and calves, the piglets and the sows had walked about a few times, you would not have known that she had been there the day before, above the ground, and that she was with Oubaas Dawid now, only a day later doing their mouldering together. It was a great funeral. There wasn't a kaffir on this farm sober for two days, except for me, because I was looking after you."

I had telephoned my sister Maria and she was due to arrive the next day after having served for many years as a nurse in the Pretoria Military Hospital. It had been decided by old Bertie Theron and the Reverend Doctor Webb, on my recommendation, that she would be the ideal person to look after Daan. The salary was good, and it was a private place. She had agreed to come away from the city because her work there had been done. The old patients of the second World War had all left, or died, and there was no real need for her to stay on in an almost empty place, doing paper work.

Although I spent the night of Bettina's funeral in the Great House, even I didn't have the guts to use the main bedroom that had been prepared for me after her body had been placed in its coffin and it had been removed by Karools and Piet and the other boys. Not that they could touch her corpse, actually make physical contact, I mean, because coloured men are not allowed to touch even the corpses of white women. Mina and I had put her in her coffin, the others had carried it to the church.

It was a rather trying night for me, because of the strangeness of being in that house again, and all the ghosts it awakened within me. Mina had gone to bed after assuring me that Daan had also gone to sleep. He was like some animal. All you needed to do was to fill his belly and he would curl up in the cell-structure his father had made, needing no blankets nor pillows, everything being soft leather. With the invention and coming into general usage of thermostatically controlled air conditioning in the late thirties, the temperature of Daan's room had been set and he lived in air conditioned comfort that was never too hot or too cold. His father had been anxious to make him as comfortable as possible, and had spent a great deal of time and money to make sure that he would never have cause to be distressed by any factor in his environment. He had taught Mina how the thermostat was used, and whom to call on the telephone if anything should ever go wrong with the machinery. He had never been a morbid man, but he knew of his own mortality and never ran away from it. That is why his preparation for his own death, and his arrangements for the care of his people after it had happened, were a model of consideration. Financially, the farm would continue to support his dependants as well as the money that had been invested in a carefully selected portfolio of gold and diamond shares. Giving his own retirement as his excuse, he had hired a well-qualified farm manager and had installed him in a renovated cottage on the estate, an excellent person called Andries Burger, who had been provided with an income far in excess of the usual wages paid to farm managers. Maintenance and care of Daan's equipment and quarters were supervised by Burger, never in Bettina's presence, though, as discussion with her was forbidden.

Mina also fed Daan. This must have been a difficult business, because knives, forks, or spoons were out of the question, there being no sense of knowing, no way of teaching him about the use of teeth and chewing, for instance, and there was no sight of the descending spoon to guide him. So it had to be what Mina had long since perfected, a kind of breast feeding. She used a piece of equipment that Dawid had obtained from Doctor Anton Cloete senior, the father of the young Doctor Anton Cloete who had been at Bettina's funeral. This piece of pottery had been made by the Royal Doulton Factory in England, and it was actually called a "feeder" looking like some sort of bastardised teapot, but allowing for the spout to be stuck into the patient's mouth, when reflexes would take over and allow a sucking motion, so that portions of gruel or other semi-liquid foods could be assimilated into the body. That was the only sort of food that Daan had been given for the first fifty years of his life.

His diet was a kind of gruel of mashed meats and vegetables, vitamins and whatever else Bettina had come across in her reading on the subject of dietetics, and as he had sucked at Mina's black breast with the unknowing instinctive appetite of the infant, so it became habit with him, whenever Mina stroked his lips with the Royal Doulton Feeder, pushing them apart, to open his mouth and to let the feeding happen. These people who took such good care of him had no idea of the extent to which he could feel, taste, or smell. He tells me that he had always been highly developed in these senses, though, because of the care with which these unknown factors had been catered for throughout his life, in case he was normal.

"So, if there is pity for my grey tunnel stretching back into the past," he says, "it must at least be partially balanced because of the wonderful flavours of the food that I was fed and the perfumes that had been introduced into my environment. There were also the senses of shape and texture of my silent world that were very important to my growing up and maturity."

He must have been the most frustrating thing in the world to feed, he says. He often refers to himself as a "thing" when he thinks of what he must have been like; and I keep telling him that we do not use such words in connection with people who are ill. It upsets Maria too, to the point of tears, and when he does it Mina calls him a "blerrie silly fool." But he does not want to hurt us, it is only modesty. One of his favourite characters is Saint Francis, besides Maria. But he also loves Jesus and everybody else in the world. If he could sing of his appreciation of life, Daan's songs will be mightier than all the Psalms together, had they been put to music by Bach.

I kept vigil in the Great House on the night of Bettina's funeral, because Maria arrived only the next day. Although I am not a person who is scared of things in the night, the thought of spending the night alone in a house with a drooling lunatic idiot, with goo in his eyes and snot-dried stains on his lips, was an unpleasant experience for me. I had seen Daan that same afternoon, combed, groomed and cleaned after Mina had finished with him in order for him to be presentable to the corpse of his mother, but when I saw him later that evening, by torchlight, sleeping in his cell, while I was checking to see if everything was well with him, it gave me a severe shock. Mina had of course cleaned Daan up again after his supper, and wiped all the exudations from his face. But you know how babies are, and within a matter of a few hours he had drooled and snotted again, and the thing I saw lying, chained in the little rounded cell, which had been constructed and padded so as to be without sharp edges or corners, chained lightly, with his right arm in the sky, because of the height of the blue wire, was not human any more. It had once again become an animal, not even worthy of the name of beast, an ugly, unfeeling vegetable. But those were phantoms of the night. In the daylight he was acceptable. I knew that I would never be able to care for him myself, and I was ashamed as I stood there in the light of my torch, trying to decide what to do with Daan. Mina came, because Mina had come to him every four hours of his life.

"What," asked Mina, "what are you doing here?"

"I was looking to see if he was all right," I answered.

"When you want to see if he is all right, come to my room first, and wake me up. Then tell me that you want to see how he is, and then go and make yourself some tea, and when you have had your tea, then you can come to see if he is all right."

I lost my temper at her words, because I was still ashamed of my feelings towards Daan.

"I need no instructions from you as to how to behave with sick persons," I said. "I will look on him at any time I wish, to see if he is well."

"Then do so," said Mina. "I am going to my room now, to make some tea. Tell me, call me when he is ready, so that I may see if he is all right." And she turned her back on me and walked away.

So that night I, not to be outdone by a snotty servant girl who had been insolent, fetched basins of warm water, and I stripped him of his clothes, and cleaned him, I soaped his penis and sprinkled on Johnson's Baby Powder, gently cleaned his armpits and with buds of cotton-wool wiped his eyes. I rubbed Vaseline under his reddened eyelids, and made long plugs of cotton-wool and de-snotted his nostrils. I wiped the hard packings from the corners of his mouth, and then for the second time in that twenty-four hours, his hair was cleansed with a dry shampoo and his pathetic grey curls were brushed, and he was dressed in a fresh pair of pajamas. Only after I had done all these things did I look about the room. I picked up the stained vest of an hour ago, the sweaty pajamas, the half dozen towels I had used, the cotton-wool plugs and the Vaseline-stained face-cloths. I went into the laundry and, finding an electric washing machine, washed all these things, and then I went to Mina's room, close by.

But as I walked there I had to go by way of his "run," and it was a dark night, so I noticed the things that Bettina, his mother, had planted along the blue-wire galvanised walk. Into my nostrils came the long-beloved perfumes of rosemary, basil, thyme, of carnation and gardenia, and forget-me-nots, and those saddest of all perfumes, three in one, purple, pink and white, yesterday, today and tomorrow. I wondered then if he had been aware of the perfumes and the soaps and the powders, of the cinnamon of Pears and the lavender of Johnson's, while I had been cleaning him. I knew, somehow, in my heart, that blue soap of fat and lye would not have been all the same to him. I was glad, and when I am glad I become coarse, so that when I reached the door of Mina's room, where a light was still burning, I yelled out loudly, "Come on out, you black-arsed bitch, and see how you take care of a sick man."

Mina came out and followed me to the rounded cell, and looked at everything that had been done to Daan.

"You have done well," she said. "It is now midnight, and at four a.m. I will do it."

"You go and get stuffed," I said. "I have work to do, all day, all over the district, but my sister Maria is coming tomorrow, and I want to be proud of the way we do things here."

"This is how it has always been done," said Mina. "I do not need teachers to tell me how to care for him. Remember, he drank at my breast, and the only time he had tears, I made them. I helped you to take him to his mother this afternoon. He needs no dry spinster from Pretoria to teach me to care for him. Your sister can sleep in the house, but tell her to keep her hands off my work."

"You're over sixty, Mina, and Maria is still strong. You must let others look after him. And you need also to rest for more than four hours. You know, Mina, that most people in the world sleep for eight or nine hours. And it is a half century now, since you've been seventeen, that you haven't slept for more than four hours."

"He is mine," said Mina, "because I have made him mine, because I have been willing to work for him."

"Is work then, the yardstick of all?" I asked, stupidly, because you don't talk in this way to a Balobedu, and I should have known it.

"There is only work," said Mina.

"And love, surely there is love?" I compounded my error.

"It expresses itself in work only," said Mina.

"And friendship?" I asked.

Mina looked at me carefully, as if she had never seen me before, and I had the decency to blush, because I knew that I had been far too talkative and importunate, European, asking about friendship. But Mina had been so long with white people that she understood their lack of manners as well as their abrupt way of coming to the point of a conversation, and, on that morning, when the stars of dawn were already on their way, she was, herself, a little importunate, a little impatient, a little unwilling to spend the remaining moments of the night in African subtleties and diplomacies. I had asked about friendship, and it was an enormous matter, like a leaf, or a stone.

Then Mina said: "The towels and the face-cloths, are they washed? Because if they are not, let us go and wash them, and, while we are about it, let us see that the pajamas are also freshened by the wind of the dawn coming soon."

And Mina also, beneath her dark skin, blushed, because she had, precipitously and in unusual haste, allowed her words to express an admiration, which is something that is simply not done, not even in the worst of circles, in Africa. Even Machopis do not do such things.

"Come," I said, "come to your bed and sleep. It is all done."

"Then," said Mina, "then it is done."

"Thank you," I said.

"No," said Mina.

"No?"

"The days of such words are past."

"Past?" I asked.

"Yes," said Mina, "he who sleeps there, not knowing that he is asleep, is now ours, made ours by the sweat of his armpits, the sweat and the snot that we have cleansed. We now have the same child, we are his mothers, and I am not displeased. All other words between us from this day forward, are meaningless words. And please, Miss Nurse van der Kolff, we who have lived through these last twenty hours together, we are both tired. Not in our spirits but in our bodies, and, being tired I say too much, because the things that have to be said are never worth saying, so, let us go and drink tea, quietly, in the kitchen of the Great House, and let us then go to sleep, before I, or you, say too much and lose things by using words."

"Only one thing," I said. "Only one more thing, let us go and drink the tea in your room, what do you say to that?"

"But," said Mina, "my room is not worthy, it stinks of kaffir!"

"If you can take my smell, I can take yours," I answered.

"You smell beautifully of lavender and cologne," said Mina.

"That is to hide the white woman's natural smell of freshly slaughtered pork, you snobbish kaffir bitch," I told her. "I'm thirsty. Come to your room."

"To my room then," said Mina. "We can both hear him from there, should he whimper."

But Daan did not whimper that night. Is it possible that the addition of new ones to care for him penetrated through, somehow; that even if sight and sound were absent, there may have been other factors, more mysterious than scientific ones, that could have penetrated his blankness?

3

DANIEL CILLIERS

If I am to begin with my initial awareness of things it must be with my first knowledge of something outside of my darkness, something outside of my feelinglessness. And now, looking back over all that I have been told, and thinking about it most carefully, I would say that the first human being to have broken through the black curtains of my world must have been Mina, and that it must have happened on the day that she attempted to make me cry. Well, I certainly did not cry, because I did not know what sadness or love was, or that throats could be lumped, or speech thickened by emotion; those were universes denied me at the time. But I do remember, somewhere far back in my experience, some of the deep-seated pains that I had at times felt inside me, when I must have suffered from dysentery or some other vapour of the time, I remember feeling that experience of there being something in the region of what I now know to be my head, and what I suspect must have been my eyes.

Mina told Maryna van der Kolff, the district social worker and nurse, of the day when she tried to make me cry, and her description, which I was told of later, of one of my eyes becoming red-rimmed would seem to be consistent with pain, with being forced to keep awake, and the heat of the six-cell torch must have caused a tenderness, because I do remember a feeling there, as if I wanted to evacuate my bowels or pass water through a place far above the normal place for such a sensation. And I remember a greyness. That's probably the most stupid word of all but I can't do better. I must try my best and not work from hindsight, so I can only describe my first use of my eyes as a greyness, although it is like describing your first view of the ocean as a wetness. I think you can understand my problem. I must make words, and I can't because all the words have already been made up, and there are none that I can use. But yet, there was a something up in these top regions, where I now know my head is, and I did know something that day, something that extended the boundaries of my tactile senses, that made my world a bigger one, quadrupled it. I had sensed my abdomen through the pains of childhood diseases and the knowledge of coming evacuations and urinations, and now, what seemed to me to be miles away, universes removed from those nether regions I had felt something external. Naturally, I have always been aware of my head, strange as that may sound. My senses, and the irritations, itches and pains on the surface of my skin caused a certain knowledge of my outer shell. My eyes had felt changes in light conditions, but they had never been hurt deliberately by too much light.

I had felt something is all I can say. Wetness is too strong a word, pain excessive to describe the slight discomfort, greyness too huge a word for the slightness of what I believe must have been sight that day, when the six Eveready batteries pierced into a cornea that did not even know of its own existence. I know there was something and it was the first time.

This is something that has occupied my thinking for some time now, the possibility that something exists that is a form of communication between people, even if they are not aware of it, and I have even read some of the books about extrasensory perception, because if anyone in this world needed that kind of perception it was I. But I cannot remember any form of communication at all, except the perfumes, tastes, and touches that I have told you about. Maria and I have often talked about it, because she also believes, with many other people in the world today, that if you feel strongly enough about even a piece of rock it will receive your message, or your vibrations, or the atmosphere you spread around. And lately, in the books people are writing about the feelings of plants and grasses, trees, flowers and other supposedly unfeeling things there seems to be a new awareness of the hitherto unsuspected capability for life of all the things that make up the earth. Soon, I am sure, we will all understand that the greatest of all scientist-philosophers was Saint Francis. This is the view of a simpleton, I know, but I wonder why it was that, although some scientist in America could take a simple lie detector and use it to make a rubber plant register joy, fear, anguish, and a number of other factors including love, why the half century of my grey world and its incommunicatability should have been so thorough, with so very little penetrating to me. But then, I suppose the measuring devices were primitive in those days, as was the care and feeding of lunatics, and even their identification. Today there seems to be, at least, some idea as to diagnosis. But I do feel that we are living in a world that is in its intellectual and scientific infancy. Therefore, the fact that I have been studying for only seven years doesn't make me feel at all inferior.

I know now that I was no madman, that I wasn't any kind of man at all, and that the silver chain that my father had attached to my wrist by the leather wristlet was put there to satisfy some obscure and idiotic local ordinance of those days, insisting on the physical restraint of what they called the "mentally incompetent." The reason for the ordinance was fear of the unleashed lunatic stalking the night, dribbling and drooling, and getting up to all sorts of nefariousnesses according to the promptings of his under-developed mind. People were afraid of the possibility of rapes and murders accompanied by the sounds of strange piglike grunts and groans, especially in the baleful light of the full moon. I suppose that there must have been incidents of that kind because a whole generation of Gothic authors made their fortunes by descriptions of these strange half-man-half-beast-goo-mouthed-droolers that stalked the night. But I was not one of them, and my little chain was actually pathetic. Any reasonably strong man could have snapped it with ease, so it wasn't there to restrain me from violence, but to prevent me from disappearing without knowing what I was up to, and it also helped to balance me in the first stages of walking. My chain kept me to a world to which my parents had, in their kindness, confined me, and it was a protective rather than a captive device. I still have it, and often wear it, wondering if it will remind me of all those years, but there has been no break-through. Chains are quite in fashion again, and men wear them around their necks. Mine is beautiful, old, and of hand-twisted silver.

Theories of communication by sentimental reasons like the strength of the love of my parents or of Mina have been plentifully explored by the little group of acquaintances of mine who are interested in such things. Only the other day Doctor Cloete, son of the old Doctor Anton Cloete, who originally talked my parents into caring for me at home, advanced the theory that Mina, with all her strength, and her enormous tenderness, must at times have brought forth a reaction from me. And we discussed it with her, but she was most embarrassed by that sort of talk. She has an abrupt way about her when such things are mentioned, not rude, but dignified, even a little overbearing, as if some royal prerogatives of decorum are being misused. "I am not a person for words like love," she said. "I only did what I felt I had to do, and those things that the Oubaas and Ounooi asked of me, and I did what I was told, as well as I could."

"Yes," said Doctor Cloete, "but that is just the point. You did it as well as you could. Others would have been satisfied with a quarter or a half of what you gave Baas Daan, so surely it must have been love, such as you felt for your own children?"

"I know of no word like love," said Mina. "I have heard it spoken and seen it written, and once, when I went to a bioscope, there were a master and a madam, and they used the word 'love' all the time, for what seemed like hours to me, and then, right in the bioscope, they started holding each other, and kissing each other, and they were using that word 'love' all the time, while they were kissing each other on the mouth, and I thought it very improper for a master and a madam to kiss each other like that in front of a lot of kaffirs."

But Doctor Cloete was persistent, and he kept at it. "What," he said, "is your feeling for your own children?"

"They are my children," she replied, "and they must be clothed and fed, and they must sleep warmly at night, and they must come in out of the rain when there is lightning or thunder about, in case they are hurt. My mother and my mother's mother brought them up, while I worked for the money, as is our way. Even in the old days, when my people lived in the Devil's Gorge at Duiwelskloof it was like that. Our women worked in the fields, and the old people looked after the children, because the little ones were their life, as an old tree shades its saplings."

"And what," asked the doctor, "is your feeling for the children of your neighbour?"

"The same," she said. "Children need the same things, more or less. There is very little difference between children. It is only later that the differences start. All of us are the parents of all the children. That is our way."

"And if your neighbour died, or became ill, what of her children then?"

"We would take care of them," said Mina. "It is our way. We do not have the things that white children have, like the house for orphans in Krugersdorp, where the white children are sent when their parents die. We would not, in any case, send our children to such places, because they are not at all necessary. It is no trouble to care for children."

"So," said Cloete, "with the African, the care of all children is a sacred trust."

"No," said Mina, "not a sacred trust. It is just something that one does. A sacred trust is to care for our Queen, she-who-is-forever-young."

"You care for the children even if it means a whole lot of trouble?"

"It is no trouble to look after children."

"And when you looked after Baas Daan, and saw to his needs every four hours for over fifty years, surely that was trouble?"

"No," said Mina, "I was the one who looked after Baas Daan. It was no trouble."

"Over fifty years," said Cloete, "six times a day, two thousand times a year, one hundred thousand times have you cleaned him, dressed him, fed him, seen that he was well. And you try to tell me that you didn't feel love for him, that all those years you were just doing what had to be done, with no feeling on your part? That's bullshit, Mina, and you know it."

Mina smiled. "You have a strange way of talking, Doctor Cloete. It is not dung. You must not use dung as a swear-word. It is a sacred thing, because it makes things grow. But, doctor, one does what one does, and that is all. May I ask something? Do you, when you see twenty or forty or a hundred sick people every day, do you keep a score? And do you love them? And when you wash their wastes off your hands at the end of the day, or their blood, what do you feel?"

"Like resting," said Cloete, with a wry smile. "Like a double Scotch whisky and a soft chair, and rest."

"That is how it was with Baas Daan," said Mina. "When I had finished I would go to the great kitchen in the Big House, and

I would tell the kaffir cook James, who is a Shangaan, to make a big bowl of tea, and I would sit down, and then I would enjoy my tea. Shangaan men are the right people to work in kitchens, because they have soft hands, and they are not allowed in the Royal Stockade." She looked at Cloete for a long while. Cloete was nodding acceptingly.

"We who work with the sick ones, doctor, you and I and Miss Maryna, and the other one, Miss Maria, and your father when he was alive, we have to be very careful of words like 'love' and of hearts that get too full of feelings. These are things that must be avoided in our work."

Cloete accepted without question that they were colleagues. He didn't pursue his enquiries any further. And all the things that she had said between the lines were not lost on him, and I knew that he was a good man. That meant that he would suffer along with his patients. Whether that was good for him is open to question, but I think that feelings of any kind that make you conscious of the preciousness of life are good. Mina's sympathy and identification was a deep-rooted part of her personality. You see, the African has too vast a history of personal disaster, and therefore a built-in disaster-dignity, as I call it, to be probed. And I have found that the African who is too eager to use his emotions is, as a rule, quite phoney, and is better avoided when he discusses these matters, because some sort of play-acting will result, usually for gain, because not all Africans are like Mina.

There is a true story of an African murderer who was to be hanged at Pretoria Central one day, and they asked him if he wanted anything, so he requested a pipe and some tobacco. He sat smoking all night, until they came to fetch him for the hanging, and puffing contentedly he was placed on the gallows. The lever was thrown, but the rope broke, so they had to get him upstairs again, and he walked up the stairs to the gallows, complaining bitterly.

"See," he said, "with all your fucking about you've broken my pipe."

That story, and variations of it, may be heard from the Sudan down to the Cape. If they are all one vast true story or not I cannot say. But I do know that if you are one of the twenty-or-so murderers who are hanged at Pretoria every few months, you would need some sort of stoicism. You have to be somewhat of a stoic to live in the conditions where such a great number of murders are just a part of everyday life.

But the point I am trying to make is that Mina was very careful never to admit to any feeling at all for me and that she never complained to me afterwards, or expected anything, or wanted to be treated as a favourite. That must have taken something more than guts, to keep a straight face, and we will have to examine what it was in Mina that made her seem indifferent to the things that happened to me afterwards, and who, now, when I have been the subject of a number of things that call for rejoicing, shows neither delight nor any other feeling. Is Mina the greatest of fatalists? Does she accept everything life has to dish out? It certainly dished out a great mixture of good and bad to her. I prefer to think of her as a tree, untouchable by rain or mist or drought, straight-backed in the wind, only the tenderest branches flying, like the hair of a woman walking in a slight breeze. Beyond that I have nothing to say of Mina, except that she cared for me. And if the word "care" has two meanings, then I am quite happy that it should have both of those meanings. And if you are unable to choose one of them, I cannot either.

The next day Maria arrived, and the changes began.

4

MARIA VAN DER KOLFF

There is something that we must get out of the way before it gets dragged out into some lengthy melodramatic bullshit. I am an ugly woman. I am, perhaps, the ugliest of all women. I wasn't born that way, it happened by accident. A real bloody humdinger of an accident.

It happened one starlit, lovely night, that had been the most beautiful of my young life, in the year 1936, when I was twelve years of age. A little large for my age, tall, over-slender, with the first suggestions of womanhood beginning to ennoble my adolescent flesh. I use that word "ennoble" very carefully, especially for someone whose speech habits are as clumsy and coarse as mine. "Ennobled" because I was in the throes of my very first, very true love, as both adolescents and mature people were inclined to speak in those days. He was a boy called Johannes, whose nickname was Hansie, and I was totally in love with him. He loved me too. I knew because of the way he stared and stopped speaking in the middle of sentences; was unable to speak or even stutter, or offer me a sweet, or anything at all, except for the devotion in his eyes, which was majestically intense, overwhelming me with a desire to be held in his arms, and to be kissed.

The accident happened on the night of my first kiss, and his. We had been, in two cars, ten students and two driving teachers, to an Eisteddfod in Warrenton, fifty miles from Kimberley. There we had taken part in competitive recitations, songs, dances, oh, the usual things that happen at such occasions. Walking to the hall where the competitions were to be staged, I had slipped, not deliberately but because it was a wet and rainy night. There had been a mud patch in the middle of the gravelled path. Hansie had been near to me. Seeing me about to fall he had grabbed me by the arm. I did not fall. I looked up, and before seeing his face I had known instinctively it was Hansie who had hold of my arm, although he was standing a little behind me. I had held the hand that was supporting me, and I had turned my head, closed my eyes, and offered my lips for a kiss. It had taken him an eternity of seconds to realise that my lips were his, and then he had kissed me.

It seems to be a hell of a lot of fuss, doesn't it? I mean what a cadenza to make of a bloody little kiss for Christ's sake, and to take all that time describing it. Now, I'm not an over-emotional old middle-aged ugly cow telling you about something nasty but nice that had happened to me way back in my youth, holding on grimly to a memory that everybody has, and has had repeated a million times in their lives, please don't be shitty and think that. Also, please don't think I'm making too much of a drama of it, but that was the last and first time that I was kissed on the natural lips God gave me. My kisses afterwards were on other manufactured lips, because of what had happened that same night, only a few hours afterwards, at a place called the Kamfersdam bluegums, a clump of trees about twenty miles before you get to Kimberley, on the left-hand side of the road as you come from the north.

In those days motor cars did not have safety glass as standard equipment and fire controls were even more inadequate than they are today. In spite of Ralph Nader and his team of investigators, things are not all that much changed, and the things you see in the casualty sections of our hospitals on weekends and public holidays are much the same, in appearance, as the victims of the time of my youth.

The two cars had been brimful with singing, laughing children. The two fun-loving yet sober teachers were also singing. No blame can be attached to them even if it is almost imperative that someone should be searched out to be the scapegoat. They were canvas-roofed touring cars, but, although the roads were a little wet and misty, visibility wasn't all that bad. Hansie and I were sitting next to each other, nervously and surreptitiously holding hands under the touring rug. We were in the front seat, next to the teacher who was driving, a nice, popular young man called Roux who had been our art teacher and who took care of all the activities of the dramatic society. I remember him so very well, because, one day, in front of the entire class, after I had recited a piece of the Ophelia "rosemary for remembrance" speech, he had said (and God forgive me this sin of pride in remembering it), and I hesitate to repeat it, that I was very beautiful, and very talented. Now, wasn't that bloody nice of him? Wasn't it? Let me tell you it's something I treasure the hell out of, because he had said it, to me, one day in 1936, when I was young, and the whole of life lay before me like a dream that I was awaiting over-impatiently.

I treasure a lot of other stuff that's just crap to other people, stuff they won't even notice because they lie so far back in the obscurities of memory; people, well, most of them, ninety-nine per cent of them, have forgotten most of the bloody awfully beautiful things that have happened to them. People have thrown away some of the most wonderful things that can ever have happened to them and they don't even think of them any more. When they come across reminders, like a set of initials in a diary, or a pressed flower in an old school-book, or a ribbon, they stand holding these mementos in their hands, and wonder how they came to be preserved, what meaning these little mementos could possibly once have had for them, to have been treated as something potentially precious.

And so people look at their enormous, dusty treasures, and flush them down the loo, wondering what the hell that was all about, once. Worse, even, they would have forgotten the magic of youth, and they would wonder "what a silly little thing I was once, to have thought this important."

The night that Hansie had kissed me we had also presented a play at our hosts' school, so it was quite late when the two cars left on the fifty mile trip back to Kimberley, a trip that would normally, at that time, have taken much more than an hour, because 50 m.p.h. was really beating it out in 1936. But it had been only 10.30 when we had set out. The next day would be a Saturday, and our parents had all been warned that we would arrive home well after midnight, so no one had been particularly worried. I was one of two sisters, the "late-lamb" of my parents' near-middle age. My sister, Maryna, was eleven years older than I, and it was she who had woken up at 4 a.m., and, noticing that I had not arrived home, had gone to my parents, and told them that I was not in bed yet. We did not have a telephone so my father had thrown a dressing-gown over his pajamas and cycled down to the police station a mile away, where he had heard of the several other parents who had also been 'phoning in, or calling personally, worried about their children.

The police at Kimberley had phoned the police at Warrenton, and they had contacted the Warrenton school principal, who also did not have a telephone. And he had told them that we had left nearly six hours previously. We should have been at home many hours ago, even if we had been travelling at the slowest possible speed.

Now there was real reason for concern, and my father and the policemen, as well as several parents who had cars drove towards Warrenton in the mist of early dawn, until we were found, twenty miles away, at the Kamfersdam bluegums, just as the sun was rising, illuminating what must have been a dreadful scene. I don't ask for pity when I describe it briefly. I can tell you about it because I am the only one who is able to do so, of all the participants.

There's something about mutilated children that always touches the heart more strongly, so it is unnecessary for me to tell you any of the details, only that I was the sole survivor. Mercifully, it had happened at a moment when my eyes must have closed, or it is possible that my memory may have clouded it over, as memories have a way of shrouding those most deeply shocking moments of one's life, so that they are ever afterwards seen as through an almost opaque veil. From a reconstruction by the police it seemed that the two cars had, perhaps, been driving too closely together, one following the other. On the untarred gravel road, one of them, possibly the one in the lead, according to the skid-marks, had gone out of control because of the over-cambered hillock, which had been wet and muddy with potholes, as well as being corrugated, as roads were in 1936. The great National Roads programme was still in the planning stages. At best, roads were only tracks originally made by the ox-wagons of the transport drivers. These tracks had been only slightly improved, and a few essential bridges had been built, but the massive schemes for a network of tarred roads were still very far from reality.

The lead car having gone into a skid, all the children still unaware of danger, only the two teachers had been in a real and immediate panic, and both drivers had slammed on their brakes. In those days brakes were badly used by almost all drivers. They were meant to bring vehicles to a stop, and people knew nothing of controlled drifts, and four-wheel skids, or round-about stopping. Our two cars must have locked together, according to our skid-marks, and then they must have slid down to the great solid trees known as the Kamfersdam bluegums, sliding, and gaining speed on the muddy downhill, the children too shocked to scream, others closing their eyes in fear, little minds shutting off as they hit the trees, the razored fragments of glass flying. The fuel tanks and oil sumps and the soaked greasy wiring must have burst into an immediate holocaust.

Of all the children, and the two teachers, I was the only one who had been still barely alive when the police and the parents had arrived in the smoky mist of dawn, always so beautiful to me before, in both actuality and in the dreams evoked by my favourite romantic poets.

Since then I have never seen a misty landscape, or a smoky city, or even the smoke curling up from a cigarette held by an unaware hand, without wanting to use a violent word.

They say that accidents and misfortunes make gentle people, but it certainly didn't do anything of the sort for me. Even as I write here of that horrible morning, I find it very hard not to use a selection of the worst and ugliest words I know, although I need not be reminded that when you tell of such things you must behave, out of respect for the dead, and the people who are listening, and all the relatives who were involved.

Some of the children had been flung far away, and had suffered only the smallest-seeming, not-at-all serious contusions on their skulls, but they had nevertheless been fatal. Some had landed among the sharp, weathered granitic rocks of the area, while others seemed to be merely asleep. Others were, at first glance, missing, although all had been where they could be seen, only they didn't look like children any more. Still others had merely become unconscious and had suffocated. My injuries, especially about the face that Mr. Roux had once described as beautiful, were, according to the photographs in the surgical records of the hospitals where I was treated, of a spectacular nature, representing an unusual, impossible challenge to the plastic surgeons of that time of peace. Only a few years later, with the coming of the second great war, the world would erupt into a plastic surgeon's heaven, or hell, depending on his own point of view, but I can assure you that a glass windscreen on a '34 sedan can often equal a hand grenade or trench mortar. The First World War had brought about only an infant science of cosmetic surgery. It would be many years before it would mature, but never enough for my injuries.

Strangely enough, not one sliver of glass had found any of my arteries, and although I had been burned about the arms I had, by some freak accident, landed in a small trench of water, just filled by the rains, and the flames consuming my clothes and hair had been extinguished before the burns could be fatal.

When the ambulance arrived, I was all that was worth taking to the hospital. The others went directly to the mortuary. I do not remember mourning for my Hansie, or even of thinking about him. I believe that it was more than six years before I even said a word again. I know that it took many more years of speech therapy before I, Mr. Roux's "talented" actress, could speak again without stuttering.

I was certainly in a state of utter shock, and (it is silly to underplay it) I was very gravely and severely hurt, and in a condition as near to being terminal, and yet alive, as is possible. I was destined to spend many years in various hospitals. Many doctors, distinguished and later to become famous, and many professors of several medical schools were to use me as an example of a challenge to their great science, but I was the insuperable problem, the most impossible one, because of a series of circumstances which neither I, nor they, could control.

We must remember that the great antibiotics had not been invented, or, in the case of Fleming and penicillin, discovered, and that every surgical venture was a grave risk to the life of the patient. Wounds that are commonplace today easily became septic, in spite of sterile procedures, and so were nearly always fatal. In the 1930's a cold in the nose could become laryngitis within a few hours, and a day later a "spot on the lungs," then pneumonia, then death. I was the most gravely injured of all the patients of all the hospitals, yet I had managed, miraculously, to survive, in spite of sepsis, bone-structures revealed by non-growth of tissue, open wounds spreading, almost winning, then gradually subsiding. I remember all the doctors' hopes and those of my parents and family, and the anguish of their waiting. I know that there were members of my family who prayed for my death, for what they called "a release from my hideous suffering." I know also that some of those prayers were sent up to God in fear that I might live, and He was asked to take me up to heaven, in case an awful face like mine would one day officially become part of my family.

But, year by year, I survived, in spite of all the odds against me. I now believe that the greatest of all those negative factors was that I myself just did not care a tuppenny damn whether I lived or died. At no time was I ever allowed to look into a mirror, and I knew the reason why. That is why I tortured myself by taking a look, at every conceivable opportunity, whenever I was allowed out of bed, in every reflecting surface around me, from the polished trays my food was served in, to the mirrors, enamelled doors, cupboards, windows, and the porcelain baths and lavatories. I stared at myself reflected in the bedpans and the distortions on bottles and pipettes, surgical instruments, or the depths of my bowls of washing water as well as the opalescences of my clear soups.

In spite of myself, I survived. After six years of what must have been extremely devoted surgical care, the stitches took, and all of the bones of my skull had at least some kind of covering of skin, as well as flesh of a sort, a kind of lips, though nothing like those that Hansie had brought to life that night on the gravel path of the school at Warrenton. Once again, I don't want to seem to be flaunting my ill-fortune, or to be possessed of too great a sense of the gruesome, but it was fucking tough, knowing you look exactly like a child's doll that had broken into a hundred pieces, and that had been put together again with a glue that was the wrong colour of red.

Year by year, the psychological anguish, which caused withdrawal symptoms, had subsided, only to be brought up to the surface again by the continuous series of operations, each of them a major one, each potentially fatal, each holding as part of its explosion within the human system the subtleties and the grossness of shock, so often terminal. But a far deeper state of agitation existed within me, one that the infant science of analysis has only recently revealed, and I will gloss over it because too much bad luck, recounted interminably, can become a pain in the arse, and Daan and I are here trying to tell the doctors a hopeful tale; but from the sounds of it we are giving them a hard time, although I must say Daan seems to have more guts than I have. Recently I had the opportunity to take analysis, and deep therapy has revealed that I had been conscious on the night of the accident. Aware only in the subconscious sense, as if in hypnosis, I had lived through that night with its first illumination of the bodies of my burning friends, among them Hansie. Gradually the light had become stronger with dawn's approach, and I had seen and experienced everything visually. Orally, I had shouted and screamed for many hours, until my vocal chords had become dreadfully damaged, and my eyes, with their lids burned off, could not be closed as I lay looking at my own blood and that of my friends mingling in the water in which I was immersed up to my breasts.

The medical, physical, and psychological shock to my system, caused by my wounds, had been re-instated with almost every operation, and I had been on the point of death many times, but this was between the wars, when plentiful supplies of plasma were available in progressive cities like Kimberley. Shock could always be treated, could always be a little nullified, as I grew stronger in the hours and days after every operation. But the other damage, to my mind, as I lay there in the long hours of the deaths of my friends, was a greater one. It took hold of me and made me run away from life and awareness, as well as hope, and I withdrew almost totally, refusing to communicate except in a hurt whimpering as the pain wracked my body.

For many years social workers and speech therapists worked side-by-side, attempting to get me to speak again, because they knew by the sounds I made in my sleep and during the post-operative periods while still under the anaesthetics that I was capable of making sounds, and that my vocal chords were medically undamaged. There was also nothing wrong with my sense of hearing, tests had proved that quite conclusively. And, strangely enough, there was no harm to my brain, physically, and none to my memory or intelligence mechanisms. I had, as one succinct report put it, "been shocked into silence" by what I had experienced on the night of the accident, and the cumulative pain-experiences of the almost ceaseless operations had contributed to my silent state.

It was six years after the accident that my mother died, in the same hospital as I was, of a cancer of the cervix, and my sister Maryna, who had been away at University, studying in the social sciences, had returned home. It was Maryna who made me speak again. When I come to think of it, it was Maryna who made me live again. She was always the one I saw only dimly, because I was a prepubescent twelve when my accident had occurred and she was by then a breasted, menstruating twenty-one who had been loved and kissed, and who wore straps with cups in which her ripened breasts were suspended.

I had, in that time of her maturing, been a gawky, long-legged girl, all shyness and knee-caps, but with the little buds of growth around my nipples that made my breasted sister seem so greatly superior, so much older, so much wiser.

And I believe that Maryna has remained the wiser of the two of us, in spite of the often-heard adage that "suffering brings wisdom." I don't, for God's sake, want to brag about my bloody sufferings, but whatever Maryna's may have been I'm damned sure she hasn't had a hundredth of mine, and I'm a stupid clot compared to her.

She made me talk, that day when my mother died. She used it, my mother's death, as a tool to make me break my silence, and I'm grateful that she did, although at the time it seemed like a dirty trick.

She came stalking into my private, beautifully-flowered ward. She had been around for the past three months, ever since my mother's condition had become such that she had needed continuous treatment. Mother had been in hospital twice, for radium therapy. It was 1942, and there was a shortage of doctors and nursing staff. I was again, after six years as a patient, recovering from an operation. This was the last one, to cover a final bareness of bone above my upper lip, and it had healed well. At last the exterior of my face was skull-less. Mother and my father had cared for me in the most expensive ways, being moderately wealthy and not wishing to expose my condition to the stares of patients and visitors in the public wards. My final operation had been a relatively painless one, because by then I had become used to pain, and it had also been relatively successful. The miracle sulfa drugs had been discovered and were in use. Plastic surgery had made giant strides in three years of war. But there was only so much that could be done for me, and it had been done. The warm, although painful, cocoon existence of hospital life in cozy private wards was a part of the unfortunate past, and I was about to emerge into the world of the living. Strange then, that at that time, my mother who had had such a hard time of it during my long years of patienthood, was in the process of withdrawing from life. She had always done things with infinite gentleness, and it was a pity that it was impossible for the fates to see to it that her death should also be gentle. But that's the way things are, they never really work out right for the really good people of the world, do they now? If you are a really good person, and I don't mean most of you, you bloody shits, you will find that your life has always had, hovering above your head, a liberally laden fan.

Maryna came, as I have said, storming into my ward, looking and speaking like someone in a fury, a tempestuous, a storm-filled person. "Okay," she snarled, "so you're sicker than mother, she's only bloody fuckingwell dying, whereas little Maria's going to be sick for a long bloody time. Little Maria's little head is full of bloody stitches. You should see your mother, you bloody self-pitying little bitch, she's hemorrhaging out great big chunks of herself, along with the blood. Come and take a look at the way she's dying, you gutless little shit."

Now Maryna had never in her whole life spoken to me like that or to anyone that I had heard of. Whenever she had been on the long visits home from University she had been kindness itself to me. She knew that I could hear, but that I couldn't answer back, that my powers of speech were gone. So I was absolutely thunderstruck, buggered, bewildered by this outburst of hers. And what's more, I understood every word of it. Not just the words themselves, but the bigger meanings.

I had loved my mother. She had always been the loveliest, most understanding, kindest of persons. And Maryna knew this.

"Come on," she said, "no more beddy-byes for you today, you shitty little turd." She jerked the bed-clothes off me, pulled me out of bed roughly, put a gown over me, and steered me out into the corridor. I was ashamed of my face. The bandages had just been removed and there was still a big red scab, so I grabbed a towel and pressed it to the side of my face, but Maryna wouldn't let me.

"Take it off," she all but screamed, "let mother see you as you are, all covered in skin, for the first time. And not the bloody slightest expression of self-pity or I'll kick your arse from here to casualty. Smile, when you see her, and bloodywell keep on smiling, so that she can at least die knowing you've got some guts left; and don't let me see the slightest bit of that smiling-through-your-tears-bravery act, you little shit."

My expression must have asked questions, even if my tongue

couldn't, because the puzzle of her behaviour and violence was too much for me to take. My face broke into a million pieces, and, so help me Christ, right there in the hospital corridor, being frog-marched to my mother's death-bed, my sister Maryna kicked me, hard, and without mercy, right up the arse.

I was so shocked by this that I stopped crying. For six years no one had shown me anything but love and tenderness, and now, at the moment when I thought that I really needed it more than ever, I was being handled with extreme arrogance, insolence, cruelty, lovelessness, hatred, and violence by a bullying harridan of a sister who was a total stranger to me.

"Yes, you little twit," she yelled at me, so that the whole hospital could hear her, it seemed to me. "You think this is when you need love most, do you? Well, let me tell you, you've been taking it for the past six years, every bloody drop there's been, from all of us, from Mamma, Papa, me, the nurses and the doctors and the rest of the family."

Then she started acting very strangely. She put her arm around me as we got to the door of mother's ward, where I had visited mother every day since her admission, and Maryna said: "She's going, Maria, our Mamma's going, very soon now, in a matter of hours. She's the one who needs the love now, and all the braveness must come from you. She'll want to know that she's not only done everything she could do for you, she'll also want to know that it helped, that it worked. Do you understand?"

This was more like the sister I knew. So I nodded, and gave her my bravest smile, hideous though it must have been.

"Do you understand, little shit?" She shook me roughly, her whisper fierce, because we were almost in mother's ward, at the door. "Do you understand, you must show her guts, you must prove to her now, that you have guts. Do you understand?" Again, puzzled, thinking that I had understood her, I nodded.

"No," she said, harshly pressing my arm, emaciated by years of hospitalisation, bringing blood and five bruises to its surface with her fingers, the nails drawing blood. "No," she said, "you don't bloodywell understand. Now. Let's damnwell try again, and if you nod your head again you'll get another kick in the arse. Now tell me, do you understand what you must do to make her happy, something you've not done in six years?" She made her whisper sound like a scream. "Do you bloodywell understand?"

The noise that came from my throat was a horrible, stuttered, shameful sound, but it was the best I could do. Maryna embraced me, held my broken head between her hands, kissed my dreadful calloused scar-tissued lips, because I had said "yes."

"Lovely," she said, "that was lovely, darling." All her tenderness towards me had returned, and I knew immediately what love her actions had needed.

When we went into my mother's ward, she lay there, all exhausted, pale, bloodless, because the nurses had cleaned up all the gallons of blood that had spilled from her, and there was very little left.

I went to my usual side of her bed, and Maryna to hers. Knowing that sound quality or volume made no difference at all, when my mother looked at me, and at the face now flesh covered, horrible though it must have been, and smiled at me. I tried to smile back. I managed something close to a grin or a grimace, and, with all my might, straining every nerve and muscle, every bone, gristle-atom of me, every sinew, vein and corpuscle, I managed to whisper "mamma." Again, barely audible, ugly and most rasping, lengthily stuttering, but the word, unmistakeable. I like to think that she heard my little awful effort that day, but when I opened my wet eyes from the straining and the painfulness of the stutter, she had died, and Maryna had taken my hand from hers. She pressed it gently, saying softly: "That was very lovely, darling." Then she stooped and kissed my mother on the pale and bloodless lips, and whispered her own goodbye, which I think was a little too private for me to repeat here, as I do not want to say anything to displease her or bring back any pain to her.

I had had six years in which to look at the world, so I knew that Maryna had that day started my process of rehabilitation. And how very strange a coincidence it is that on the day Daan's mother, Bettina Cilliers, died, she was also to start on the rehabilitation of that strange, dumb creature that she knew lived in the yard. And he had also, in his strange way, but with even less communication than I had managed, said his own goodbyes to his mother, without knowing of it. Bettina Cilliers had died in 1971, and Mamma in 1942, twenty-nine years apart, but I still sometimes wonder if there is a connection between the two events in Maryna's mind. If it is not so, why is it that she knew that the one person in the world that Daan would need would be me, although I was as unaware of his existence as he was of life itself?

5

MINA LONG

If anybody knows anything at all about Baas Daan, it is me. After all, I have cared for him since 1921, when his birth certificate says he was born. My own first baby, the one that gave me my milk, died two days after I had pressed him out in the hut there, next to the church, the one with the pulpit that Baas Dawid had made for the Methodist Church, that is now our church. Baas Dawid made other pulpits too, like the one in the small chapel on the farm, where Nurse Maryna sits.

All sorts of people are now coming into the house and upsetting everything. I didn't ask for any help. They tell me that when the Oumiesies died the will she and the Oubaas made said that other people had to come and live in the big house and look after Baas Daan. I tell you that that is not really necessary because I know what must be done and if he ever gets sick or anything like that I can call a nurse or a doctor and they can all go to hell, coming here and talking to me.

Ag well, I don't really mind, long as they don't bugger me around too much, because I know I'm getting old. It's only that they keep coming and talking and asking me personal questions, I mean really personal questions, about words like love. And I answer them with the sort of words you use with white people, because they can't really speak. They only know words. That's all. White people know only about words, and that is what they use to speak to each other with. I tell you, if I had to use so many words as white people do my tongue will wear out and my throat will become twice its size, because white people speak so much, they are like windmills that have not been properly greased, so they make a noise all the time, day and night. You never see a lot of white people who are just sitting, or standing, or working.

Even when they are in bed together, doing, you know, they talk. And sometimes they make a big noise together, like wild animals. It is because they talk so much that they do not have any manners, and now they have come here. That's all right, so long as they know they mustn't take Baas Daan away from me. They must understand that after fifty years he does not belong to any of them any more, only me, now that all of the other people are dead, so why they want him, what they need him for, I don't know, and I don't care, but as long as they do their things after they tell me about it, and I say it is okay, then they can carry on with their nonsense.

He is just like my own baby. I know that he is fifty and that I am sixty-seven but that doesn't matter, I never look at him in that way, the way people think. But people don't know that I have to wash him, they do not understand it, so it is better that they do not know. Of course, the Oubaas and Ounooi knew, but they also knew that I went to church, and I had a husband of my own, and I would never play about with a white baby's things, no matter how old he is, because all my life I have had my own man who comes from working at Baas Billie's on the other side of the hills, and all his life he has been coming to me every Saturday and Sunday, and on Monday he goes back to work. And once, we even went to the old Minister, Doctor Webb, the Reverend, I think you call him, and we let him marry us. But it was not private because of a thing that I will tell you about.

You see, Missus Bettina asked me, one morning, what about me, didn't I want a husband and get married? I said no, I had my own man. And she asked me who he was? I said it was Adam Long who worked at Baas Billie's farm over the hills and came to me every Saturday and Sunday. And she asked me if that was the man who had given me the baby that had died, the one I would also have called Adam, because he would have been my first-born, and I said no, I didn't know, because before I got the baby and it died I had been a little on the loose side, and I had played with a couple of the men around here, and I thought it was good, to have fun like that, so nothing bothered me about it.

And then it happened that my periods stopped and I started to swell up and I got these very big breasts with their big nipples.

I swear to God man I thought I was going to burst, the way I swelled up. And while I was swelling up like that I met Adam Long, and it's just his name really, he's just average, and you mustn't think dirty about him. I met him and he said he would look after me. So I said to him: "Look," I said, "man, it's not even your baby here in me," because it wasn't you know, because my monthlies had stopped long before I met Adam. And you know, Adam Long said: "That's all right." Just like that, you know, he said, "that's all right." I'll remember it as long as I live, man, for the rest of my life, the way he said that. And I said to him: "Listen, man, just because you been with me a couple times doesn't mean you got to look after the baby. They take a bleddie long time to grow up and he's not yours. I been a naughty girl and I am being punished by God, so the Reverend says, so you don't have to look after someone else's kid, so why don't you just forget it?" And then Adam give me a clout on the left cheek.

"Listen," he said, "I told you it's all right."

So I said, "all right, if you think it's all right."

But we didn't get married right-away, because black people don't have to, just because babies are coming. Black people don't have to do anything. That's the difference between black people and white people. Black people don't have to do anything and white people have to do everything, even if it isn't really necessary, because they are busy-bodies, and talk too much. Adam Long came from a black mother and a half-a-Portuguese father, and he also had some English in him, and some Boer, but I was nearly all black, and he liked me that way. He said I was all right.

My time came and there was a big party. The baby was born and we called him Adam, after Adam Long, even when we were not yet married. We had a very big party on the Saturday, the day after little Adam was born, and I was there too, but I couldn't dance or anything, I had to stay still, because I wasn't quite right yet, and we celebrated little Adam's birth right through the night, until it was Sunday. Then a message came from the house, and a lot of wine, because Missus Bettina had gone into labour, and the doctor was there and there was a lot of drinking, because the people were having babies like it was lambing time on a sheep farm in the Karoo.

Now, I don't know what happened that night. That Sunday night, when everything was quiet. I still don't know what happened, but I went into the hut, that one there, next door to the church where Adam Long and I lived, there where those four huts and the thresher is. I was going to feed my little Adam, but when I got inside the hut, I could see him lying all wrong in his little bed, so I called to Adam Long, and he came. He called some of the older people. I remember my mother and her mother were there too. They came into the hut and they held me fast to them, and they were crying. My great breasts were heavy with milk, but my mother and Adam Long were both crying. The people outside the hut had already gathered for the death, and they were crying also, but singing as well. We sing, you know.

We sing, when there is nothing else to do because singing is something that you can do, that has the right sound. We don't mind children, you know, even if they don't have legal fathers, we don't really mind, because we have them, you know. That is why Adam Long had said: "it's all right," because it was. I don't even know why I make such a fuss of it, I would have loved that baby, and all the other people would have loved him also.

I was feeling faint, like I didn't have enough air to breathe in. I couldn't understand anything, except of course I knew that my little Adam had died. They took me outside and I sat at the door. It was now the death-hut. Adam Long and my mother made all the arrangements, they slaughtered the chickens for the people who would come to sit by me until the time for the burial. The people cried, and sang.

One way or the other, I didn't mind, because I had done something wrong, and my baby had died. So, when I had sat by the door of the death hut for hours I felt too sick to carry on living and I just allowed myself to fall off the chair, to one side. I curled up in the position of a baby inside a mother, and I let myself die.

It was a whole day later that I started living again. My eyes opened and I saw old Doctor Cloete, the new one's father. He had done something to me to bring away something that had not come away with the baby. I don't know what it was; the old women who had helped with the birth must have missed something, and it had nearly killed me. I didn't mind living, if God wanted me to, so I stayed alive, just in case.

Doctor Cloete had been at the Great House when they had come to tell him about me and my baby. There, he had just delivered my Oumiesies Bettina of a baby called Daniel, whom we were to call Daan, the little Baas. Because the Oumiesies was always a little woman, with almost no breasts at all, and I was suffering with too much milk that was hurting me, I became the young Baas Daan's wet-nurse, who would look after him and see that he grew strong because of the rich Balobedu milk of my great breasts, which is the best milk you will find in Africa.

I must also tell you about the time that I got married to Adam Long because it is something I did because I was told to, and it was unnecessary. In any case, it was a trick, and Adam Long always liked people who played tricks on other people, so he didn't mind, because he liked playing tricks on other people too. It was Missus Bettina who had asked me to do her a favour and marry Adam Long. She had arranged it with the Reverend George Webb, one weekend, but by that time Adam Long and I had been man and wife for almost four years, and we had two children. Everybody knew he was my man and I was his woman and that we would never leave each other. But Missus Bettina didn't want a black whore woman to look after her boy, Baas Daan, because he was already getting on for three years of age then. We black women, who lived with men, they called "los hotnots" which means loose Hottentots, because Afrikaans people call coloured people Hottentots, or hotnots. I suppose there must be some Hottentot blood in us, because we've got all sorts of blood in us and some of it must be from the early Cape Hottentots who once stayed there and other places before they became lost. Now nobody really knows if he is a Griqua or a Koranna or a Hottentot. The Zulus and the Machopis and the Tswana and the Swazis know what they are, so do the Basutos, but the Hottentots have become lost, even more than the Bushmen, because sometimes when we want to be insulting to someone we call him a Boesman. But when we love someone we also call him a Boesmantjie, or a little Bushman, and I know some white people who call their coloured people "Hotnots" or "Boesmans" out of love, and we can accept that, because it is in the eyes that you see things, so the words are not important.

I only had a little white blood in my veins, that went back many years, and so you will see that I am nine-tenths black. My real race is the people of Vendaland, and I come from the best of the tribes, being a Balobedu, the people of Modjadji, the Rain Queen.

And we of Africa, those who have blood that is mixed with that of the Arabs and the Whites, and all the other tribes of

Babel, and also the ones of pure blood, you will see that we speak with our eyes. If you don't believe what the eyes tell you, you're better off without eyes, like Baas Daan.

Adam Long and I went to the Reverend George Webb one Saturday afternoon, and he married us, but we tried to do it quietly, because we felt a proper pair of bloody fools, because we had been man and wife for so long already.

But we couldn't do it quietly because the Reverend George Webb had read it out in the church for three weeks before the wedding, and everybody had shut up about it. I didn't know a bloody thing about it because I was working and I never got to church very often. Adam Long, God bless him, never went to church at all except for weddings and funerals and christenings, because that's when you had parties afterwards for all the people who had been to the church. Why it was a secret I don't know, but they all shut up about it, and when Adam Long and I walked into the church to get married that day the whole blerrie place was full of people. I had to run back to my hut to put on a proper dress. Thank God I had a white one. Adam Long came and put on his shoes and socks, and I found a scarf to go under his jacket. In two minutes we were back at the church where the singing had already started. We walked down the path between the two rows of benches, and some blerrie twerp was playing "here comes the blerrie bride" on the blerrie organ, I ask you, with tears in my eyes.

It must have been Missus Bettina who had arranged this surprise wedding, because she was there with the Oubaas. They were sitting in the front row of the church. This was after the church had been taken over by the coloured people because there were almost no more Methodists among the white people, and most of the other Europeans were Dutch Reformed Church. The Reverend George Webb was a retired minister who had been out of work so long I think even God had forgotten that he had once been a proper minister in a white man's church, but he liked preaching. He was a nice old bugger, so after he retired he stayed on at Skeerpoort and us coloureds and black people took him over, and he preached to us ever-so-often. He also did the big jobs like funerals and weddings and christenings. He taught some of us people to preach also. They did most of the ordinary preaching, and they were called lay preachers, I don't know why, and I don't want any lip from you either because that wasn't it at all.

So there we were, Adam Long and I, feeling a ripe pair of blerrie paw-paws, standing in front of the whole churchful of people. The Reverend Doctor George Webb was marrying us, and pretending that Adam Long and I were not married at all, but that we had just met each other, and that we had never been to bed together. I have heard that this is something that often happens to white people. They have even told me stories about girls who were eight months and big-bellied, or "boepêns" as we call it, white girls, getting married to someone just to, what they call, "give the child a name" and getting a divorce afterwards, but that isn't our way.

Now, I don't know what I felt that afternoon, but Adam Long was very good about it, I mean us making a blerrie fool out of him and all that. I still feel bad about it when I think about it, because Adam Long isn't the sort of man you bugger about. Because Adam Long isn't the sort of man who buggers people about, but he's very strong and nobody likes to tangle with him, because once a donkey kicked him and he kicked the donkey back, and the donkey had a limp for four months, so you don't bugger about with Adam Long, and this whole church thing and wedding was buggering about. But Adam Long didn't mind, that day, because it was a funny trick, and there was a lot of drinks and cakes. Adam Long likes wine and cakes, and after the wedding, there was a wonderful party with Missus Bettina and the Oubaas staying on and having a drink and a song with us.

Someone else was looking after Baas Daan that afternoon, I forget her name, but she was a big Zulu girl who only stayed in the district for a year or two before she ran off with an old rich coloured man and they were to live in Natal, by the sea, and I never found out how much money he had, but they say it took an hour to count all his cattle and sheep and goats, so he must have been very rich. Lots of coloured people got rich in those days, because there was a lot of diamond smuggling from the diggings, and cattle smuggling from over the border, and game poaching in the biltong trade.

Adam Long never got rich in all his life, because he always had a job, and he liked to take a drink. White sweet wine, Muscadel or Hanepoot was what he liked, or Old Brown Sherry, thick and sweet, or Malmsey, any of those, even Hock or sweet White Port wine. He could drink a whole gallon on a Saturday afternoon, and again on Sunday, and still go to work on the Monday, without too much of a hangover. On Monday, at four in the morning, he would make a black cigarette out of brown paper from a cement bag, and B.B. tobacco, and smoke it, and it cleared his head one-two-three.

A lot of coloured and black girls made extra money by being whores, and sleeping with just anybody for fun and money. Once, when I was walking along the road, a white man offered me a lift, and then he started playing with me. I knew he would because white men don't just offer black girls lifts, just out of the kindness of their hearts, oh blerrie no. But I didn't mind that day, so I let him drive into the bluegum plantation, and then he gave me ten bob, and called me something nice, like "my dear." I didn't ask for the money. He just thought I was a whore. This was when I was about twenty, three years after I had started looking after Baas Daan.

About eight years after that Adam Long asked me if there had been another man, since him, so I told him not to be silly. He fetched me a clout on the side of the head and said: "You were seen, about eight years ago, in the bluegums, with a white man. My sister-in-law, Silver Adams, saw you, because you and your white man nearly rode over her and Flash Port, who was with her, and they got into a big fright because she was still married to Petrus Long, my brother, because that was before he died in the train smash at Langlaagte."

So I told Adam Long all about it, and the ten bob, and how I had not asked for money, and also that I had known it would happen once I got in the car. And Adam Long said to me: "He made you feel like a whore, with the ten bob?"

I said, "Yes, that's what made me feel like a whore. Without the ten bob I would have been just an ordinary sinner, but the ten bob made me feel like a whore."

Adam Long asked, "What did you do with the ten bob?"

And I felt like telling him that I had torn it up, I was so blerrie insulted, but I had to be careful, because you don't bugger about with Adam Long, so I said the truth: "I took it," I said, "back to the shop, where I had just been, and bought myself a scarf and some chocolates, and the change I kept and spent over the weeks afterwards, and I never told you about it because I didn't want you to think that I was a whore. But Adam, why did you wait for eight years before you told me you knew about it?"

"Because," said Adam, "last Wednesday I took a girl into the bushes, and it's been bothering me, and I don't want it to bother me, so I wanted to tell you about it, because I enjoyed it, and I didn't want it to worry me any more. I knew about your white man, so now we're quits."

I didn't like that at all, and I told Adam Long about it, but he wouldn't let me scream at him or clout him back. He just held my hands and told me to shut my trap, with a smile on his face, so I let it go, because you don't bugger about with Adam Long, and I knew that he wouldn't bugger me about, so I left it. A man is a man, and so long as he comes back to you afterwards, and you get your share of him, you can't complain.

But I was telling you about the party after our wedding that day, when we felt such a pair of blerrie fools. It was a wonderful party, with all the food and drink that anybody wanted; paper plates with blue paper serviettes; salads and cold meats; polonies, hams, slices of cold beef, pork and mutton; all the puddings that you could buy in the shop, like jellies and custard, sponge cake and biscuits, and a lot of stuff like raisin bread, butter, white bread, with butter, peanut butter, and jam. And canned fruits.

That day Adam Long was very gentle with everybody, especially me. He knew why the Oumiesies wanted us to get married, because she had a low opinion of me and this marriage was to stop me from being a "los hotnot" or a "hoermeid" which means "whore of a kaffir girl." He kept on laughing, because he said it was a blerrie funny trick, and he was drinking, eating, and putting his arm around me, and he kept on looking into my eyes, to see if I was not too unhappy, and he kept on saying to me: "It's all right, Mina, it's all right."

That night, he was very sweet to me, the way he sometimes is when he hasn't seen me for two or three weeks, because of his work, or sometimes when he wants me for a second time, right after, he is also like that, very sweet and very kind. I felt like a woman who had just been married, and I told him so, and he said: "That's all right, that's how you should feel. I want you to feel like that, so it's all right if you do."

I tell you all this because I want you to know that I have nothing to complain about. Even though I had to get up every four hours of my life, it was good, and Adam Long understood for all the years. I don't want anybody to think that looking after Baas Daan was trouble, because it wasn't.

I was made his wet-nurse that day 1921 when my own baby died, and after that I didn't live in my own hut again, except for weekends when Adam Long came home, for four hours at a time. I had to go to Baas Daan every four hours, but, with Adam Long about, you can have a lot of jollifications every four hours. During the week I was given a room next-door to the one that was the nursery in the house. It was a lean-to, just off the side verandah, and I could get into the baby's room from my own without waling anybody, whenever he got restless during the night. He never cried like other babies, just a very quiet sort of a whimper, or you can even call it a kind of a grunt, like a little baby piglet makes, but very quiet, and it didn't mean anything. I mean, most babies, or all babies, when they want to be fed they cry out and you give them the bottle or the breast and they shut up, but with Baas Daan it was quite different, he didn't know about making a fuss when he was a baby, the way other children do. He never sucked his thumb, and he never cried, and he never screamed, not for anything.

He was a little baby saint, I thought, and I often told his mother: "Missus, little Baas Daan, he is one of the saints, like in the book of the saints, and he never asks for anything at all." I never knew why Missus Bettina smiled the way she did, because I was simple, and in those first days while I was nursing Baas Daan I had no idea, and neither did she. But she was a mother, and she did spend long hours with him, and I think now that even then, in those first few weeks, she must have known that there was something wrong, although she could not have told anyone what it was. It must have been just feeling, because I never heard her mention it to anyone.

Baas Daan grew up just like any other baby, but only us who cared for him knew there was a difference. To the visitors who came to see him in his cot he looked like an ordinary child. In those days it was a big thing for visitors to come to the nursery where the nurse, that was me, was rocking the little one in his cot. And all the women would say what a lovely little one he was, and how he looked like so and so, and what a pretty face he had, and how he reminded them of his great grandfather, and that he would one day be prime minister. Sometimes, people would come in while I was changing his nappies, and the women visitors would look away, because in those days you didn't look at a man child's things unless he was your own or you were his wet-nurse or a grandmother or something very close. But the men, in their watch-chains and waist-coats and moustaches and the sideburns of those days when men were funny about their face hairs, like they are again today, those men visitors would crowd around close, and slap Bass Dawid, the baby's father, on the back, and they would make ugly and rude remarks about the baby's things.

"Just like his father," one of them would say.

"More virgins bite the dust," was another thing they liked. They must have, because they laughed.

And Jock Travis, who had once been the village farrier and blacksmith would say: "He's hung like a bloody horse, that one."

I always thought it strange, that they should talk like that in front of their womenfolk, and in front of me, but those days are long gone, when anything a man says in front of a woman is strange. I am now over the age of seventy, and I've seen all sorts of fashions, and I've heard all the fashions too, in the way people speak, but you know, the things men say when they see the things of a man-child are still exactly the same as they were fifty years ago. The same words, the same expressions on their faces, even the same silly pride on the faces of the fathers. I know because the fashion has now spread to the coloured people as well, and, whereas once it would have been unheard of to discuss anybody's things in front of women, or a coloured man, now it's common. And to me too, I also think it is common, and I wish people wouldn't do it.

But nobody, not any of the visitors had any idea that there was anything wrong with Baas Daantjie, the little one, whom I called "Kleinbasie" meaning "my little boss" in those days. I saw nothing wrong with it, and they tell me now that it was part of slavery to call a white man "Baas" and a white child "Basie" or a white woman "Miesies" or her daughter "Nonnatjie." These were the words of the time and we lived with them, alongside of them, and they were in us and around us, and we had no resentments or acceptances, it was the way things were. "Basie," "Kleinbasie," or "Baas Daantjie" were just what he was called, there was no subservience or slavery in it for me, and there would have been no superior feelings if I had not used the correct polite expressions, except that I would have felt that I was being rude. And I have never been really rude to any person in my life. I have hurt people, but I didn't know that I was doing it, so I think God will forgive me.

Baas Daan's trouble started when he was born, and it was all my fault, because Doctor Cloete had been called away to attend to me and my illness when my baby had died. He had not finished treating Baas Daan, and he had not put the drops into his eyes, that would take away the germs of the gonorrhoea, as all doctors and midwives had to, so that the child's eyes would be safe. Only three weeks later did he remember what he had forgotten, but by then it was too late, and the germs had eaten out a lot of the middle of the eyes. Although you couldn't see it from looking at him, he was blind.

I have tried to blame myself, and I take the blame gladly, but Adam Long says I am talking rubbish. I have asked the Reverend Webb about it, and he also says I am talking nonsense. So I feel bad, but it is nonsense. It's something I don't understand.

That day Doctor Cloete told the Oumiesies Bettina and the Oubaas Dawid that the child had become blind because of trouble with the dirty sickness, and they wanted to kill me. Doctor Cloete told them that he had already examined me, and I was clean, and so was the Oubaas. It was from the mother. I was sent out of the room. There was a lot of shouting and crying, with bad words, and Doctor Cloete rode away, while the Oumiesies was shouting like a mad woman. Then I heard my Kleinbasie screaming, so I ran into the nursery. He was lying on the floor and blood was coming from his mouth and ears. Missus Bettina was also lying on the floor, outs for clouts, with a big bruise on her jaw, like she had been knocked out. Baas Dawid was sobbing his heart out in the corner. It was the only time that I ever heard the Kleinbasie scream. He was quiet for a long time after that day, many years. As if he didn't want to live any more. I often wonder what went on in that little brain of his, but I never found out anything.

That day, we called back Doctor Cloete, and he left me with the Kleinbasie, who seemed to be dead, except he was breathing. The doctor spent a long time with the Oubaas Dawid and Missus Bettina, but I don't know what they said to one another. The best thing, with gon, is to cure it, says Adam Long, but white people make a big thing out of it.

That same day Oubaas moved into his own bedroom.

Some people might still say that it was me with the gonorrhoea.

Well, you can ask anyone who has ever known me, and you will hear that it is not the truth. I have always been afraid of being called dirty, and filth is something that I guard against, just as I will, with my life, guard the things that are mine from coming to harm.

But in those far-off days my charge was my Kleinbasie, and I did all that was in my power to make him comfortable after he had been made sore. Because he never seemed to ask for anything, or to need anything, I felt that I had to do more for him than I normally would have done for a child. He was always awake when I came into his room, no matter what the time of day or night it was. Because he lay on his back, or his stomach, or his side, it seemed to me that he was looking in whatever direction he was facing. It never entered my mind that his eyes were open because he didn't know about closed eyes. I had always thought that eyes opened because of noises, or light. You see, his eyes were eyes that moved, from one side to the other, and up and down, and if they had a slightly misty look people thought, "what lovely eyes he has."

They painted portraits of people in the early days, before the box Brownie camera, and they used ordinary house paints that came from little tubes, but with the same linseed oil and turpentine from the chemist, that you use for medicine. In those portraits, especially the ones of children or beautiful ladies, they always painted in the eyes a little misty, and my Kleinbasie's eyes had that same look about them, like some painter had tried to make him more pretty.

And, I won't tell you a word of a lie, but it was eighteen days after I started looking after him that I first found out that the poor little bugger was going blind. And remember, he drank all those days at my breast, so it makes you wonder, doesn't it? I mean, do we see only what we want to see, or do we ignore things we don't want to know, or what? After he was injured he never cried for his feed, so I thought that he was a very uncomplaining child. I fed him every four hours, as I had been told to, by his mother, the Oumiesies Bettina. I would go to the tap in the yard, draw a pail of water, then I would go to my room and wash my hands and my breasts in soapy water, the way you wash before you milk a cow.

Wait, that sounds like I am complaining that they treated me like an animal. They didn't. It was just as it should have been.

We who grew up and lived on farms have never been insulted by being likened to our livestock. Our tender names for our loved ones are words like "lamb" or "skapie" or "bokkie" meaning 'little goat' and so on.

I would soap my large breasts, heavy with milk, and dry them with some towels, threadbare but still of good quality, of which I had a big pile that the missus had given me. My soap was a red carbolic like white people used, and I had a good iron bed with a mattress, not just a bag of straw on the floor. It was a coir mattress, which was a luxury. Adam Long beat it out for me once every year, so that it was all fluffy and soft again, before he stuffed it back into the ticking bag. I would then take new leather washers that I made from the uppers of old boots, the size of a half crown, and string, and with an upholstery needle I would quilt-stitch my mattress every square ten inches. Oh, it was a lovely mattress. And, you know, Adam Long never once used it with me, because it was my house mattress, and we people were not supposed to sleep together in the same house where white people slept. It would have been very rude.

So much of what I say seems like I am moaning, now that it is past 1970 and the world has changed. You may, if you want, feel bitter about it, but I would prefer it if you didn't. I'm just telling what happened, and how things were done in those days, so please don't get the idea that we even gave these things a second thought. Oh I know now that there were people, what do you call them, agitators, or revolutionaries, or Bolsheviks, or just cheeky people, but Adam Long and I, we were never like that, although we heard a speech once, but I will think a bit before I tell you about it, because I don't think it is my place to report speech by agitators. No I don't think I will tell you about it at all, because, although it made me think a bit, it isn't my place to tell about it. You see, I have always known my place, and I think I will stay in it. Sometimes, when I say "blerrie," it's because I'm shy about something, or angry, but it isn't meant to be rude, it's just one of the sounds I make. For a black girl in those days, I was very well off. I ate the same foods that the white people in the house ate, and much more. They gave me all the rich things, the gravies and the marrowbones with the marrow still in them and they never gave me separated milk, always the richest from the Jersey cow, which I loved, and I was fond of puddings also. All the cast-off clothes came to me as well, because

Missus Bettina and I were nearly the same build, although she had to put cotton-wool into her bodice to make it look like she had breasts, because for a while, breasts were fashionable, before about 1926, when they went out of fashion right up to 1936, when they came right back into fashion again. I see by the magazines that they read in the Great House, and throw away, that now breasts are out again, and I'm in fashion, because they are now so out that you mustn't even see them, and mine have finally disappeared. Well, to tell you the truth, they are still there, but they are flat, and long, so you can't see them at all when I am dressed.

But I had what Doctor Cloete called a "truly magnificent bosom" when I took over the job of looking after my Kleinbasie. Big, pointed ones, with willing, jutting-out nipples. Thank God I never became very fat, it seemed that all the good things they fed me at the big house went into my bosom, which, of course, is what they wanted. Adam Long never had to complain about my figure, because, while I wasn't thin, I was never really fat. I asked him about it once and he said: "It's all right, Mina, it's all right."

Now when I come to think of it it seems that all that Adam Long ever said were those few words, and you may think I'm lying or trying to make him sound stupid. But he was the foreman at the farm, Billie's, where he worked, on the other side of the mountain, and he didn't speak much, never needing to say a lot, because he wasn't ever a man for talking rot or buggering about. He just said the few words that he thought were right. Or maybe he didn't even think so far, because he was always better at doing the right thing. He never bothered about saying the right thing, because, he says: "If you talk too much you can talk yourself right into trouble."

Before I fed the Kleinbasie I would soap and dry my breasts, and put on a clean blouse, of which I had nearly twenty. The wash-girl at the Great House, Silver, used to say that I had more laundry to do than the white people. I would sometimes change into three clean blouses a day. Not that people were strict with me. They didn't have to be. It was just that I was a clean person in my own way and while it was possible to be clean I made a big thing of it, and I would often hear people say, behind my back, when they thought I wasn't listening, that Mina was the cleanest "meidjie," that means "little black girl," that they had ever seen. It was one of the reasons why I was employed in that one job for so long, because if you are dark-skinned and people can describe you as "clean" you will never go short of a job. But that wasn't why I was that way. It was just that that's what I liked, and how I liked people to think about me. I remember the first time that I had gone through the cleansing ritual when the Kleinbasie was only one day old. I was carefully watched by Missus Bettina, who had had my washbasin and jug brought into her room, so that she could see that everything was right. Baas Dawid was there too, and in those days black girls were not supposed to be shy of their breasts before white men, and many were not, but I always was. But it was his boy-child I was to feed, so I felt that it was all right, and I stripped myself to the waist, and washed in the warm and soapy water, face and all, bending, or rather kneeling over the wash-basin on the Persian rug that covered the yellow-wood floor. But when I had finished washing my face, before I soaped elsewhere, he had left the room. He was like that, Oubaas Dawid, and I often think he was kinder to me because he had embarrassed me. After I had washed and dried myself I picked up the baby. He had been in the world for only a few hours, and he was already greedy. When he had filled his little belly he let go and I put him back into his cot, a kind of crib, really a woven wicker thing that had been made by blind people in England, because it was only a few years after they had had that horrible war that left so many people blinded and without lungs because of the gas, but in spite of the sad story of its making, it was a very pretty thing, with many fancy bits of weaving of canes of different sizes and thicknesses, and it had been decorated by laces and all sorts of frilly things. He was lying between blankets of the purest Waverley lambswool, covered by sheets of Egyptian cotton, and all in blue, like his pale misty eyes. I had been to school and I could read all the labels, even the little brass one with the black lettering on the canopy that said "manufactured by the Sheltered Employment Workshops, St. Dunstan's, London."

Because I had often had to work with babies in the huts where we lived, especially my mother's steady stream of children, I knew how they were handled. So I took him up, very carefully, that day three weeks later after he had been made so sore, and, with a clean cloth draped over my shoulders and skirt, I held him to me. I knew that he had run away, in his head, as people do, when life is too much to take, and he was making that tiny little noise of his. But, when his mouth was put next to my nipple, nothing happened, and I bent down with him, and I gently stroked my breast, downward, with my fingers, so that a little trickle of milk ran into his mouth. After that his throat took over, and he swallowed. Thank God there was that hunger feel, that impulse to feed and to swallow, and now that he tells me that he does not remember having been fed by me, I do not quite believe him. I think it was so tiny, that feeling for the breast and its contents, that it just didn't become a part of what his nerves or his brain could cope with. I know that the doctors have a lot of stories about how he managed to eat all those months after he had been hurt, when he went away from the world, without choking himself, but that is what I think and it makes sense to me.

The doctors can say what they like, and they will, but I will stick to what I believe in. I think that he did it because pigs and dogs and all the animals of the world do it. They eat food when it is brought to their mouths by mothers or by nature, and half of the creatures on earth don't even know that they are eating, and that is what I believe happened to my Kleinbasie on that terrible day. I knew then that he didn't want to feel anything or taste anything, I knew only that the rich life of my breast-milk had to go down into that little throat, and I got it down there, and somewhere in him was something that made him move his throat in the right way, and he swallowed. I know now that he had no need of food at all, that he would have told me to go away if he could have spoken. An older child would have run away, and hidden himself from the world. And that is what the Kleinbasie did, deep in his brain. But I knew he was still in there, hiding away from the people or the things that had given him pain. He couldn't get away from me, though, because I could comfort him with my rich milk, and the warmth of my breast, even if he pretended that he didn't want to. And luckily hunger starts deep down. The stomach is far away from the brain, and it was that thing he had, of feeling deep down, that must have made him take that first swallow. When all the spillage had been wiped off, I knew that he would be, in Adam Long's words, "all right."

But, in spite of the fact that I knew that I could get food into him, I also knew that there was trouble. The reason I got that feeling was because of a strange voice, inside me, that made no sense at all. It was saying "he's too beautiful." And it made me go cold all over. It is difficult for me to tell you about what the doctors said, because they have a way of telling you nothing while pretending they know something, and I was almost always present when there was a doctor around. They use words like "motor responses" that made me think of spark plugs, but Nurse Maryna tells me that it means only that you do something out of instinct, or feeling, or something, so she doesn't really know anything either. But she is good with sick people, and so am I, so I will not speak ill of her. Although she has had a hard life, she has never harmed anybody, not even the bad people who have given her a hard time.

Now I have told you how it happened that I found him lying on the floor that day, and how I tried to do for him what should be done.

Day after day, for many months, I held the Kleinbasie to my breast, and milked myself into his mouth, that I had to hold open with a spoon. It helped to funnel the milk to where it was supposed to go, down his gullet. Then I had an idea. I would simply wait until one breast was so swollen with milk that it would start leaking of its own accord, and when that happened, I took him to the nipple and fastened his little lips around it, and the milk flowed out into his mouth. This went on for a long time, and I despaired that he would ever get it right, but one day, about nine months after that horrible day, I felt, for a small moment, a distinct sucking, an outward pressure caused by him, and the milk flowed freely. Now the doctors tell me that if I had not persevered, taking him from my breast and de-choking him, upside down, slapping him hard, he would have died, and that this "response" thing is what they called his first sucking, when he started to come back after running away. It didn't happen again for quite a long while, several weeks, and then, one day I felt it again.

It began to happen more frequently, even regularly, and the day had to come when it happened every time he put his mouth to my breast. By this time more than a year of his life had passed, but he was at least sucking and swallowing, and those were the two great events of his first year.

I have often heard people call him a vegetable, but I can tell you that that was a real baby who sucked at my breast and he felt like a real baby, with all its helplessness, and all its needs, and all its warmth, and I felt for it the way a woman feels for a real baby.

I did not want to wean him from my breast, so I kept on allowing him to feed there, until Missus Bettina started to get worried. She thought the baby was "backward" as she called it, and one day she spoke to Doctor Cloete about it. But he was a very old-fashioned doctor, and I remember the way he spoke to Missus Bettina, because I was in the room, suckling the child.

"Mrs. Cilliers," he said, "the child is a little slow in learning. I know you're worried because he hasn't said any words yet and he doesn't seem to recognise people by their voices. This is quite common."

I could have told him something. But I shut up, because it wasn't my place to talk when a doctor, who had been to the big university at Cape Town, told her not to worry.

I wanted, also, to tell her not to worry. But it was only because I knew that I would take care of the little one, no matter what happened. We all hoped for the best the first year, thinking that whatever was wrong would be fixed up, somehow, by nature, or by God, or by miracles, or by prayers. I had already started asking God for a miracle, because all the little games that I had taught my brothers and sisters by the age of one year didn't mean anything to my Kleinbasie. He couldn't clap "handies" or "hush-a" or any of the things that make a one-year-old child. He just lay there in his cot, looking very beautiful, wearing all the beautiful clothes that his mother had made and bought for him. And she too, often sat by his cot, looking very worried.

His father came right out with it one day, right in front of me, and that is how the question of his being backward came to be asked of Doctor Cloete, and I knew then that the troubles were starting, and would never stop. They did not give me much of a bad time, they just became part of life at the Great House.

Doctor Cloete had set their minds at rest for a little while, telling them of children who had reached the age of thirty months before they could say "mama," but he didn't know of the swallowing, and of the little noises that never changed. And nobody explained to him that there must be something wrong with a baby who never cries. Nobody told him. He was told only enough to make the silly statement he was forced into, because there was no way out for us, for Missus Bettina, or his father, or me. If we talked we would have to tell of what we really knew, and it was too early to stop hoping that a miracle would happen. Babies are supposed to be helpless, and if they are a little more powerless than usual in the first year, people don't as a rule say much about it. I wonder now if I should use the word "powerless" instead of saying "crippled." Or that his parents knew it, and I knew that they did, because it was in their eyes.

If they could have spoken to me, the way it is possible to speak without words, I would have told them, in the same way, without words, that what they knew was fact or truth, anything you like to call it, but real trouble. And I am sorry to have said that old Doctor Anton Cloete had made a silly statement, because that is rude. When two people deliberately hold back things they know they should tell their doctors, then it isn't the doctor's fault that he allowed the Oumiesies Bettina to lead him to another room in the house where the tea things had been set, and to continue his speech there, instead of next to the baby.

I heard their voices in the drawing room for a long time that afternoon, and a lot of their words, but what it all came to really was that Doctor Cloete thought that the trouble with the Kleinbasie might still come to its own end, except for the blindness, and that was really what Missus Bettina wanted to hear him say so that she could tell it to her husband, Baas Dawid. And Baas Dawid wanted his wife, Missus Bettina, to hear the same thing. So they were all fooling each other.

I sometimes wonder about those three people that day. The Missus and the Doctor, both knowing, and Baas Dawid, who wasn't there that afternoon; he was in town, so he said, but I think he had left the house so that the other two could make up the story that they would tell him. Did Doctor Cloete know what was coming their way, and was he just postponing the time of telling them out of kindness or, well, any other reason he may have had? I don't know. The new doctors who came to look into Baas Daan's head after Missus Bettina had died, say that they don't believe it, that he knew all the time, and that he was letting nature take its own time to break the bad news to the parents. Perhaps that is so.

I do not wish to speak ill of the dead here, he was a clever doctor for the croup and the whooping-cough, and he could break a fever and get bowels to work; he set broken bones and sewed up open sores, and he managed to get people well oftener than other doctors, but he never seemed to me a man who would take it on himself to tell the parents of a child like the Kleinbasie everything he knew. Perhaps he was too soft, or too gentle, for such a thing. Or perhaps he did it because he did not have the wisdom.

Who am I to say that doctors should tell their patients everything? Perhaps that is one of the things that they are taught at the university, not to tell their patients everything, or as little as possible, or, the more serious it got, nothing at all. Who knows?

I have never pretended to understand what goes on in a man's mind. They, the men, always talk about what goes on in women's minds, and that they will never understand them. But I think women are very straightforward creatures, easy to understand if you've got a half-a-brain, something like my Adam Long's, but men, they are a blerrie mystery to me that I will never understand at all, and it is possible that Doctor Cloete was really a deep one. I often ask myself of the other one that day. The father, Oubaas Dawid, who knew that the doctor was coming in the afternoon. And he had always slept a little after the midday meal, which was the big meal of the day in the big house, before they called it "lunch" and changed it to cold meat and salad.

The Oubaas liked his food, and he ate a lot at noon, and he would sleep nearly every afternoon, but on that afternoon, when the doctor came, he had made some excuse about having to go to the shop or the lands or something that was supposed to be urgent, I forget what and he almost seemed to me to be running away from what he thought the doctor would say. A sort of afraid, funny look in his face as he drove off in his new 4-cylinder Chev, making too much smoke and noise and dust, as if he was scared of running into the doctor. Nothing had ever scared him in his life, and I was worried for him.

Did he know, that day, if he stayed, and we all talked too much, Missus Bettina with her fears that was knowledge, I with my eyes that knew, he with his good sense that had already told him, and the doctor with his almost certain knowledge, that the Kleinbasie's secret would not have been a secret any longer? Did we, that day, deliberately put off the troubles for another day in the future? Now that I think of it I'm sure that we did, and that it wasn't cowardice. No, not that. Maybe it was what we call love, but I doubt it. Maybe the Oubaas was trying to spare the feelings of his wife, but I don't think so. I wasn't trying to spare anyone anything. I knew he was mine to look after, no matter what was wrong, and I had already hidden from them the knowledge of the swallowing and the sucking. And the doctor, he may have been waiting for the miracle injection that would cure all the illnesses of mankind, but I don't think so. No, I think we were playing for a little more time, all of us, to plan a little better, now that we were face-to-face with it; that he was a backward child, and that, even if he was the most beautiful baby of all, there was something terrible, somewhere, something wrong.

But another six months were to go by, making eighteen months in all, before we all admitted to each other what the real trouble was. It was my fault. I had been feeding him at my breast for all that time, eighteen months, and although they were still producing food for him with a reasonable willingness, not as much as before, I felt it was time for him to have a feeder. So they got him one of those spoon-and-pusher sets, and I made the right kind of mush that you feed to the little ones, strained vegetables, and porridges from corn and oatmeal, and the best rich Swiss goat's milk, and I tried to wean him from my breast. Of course it broke my blerrie heart to try, man, but it had to be done, because he was eighteen months, dammitall. Sorry hay, sorry. I didn't mean to talk like a kaalgat Koranna, that is, if you'll pardon me, a bare-backside kaffir of the Koranna tribe, but it happens every now and then that I forget my manners and all the words I learned by staying for fifty years in the Great House. Sorry. Anyway, I made some of the stuff and put it in his spoon and pusher feeder, and I tried to feed him, but of course he knew only what a breast was. Food was something that you put in his mouth and he sucked and it fixed him up inside where his stomach was, that's all he knew. But, with this new food his good hand came up, just a movement, because he moved quite a lot sometimes, and other times he just lay there, and it splashed a lot of hot food into his eye, and he closed it, and then opened it again, as if nothing had happened. I washed it out, but he could not move the muscles of his eyes properly, so I knew he was in bad trouble with his body, because he could only jerk, without any control.

Now I must tell you that I had seen him, sometimes, not very often, with his eyes closed, specially on hot days when we had him on the stoep, his eyes would close, but not very often, and always, in his cool, shady room, they would be open, but they would move about, like he could see. But these movements were bad, like a madman's, and jerky. And his one arm was all right, but the other arm, and the two legs, they just jerked about. So that day when I splashed hot food in his eye and it opened and in the wrong way closed I knew something important. The eyes were blind, but not dead. Of course I had wiped his eyes out, but only at the corners where a little sleep would gather. Open-lidded sleep. And of course the tears had washed specks of dust and even tiny insects to the corners, but I had ignored all of this, because I knew, and Missus Bettina and his father didn't know, and of course Doctor Cloete knew that he was blind, but he also did not know that although the Kleinbasie's eyes could not see, they were still alive.

The biggest thing that they didn't want to talk about was that the child had bad muscles that didn't work together with the sinews, what we call paralytic, not paralysed, like the white people say spastic. So that night, when they came in to say goodnight to their child, they found me feeding him from the breast again.

"Didn't the feeder work, Mina?" the Oumiesies asked. "Never mind, he'll get used to it."

"He is blind," I said, "but we must admit it that he is also deaf, and he is a paralytic too and it happened that day of the big trouble, when he was three weeks."

"Nonsense," said Missus Bettina, "I don't want you to say such things, never again, do you hear, Mina? Never again."

She left the room, and the Oubaas Dawid stayed on.

"Mina," he said, "I don't know how long you have known, but it is a knowledge that has grown with me through these months, for a long time now. I have kept quiet about it, because there is nothing you can do for a child who is deaf and dumb and blind with a brain that doesn't work with his body, except to give him the best possible care. Do you understand?"

"We should have spoken, Oubaas, you and I."

"No Mina, it wouldn't have helped. There is no way to speak to him, or to help him. We can only love him. He doesn't know. He lives in a world without sound, without light or colours. To have spoken of it would have been to no avail."

"And now," I said, "now, do we speak of it now?"

"You and I," he said. "When it is necessary. He will be a child for many years yet, and the world may change. Let us spare the Missus all of this, because she has put it out of her mind. It is a weakness, but she has done it, so let it be as it is."

"It is not a weakness, Oubaas. It is a wound. So she has put a plaster over it, so that it cannot be seen."

"Then we must respect it, that she doesn't want it known," he said.

"I will tell no one. I have told no one thus far, because I was as you were, afraid of telling myself the truth, and now, as you say, there are still years of childhood left, and I will look after him. There are things that I need, and you must go to the city and speak to the doctors at the hospitals. There are shops where they sell things for such people to help with their feeding, and the training of babies, and you must get all these things, because I already know much of what I need from the things I have heard people say. But Oubaas, what of Doctor Anton, should we tell him?"

"He knows," said the Oubaas, "as we all knew. And he told me about it a long time ago, about its possibility. But he did not want us to speak of it, because of his hopes."

"And where are his hopes now, Oubaas?"

"I don't know. I think they were false. To encourage us, to make us feel better. He reads all the books, all the papers on the subject written at the great universities, but he has no faith. The operations are too enormous, the risks too great, even for the deafness they have something but it is too near to the brain, and any germ, from the knife, would mean that we have killed a defenceless thing. Even so, the other doctors who know all about the ears are still afraid of operating."

"You mean they have no faith, in their own work?"

"That's about it, Mina. But you must try to understand Doctor Cloete. He has sent too many people into hospital from here, with blood pouring, or scratches, or wounds, or appendicitis, or tonsillitis, or any of those things. A lot of them died in the hospitals. They are not dangerous things in themselves, it is the knife that is dangerous."

Well, I don't know about such things, but I do know that in 1923, when you went to hospital for an operation, you were in deadly danger. Very few people escaped the knife, but, although a lot of them lived, a lot of them also died. And now, you young doctors who tell me you don't understand Doctor Cloete's behaviour at that time, let me tell you that I understand and I forgive him, because I was a young girl in 1923 and many of my people, and the people I had known white, black, coloured, and Indian, had gone off to hospital. And very often the next time you saw them they were in a long box. So don't tell me he was backward. He wasn't. He was afraid. Blerrie afraid. And I don't blame him. And if they had asked my permission to send Baas Daan off to the hospital, so that they could cut out the things from his ears that made him deaf, let me tell you that I would have sent them away, because I was also just as afraid as Doctor Cloete was. A long time later we found out that the ear operations of 1923 would not have done anything for the Kleinbasie, anyway.

So, it was good to know that Doctor Cloete was a good man, and that he was worried not just about the Kleinbasie, but also about all of us who cared for the little soul.

And that is why I kept to myself the other knowledge that the Kleinbasie had run away from the world for a while, and that he didn't care for taste, and feel, and smell, and even pain. And this is something to talk about, at some other time, and I will, but now I can't go on any more, because my throat is getting dry, and I don't feel like talking any more.

Missus Bettina was like this, as I am now, too full to speak, most of the time after that day when the horrible trouble happened. She would make it known that she was about, and that we couldn't misbehave in any way. I knew that she checked the Kleinbasie regularly, several times a day, and even picked him up, because when I came back from washing his nappies or cleaning things, the blankets would be different. But she never again spoke of the Kleinbasie to me, I mean, about the things that were wrong with him.

She had put her heart out of sight, so that there was nothing for people to see, except a beautiful young woman who was growing older more quickly than other white women do. And she asked the Oubaas to let her have her own bedroom, and he allowed it. They would sit together at table, and pray together, and do all the things that married people do, except that they did not share a bed any longer. This isn't any of my business, but it is something that was caused by the troubles of the Kleinbasie, and I don't want to talk about it.

It was so sad to see her sitting at the window of her large bedroom, writing in a book that she called her journal. Of course

I never asked what she was putting in the book, and I couldn't have peeped anyway, because she kept her little gilt desk locked. I suppose they found the book that she wrote in after she died. I wonder what she put in it, sitting there, alone, year after year, and, sometimes, writing words.

6

BETTINA CILLIERS

From my window I can see all the way over the fields to the low hills beneath the Magaliesberg that loom up like a larger, bluer silhouette, and I often wish that I had a talent for painting. If I had I would have liked to do a good watercolour of that scene; the picture before me now, as I glance up from this page.

It is a beautiful journal. My husband Dawid gave it to me a number of years ago, before Daan's birth, but I have only recently begun to use it. To look at it, one would think it a Bible, or some such great work, so beautifully is it bound, with little gilt decorations around the leather bindings, and with its own little clasp and lock, so that when it is put away in my desk, it is doubly secured against prying eyes.

When Dawid gave it to me, I asked him what he wanted me to write in it, because I was not sure of his intentions. And he said what I thought was a strange thing for such a practical man: "Everybody has need of a special, private place. Sometimes, in the past, ladies used journals such as this to put in those words they wanted to remember, or thoughts, or descriptions of days. Even little fragments of poetry and enlightened thoughts, or texts from the Bible. Such things were kept in their journals, faithfully copied out from their sources. Some ladies used their journals as diaries, others as grand recipe books. Other ladies were amateur poets, or fancied themselves as deep thinkers, and they used such journals to record their thoughts and their fantasies.

"But I want you to have it, to be a private place for yourself, and you may put into it whatever you wish, and I will never pry into it, or ask to see it, or anything that is in it, unless you ask me to look."

Now this kind of thinking, from Dawid, was not really in character. He was a violently jealous man, and would never allow me to discuss any previous romances I had had. He always said that those things were none of his business. In the first days of our marriage he had been under the impression that he had taken me as a virgin bride, and I was well aware of my fraud, and I suppose the whole world must be by now. We have tried to keep our secrets, but the gossips are ever-active in the little village.

I would have given all of my life if I could have spared him that day when I was reckoned with, the day that Doctor Cloete told me the reason for little Daan's blindness. The infection had not come from Dawid, but from me. I had, once only, a few years before, allowed a man to touch me, and I had even allowed a limited penetration, which I had stopped as I came to my senses with the pain of the imminent loss of my virginity. That moment had been the mistake, and it hadn't even been a pleasure. It was a silly little war-time romance, not even necessary as a soldier's farewell because a few months later the armistice had been declared, long before he, newly joined, could have reached the front. I never heard of him or saw him again. I know his name was William Clark, and that it had happened after a ball, in Pretoria, at his regiment's headquarters. My head had been turned by the glamour of the occasion, I suppose, but don't let me allow myself to make excuses.

This confession is to absolve my husband, Dawid, from responsibility. I know that the man is always accused of being the carrier of those diseases, but in this case I was at fault. It was a very light infection, almost impossible to diagnose, or even to notice. I had certainly never thought of it after it had disappeared, because I had treated the initial slight discharge with a solution of Lysol. I had had no idea that it was a venereal infection, simply because I didn't know that such things existed. So it had been only partially cured, to show itself again at little Daan's birth.

I made my confession, on the day of the discovery, after my husband had sworn to God and on the souls of his parents, a huge oath indeed, that he had had only me, and that he was entirely free of symptoms of any kind, which Doctor Cloete confirmed could be the case if we had been intimate during the dormant phase. After I had fallen pregnant we had respected the custom of those days and stayed apart sexually. It must have been then that the dormant phase ended, and the bacteria became active again. There had been no pre-natal internal examinations, also a custom of the time, and the slight irritation I had felt I ascribed to my condition. Doctor Cloete could, and did, cure me easily, but there was no solution for the violence of our argument over the blind child that I had brought into the world. In a moment of deep despair, when I must have been quite mad, I had tried to destroy him by literally beating out his brains. I had been stopped by Dawid, who had knocked me unconscious, and so relieved me of my hysteria. So there you are. As unimpassioned a record of the happenings of that day as I can manage.

Lately, now that the trouble with little Daan has come out, I find it a solace to sit at my little gilt desk, to take out my journal and to write a few words in it from time to time.

I do not allow discussion of Daan's condition with anyone, because it would be to no avail, except as an exercise in masochism or self-pity. People may think that I am hiding away behind a mantle of silence, but this is not so. I just fail to see what useful purpose could be served by discussion of the subject, except to stir up gossip. I will never allow them to take him to a hospital anyway, because of the great risk to his life, once they start with their operations. So we will care for him here until they know more about such things. Doctor Cloete, who is a dear and sweet man, and a gentleman, has, in his reserved way agreed with me, and he has shown me some figures of a statistical nature that paint a horrifying picture of life in the surgical wards of our time, in spite of the great advances made by the science of medicine during and after the great war that ended at the eleventh hour of the eleventh day of the eleventh month of 1918.

(If this appears to be a continuous chronicle, written at one time, it is only because I have not bothered to date any of the entries. That is one reason. The other is that everything in this journal concerns little Daan, and was written many years after the events I describe took place. Daan is the only privacy of my life, and my feelings about and for him are the only things that I want to hide from the world, and that is why this book is doubly locked.)

I knew, of course, that something was wrong when the infection in the eyes became obvious, ten days after birth, but I bathed them with a gentle eye-wash; only on the eighteenth day did the doctor call, too late. A knowledge of his deafness came only a few months later. And of course I knew, also right from the start, that he had withdrawn his mind from the world, because of the way in which he had been hurt. He has vocal chords, but of what use they can be to him is hard to imagine. There is absolutely no known way of establishing any form of communication with him. His jerky movements are a source of great distress to me, but there is nothing that can be done for a brain that has been damaged. He is growing at the normal rate of growth for children, so I suppose that that is something to be grateful for. He will at least not develop into some sort of dwarf, or huge monster. I shudder when I use that word, because I keep seeing in my mind's eye an image of Daan as a grown man, and still without his senses.

Doctor Cloete had defined his illness for us. The violence of my action had brought about a state known as cerebral palsy. In 1921 it was a little known disease, some doctors confusing it with infantile paralysis, because of the similarity of some of the symptoms. Infantile paralysis, later to become known as poliomyelitis, is quite a different ailment, largely incurable once it has done its damage, which is initially determined by the severity of the attack. Cerebral palsy could manifest itself in many forms, but the apparently paralysed muscles could be made to work and need not be wasted away through disuse. The patient's brain, the thinking part, need not of necessity be damaged, but in Daan's case, the blow to his head had also caused him to become deaf. I put this down, dispassionately, because I want to read it over and over again. I never want to forget the evil that I had done to my husband and child, the two people whom I love more than anything in this world. A broken-hearted man, too strong to weep, whose life I shattered totally within a few moments, and a child, blind, deaf, unable to allow himself to live in the world, withdrawn, shocked, senseless.

Being bereft of sense, being senseless, does that mean my son is a lunatic? A simpleton? What words of derision will be used in the villages from Broederstroom, Schoemansville, Skeerpoort and Hekpoort, to Magaliesburg and beyond.

No words of derision will ever be used against my son. He will never be described by anyone except his father, and perhaps his doctor. And, in these pages, I will attempt my description also, of my love, now that I have described his hurt. No, not even his faithful Mina must ever be allowed to say more about him than to give a description of his needs, and that to me or my husband only.

Six months have gone by since his birth and I should have thought that the revelations would have been fully made by now. I shall have to wait for the doctor, or Dawid to speak their minds. As for myself, there will be absolutely nothing to say. I will accept only the doctor's assurances that children sometimes grow out of this kind of condition, if nature is allowed to take its course. Of course, we will allow nature to attempt just that. There must have been some design, some reason why God allowed that germ to survive, in wait for Daan's infant eyes, and I will sit with, if necessary, excessive patience, until He has made it clear to me why He chose this punishment, or trial, or tribulation, for us.

My conscience is very active so it does not allow me to, in any way, blame Daan's condition on anything but the things I have done, no accident. I am over-rigid, too straight-laced. There was a time when Daan was being conceived that had brought out a great deal of warmth in me, but I did not allow myself to do anything with Dawid except the act of conception, and I quickly shut that out of my mind. I have a guilt, because I enjoyed creating Daan, and he emerged with the seed of blindness from my womb, and then I hurt him, made him into a lifeless, listless monster.

I knew that that was a strong word to use when I wrote it some weeks ago: the word "monstrous." But it is so pathetic, when I take him in my arms, and hold and kiss him, to realise that, beautiful as he is, he will never know this love. And it is his very beauty that makes his lack of senses so dreadful.

Mina plays with him, children's games, trying very hard to make some sort of contact, and the passing of the months brings us nearer to the day of confrontation, when the scales will have to fall from all our eyes, and we will have to face facts.

Already there have been discussions, decisions postponed. And soon we, the four of us, will have to face each other with a confrontation that will reveal our dishonesties and cowardice.

But time has given me the opportunity to plan my own actions, and now that the time for the facing of facts is very close, I am grateful for having had the chance to work out what I intend doing.

Mina was the first to find herself unable to continue with the charade, and with typical abruptness announced, as if she was serving dinner, that Daan was blind and deaf, and withdrawn.

But my plans had been made months beforehand, and I knew exactly what to do about it. I merely forbade any further discussion on this matter within my hearing, or that of any person not connected with our household. Oh, they could all go on discussing it, in the house, as much as they wished, but I did not want to be part of those discussions. I would help as much as possible with his creature comforts, and do everything in my power to make contact with him, on whatever level.

I had tried hurting him. Little "accidents" with pins that had been dipped in disinfectants, to see if a little tremor could be roused in his face, but it gave me the kind of guilt feelings that I found to be unbearable. I felt like a mother-vivisectionist, a botanist who killed or bruised a plant to see what would happen, or a medical man cutting open a live animal to show his students the heart beating. Often, I have had that kind of dreadful nightmare, that wakes me in a sweat, with my heart beating horribly, so I push from my mind the nightmare images of my dreams, cutting him open with the meat knife, going in through layers of skin and muscle, to find a place where he had not been hurt. Because, somewhere in him there is such a place, of that I have always been sure.

Once, visiting a friend who had a baby boy of about the same age, and listening to the unintentional brutalities of her conversation, which concerned our mutual offspring going to school together, wondering in what fields they would excel, if they would be great scholars, or great sportsmen, I saw her soaping the little boy's penis, and it grew erect. The little fellow's mother was quite brazen about it, making coarse remarks about that appendage one day giving a lot of girls a great deal of pleasure. But there was no doubt about it, the soaping had caused the pleasure that had resulted in the innocent rigidity. When I got home that day I gave Mina the rest of the night off, telling her to be back by midnight, and she was delighted because her common-law husband, I suppose you can call him, one Adam Long, was on his usual weekend visit, which was the only thing about Mina to which I objected: her loose living. I had virtually to force them to the altar by trickery before their relationship became respectable and not just a series of loose adulteries.

That night after the visit to my friend, I also bathed little Daan, and soaped his little penis. I rubbed it dry afterwards, using deliberate gestures that I thought would stimulate him, and then I kissed every part of his body, lingeringly. I suppose that, strictly, it was a form of incest that I tried to practise there that night. If so, God strike me dead, if He wishes. If I could have managed the slightest form of communication with my son there, that evening, my capacity for the vilest of debaucheries would have been endless, as would have been my enthusiasm and inventiveness. But nothing happened. Only time would heal the wound to his inner mind. I contemplated his private parts with an immense sadness. Here hung the little scrotum, all wrinkled and pink, that would one day contain the testes. Would it happen, I wondered, that he would one day develop a reproductive urge, and that he would in that way achieve his first communication with a fellow human?

Straight-laced, you call me, but if that were even a remote, faraway possibility, I would have imported every attractive prostitute from every possible country, broken every possible moral and legal law, and watched greedily as he consummated a communication, no matter what form of fornication it might require.

God forgive me, Dawid, for what I did to your sex life. I knew you for a virile man, but when the obvious result of our coupling became a household fact you had already become used to the death of my passion, as my guilt took over my personality. I never struggled or pretended that I could still have enjoyed you, my movements would have been those of a whore. Thank God you understood, immediately after the so-called accident, that I would never again want to have anything to do with sex. I can say all these things to my journal, because it enjoys the privacy that you promised the day you gave it to me. But every time you tried to reassure me that you still wanted me if I should ever change, every touch from you was abhorrent to me.

God forgive me, my dear husband, I love you as much as I ever did, but the product of our coupling is too strong a reminder, there in the next room, and we must never again attempt reproduction. The only thing to be grateful for is that you had always taken it upon yourself to prevent conception until we were ready to have our first child, and that the night of his creating was the only time that you had been exposed to infection. You must have removed the bacteria that I had allowed, unconsciously, to find their way to you because of your habits of scrupulous cleanliness. You always used to leave me to go to the bathroom as soon as possible after we had done, and although I resented it at the time I never spoke of it. Now I am happy because of it. That must have been the reason why you were not infected. We never made love after I knew that I was pregnant, as it was not the "done" thing then.

I gave you your freedom from our marriage. I offered to take little Daan and his nurse to a strange place, where no one knew us, and I proposed that I should look after him there. I offered you a divorce on any grounds you wished to choose. But you rejected all these plans of mine with just two words: "Bloody nonsense." Why do I write these words as if they were part of a letter to you. I suppose that, when I am dead, I hope you will find the keys to my book, my beautiful golden private journal, and that you will unlock it and take a peek. If you do, please remember that although I stopped making love with you, I even loved you to my last day.

When Dawid had rejected my plan for a divorce, which would have freed him from the responsibility of little Daan, I had become very worried about what would happen to his sex life. A man, they say, has to have it more often than a woman, and I have heard it said so often that I suppose it must be right. I didn't want any scandal connected with our good name in the village. We had always been respectable people, and I wanted Dawid's happiness, so I gave him permission to do as he wished, go to the city as often as necessary, have a woman, and return to me, and I would understand.

I am afraid that when I made this suggestion he turned it down with an expression of excessive vulgarity. Even though this is a private journal I'm afraid that I shall never be able to report it accurately, not even by suggesting, with blank spaces, or little dots, the number of letters, or the first letter, or even what it rhymes with. So you see, where my own morals are concerned I stayed as straight-laced as ever, never so much as even permitting myself a fantasy or a dream, but I hoped very much for an adequate sex life for my husband and later, for my son.

I tried to communicate with little Daan by other methods. My husband had, over the years of our engagement, purchased for me gifts of all the world's very finest perfumes. It was, he knew, my weakness, and in the first few years of our life, just before and after our marriage, he spent extravagant sums so that I would be able to wear a really wonderful perfume to a party. Dawid always noticed the perfumes I wore from day to day, because I had taught him, made him an expert, until he knew more about the subject than I did. With both parents having such highly developed olfactory senses, I thought it reasonable to suppose that little Daan may have been left with at least this one talent: to be able to enjoy and distinguish the subtleties of different scents. Therefore, I placed a different perfume about his room each day of the week, in the hope that he would come to recognise certain days by their aromas, and that this would give him a sense of time. I never knew whether he ever noticed any of these attempts, but, once started, I did it continuously, just in case it worked, even to the most limited degree. I still do it, every day, and will continue for as long as I am able.

Once, many years later, I asked Dawid what the perfume was that I smelt on him when he came home after having been away all day and part of the night. It was a woman's perfume, and I was curious, because it had been chosen and used with good taste. When Dawid pressed his cheek to mine, which was the way in which we perfunctorily greeted each other now that I was not able to bed with him, I had noticed, about the lobe of his left ear, the faintest of traces of one of the world's most expensive perfumes. I was, naturally, curious of my rival, but he quashed my curiosity by saying that he had been caught up in a crowd of females at the shop in Magaliesburg, and any one of them might have rubbed it off onto him. It wasn't a good lie, but I had to accept it.

"In any case," said Dawid, "we don't talk about such things, do we?"

It was as close as he had come to being abrupt with me since I had first met him. So I suspected that a woman had been with him, and that he did not want to discuss it with me. And he was quite right, too, because knowing would have hurt me, but curiosity never hurt anyone. I hope though that it wasn't just a casual medicinal thing, but that there had been something more to it than just physical need. My hoping hurt me tremendously. I had no right to be troubled by jealousies of a husband whom I could not love as a wife should, but I was nevertheless distressed.

One day, long after the incident of the perfume, I told Dawid that I sometimes imagined him making intimate love to another woman and that it hurt me and made me jealous.

"Quite right too," he said. "I still love you, you know."

I kept pressing him on the subject that day. I had the feeling that something was happening to him, sexually, somewhere. It just was not natural for a man of his virility not to have regular sexual release, and I desperately wanted to know about it, to, in a way, share it, and, in so doing, to share a little of his happiness. I was now on my way to the second stage: First there is the straight-laced prude, then there is the dried up old hag.

I had always looked after myself, seen to my appearance, but in the middle years, and I am now speaking of the early thirties, I have seen that the time and the passing years were making their marks on me. We had been born a few months apart at the turn of the century. But, no matter how hard I tried, my husband would give me no clue to his private life, except to deny that he had one. I never quite believed him but there was never enough evidence to be sure. So that part of his life was a total mystery to me, and I suppose it was wise of him not to subject me to a knowledge that could only pain me. I never, from the day I stopped him from sharing my bed, heard even the slightest breath of scandal about him, and to this day, now, I still do not know if anyone has shared that part of his life, or if I have turned him into a monk.

For the first years of his life, after the initial eighteen months during which we deceived ourselves, or hoped against hope, there were positive things to do. Doctor Cloete kept reading up on cases similar to Daan's, but there was very little that he was able to suggest. There was talk, once, of taking Daan to one of the great hospitals, somewhere in London, or even in Europe, and correspondence of a sort was entered into by Doctor Cloete, but I never got more than the flimsiest, most indifferent encouragement from him. The trouble was that he believed only in himself and what he could do, house by house, patient by patient, as a family doctor. His faith in the research that was being done all over the world was tremendous, and I know that he contributed to research by sending in, regularly, findings of a statistical nature, from his experiences as a country doctor.

Although he was a bachelor of surgery as well as of medicine, he had an abhorrence of surgical techniques. There were very few surgeons, specialists as such, on the scene then and it was often necessary for him to use the knife, but he never did if it was possible to send the patient to any of the nearby cities, like Krugersdorp, or Pretoria, both forty miles away, or Johannesburg, which was twenty-five miles beyond Krugersdorp. There were many doctors who preferred the knife to most other forms of medicine, but their knowledge, in those days, was not what it is today. Doctor Cloete did not believe in the bolder solutions offered by his own profession, and, as our family doctor, his caution was an influence upon all of us. Neurology, and all the other delicate procedures, as well as ordinary surgery, were, in any case, only infant sciences. The thought of tampering with the ears and eyes, so near to the brain, so directly connected, was more than other-worldly. It was, as far as our thinking went, not even a matter to which the slightest consideration could be given.

After our cataclysmic scene on the day that we had had the discussion of little Daan's troubles, order was restored to the house, and things settled down. My husband withdrew to his bedroom. I took refuge in this little journal, or just sat at the window, feeling guilty at seeing all the lovely things that my little boy could not see, and being conscience-stricken at hearing the singing of the birds.

Often I would join my son in his world by stuffing plugs of cotton-wool into my ears, and taking a length of black crêpe with which I masked my eyes from the world. I would sit as quietly as I could, at this desk, on the softest chair, so that my body would feel as little as possible, and I pretended to myself that I was deaf and dumb and blind. The experience at first filled me with a sort of terror. I knew that anyone knocking on my door would think that I was in a deep sleep, and no one could see me through the drawn curtain at my desk. In that gloom, that total blackness, with the complete lack of sound throbbing at my temples, I would spend many afternoons of my life, keeping my son company in his world, or as much of it as I could create. I had, of course, experienced all the wonderful knowledge of the world that the senses can give to a life, and these things were all in my memory, so my sense of loss was not at all what Daan was living through. Still, it was an attempt to be close to him, and it made me feel that I had at least done something.

I tried many experiments to shut out the persistent things that came flooding into my thoughts, memories of experiences already lived. I tried, many, dozens of times, even, now that I think of it, hundreds of times, to clear my mind completely of every possible thought or memory. This I found was best done by concentrating on absolutely nothing, and finding a zero symbol for the concept of nothing.

Doctor Cloete and I discussed nothingness one day, not in the context of Daan's life, because I never spoke of my son with him except at times when he had become ill, but a conversation concerning the concept of the complete non-existence of everything, as if one could imagine a dreamless sleep, or a death without an afterlife. He had read widely on the subject, and was able to obtain for me certain books on the lives of the saints, and other mystics, as well as books concerning the holy men of the Eastern religions, those whom we called the "heathen." I had these books in my locked desk, because it would not do for a good Methodist such as I to be known to be reading books about Catholics, and Buddhists, and Blackamoors, and the strange godlessness of their so-called "holy rites."

I write this with hindsight. It took many years for me to become a person who understood the philosophers and religions of the mystics before I developed a respect for things and people other than the objects and personalities of my own life. I did formulate, like a Buddhist, an understanding of the concept of nothingness into which I could allow my personality to go, on a journey into a world of immense tranquility, where I could exist in a sphere of living far away from the everyday demands of life. A world where my guilts were, for a while, forgotten in nothingness.

Of course, it defeated its own purpose, because my original ambition had been to find a place of blackness, silence, and lack of consciousness where I could also feel myself to be a part of the world of my child, so that we could, through a total inability to experience anything at all, be part of each other's life, and so that I could know a little of what life must have been like for him, in his time of withdrawal.

And many times, I did not allow myself to experience the tranquilities of the East, because it was too delightful, too spiritually satisfying. So I penetrated only the first of the veils to the unconscious, where things like blackness, deafness, and horror existed. Perhaps it was wrong, perhaps little Daan had never experienced any of these things and it could be that I was making a world where I could join him, and accompany him, in horrors that he had never known. It is possible that I was torturing myself for nothing logical, no reason at all. But I think you can understand why my preference was for the creating of a world that was at least uncomfortable, disconcerting, and painful.

I sat quietly, not moving, for many hours, neither shifting my position nor flexing so much as a muscle anywhere, not even my eyeballs, because I wanted to experience the lack of the physical which I knew to be part of Daan's withdrawal. I would sit there in total darkness and deafness, only allowing myself to breathe, concentrating on my early, primitive zero symbols and concepts, until I could feel the calcification of response in my muscles, which was a kind of dullness, like the lack of life one feels if one is about to get "pins and needles" in a limb. I would hold on for as long as I could, until the onset of actual physical pain, which I would endure for hours. When the pain started I moved but only slightly, allowing my cramped muscles the agony of a limited renewed circulation, which was usually accompanied by excruciating physical distress, because I thought it possible that he allowed himself the experience of pain, and I wanted to stay in his world, if I had ever been there. I will never know if my attempts at joining him in his life were even vaguely successful, but I feel better because of having tried my best.

After such a session of blackness the heartbreaking beauty of returning to the glories of the world was always almost too much for me to bear, its sights and its perfumes, and the sounds of the cattle coming home to the kraal, where Dawid and I had decided to be buried one day. No matter who inherits or buys this farm, they will always raise cattle and sheep here, because it is that kind of place, as well as the other crops of those other fields more suitable to being planted. The kraal would always be near to the big house, and we will always have animals about us in the long night of eternity. And that is how we both would like it to be. I do not know if I have forfeited my right to be beside Dawid in the millennia of eternity, but I will keep quiet about it, and not bring up the subject, in case he forbids it.

Of course, I joined little Daan in other ways too, the world wasn't just a place for a little boy to lie about in. We had to teach him to walk, and I made that a part of my job. It wasn't that I mistrusted Mina, but she had so much to do. She was more careful of him than any mother could have been. It seemed that, knowing of the many things he did not have, she tried to make up for it by the extra care and attention she gave him. Every four hours she would turn him, rub his little body with a special formula of oils and unguents made for her by Doctor Cloete, to which, I suspect, she added ingredients of her own. She would see to it that his room was airy and cool in summer and warm and comfortable in winter. She would always use a warm, soapy water, and lots of Johnson's Baby Powder after she had changed him, and she would sing bright childhood songs often, although I knew that she was sad too, as we all were. She would sing the sweet, happy songs of childhood that the coloureds and black people have, into his little deaf ears, and I would cry.

It seems, reading some of the little thoughts that I have put down, that there is, as in that last sentence, an excess of emotion. My impulse is to scratch it out, because of the dictates of good taste. But this is my private journal, and if you read it after my death you may say to yourself, "The old girl went a bit too far sometimes, didn't she?"

My generation had a saying: "You must know where to draw the line." For instance, how much of one's breast should be revealed in a ball gown? You were on thin ice there, as you were on all of the "draw the line" questions, because too much revealed meant that you were anything from a "common bitch" to a "whore," a "Jezebel" or a "brazen hussy." There were the minor infringements, too, such as "shameless" or "painted lady." What we all strove for was something between "sweet" and "forward."

Therefore, in our generation, we had to know where to draw the line. What we did in our private thoughts were things that knew no boundaries, and we certainly allowed our imaginations riotous freedoms and the most bizarre fantasies. I suppose that is why the Rudolph Valentino films were our favourite entertainment. But now I have come to a question of honesty, which is probably the most abused word of this century. I write here as if this journal is totally private, but I hope, all the time, that sometime, someone will read it. There! I have said it (and that is the only exclamation mark you will find in this entire journal, because I am not a demonstrative person).

I do hope that these words will be read by someone, and that I am not judged by them, but that they will allow a person of the future an insight into my problems, and an understanding of why I was as I was. Sometimes I hope it is my husband, Dawid, and at other times, his mistress, if he has one, so that she may know how I felt, and why she had to do what she did for him. Perhaps it would be best if a doctor who works with the minds of people were to dig here. There are no diamonds, or gold, but there may just possibly be something of another kind of value. And, if my husband had a mistress, I would want her to know that I was jealous of him, but that I nevertheless wanted him to be happy in any way that he could find.

Oh I can see Dawid reading that last sentence and snorting: "Tripe and nonsense." But, my dear, do you really blame me for wondering to just what extent I damaged your natural life? But I would not like these words to be read before my death. Afterwards, when I am aimlessly decomposing beneath the hooves of the farmyard animals, yes, but not while I am alive. I have always dreaded the thought of someone washing my naked body and dressing it in its funeral raiment. Mina will have to do it, she is wise enough. I also do not want my nakedness observed, ever again, by anyone, while I am still alive. And I hope I never become so ill that it has to be done to me, because the shame would be very great.

And now that I have confessed that my privacy may be invaded after I am dead, I shall continue. When the subject came up I was in doubt about whether certain, what seemed to me, over-flowery emotionalisms, sentiments, or sentimentalities, the melodramatic, the over-illustrative, the moving, should be excised in favour of greater objectivity. But I am of an age where women's lives were manufactured of these frailties, and I must not lose my identity in objectivities and dishonesties. I know there are simpler ways of speaking, but when you have had your life made into a Baroque disaster, with Gothic overtones, it is very difficult to express it in the oversimplified terms of today.

Dawid is the purist of this family. Everything he does has a grace about it; even when he grunts "women's nonsense" he does it with a charm that never offends. I suppose, if there is such a term, or description, he could be called "coarsely elegant." He knows how to live by saying the least, and doing the most.

But my own extravagances are the result of an over-emotional set of circumstances.

I took on the job of helping to teach Daan to walk, and of course my husband and the doctor also took part in it, because it wasn't just a matter of holding him up. He had to be continuously supported. My husband had made a little kind of cart for him, with pram wheels, something that he had seen on a larger scale in a book on the rehabilitation of war wounded, that allowed the wasted, torn limbs of Flanders (see, how I am unable to "draw the line") to exercise without using the full weight of the body on the legs. My husband was a wonderful carpenter, and he made his exerciser, or "walk trainer" as he called it, using only the softest of woods with the nicest grains, and, except for the three ball bearings that he used on the three little wheels, and the leather supports that held up the little arms and shoulders, it was all made of wood, and a very beautiful thing it was too. Then, in our private garden towards the back of the house, where only we ever sat, he made a kind of sunken walkway, in which, like a track, the little wheels could move and be guided, almost as if the little device was a train, but all tastefully recessed into its own little concrete path, so that if you saw it you would think it only a shady walk between the bushes.

There I planted shrubs and herbs of the greatest fragrances that I could find, even writing away to as far as Kirstenbosch Botanical Gardens in the Cape and Kew near London. They sent me plants of many strong, sweet odours. They also sent me the address, in London, of St. Dunstan's, the international organisation for the blind, that had established special gardens for the sightless in many parts of the world. They were experts in this field, giving a greater dimension to the sense of smell of people who could not see, stimulating a normally neglected sense to compensate for an absent one.

There again, with those words, I question my "drawing the line" feeling. My sentimentalities, my clear but pretty phrases. I hate people who sacrifice clarity for the pretty phrase, but what of women like me, who sacrifice good taste for the phrases of her youth? Surely we have a right to exist also, and to bring faded remembrances to your attention? And, in my case, am I not allowed to exceed certain boundaries? I have no regal background, so there is no reason why I should not bend before the wind, no reason for a ramrod to exist between my corset and my backbone (I can think of the phrase my husband would have used instead, and I am excessively tempted, but I will refrain).

We made, for little Daan, a place where his little feet could walk. They never touched the ground, because they would only have dragged, and that would have been of no use whatsoever.

The system of wheels and pulleys, and the slight inclines made use of by the ball bearings were all that were needed to make his feet and arms use themselves in the pedal-motions of walking and arm balancing, so that, if you did not know of the little feet strapped in the pedals, you would have sworn that his walking was the cause of the movement. Is there such a thing as a muscle that thinks for itself? I have spoken to people called physiotherapists, and physiologists, and physicians, and they all have different sets of theories. It all boils down to something they call "motor reaction" which I have previously mentioned. Now, although I have been into it more thoroughly since my last mention of it, it still remains a mystery, and I am unable to tell you anything about it, although some years have passed since that entry.

The field remains murky, full of shadows, and I cannot make head or tail of it, and nobody in the medical world is able to help me. Yes, yes, they have grand phrases, because we have come to live in an age of professional argot, the phraseology of the experts, the art critics and literati, the medical people, the businessmen, the advertising experts, the film men, the journalists and the motor mechanics, and when they have been allowed to talk, and charge good money for their talking, for hour upon hour, they have only managed to convey to you that they suffer from delusions of adequacy. They do not know, although it is their profession to know, and their field is to make mysteries of the obvious, or they would have no reason to exist. I know that I am being harsh on some people of real skill and achievement, deserving of true admiration. They are the ones, who, when reading of what I said of their professional skills, will have said to themselves, "how true." The others, who said, "nonsense" whenever I mentioned their professions, had better retire now, before they compound even further the harm that they must have already done. I am sick to death of professionals who are charlatans, and experts whose lives are made up of confusions.

Nothing is really known. Facts can all be denied, or manufactured by the million. There is no reality worth embracing, and, for me at least, no embrace that is real. Even when I dream of Dawid taking me into his strong arms, which is the safest place I know of on this earth, or the next world, for that matter, I will always doubt the reality of truth, or the falseness of lies, because so many of the lies that I have lived through have been the truth, and so many of the things that I have pretended to myself to be real have been lies. And virtually everything that I have shown to the world outside of my own private world has been a lie. I have allowed no outsider to see even a part of what I, in my madness for privacy, know to be the truth of myself.

So, here is a speculation. Have I, for all these years, been just like my son? Has no one ever seen the person known as Bettina Cilliers, née Paulson? Have I been as much a mystery as he has been, to those who have tried to penetrate the bastions of my boorishly-protected privacy?

It seems strange to me, when this thought occurs, that I have been as blind and deaf and dumb, as unfeeling and incommunicable and uncommunicating as little Daan. And then the thought occurs to me, is it really my duty to make contact with people? Is there perhaps not too much of this making free of ourselves in the world? Are we not too casually generous with our words and our feelings? Is it not time for an honest withdrawal from the world? Why not be like Daan? What's wrong with him as he is? We are all like him, to a certain degree, are we not? Rhetoric, I know, but doesn't it make sense, to be like Daan, to be like the three little monkeys that are always removed from the mantelpieces whenever my husband and I go visiting socially: hear, see and speak no evil? Funny how the most tactless people become diplomatic in the most grotesque ways. Funny how the people found out. We never told anyone. Strange how gifts of aromatic plants were made, as if Kirstenbosch or St. Dunstan's, London, had been in touch with the most clear-sighted citizens of Skeerpoort, Transvaal.

I would not like to leave the subject in the air, which may perhaps be the understated, tasteful thing to do. But I will not "draw the line" at the thought that, in some way that I beg you to investigate, we are all just as blind and deaf and unfeeling as Daan. In my time we have lived through some of the world's great holocausts, and I have felt, time and again, that if only people can get together and talk to each other on an unofficial basis, there would be no further fires on the skins of children.

This is my, Bettina Cilliers-Paulson's contribution to international politics and the centuries to come: We have been too official. Everything has been a matter of official policy. In our homes, our parent and teacher meetings, our church gatherings, our picnics, and our parliaments. Whenever we have gathered we have been a group of official beings, bent on stating our collectively worthless thoughts, which we have arrived at in committee. Our faults lie in our gatherings because we do not trust individuals. We do not love each other and therefore we do not trust each other, something like that. I'm sorry I can't say any more on the subject, but it seems to me that this is all that one can possibly say, and that the trouble lies there. Why can't we be earthlings-unofficial? I apologise for that venture into a sphere that is not mine. I have not been officially appointed to speak.

Daan is, in this journal, no symbol of international inabilities to communicate. My concern was, since I knew he could not see or hear, perhaps he could smell. And I made for him the most fragrant world that it was possible to make, for all the years of his baby- and boyhood, and all the years beyond. For instance, when he was an encotted baby he smelt only the most delicate perfumes of Paris, Rome and London. A few, a very few from New York, but I have only a slight admiration for the Americans. The French are my people for perfume, because of the trouble they take. Oh I know that extraordinary fragrances can be created in laboratories, but the French will always go to the plant, and that, to me, is somehow more precious, although the synthetic perfume may, in terms of its olfactory powers, perhaps be more effective. But then, I think a blunderbuss is a more beautiful firearm than an F.M. rifle.

I say these things to get you to understand that I knew what I was doing when I imported frangipani and the odours of the East for the first of the little gardens. Others were to come later, which I planted in the sill of his window, in a box carpentered by his father, who was careful to use only aromatic woods like tamboekie and sandalwood in everything he constructed. You see, we had no idea, but we hoped, and we prayed, that he could smell the odours of living, and, if he couldn't, we had to try, in case. Do you understand that, just in case he could smell, we wanted some of his days and times to be occupied by the delights of the olfactory sense?

It is difficult to realise these things now, so many years after these events have occurred. Tests have by now been devised that measure all responses to a great degree of accuracy, but at that time we did not really believe that Daan could experience anything. There was only an extremely slight chance, but we had to give it to him.

The same applied to his food. He wasn't a chewer, we knew of no way to stimulate his jaws to actually chew food, and we were terrified that any solid would choke him. Mina had let him swallow, and I know that it had not been easy for her, but she had managed where I think, to be honest, that I would have failed.

Strange now too, when I think of it, that I preserved my hard, pointed-skyward, diminutive breasts for a husband who would never again . . . but I go beyond myself. I would, in any case, ever after be buttoned to the neck and skirted to the floor.

Little Daan was fed, all his life, on soft gruels, the consistency of mother's milk. That brings a lump to my throat, because he had never tasted his mother's milk, only that of Mina. Can you believe me that I had no idea as to what anguish I was causing myself that I was only being empty-headed and fashionable because we could afford a wet-nurse? After the horrible day that hurt all of us so much, when the truth of my infection became known, I was afraid, for many months even to touch the child. I lived in a kind of terror of him, like a person drawn to the edge of a precipice. There was a distinct feeling in me, that if I came too near to him, I would again hurt him.

Only after he had allowed his mind to be healed, and when he started coming back to the world in his own slow way, did I allow myself the privilege of mothering him again. But I remained afraid that my milk might be tainted. Can you accept such an excuse; that I blame both disease and fashion? No, I don't suppose you can. So I accept your censure. I can only say that now, I would have looked with pride at a pair of leathery, flat dugs, had they fed Daan. Imagine the disgust with which I look at my aged, proud, beautifully pointed, pink-nippled breasts. I am able to describe them to you unashamedly because I am so horribly ashamed of them. They are not, to me, the mystical, lovely things of love that they were supposed to be when I denied my son their milk, but monuments to pride, conceit and vanity and infection, pointing their way to my eventual damnation among the stars, if God wishes to be unkind. That bears thinking of too. Does God ever wish to be unkind? In the case of my breasts, I would not blame him. And does God ever wish anything, or do

God's things just happen, as He did? So I believe anyway. If He didn't just happen, Who, with a capital W, created Him?

Edwardianisms of thought written in the new Georgian age. Of what interest can my little apology for a mind at work be, except that it tells in part the story of Daan, and I believe in him. Somehow, Mina's early calling him a saint meant something to me, and I believe in him. What of him, what part or way of him, of the twistings of his life or of his death, I don't know. But as I am him, he is me. As I am faceless to my husband, my neighbours, my servants and my God, so is Daan soulless to me. And I know that I have a face, and that Daan has a soul.

Daan has the loveliest face of all the children I have ever seen, and looking at the beauty of it makes me catch at the throat, as if it will never be wide enough to admit the air I need to live, like a man with tuberculosis, whose lungs are finally gone.

In his window box went all the things that would be killed by frost in the open air, and on his "walk" as we called it, although "forced arm and foot-pedalling motion" might be a better way of saying it, I planted other flower fragrances which I chose to suit his age, because he was a baby, and flower fragrances are the right things for a child.

In the kitchen, I knew that curries and such powerful flavours were for his later years, and that the blandnesses of custard, blancmange and jelly, the sweetness of sugared chocolate, the mildness of a watered turkish delight, and the almost nothingness in the kind nuance of a watercress soup, a vegetable purée with just a hint of pepper-root, or, as you call it, horse-radish, were the flavours that his little tongue would roll around with delight. I would spend the hours of my days searching for the mild nuances of flavour that may have pleased him, if he had allowed himself a sense of taste. I will never know. He had withdrawn too well. They say that the food for babies, bought in bottles, on sale in the shops commercially, is quite adequate and also acceptable to the little palates. But once, I tested the temperature of one of these concoctions, so that I would not burn his little tongue. I had diluted it with a rich creamy milk, from our prize Swiss goat, that had won the gold medal at the Rand Easter Show for ten years running. She was a magnificent animal, of noble appearance and her product had an incredible taste and richness. After I had mixed this amazing blue-riband product of our farm with the bottled product, I tasted it, and even with its glorious additive, and although the temperature was just right for a little boy's tongue, I said one of the few swear-words of my life. I took the name of the Lord in vain. I tasted it, spat it out, and God forgive me, said, "Jesus Christ" using it as an expletive and not as an adoration.

I have had several other experiences, usually as a guest or a restaurant customer, when foods of this nature have been served to human beings, so that they may consume it and be, God help us, not only nourished but also entertained by persons who, one would have thought, had a modicum of taste or even of professionalism, and each time that awful expletive, in all its blasphemousness, would come up, right from the depths of my spirit, and I would exclaim, in my mind's irreligious irresponsibility, that name, so precious to me: "Jesus Christ." Never loudly, though, and always with a sense of shame.

Stupidly enough, it is canned baby food that made it clear to me why men sometimes used the name of the Lord in vain. We, whom the men protected, seldom came into contact with the awful products of this century of blasphemy, as you can call the time in which we live, and only when you have to use the rubbish that people consume can you understand why men curse and damn the manufacturer's souls, as I did when I tasted the ordure that some idiot had considered good enough for my child.

While Mina concerned herself, and I use the word "concerned" advisedly and with love, with the physical comforts of my baby, I would spend hours and days in the kitchen, working at flavours that would give him a pleasure in flavour in case he had a reasonably developed sense of taste. I was trying, as I had done with the perfumes, to establish a form of communication. I wanted him to know, if possible, that there was someone, out there somewhere, some place that he could not reasonably know of, who wanted his tongue and his taste buds to tell his brain, "You have a thing called a mother, and it loves you." Go to blazes with your feelings of good taste in telling things, in what may be said or not. You are the intruder here, so go to blazes, or the next page if you wish.

The above expletives were the result of a bad mood quite a long time ago, and I beg your pardon for my rudeness. Rudeness. I wonder if I fool you by using that word. It is a matter of complaining, and, being unable to complain, having forfeited the right to do so, I lost my temper. I suppose all four of us who are involved with Daan say: "I must be the strong one," because the others are certainly showing a stoicism that I am trying to emulate. Perhaps they are trying to be like me. If it is so, the situation is ludicrous, but better not spoken about. The only alternative would be to collapse tearfully, and that would be most embarrassing. Only Doctor Cloete, of the four of us, could do something concrete, if there were something he could do. But there isn't, so we can do nothing but live on in our half-worlds of doubt, wondering if we are doing the right thing.

Often the thought has come to me that little Daan would be better off dead, that there is no promise of any sort of life for him anyway. Any neglect of the diseases of childhood (and he went through all of them, in spite of the antiseptic conditions of his life) could easily have been fatal. One day, when he was about five years of age, the thought came to me that we were raising a turnip. The words "vegetable existence" was one of the better-used clichés of the time, and it was a thought that persisted, especially the word "turnip" which is the name of a vegetable that I have never successfully cooked. There is, about it, a bland idiocy that well suits its relationship, adjectivally, to morons and droolers in asylums.

Several times, after that, the words "turnip" and "living vegetable" became so strong in my consciousness that I actually thought it as I looked at my son, saw it in my mind's eye as a description of him. One day the thought became too strong, and as I shut it out of my mind, another took its place; would it not be better if the tiny little life that he had were shut off? It would be easier done than snuffing out a candle, and all the futile years facing little Daan would cease to stretch out before him like a long black tunnel that he was not even aware of.

It was a thought that I wrestled out of my mind, shudderingly, wondering what sort of hideous monster I was, who could even begin to allow such thinking about her child who was ill. I had always seen it as an illness, and now my mind, with its desperate by-way escapist thinking, was trying to change the concept of "illness" to one of "living death." It went against everything that was in me, everything that I had ever been, or believed in, or wanted myself to be, but it was also persistent. I have always been amazed at the persistence of my mind. I suppose if there were a one-word description of me it would, perhaps, be "persistent." But it would describe me only from the exterior point of view, from which persistence might seem to be an admirable trait.

Deep and dark within me were other things that persisted, of which I am ashamed. I have told you of some of them. For instance, I never looked at his little penis without wondering if there were not perhaps some way to stimulate it to erection. That stayed with me. But what I am really ashamed of is the persistence of the death wish in relation to my son. I know now, after all I have read about the mind, that a death wish is a fairly common thing that lurks in just about everyone's brain, and that it is as a rule unbidden and unwelcome, as it most certainly was in my case, and still is. But the shuddering sense of shame will not go, and, although I have made a bigger thing of it than it deserves to be, it still plays its horrible part in my outermost fantasies, when my mind threatens to lose control of itself.

I was in town once, and I had left the shop where I had bought a few things, Calitz's shop in Skeerpoort, next to the post office. Suddenly I realised that I had forgotten something important, candles I think it was, and I went back. They didn't see me re-enter the shop, and I heard them talking behind a pile of groceries, Calitz the shopkeeper and one of his customers, an old gossipy woman called Watson. In Wales she would have been called "Watson the Gossip." Here in Skeerpoort she was known to have slept with Jock Travis the farrier, later of Travis Motor Engineers. Now, who is a gossip? I am trying to hurt her in your mind before I tell you what she said that hurt me, so that you may be my ally against her.

"More and more," she said to Calitz, "Bettina is becoming a little mad herself, like that lunatic son that they are keeping in the Great House." That was all she said, but it cut very deeply into me, so that I had no courage. I couldn't go into the shop where they could see me, at the other side of the pile of groceries. I just could not face them and make them stop saying such things about us, or threaten them with a lawsuit, or even slap her gossipy face. I tiptoed out of the shop, and I went to the post office where I collected the mail, and sent off my correspondence. When I got back home I pretended to have forgotten the candles, and someone else had to go back to the shop to get them. After that I never went to that shop again. Slowly I transferred my account to Moosa, the Indian, and after that he promised to get me everything I could possibly want should I give him a few days' notice. Within one month, he promised to keep in stock, as a matter of course, all the groceries needed at the Great House, and he also promised to deliver whatever we needed, so Watson the Gossip had really done me a favour by speaking as she had done, but it was a knife that twisted horribly in my mind for many years.

So I was, in my own mind (because these things prey) a potential mindless murderess, in a small way of course. I didn't really think that I could kill my own son, and my mind seemed lucid enough to me in the moments of control, the daylight hours when I kept myself busy attending to the running of our house. The lonely nights were the times when these thoughts came in like soft-footed black panthers, through the dark windows, in the black moonless nights. I would be too afraid of my own phantoms, of myself as it were, to get up out of bed and read a book, or draw the curtains. Only when I heard Mina, on her four-hourly duty in the nursery next door, whispering softly to the baby, did I feel better and less afraid, not quite so lonely. And I would wait for Mina's sounds next door, the little clicking of the latch, the soft sounds of warm soapy water, the shaking of talc in the baby powder tin. Daan's tiny little grunts as he was turned and changed. I would wait for these sounds in the long and terrible nights when my fantasies grew too much for me, sitting up in my bed like some invalid in hospital, unable to sleep.

Never in all those years did Mina know that she had two charges; that the grown-up woman in the room next to the nursery needed her presence even more than the little boy she was tending. Never did I make her, or anyone else, aware of my terrors, and she never knew that she was my nursemaid, also, in all those long hours of darkness. How awful it was for me when, some nights, my conscience would force me to allow her the whole night off, awful for just a moment, because she would never take advantage of my offers. "No," she would say, "my Kleinbasie needs me every four hours, and I wake up every four hours out of habit anyway, now. I don't even need an alarm clock any more."

"But," I would protest, "your husband. Doesn't it annoy him, on weekends, to have you get out of bed and come over to the house every four hours?"

"No," she said, "Adam Long says it's all right."

"Perhaps he's just being kind and understanding, Mina, have you ever thought that he might be angry about it, really?"

"Adam Long," she answered coarsely, "doesn't allow anyone to bugger him about."

7

THE REVEREND DOCTOR GEORGE WEBB

The year was 1930, and after having experienced many of the trials of doing missionary work among the heathen in the Northern Transvaal, Barotseland, and as far afield as Rhodesia and Tanganyika, I had been for a few years settled down in the village of Skeerpoort, near Krugersdorp, also about forty miles from Pretoria, the capital city of the Union of South Africa, part of our glorious Commonwealth. I had been invited there because of a bout of malaria which had laid me low, and various other tropical diseases, indescribable here, because of their intimate nature. But I had become reasonably well after several spells of being bedridden, and I had been made comfortable by members of the little congregation of Skeerpoort. Lodgings had been provided for me by a prominent local family, the Paulsons, at the edge of a little grove of fruit trees facing the main road, in the form of a charming little cottage that they owned. This was to be my home for many years, because of the decline in church affairs in the Transvaal. I felt myself lucky to be settled in such a delightful, tranquil village, where I knew and liked the people, white, black and coloured, whose spiritual needs were my province.

The Paulsons' daughter, Bettina, had married a Boer farmer called Dawid Cilliers, a man of French Huguenot descent. I am happy to say that it was I who confirmed him in the Methodist Church a few months before their marriage. Later, when Bettina's parents had died, she and her husband had inherited the estate, which, in addition to his own great material assets, make up a very large part of the wealth of the village.

Cilliers had built a very sweet little church, with a thatched roof and small flying buttresses to hold up the unbaked brick walls. It was painted a serene ochre, and there were pews for over a hundred people. The pulpit was a little primitive, only a yellow-wood table with a Persian mat of some sort flung over it, I believe a camel's saddle-bag, but all very acceptable. Cilliers had promised me a grandly constructed pulpit, and I had no idea that he had spent much of his own time in his workshop at home, making the pulpit that was to be my joy.

He was a fine carpenter, and a man of his word. In his own abrupt way, he was a servant of the Lord. And more than that I don't care to say about any man. It is surely enough. His wife, Bettina, was a refined lady of great sensitivity, and it was my pleasant duty to instruct her in the many mansions of our Lord, referred to by Jesus. I never was much of a theologian. Oh yes, I had passed all the appropriate examinations, and I was a Doctor of Divinity, but dogma and rigidity of rule have never been my strong points. I was able, for many years, to preach with a certain success where others had failed, because of my flexibilities, which once would have caused my expulsion, but which now, I believe are "part of the scene" in places like America. But I digress.

These poor people, Bettina and Dawid Cilliers, had been most sorely tried by the Lord. In 1921 Bettina had given birth to a son, an extremely beautiful child, who was completely without any of the normal senses of sight and hearing. Of the sense of touch, I was not sure, nor was I of the sense of taste or smell, but this is because they were not sure either. Apparently the boy had been involved in a domestic accident three weeks after his birth. With the aid of a servant, they had brought up this child as best they could, but I will not go into detail on that point here, as I have only a specific incident, in which I was involved, to tell you about. It concerns the intrusion of authority on private lives, a question that has always intrigued me.

Bettina and Dawid Cilliers had always wanted to keep their child to themselves, a well-kept secret in their own home. Of course they knew about a certain amount of village gossip, even speculation as to the eventual fate of the child, but they, themselves, did not ever allow any discussion on the subject, not even with me. Often, when visiting them, I would mention tactfully that their source of sorrow and unhappiness was, on many occasions, part of my prayers, but they would shy away from the subject with generalities about the lot of people around the world and the unusually sorry state that it was in.

Once I was even involved in a little deception. Doctor Cloete was the only confidant they had in this situation, and he knew of my collection of books regarding other religions. I was especially fond of reading of the lives of the Catholic Saints, not really the right occupation for a good Methodist preacher, and funnily enough, whenever I spoke of the great martyrdoms to the coloured and black people of the area their attention was gripped, even as the story of the crucifixion always gripped them. They had no feeling, or not much, for the golden words of the sermon on the mount. They preferred the stronger meat of the martyrdoms. And the "Book of the Saints" was as popular in my parish as the Bible.

Knowing that they liked a bit of exaggeration, I had once, during a sermon on thrift, mentioned that they all knew what a careless person does with his wealth, against the wall, and that they would find it in the First Book of Kings, chapter 14, the 10th verse. According to what was told me later, all the servants in the village who did not have Bibles had then asked their employers to look it up for them, and my congregation of whites were angry with me for drawing the attention of the coloureds and blacks to the verse: "Therefore behold, I will bring evil upon the house of Jeroboam, and will cut off from Jeroboam him that pisseth against the wall, and him that is shut up and left in Israel, and will take away the remnant of the house of Jeroboam, as a man taketh away dung, till it be all gone."

The Bible, especially the old Testament, abounds in this sort of thing, as any diligently searching schoolboy or moderate reader of it knows. It was, of course, a little naughty of me, but, as I have said, I never was one for keeping too strictly to the rules. On occasion, I even sinned, but that is a matter for discussion between the Lord and me, and no doubt I will, in a sense, be hauled over the coals for it in due time.

I also possessed, apart from my books on the Catholics, a fair collection on the other great religions of the world. Among them were certain works concerning the mystical Eastern religions. Doctor Cloete, feeling that reading these books may have some therapeutic effect on Bettina Cilliers, suggested that I lend them to her, a few at a time, so that she could, in her solitude, read of the great advantages of meditation. The Bible, as we all know, also stresses the need for meditation, but not quite as strongly as the Eastern theologies. I was quite willing to make these books available to her, as I could not see any possible harm coming of it, and I promised Doctor Cloete that I would initiate a discussion on the subject the very next time I saw her. But he felt that she would not wish to talk about so personal a need and that it would be better if I let him have the books in question, so that he could let her have them on loan. That is how a man of science became a messenger of God, ferrying religious books to-and-fro. At times I was tempted to subtly mark a passage or two that I thought might be of value, but I refrained, and probably better so.

In those days, around 1930, when the little senseless Daan Cilliers was about nine years of age, a compulsory schooling act was part of the law of the Union of South Africa. It applied to white people only, because things were still very primitive then, and even today, although there are seven black universities, it is still excessively difficult for a lot of black children to get to a school. A census was taken, and unfortunately, along with official records, like his birth certificate, this poor child was included in the lists as an official citizen of the Union, a British subject.

Certain eyes had been closed when he had become six years of age, but it was no longer possible for officialdom to ignore the existence of this child, and Sergeant Hendricks of the Thornhill police station was concerned that he would get into trouble with the law if he did not do something about it.

The sergeant went to call on the Cilliers home, "the Great House" as it was called by all the villagers, and asked to see Bettina. When he had asked her what her intentions were with regard to "their mentally defective son," she took a broomstick out of the hands of one of the servants who happened to be sweeping the porch, and chased the sergeant all the way to his horse. He had to mount in a great hurry and get out of the yard at a gallop, with the black and coloured people, employees of the nature of servants and gardeners, laughing at him. The sergeant found Dawid Cilliers in the fields as he was supervising the harvesting of some crop, and put the problem to him. Once again he was met by a total lack of cooperation, and, so it also seemed, a complete lack of comprehension as to what he was talking about. It seemed that the Cilliers family had no intention of admitting to the existence of a mental defective in their home, and in the village little Daan had always been described as such.

The sergeant returned to his police station where he telephoned through to Pretoria, asking the district commandant what he should do. Back came the instruction: "The child, upon certified to be mentally defective by a doctor or minister of the church, will be placed in a state institution for expert care, supervision, and treatment by persons qualified to do so, duly appointed by the state."

The sergeant then went to Doctor Cloete, and asked him to provide a certificate of lunacy, or whatever the official document was called, in respect of Daniel Cilliers, aged nine, known to all and sundry as a mental defective, and living in the home of his parents, Bettina and Dawid Cilliers, of Skeerpoort. Doctor Cloete was also informed of the "disgraceful conduct" of Bettina, and of the intention of the sergeant to prosecute her for hampering him in the performance of his duty, and her husband for the same reason, or any other that he could find, after he had looked it all up in his law books.

Very often, tragedies are made of such simple, even humorous elements. That, Doctor Cloete knew only too well. A situation was growing around him that he had to prevent at all costs. Not to certify the child as insane meant that it had to go to a school, duly registered, where its education could be supervised by the appropriate officials appointed by a government that was concerning itself more-and-more with the problem of illiteracy. To certify him, on the other hand, meant that the boy would have to be admitted to the appropriate state institution. There (and there was no doubt of this), he would die.

Only a very special set of ways of keeping the little heart beating had kept him alive thus far, and already his survival had been nothing short of a total miracle. Doctor Cloete doubted, in his own mind, whether any doctor in his right senses would believe that a creature such as Daan could have lived for more than a day or two after his accident. And yet, because of the care he had been given, he had survived. That kind of care was just not available in the institutions of that time. In fact, there are very few places in the world today where such devoted treatment is to be had, at any price.

But an offended police sergeant, blown-up bull-frog-like by

his own sense of importance to the community, had been roughly treated and badly degraded in sight of a large number of his charges, and the fame of the broomstick incident would spread throughout the village within twenty-four hours or less, so strong was the gossip grapevine in the days before there were other entertainments to keep people occupied and their minds diverted. Except on Sundays, when *I* did my work. It was a flare-up of the Daan-scandal, something that had been kept quiet about except by a very few gossips. Some of these scandal-mongers were also personally involved in sinful acts that would eventually reach my ears. There was the case of the farrier and a certain gossipy widow, for instance, that was to divert the village for a number of years, but it is not my business to go spreading even more loose talk around, although I was, myself, also amused at the time.

Please accept that as a confession of childishness, and not as an attempt to prove my man-of-the-world qualities.

Because of their rigid disapproval of any discussion on the subject, it was doubtful if Bettina and Dawid Cilliers would even listen to any person representing the law. The only alternative was the use of force, the issuing of summonses, arrests, recriminations, and all the other unpleasant things that go hand-in-hand with legal action. I have always found that the only legalities that are necessary in this world can be handled by an attorney, and the only one we had around at that time was a person whom everybody called "old Bertie Theron." He was still a young man in 1930, and he stayed in the village all his life, doing all the legal bits-and-pieces that cropped up from time to time, including the necessities of accounting and auditing, although he was a qualified attorney. He had no heart for the law, and would rather have run away than issue a summons. That was why he had set up his offices in such a quiet backwater of the legal world.

Doctor Cloete knew that the law meant trouble that day, although everyone in the village was laughing, and he took the sergeant to my home, asking old Bertie Theron to meet us there as well, as a legal problem had come up.

"Gentlemen," said Doctor Cloete, when we had all settled down in my best chairs, in the lounge, that was hardly ever used. "Gentlemen, the sun is going down on another day, let us try to get this matter of little Daan Cilliers out of the way before it is dark. I can't get myself to sign the boy away to a lunatic asylum. Can you, Reverend?" he asked me directly, to my face.

"No," I said, "from what you have told me it would be tantamount to signing away his life."

"And," asked Doctor Cloete, "Attorney Theron, are you willing to assist us, and the parents, if the law insisted on their cruel solution?"

Attorney Theron, old Bertie, was so delighted at being even noticed that he said, with a fair amount of dignity: "I will do all I can to assist the Cillierses, who are very valuable and valued clients of mine. I am working on the preparation of a case now, based on precedents in law, that will be so strong, when all has been done, that no case for the removal of Daniel Cilliers from the custody of his parents will ever stand up in court. This information is confidential, by the way. No, I won't sign his life away."

"So there we are, sergeant," said Doctor Cloete. "None of us will sign, and if it goes to court we have a lawyer ready to act for us."

"That's okay," said the sergeant. "I don't mind going to court. Us in the police, we're in court all blerrie day long, it's part of the job."

"But I'm sure," said Doctor Cloete, "that there is an easier way out. What if, for instance, we certify that the child needs specialised medical care which can only be obtained at his home?"

"No good," said the policeman. "You think I'm blerrie cruel, hey? Well I'm not, I already spoke to them in Pretoria, and asked."

When he said that I knew that we had already won, hours ago, and that the situation was far less dangerous than I had supposed it would be. What Sergeant Hendricks didn't know was that, out of the list of names he himself had submitted to Pretoria, of worthy persons of the town to serve as Landdrost, or Magistrate, at the next court session at Thornhill, commencing that coming Tuesday, four days away, I had been selected by the authorities in Pretoria, for the job of Landdrost for the next six months or so. I had not yet had the opportunity to hand in my credentials, but my word, as magistrate of the district, would be law as from then, and it was only four days away.

"Very well, sergeant," I said. "You must obviously do your duty according to the law. We can all see that."

"Or the law will get me," said Hendricks.

"But," I said, "I don't want you to proceed against Mr. and Mrs. Cilliers. They have had a very bad time of it, and we don't want to drag their anguish out in open court, do we? Have a heart, sergeant."

"Have a heart" was one of those old-fashioned phrases I had learned in my uniformed days, when I had been seconded to a unit of the British Armed Forces doing service among the blackamoors in the interior. I thought that the phrase would appeal to his military sensibilities, and I was right.

"What do you want me to do?" he asked. "Pretoria knows about this case, and they will want to see it settled in Tuesday's court report."

"I want you to charge Doctor Cloete," I said, "with obstructing the course of justice."

"All right," he said. "What will that help?"

"Then the magistrate can order him to sign the certificate," I said.

"Oh," said the sergeant. "That's clever, but how is that going to help Mr. and Mrs. Cilliers, and the little boy?"

"That's up to Attorney Theron," I answered. "He must prepare a defence for Doctor Cloete that the magistrate will accept."

"But how can you expect me to do that?" asked Theron. "I'm not finished with my defence. It will take at least another year before I'm ready to go to court."

"Then," said Doctor Cloete, "you will have to place me on the stand, in my own defence, and I will make an impassioned speech, and the magistrate will be so moved that he will dismiss the plea."

"That won't work," said the sergeant. "The law is strict, and the magistrate will have to stick to the law. Magistrates can't be dishonest, you know."

He had me there, my whole little plan going wrong because of that word honesty. I knew that, as magistrate, I would have to uphold the letter of the law. Sometimes, as we all know, judges and magistrates have to make shockingly unjust decisions because of the evil ways in which the law is most often used by unscrupulous persons, or people who commit perjury, or for any amount of reasons. The law is the law, and sometimes it can be very unjust.

"Yes," I said to Sergeant Hendricks, "you have me there."

"I have you there sir?" asked Hendricks. "How do you mean?"

I took out the magistrate's letter of appointment from my desk, which was in the corner of my lounge, my little home not having a study.

"Oh Heavens, sir," said Hendricks, "this is a nonsense of a situation."

Of course he used other words, more suited to his military background and his perpetual association with blackguards and the criminal elements of the community. He even committed blasphemy, but had I been a priest of the Catholic faith I would surely have forgiven him.

"But sir," he said, "magistrates and doctors, acting together, have other powers, and I would like to suggest a drastic course. What I mean is, why don't you just declare the little bugger dead?"

"But," I said, "he's not dead. The whole thing is a matter of honesty."

"Mr. Theron," he said, "you are an attorney. When is a man dead."

"When he's dead and buried, he's dead," said Attorney Theron, and I could see by the sentence why there had been so very little chance of his ever becoming a trial lawyer, and why he had chosen to come to the quietness of Skeerpoort, instead of fooling himself that he had talents for bigger things. But fortunately Doctor Cloete came to the rescue.

"A man is dead," said Doctor Cloete, "when he can no longer see, hear, or speak, and when there is no likelihood of it ever happening to him. He is doubly dead when there is no certainty that he can smell or taste anything."

"That," said the sergeant, "is a good description of a dead man. Do you see what I mean, Reverend?"

"But," I said, "surely he can feel, touch, smell, taste, surely?"

"This is between us," said Doctor Cloete. "A privileged communication, and we all know what that means. No, Reverend, he may have a sense of taste or smell but it is highly unlikely that he uses it. It is a miracle that he is alive, and that is solid, scientific fact. He answers to all the requirements of what death is, technically and medically. All he can do himself is to void his bladder and bowels, which are also the only acts of death."

"Then," said the sergeant, "there's no problem. Except about the burial, we will have to have a burial certificate."

"You sorely tempt my conscience and my honesty, sergeant," I said.

"You don't have to bury him, or certify him dead."

"But as magistrate I will read in your records, on Tuesday, that one Daniel Cilliers, aged nine, died here in Skeerpoort today."

"That's exactly the truth," said Doctor Cloete. "That's why we are here. To make sure that, as far as officialdom is concerned, he is declared to be dead and buried. It isn't just for today. Records cannot be continuously falsified. Parents, servants, trusted friends can die. In their wills the Cillerses will make sure of his care after their death, I'll see to that, next week. But the time will come for a call-up to do military service, or the tax man will want to know why this person born in 1921 has never contacted them, or he will disappear from the census forms and some official may want to know why. No, we make sure, today, that he is killed, finally and permanently. And you Reverend, on Tuesday, when you sign Sergeant Hendricks's records, you do so gladly, because with a little white lie you save a life, although you certify that that life no longer exists. This is the official death of Daniel Cilliers."

With that, he took a death certificate from his bag, filled it in, and asked Sergeant Hendricks to witness it. Daan Cilliers was indeed officially dead. But I thought to myself, I must also make a contribution to this gracious lie, that I believed needed to be lied. So I went to my desk and wrote out, by hand, in my best copperplate, a certificate stating to whom it may concern, that I had that day assisted at what I cleverly called the "final incarceration" instead of "burial" of one Daniel Cilliers, child of this parish. I signed it, and it was duly witnessed by old Bertie Theron as well as Sergeant Hendricks.

"Now," said the sergeant, "I am now folding up these two certificates and taking them to the police station. I will make out all the reports and they will all be correct and the child will be officially dead. Then I am going down to Fritz Smit's bar at the station, and I am going to get pissed. I invite you all to join me at the wake to Daan Cilliers this evening at Fritz Smit's bar. Although we will not mention the name of the deceased to anybody, at all, ever again. You hear? I will not have it ever mentioned again, unless it is accompanied by the words, "the late," understand? And the invitation to the wake is for you too, Reverend."

He blackmailed me with his words.

"We would all appreciate it very much to see you at the bar, at the station, this evening. Right boys?"

Doctor Cloete and Bertie Theron looked at me, and at the sergeant, and both of them smiled, knowing I was over a barrel. "Right, Sarge," they said.

That evening I went along to Fritz Smit's bar. As luck would have it he had a Jeroboam of champagne. It was winter and there was no reason to chill it, so I ordered it opened, and paid for it, making the excuse to the others that it was more seemly for a minister of the church to drink champagne than ordinary brandy.

I drank too much of it, with the result that it was necessary for me to engage in a biblical act. You will find a description of it in four words in the 10th verse of chapter 14 of the First Book of Kings.

That is how it happened that I made a fool of myself on the night when I, in collusion with certain leading citizens of the village, contributed towards the official death and burial of a person in order that he may continue to exist in an unofficial capacity. We never told the parents, or servants, of this matter, and we killed all village gossip about the existence, or non-existence if you wish, of the boy Daan Cilliers. To kill the gossip that was always being spread in the village I had to adopt a rather unusual tactic; that of the full frontal attack in the face of the enemy. My calling gave me the ears of most of the people of the village as well as those of the black and coloured servants and farm labourers.

Now, one of the most inveterate of these gossips was a certain widow, a Mrs. Watson, now long since departed, leaving no trace of family, so no one will be particularly hurt when I mention her liaison with a certain bachelor farrier who lived in the village once, a man called Travis. Both were Methodists who attended church regularly, but word of their scandalous behaviour reached my ears because of other gossips. In those lonely days, before the introduction of the mass entertainments, people had very little to do with their leisure time, and visiting each other, back and forth, on a basis of taking turns at it, they managed to discuss everybody and their personal business in great detail. Gossip is part of the way of life of a small community, and, as long as it did not result in too much trouble or enmity, I did not take it upon myself to do very much about it.

Occasionally, from the pulpit, I would mention the danger of the devil finding work for idle hands, or sharp tongues, or some light warning. But the fact is that, by informing me as minister of the church, people thought it their duty to point the finger. So, whenever a new love affair was being perpetrated, or an illicit liaison being practised, I usually knew of it virtually immediately, and often while the potentially guilty parties were still making plans, not actually having sinned yet.

I knew, in fact, everything that went on in the village, and as I had become its almost permanent magistrate, I found out even more than I would have known normally. So, very often, the cases that had been due to go to court each week were settled, by me, by just asking the litigants to take tea with me. (In my own mind I preferred to think of it as drinking tea, but in those days such common form of speech did not suit the dignity of a minister or a magistrate.) I practised, through the years, a number of little pomposities of speech and bearing that I thought both ministerial and magisterial, until, one day, in the middle of a particularly long and complicated phrase the words "bugger this" came into my mind. So I stopped. And after that I was often hauled over the coals, for my loose use of language, by occasionally visiting superiors. I have noticed a tendency towards pompousness in these notes, and, if they are deemed worthy of publication and distribution by the Society in London, I must ask the worthy editors to polish up my prose to a more dignified standard. The pompous is never dignified, the momentous is. The trouble is to distinguish between the two.

Here I must confess that the scandalous gossip of the little village quite often included acts of mine when I made mistakes, because often I had been subjected to temptations I could not resist. Like St. Augustine, the Lord had not been willing to bestow the great virtue of chastity upon me, and I was also willing to wait until He saw fit to do so. We were all involved, each in our sins. Methodist ministers could, of course, marry, and usually did, and there had been a time when I had been in love with a young lady who had promised to wait for me, in London. But when I had sent for her to join me I had received a note from her father regretting the fact that his daughter could not comply with my request as she had become married to a lad from Sussex and had gone with him to live on his farm. The gentleman had also made it quite clear, in his letter, that, although he admired my work among the heathen in darkest Africa (for those had been my missionary days), he did not think that the life out here would have suited his daughter, whom he and his wife had tried to bring up to be "a respectable and genteel lady." So she became a pig farmer's wife in Sussex. My, that does sound a little bitter, doesn't it? I should say that George Webb was tasting a mouthful of sour grapes again. However, be that as it may, I did not, after that, seriously consider taking a wife again. Not that I was all that hurt or mentally scarred. It just didn't seem to matter so much any more, so I didn't consciously search for a successor to my unfaithful fiancée.

However, I was subjected to an occasional temptation, and often the means of succumbing to it was at hand, so to speak. There are ladies who believe that the seduction of their doctors is proof of some superhuman prowess over men. Doctors, as I know them, are as human as anyone else, and fall prey to temptresses just as readily as carpenters do, or clergymen. I have heard many stories of the great debaucheries practised, throughout history, by the men of my profession, and of course they are true. And yet, as a group, I believe we have not done so badly as to be totally condemned. But I am here making my apologies to the wrong judges. There is a judge waiting for me, I know, and it is no use my preparing my defence now. No, these words are more in the nature of an attempt to say that I did not put myself in a position above the good, human people of my parish, in spite of the fact that they gossiped meaningfully and with good reason, because we were most certainly, all of us, sinners in all the senses of the word.

That is how things were when the question of gossip and loose talk about Daan Cilliers came up. And a rather serious question it was too, because we had, as a group, falsified official documents and we could all have lost our positions as well as our freedom, including the good Sergeant Hendricks, if word of the false death were to become part of village gossip. Apart from that, such irresponsible talk would have been dangerous to Daan's life, as well as to the well-being of his already sorely tried parents. Therefore, in private, and never from the pulpit, I told person after person that I knew of their most hidden sins. Confession of these sins to a clergyman is rather rare in the Methodist faith, as we believe in that day of judgement waiting for us on the other side, and, as I've said previously this is no time to start the preparation of a defence. No, what I knew had come from plain gossip, guilty consciences, malice, fear, holier-than-thouness, and so on, all little human things that I could excuse. But now I was in a position to bargain, gossip-for-gossip, guilt-for-guilt.

My proposition was always the same; please stop talking, or even thinking of the little boy growing up at the Cilliers's farm. It hurt his parents, and they had been good to the village, as well as to the church itself. If the talk stopped, I would see to it that such-and-such a sin would not get to the ears of so-and-so. Only through stopping all tendencies to gossip could I stop the inclusion of the Cilliers's position in the spreading stories. But that of course was impossible, people want to tell their stories, and to deprive them would have been mean.

It was, however, possible, over the years, to bring about a less malicious sort of story about Daan, turning his condition into an illness that was incurable, and gradually the tales of the little slobbering monster grew fewer, to be replaced by stories of a bedridden boy growing up quietly, being cared for with the utmost devotion. So my wheeler-dealing in sins helped the family, and much of the village gossip stopped, to become, rather, well-kept confidences among friends. And there is a great deal of difference between those two matters, let me assure you.

Many lives have been ruined by loose talk, malice, and unfair speculation, just as many as have been harmed by actual things that have truthfully happened. Neither need ever become public property, certainly not since the invention of the birth control pill, the cinema, and, lately, the television, all of which provide ample opportunities for diversion. After a while, I suppose people grew tired of the subject, or there was no-one else to tell it to. Perhaps it had just become worked out, like a stale joke that nobody told any longer, but I noticed that stories of little Daan had all but stopped in the village, and I took some gratification in the fact that I had made my contribution to the reasonable silence that was now reigning about the subject. I often discussed the matter with Doctor Cloete, who, although belonging to the Dutch Reformed Church, had become one of my friends, but our discussions were more a matter of trying to find some way whereby we would be of help.

Doctor Cloete was a regular caller at the Great House, and could see the little boy whenever he wished. He made it a practice to examine the child's heart-beat and the clarity of his lungs at least once a week. He also kept a wary eye out for symptoms such as fever, complexion, inflammation, and so on, to be quite sure that the boy survived in spite of not being able to talk of his symptoms. In his way the miracle of life within that excessively frail and vulnerable body was sustained.

There were, of course, other miracles as well. The parents, Bettina and Dawid Cilliers, having realised that their son was a beautiful creature in spite of all that was wrong with him, were determined that he should not be failed in at least that respect. With the help of various locomotory machines that could be purchased, or imported specially, a series of exercises had been devised, including a miraculous form of walking by means of a kind of upright tricycle, with horizontally moving foot pedals, that had to be pushed by a second person. This provided the bodily exercise normally available through the actual act of going for a walk. This machine, made by the father, Dawid Cilliers, kept little Daan active for as much as two hours every day, an hour in the morning and another in the late afternoon. In the house it was referred to as "little Daan's walk" and, in the opinion of Doctor Cloete, it was this machine, designed and built on the site, that was the single most important factor in the little boy's survival.

The machines that arrived at the Great House during those years are commonplace today, and mechanical exercisers are a part of everyday life, with the most magnificent ones to be seen at the physiotherapy departments of the great hospitals, and an even greater array at the health farms where people go who wish to improve their appearance or to trim down their waist-lines.

Lately, I have noticed a tendency to a slight corpulence in myself, and I am rather ashamed of it, when I think of all the time and trouble that was expended at the Great House on a little boy, all those years ago, to keep him looking attractive. But his parents were determined that he should remain a beautiful person to look at. They never allowed me to see him, of course, and I had no wish to, as my reports from Doctor Cloete were quite adequate. Over the years, on my visits to their home, I never again, after his "official death," mentioned him to them or to any other person, for that matter, except for Doctor Cloete.

Toys, in the normal sense, were of no use to the child, and neither were things like bicycles. Pedal cars were coming into fashion in the early thirties, but they had to be especially adapted to Daan's feet, because of the strapping-down that was necessary. His feet could not, of their own volition, be made to stay in one place. If he were held up, and released, he would collapse in a heap. He knew nothing of balance or locomotion, and his every movement had to be made for him by manual or mechanical means.

Doctor Cloete always mentioned his intention of writing a paper on the subject to some medical journal or other, and I know that he had amassed a great knowledge of the matter in the form of various notes, and he had written a number of pages as well. Some statistical matter had been sent to the medical schools, but he was not an academically minded man and no trace could be found of such a manuscript after his death. All that remained were the usual case histories. But that was many years later. I have discussed the matter with various members of his family, including his son, now also a doctor, but their feeling is unanimous: Doctor Cloete had had a great many intentions during his lifetime, but he was a practical doctor, never a theoretical one. He had kept up-to-date on his subjects as a general practitioner, or family doctor, but apart from that his interest in little Daan was expressed, academically, only by the reading of articles on similar cases in medical journals. But of course there had never been a case like Daan. No person with such handicaps had ever survived. In gamblers' terms: the deck was too heavily stacked against him.

And, looking back, I think Doctor Cloete was right. There was no necessity for the world to know about little Daan Cilliers. He was our own private village tragedy, and we left him alone. The world could do the same. Doctor Cloete, his parents, and Mina had done all that could be done, in fact, more than could be done. No, the good doctor was a practical man who knew what to do when he felt inflamed skin or saw bone sticking through flesh, and he lost very few patients before it was their time to go, and if others have to record their belief that the boy had been kept medically alive by him then it is our duty to do so, because he was a most unusual medical man, the only one I have ever heard use words like "I don't know."

Usually, doctors know every possible thing that you can ask them, but Doctor Cloete wasn't like that. He admitted frankly that, sometimes, he didn't know, but he also had a sort of built-in common sense that guided his hands in the right direction. I can tell you of many instances where tragedy was almost certain, and Doctor Cloete didn't really know what to do, instances of fractured spines, necks, perforations of the intestines, and so on, as well as burns and other serious hurts that could kill or maim for ever, that he managed to get right by some guiding genius, as I call it; but he, when questioned, would always refer to his most spectacular cures as a "combination of luck, common sense, and the effectiveness of your prayers, Reverend."

I prayed a great deal, it is true, because in a little village like ours, in spite of the fact that I have told only of the case of little Daan, a doctor and a minister of the church crossed paths almost daily.

We had our fair share of tragedy, in that village. Children who died for no apparent reason, long before anyone had even seen the need for calling a doctor. A little cough in the night, and in the morning the little body would already be cold to the touch. And then again, a man would go off to work with two perfectly good legs, something would go wrong with the ploughing and by that evening he would be a lifelong cripple with a leg severed at the knee.

One of the saddest cases was the death of a Mrs. Harris. She had worked on her magnificent, formal rose garden all her life, collecting the rarest and most beautiful roses she could find from all over the world. She answered all advertisements and kept up an enormous correspondence with rose-fanciers in other countries as well as her own. One day, while making a cutting to send off to a correspondent in England, she pricked her thumb on a thorn. That night, the gland under her armpit had become swollen to the size of a ping-pong ball, and the arm was throbbing painfully. She should have sent for Doctor Cloete immediately, but decided to hold out till morning and not to interrupt the good doctor's sleep. As it was, he was packing to leave for Krugersdorp early the next morning, and so she missed him and died of blood poisoning before he arrived back that same afternoon.

Doctor Cloete's job was to heal what he could of their broken bodies, and mine to attempt to mend their souls, and, as I said, our paths often crossed. Hardly had he left a house than I was called in to pray for the recovery of the invalid or the soul of the departed, as the case might be.

But I was never seriously consulted, spiritually, by Bettina or Dawid Cilliers. Yes, I went to see them about once a fortnight, just to see if there was some breakup in their spirit that I might be allowed to, if not heal, at least spread on a balm of some sort. After all, it was what I had been trained for, to bring solace to those whose spirits were troubled. But Bettina, although she looked frail and breakable, never so much as bent, as far as I knew. And her only spiritual need seemed to be a never-ending appetite for books concerning other religions than her own. I would, on my rare visits to the cities nearby, always endeavour to obtain for her as many of these as I could lay my hands on, but in those days the need for books about Eastern religions had not become a fashion and they were few and far between.

I would like to be able to report here a dramatic break-through to the spirits of either Bettina, Dawid, or their son Daan, but this was not to be. I had helped them only by providing their son with a certificate of burial, and by falsifying certain official reports, of which they knew nothing. Bettina remained convinced, ever afterwards, that her chasing of Sergeant Hendricks with a broom-stick was the end of that affair, and she never knew that the books brought to her by Doctor Cloete had been provided by me, the Ex Libris carefully steamed off and replaced again on their return. That was the only solace I could give to the man and woman who had paid for the building of my church, on whose land my rent-free home stood, and I wanted to show my thanks also for the fact that Dawid had built my pulpit, alone, because of his love of woodwork.

But they would never allow me into their torn and broken hearts. They would never break or allow any mending. And this is a complaint from me. I feel that they could have, sometimes, pretended to need me.

After all, it could have been another minister, not as strong in his mind as I am. And his feelings might have been hurt.

The boy was growing up fast, as the years were passing, and more and better ways of exercising were invented in other countries. These expensive machines arrived at the station from all parts of Europe as a result of the addresses given to Dawid Cilliers by Doctor Cloete, and in that way the boy's muscular development was assured.

And so there grew to maturity one of the most unusual human beings ever to have lived on this earth, and I have mentioned his particular case at length in this memoir because his is the case that most plagued my conscience. It was because of him that

I perjured myself as a minister and magistrate, that I became drunk and rowdy one night, in my own village where people were supposed to have respect for me. And it is strange, but after that night of drunkenness, they seemed to like me more.

The case of the Cilliers family represents my greatest failure, in that I could never, no matter how I tried, penetrate the iron reserve of the parents, or do anything constructive for the boy. How could an unfeeling, sightless, dumb person like that have had so great an influence on my life? He could not even have been aware of my existence, or of the existence of any other person, thing, feeling or thought as far as we knew, but he had this talent to influence the lives of people, to make other troubles seem small by comparison, and if I sinned with women there on the edges of his world more often than I would have normally, it was to bury my own feelings of inadequacy.

Knowing people like Daan and Bettina and Dawid Cilliers can be an emasculating experience for someone like me. I had never been too certain of myself in any case, if the truth were to be known. Hence, of course, my air of pompousness. As I write here I wonder, should I have prayed for them more? I do not know, in their case, if my prayers were even welcome. Perhaps, in talking to God about them, and asking for his hand to heal their wounds, perhaps I was interfering. I will never know, because they never allowed me to get close to them. I would make up sermons especially for them, telling the congregation how important it was that we open our hearts to each other, that we do not live behind facades. "Who knows the face of his brother?" is indeed a living question for me.

But never, never once, was I allowed a glimpse of what must have been the most private hell on earth, except through my talks with Doctor Cloete, who was also a sorely troubled man. He had several times asked me what my opinion was of the advisability of taking the boy to one of the great hospitals of London, Edinburgh, Berlin or Geneva. There was a growing new science, a branch of medicine called neurosurgery, which actually probed into the brain with the knife.

"Imagine, Reverend," he would say excitedly, "a knife in the human brain, cutting, trimming, sawing away at the surrounding bone, excising tumours and all sorts of unwelcome things. But in the brain, Reverend, right inside the human brain."

Of course, I had heard of operations round and about the

human brain, the removal of appendages, growths, and blood clots, procedures that were usually fatal. But to actually slice into the membrane covering the brain, and working in there, where we thought, felt, loved, hated, adored God and flowers, this was too much for me. I couldn't understand even the concept of it, much less the reality.

"It's like a nightmare, just the thought," I protested. "Cutting into the protective membrane around it. You and I have seen what the brain looks like inside. Remember the night of the train accident at the level crossing? That soft matter was brain. How can you slice into that with a knife, or put needles into it? How can you slice off a thought, or the message of the brain about a perfume, or the sight of a flower, how can you cut into that, and your feelings? Your feelings are in the brain, Doctor, and I have a suspicion that while you are alive your soul is somewhere in there as well. How can you take a knife and slice into someone's soul? I tell you Doctor, the thought is too much for me. It's something that gives me the horrors."

In that way I advised Doctor Cloete not to do anything about the boy surgically. I'm not sorry I did, because it was still in the early and middle thirties when these conversations were taking place, and I remember still the tragedy that was associated with having even to go to a hospital in those years when everything that we now take for granted as commonplace was still being thought about and developed. I believe that, if Daan had been subjected to one of those premature guinea-pig exploratory operations, we would never have seen him alive again.

A knife to the soul, I had said, fully realising that a knife can also be used to cut bonds, to release. And I had to ask myself the question as to whether it would not have been better to release the soul trapped in that beautiful, useless body.

Fortunately, the decision was not mine to make, or give advice upon, or, even to discuss. There were problems of diplomacy that all of us in the village had to sort out in our own way. I don't want to give the impression that the Cilliers family were in any way aloof from the daily life of the little town. They were as friendly and courteous as ever, even to entertaining in their home. There was only one proviso, and that was that there should never be any discussion of the child in the nursery, and later, in his own back garden.

In this way the shadowy creature grew up to the age of fourteen, and we had found a way to live with him. We were careful of our gay moments, watchful of the sort of Christmas cards that we sent to the Great House, careful not to use phrases like "blind as a bat" or "dumb-bell" or "as unfeeling as a pumpkin." There were many other similar phrases that had to be avoided in their company, and, being only human, mistakes were often made, chance remarks that would only have significance for the parents, but they also did not allow frozen moments of silence. It was as if, in this respect, they understood that they also had a diplomatic duty to the conversations in which they took part.

And then, one day in 1935, Doctor Cloete called on me and gave me the exciting news of something that had happened to Daan. It seems that, after all those years of daily exercising, he had walked. I have no sense of the dramatic, I can merely say that; he had walked. It had been a silly little walk, verging on the dangerous, but he had managed, somehow, to stand up without help for a few moments, and after that he had taken a few steps forward, in perfect imitation of the steps that were created for him on his walking machine. They were, said Doctor Cloete, more like awkward shuffles, one with each foot, and a further half-a-one before his balance became upset and his father had to take him by the arms to hold him up in order to prevent a fall.

But somehow, far beneath the brutal cruel unfeeling exterior that fate had so unkindly given him, he had moved. He had, by himself, caused a movement of his own that was part of the regular pattern of human life, but totally foreign in his experience. He had of course walked in his own way previously, on his machines, but they had been aimless perambulations, with no design or purpose, or aim in reality, and with no relationship to motion as we know it. But these few steps had had the definite pattern of walking. It makes no matter what had caused them, what was important was that it appeared that if the family persevered with their programme of therapy and exercise there was an almost certain promise that the time would come when he would be able to walk at will. Those words "at will" immediately, in their turn, promised the abundant joys of an identity.

I will anticipate a little and tell you that the years sped by, and with each year he became more adept at walking, if only to draw a moral with which to conclude my little talk; that love, perseverance, and the will to make something work, something that was scientifically and logically impossible, had overcome, somehow, the total lack of a natural capacity. Now he could not only swallow, he could also take a few steps.

To me, it was a great miracle, and if I seem to make too much of a fuss over two and a half shuffling steps, put it down to my faith and my belief in miracles, and my conviction that the Miracle Maker, the One who had made Lazarus rise, still walks this earth.

8

SILVER ADAMS

"I don't care, old Silver, long as I got you I don't care," said Flash, one day, after we had finished what we did together. He was talking about his job, and the way the people of the Great House didn't ever tell him anything about what he was doing.

"But it's okay, Flash," I said to him. "I will tell you the lot, man. There isn't anything that goes on in a house that you can hide from the house-girl. There isn't no place I can't get. I even been inside the Kleinbasie's room, once or twice."

"What's he like?" Flash asked. "Is he stone mad, or has he got a chance?"

"No," I said. "He isn't mad at all. He just lies there when he isn't on that walker you and the Oubaas made for him. Other times he sits there on the thing you made from that easy chair. But it's all connected up to the foot pedals that Mina uses, and so he gets his exercise. But you know, they used to put his feet on the pedals of the walking machine, and now sometimes they take the pedals off, and Mina says he is beginning to learn to walk."

"And the straps. Must he still be all strapped up to keep him straight?" asked Flash.

"No," I said. "The strap that used to keep his head up, that big red leather thing that came from England with the brass holes in, he hardly ever needs it now. It looks like he can keep his head up by himself for nearly an hour at a time now, before it falls down on his chest or his shoulders again. But it's not like it was when he was a little boy. All the exercises they gave him every day, all through the years, this has made up his muscles, so now his head just sinks down quietly when he is tired, it doesn't fall plop like that anymore."

"You know, Silver," said Flash, "if we have a baby like that, I won't let him live, you know, I will turn his neck like you kill a blerrie chicken, man, and then all the trouble is over, man."

"You musn't talk like that, Flash," I said. "If anybody ever hears you said a thing like that, and the Oubaas finds out about it, he will turn your blerrie neck around, like a chicken. And I won't like to see you with your eyes looking down your back, past your bum, to your heels. The Oubaas is very strong, Flash, stronger than any man I know, and he's very straight, but nobody must ever say nothing about the Kleinbasie or there will be big shit."

"I don't care," said Flash.

He always says "I don't care." It is the thing that he says, like Adam Long says "it's all right" when he's pissed up, so Flash says "I don't care." So he said: "I don't care, because I know everything anyway. You know they don't even ask me to go work in the lands any more, because I'm the best fuckin' garden boy in the Transvaal. There is nobody that's better'n me, for growing any blerrie thing in the Kirchoff's seed book. And I'm almost as good as the Oubaas with the carpentry and the wood polish, and I can do bricklaying and plaster and garden paths and crazy-paving with slate better than the Oubaas. So I don't care, because if he kicks my arse I will take my stuff and bugger off to Pretoria or Joh'burg, there I can always get a job if I can get the money together for a train ticket and a month's rent for a room in Sophiatown."

"It was me that took the chair out of the old store-room, sommer a old rocker that was broken, and I made the sliding back from a old Morris chair, and the pedals from that trike with straps for the feet from a old racing bike Moosa the Koelie had hanging up in his store-room. I sommer scaled the stuff when he wasn't looking. But when I told the Oubaas he went and paid Moosa, too blerrie much money, and now Moosa watches me very carefully whenever I go into his shop, like I'm a fuckin' thief, man, and all because I wanted to help. I tell you, Silver my girl, I made that sitting machine almost hundred per cent all by myself, and I don't want to hear no shit. I work blerrie hard, and I try to fix things so they will last forever, because my work is good, but they don't tell me anything, and I know what's going on anyway. It's blerrie silly man, everybody knows what they got in that room there, and I know what that machinery is for, because I got to help fix it up, and I know where all the tools and spanners are, so what they got to hide from me, man? You know, he tells me 'fetch this' and 'get that' and 'where's the screwdriver' and 'hold fast there' and they expect me to make like I don't know what everything is about. They're blerrie stupid man, and they blerriewell think I'm fuckin' stupid too."

"Flash lovey," I said, because I don't like him to get too upset when he is busy drinking, because he gets upset and I don't fight with him, so he must go out and find a fight at the shebeen where they sell that shit drink that makes blood come out of you after a couple of years. I don't like Flash to go there because there are whore kaffirs and Boesmans there that behave like common kak, and they don't even wear bloomers, and sit with their legs open. That sort. I don't like Flash to go there because they've got the pox anyway and any case I'm good enough for any man, just ask. But Flash is my special, true love, he is, because he is my regular.

And its nice because I work in the house and he works in the garden, and my room is near the house only a hundred yards, and it's pretty at the edge of the fruit orchard, that Flash prunes every July. Us that work in the house can eat all the fruit we want to, because there's too much for the house people, and the Oubaas doesn't want to sell what grows in the yard. That is for us people who work there, is what he says, but the other fruit that grows on the five thousand fruit trees in the big orchards, that nobody must touch, because that is not for us to eat: It is business.

But it is a good life in the farmyard, with lots to eat and clothes to wear, and a room with an iron roof, and a ceiling, and our own lavatory, not like on the other farms, where you live in mud huts, with grass roofs, and you kakked out in the open, behind the long grass, like common Hottentots.

So Flash had to be calmed down, like a child, when he got cross. Because when Flash is drunk on his name, you know his name is Flash Port and he loves Port, because he can go to the bottle store off-sales and say to the Hotnot behind the non-European counter: "Two bottles of my name" and then everybody laughs, every time. He drinks one bottle on Saturday and one on Sunday, half before church and half after. But sometimes he is still thirsty, because he doesn't mind a hangover Sunday morning, because he drinks on Sunday as well, so he breaks into his Sunday bottle sometimes on Saturday night, and then the shit flies.

He's a bugger in a fight, and he hurts the other boys, so I don't like to see him in trouble with the Oubaas on a Monday morning, when some of the boys got on bandages and black eyes and sore arms, because they go blerrie mad when they start fighting, man, worse than a pack of dogs. When they get into that sort of trouble the Oubaas finds the man who was responsible for starting it, and he takes him up the hill to Baas Hendricks, the policeman. He puts him on charge for drunk and disorderly, and next weekend the poor bugger has to pack up and go in the cells from Friday till Monday morning, on rice water and kak stale bread.

We who work in the house and the garden, we eat just what the white people eat. We don't even eat the meat soup and corn the others eat at lunchtime, it's too common for us. We got a good life.

So that's why I said: "Flash, lovey, you mustn't mind, man, they don't talk about the Kleinbasie to each other, either, you know. Never. They don't say a word about him, except when they talk they make it sound that he's just a normal boy, like everybody else. You never hear them say anything that will make anybody think that there's something wrong. It's the way it has been in that house for many, many years.

"The only thing you hear about is when something happens that means he has made some progress with maybe his walking, and his arms, and keeping up his neck, because every year now something seems to be happening to him that wasn't there before, and now he can sit in a ordinary chair for a long time, without looking like a rag doll, all floppy, but like a young man, and if you didn't know, you'd swear he was just like you and me.

"But you mustn't mind, Flash lovey, you must be a Christian man that Jesus loves, and be understanding, because they have had a hard time, just keeping him alive, because they say that anybody else would have died by now."

"And a God's blessing it would have been too," said Flash, taking another long sip from his bottle, that was next to us, on the floor, because it was winter and we didn't go to the long grass, where Flash always liked it on a hot day. "That isn't no human being, man, Silver lovey, that's sommer a blerrie pumpkin-head, man, and he is too much trouble to bring up, and when they get him to be a big man one day he's going to be just as useless as he is now, so why trouble, man. That's what I don't understand, why go to the trouble, because it's going to a hell of a lot of trouble for nothing. I'm only a garden boy, but I don't know, Silver, lovey, why plant a fruit tree when you know it's never going to do any blerrie thing at all, just like a dead stick, that you must tie up with grass ropes and other sticks just to make it stand, with a special roof to keep off the sun and the frost? Why don't they just throw it on the ash heap and plant another one? There was nothing wrong with them that time, they could have made another baby. Not now. I hear they don't touch each other any more. She sleeps in her room and he sleeps in his. I think that's a lot of shit. Why don't they stay together, like you and me, in all the troubles we've had, even that time I nearly killed you in that fight, we stick together, don't we, so why can't they? They supposed to be blerrie fuckin' educate, and I only got standard two, and I can tell them a thing or two, only they won't listen, and always I got to keep my mouth shut, and never say nothing about the Kleinbasie, in case it hurts their feelings. What does the Oubaas do hay? I mean. How does he manage? Does he pull his wire or have wet dreams? He doesn't bugger around with you house girls hay. Does he?"

"No," I said, "and that's the God's honest truth. He never touches any of the house girls. And I don't know what he does."

This wasn't easy for a randy bugger like Flash to understand, and I didn't understand it either. In the mornings when I took coffee to the bedrooms, the Oubaas was sometimes still in his half-sleep, before being full-awake, and I could see by the tent in the middle of his bed that he was still a man, and that he had been dreaming. And sometimes, when I did the washing, there was a hardened patch on one of his sheets or his pajamas, like he had been with a woman, but it must have been one of those other things that Flash said just now, you know, about the wire, and the dreams. Flash is a very ugly talker, when he is drinking, especially Saturday. He uses words that he is ashamed of when he is sober, except when he hits his shinbone with a stick, or his finger with a hammer, then he also uses those same ugly words, loudly, even when he is sober. But he is a good man to me, old Flash Port, and I don't care either.

So I told Flash all about all of the things a cleaning girl sees around a house, because if there's one thing I know, that is that Flash Port is not a man for talking loose all over the place. I have never yet caught him out on anything that I have ever told him. When I say to him: "Flash, lovey, this is strictly between you and me," then I know that it will not go any further. I must talk sometimes, about what my life in the big house is, or I will burst, or something. You can't sit with secrets all of your life, without telling them to anybody. What's the use of a secret if you can't talk about it? So thank the good Lord for Flash, because what I tell him goes in one ear and out the other. Sometimes, when I'm in the middle of telling him something very interesting, at least I think it's very interesting, he tells me to shut up, I'm talking too much. So, even if he isn't listening sometimes it's nice to talk and get it off your chest.

The secrets of people are all in what the cleaning girl has to put into her pail in the morning. You can see by how many handkerchiefs a lady has used what has been going on. How much tears, what has come from the throat or nose or mouth, how many times has she put on new lipstick, this you can see from handkerchiefs, and what is on them. And what they have been thinking of, all this is left on the lace-covered things, their bust-bodices and bloomers, and the things we have to clean up. I often wonder, if they got no shame, to let a Hotnot girl see so deep into what is going on. They think that they are not talking, but in the bathrooms and the bedrooms and the lavatories they leave all the things that shout out their words to you.

Often when I go into the master's bedroom in the morning with his coffee, and he turns on his side to hide his feelings that are showing, I often want to take off my bloomers, right there, and lie down on the floor, because my place is not in his bed, and say to him: "Come Oubans, let me help you, and nobody will ever know anything at all." And I can imagine that he will take off his night-clothes, and come to me on the floor, and take me quickly, with his breath held so that it won't make any noise, and after a few moments he will let go his seed and breath and everything, like a fire-cracker.

Then, I can imagine, he will get up quickly and get back to

his bed, and close his eyes. I will wipe up the spill on the floor with a hand towel, and go out softly, so that he can get up and go to the bathroom and wash me from himself. And put on ointment, because white men are afraid of Hotnot girls, in case of the pox, but, as Flash says, "I don't care."

Afterwards, I imagine, the Oubaas will buy some rubbers in town, and keep them hidden, in a private place in his bedroom, in case it happens again, so that he doesn't have to be afraid of babies or of the pox. But he needn't worry, I think in my imagination of course, he needn't worry because I have always kept myself clean and there is something wrong inside me, so I can't have babies, at least, that is what Flash says, that it must be my fault, because he says that before he met me he planted at least a hundred babies from Pretoria to Krugersdorp.

Now, all this what I have been saying about my imagination and how I sometimes feel sorry for the master, and how I would like to help him out, is in my head only, and I swear it's just my imagination, but I can't talk about it to Flash, because he will beat me up, just to get such evil thoughts out of my head, because there's a lot of evil things that Flash can do and stand, but there's other evil things that Flash will not tolerate, and one of them is a Hotnot girl who thinks too much of herself and who brags about things that are only in her head.

I can always see what sort of night the Oubaas has had. Sometimes, when he is tired and I take him his cup of hot cocoa, which is a habit with him and the Oumiesies Bettina too, he is, sometimes, as I said, already in bed and I can see that he will close those eyes and go to sleep straight away. And when I bring him his early morning coffee the bed is hardly messed up at all, like a baby has been sleeping in it, without moving. Other times the pillows are lying on the floor, and all the blankets and sheets are tangled up and not tucked in any more, and his ash-tray is full of cigarette ends, because he can smoke like a chimney, and I used to feel very sorry for him after such a night, because I thought I knew what was going through his head. Men and women are not so different as you think, and I know what makes it possible to sleep the whole night.

These things that I imagined doing to help Oubaas Dawid, that I have told you about, they are also a secret. But I must tell you that I would have been willing to help out the Oubaas anytime, even if he never asked, all he had to do was just make me feel he needed me. I would have imagined helping Oubaas Dawid out from the time he had to sleep alone in his own bed and room, for nearly twenty years, right up to 1942, when the Kleinbasie was twenty-one years old, and he could sit upright in his chair, and walk steps, and so on, and so on.

The Kleinbasie grew up like every other child except for the problems. In his body he grew like anybody else, but all the things that babies do, as they grow older, what took a ordinary baby a month took the Kleinbasie a year.

So he did grow up, and when he was twenty-one years old he was like any other baby of twenty-one months, except for the talking and hearing and seeing, so you can think for yourself how hard it must have been for his people to get him big. As I said one day to Flash Port: "You know, Flash lovey," I said. "Those people up at the big house, they punish themselves for something that they didn't even do. It's not their fault that they gave birth to the Kleinbasie, he just came, and now they think it is all their fault. The trouble with them is that they can't see what the Reverend George Webb preaches about in church every Sunday, that the Lord knows best, and that things that happen to you, and all your trials and tribbelations are all the Lord's doing, and He knows what it's all about. You can't walk about with a long face because the Lord has given you a child like the Kleinbasie, because it is the Lord who decides what sort of a child you will have, and you take what you get, like Christmas Eve presents at the Salvation Army."

"Listen," said Flash. "The Lord's got buggerall to do with it hay. If I go over to Adam Long and start a fight, and we fight because we're drunk, and we both get hurt, it's got buggerall to do with the Lord. If Adam Long kills me, and I'm dead and you're a widow, it's got buggerall to do with the Lord. By the way, you must remind me to marry you sometime, because of the pension. But if they plant a bad seed by accident, the Lord's got buggerall to do with it, it's just a blerrie accident, man, so don't blame the Lord for all the shit that flies, He's innocent, man, He's not bad, He's good and kind, and He won't make life too hard for you, man, that's the way things happen. The pisspot breaks off a handle, or cracks right through the middle. When it breaks off a handle you can still piss in it if you stand it carefully on the edge of the bed, and if you're careful not to piss a double stream, or you'll piss on your hand; but if the pisspot cracks right through and you can never use it again, it's your own fault for buying a glass one, like a cup or a plate, instead of a good tin one with enamel and roses, that can't break, only chip."

"All the same, Flash," I said. "You know, they blame themselves there, those two people, and it's not their fault. All right then, if it isn't the fault of the good Lord . . ."

"It isn't," said Flash.

". . . then it's right as you said, it's a accident. But those two up there at the big house, they blame themselves, and it's because of that that they feel guilty all the time. Mrs. Bettina, she's like a prisoner now, she's so guilty feeling that she locks herself up in her room, almost like a prisoner in jail, that's how bad it is. And she never talks to anyone any more, not even me. When I'm in to fix her room she sits in the corner, with her little book, and she snaps it shut when I come near her. Sometimes she is reading what she has wrote in it, other times she is writing some words, but she never allow me to come close without she snaps it shut, like it's full of her secret things, that I know about because I clean up her room, and she's got no secrets from me. You can't keep secrets. Secrets are all out in the open, people just try to hide them."

"Well," said Flash. "You bloodywell keep your secrets to yourself, you hear, and if I ever see you sitting with your legs open and no bloomers on, I'll kick you right in the secret, see?"

Sometimes Flash talks like a Hotnot that hasn't been to school at all.

"I sometimes wonder," said Flash, "now that he is old enough. The Kleinbasie, I mean. I wonder if he ever feels anything, down there, you know, like other little boys. Because if he does it is a good idea to get one of those young yellow bits from the location to come and give the bugger some real exercise."

"Don't talk so rough," I said. "Please Flash, the Kleinbasie isn't like other people. I asked Mina about, you know, what you just said, and she told me if I ever ask such a thing again, or talk about it, she will tell the Oubaas, and he will kick my yellow arse over the moon, that's what she said, the stuck-up bitch-cow, just because she works in the nursery, who does she think she is?"

"She's got buggerall to be stuck-up about," said Flash. "She's just a common whore, who whores with white men, for money.

You remember that day we saw her and that white man in the bluegum forest, when they nearly rode over us while we were in the long grass, you remember?"

"What were we doing in the long grass, Flash?" I asked, all innocent.

"Waiting for the bus to Pretoria," said Flash, quick as a flash.

"I remember," I said. Because it was a long time ago, and it was nice to know that Flash also remembered the days in the bluegum plantation, when I was still married to Petrus Long, before he got killed in the train smash at Langlaagte. "It's nice to know, Flash, that you also remember the bluegums, and the way it was then, for us, young with the smell of the bruised eucalyptus leaves that you used to break off, to make a little bed for us. I remember, you used to say that a single bed was enough, plenty big enough, because you would sleep on the floor. You've been a nice man, Flash."

"Ag shut up man," said Flash. He always says that when I say things with my soft voice, because he says I sometimes get too sloppy, like glue, and he doesn't like it. I like to get sloppy over him, but he says it's my only fault, and so I always get sloppy about him in my head, you know, my imagination, so that he can't hear.

"I remember because it was old Mina, in there, with the white man. And after, in the shop, she had a brand new ten bob note, spending it on sweets and chocolates and a scarf, like a common whore. So she can't be stuck-up about anything, even if she works in the nursery. I often wonder if it really was who we thought it was, the white man. Maybe it was. Hell man, it would be very funny if it was him. Old Holy Moses himself. Pity we never got a good look."

"Don't be silly Flash," I said. "Just because it was his car you can't just go thinking all sorts of things. He's a man of God, and you know that he's a very generous kind of man, and he will lend a man anything, even his car, a man's only got to ask. No, really, Flash."

"It'll be blerrie funny if it was him," said Flash. "Hell man, it'll be so funny, old bell-book-and-candle himself, Holy Moses."

But I would not let him carry on with that kind of talk. After all, we all know that a man is a man, no matter how holy his work is. Even if he is the kindest of men to work for, or the holy man who does the preaching and the burying, a man stays a man, and nobody can blame him if he has to do a little sinning, sometimes. Just as nobody can blame me if my imagination runs away with me, to places that are secret.

You see, I can keep a secret. I know something about the Kleinbasie that nobody else knows. I know that once when he was sixteen, something happened to him in the night. Mina could not have looked very well into the damp nappie when she changed him, and bathed him, because the next morning I found the nappie in the wash basket, and it was crisp to the touch, as if something like tree gum had hardened it. I knew what it was, because often, in my imagination, I had washed the same kind of crispness out of hand towels, and some of the sheets that were used in one of the bedrooms of the big house.

I kept a watch out for it afterwards, but I never saw it again. So it must have just happened to him one night, in his sleep. I wonder if he even knew about it? I don't suppose so. They say you can stick a needle in him and he won't feel much. So he must have just flowed over, like a river bursting its banks, that night.

Still it is nice to know that it can happen to him. That somewhere, deep inside of that skin that can't feel much, there is a well of hidden things. Maybe some day somebody will find a way to those dark places deep in his body, or his soul, or whatever it is that he's got.

"You know, Silver," said Flash. "I wonder, about the Kleinbasie. Isn't it possible for you to let him fall, on his head, a couple of times?"

"What the blerrie hell for Flash, lovey?" I asked.

"Well," he said, "you know how it is. When you've got a motor car, and it won't go. I once saw the Reverend George Webb get out of his car, when it wouldn't start, and he kicked it in the radiator. Then he got into the car and put on the spark and the petrol. Then he came to the front again and said 'bloody bugger,' yes, him, old Holy Moses himself, and he gave it another kick. Then he turned the crank handle and the car started up and off he went. So I thought, if you drop the Kleinbasie on his head, maybe something has been blocking the carburettor in his brain. It can't be so much different from the engine of a motor car, in there, you know, right inside his head. I don't think anything can be as full of different parts and things as the engine of a Ford T, so the inside of a brain can't be all that hard. I saw the inside of a man's brain once. That time the train ran over those people, and we helped the Reverend Holy Moses and old Quack Quack Cloete to put them into paraffin tins to take them to the police station. That day I picked up a whole four-gallon tin full of meat and people's brains, and maybe I even mixed them up a bit too. People's brains look just like pigs' and sheeps' and calves' brains, no different, lot of grey stuff, half white, with little red veins and a skin over like a F.L., that's what your fuckin' brain looks like," Flash said, thinking he was being funny.

That's the one thing I don't like about Flash Port, is when he thinks he's being funny. It's when he has been drinking on a Saturday, and he is getting near to the three-quarter mark on his first gallon, that he thinks he's being funny.

"People's brains are nowhere near as complicated as the engine of a Ford T," said Flash. "So why not give him a good few kicks in the head to get his commutator to send the spark to the petrol. Maybe the blerrie thing that's been blocking him up will go away and he'll fire down in the spark plugs. That's what I would do if he was my boy, anyway," said Flash. "I would turn him upside-down a few times and kick him in the head once or twice, and throw in a couple of good flat slaps to his ears, and maybe that will loosen him up. If it doesn't, no damage done, he can't feel anything anyway. That's what people say."

"Who says it?" I asked, because we were supposed to report all gossip to Mina. She would report the gossip to old Holy . . . I'm sorry, to the Reverend George Webb, who would have a lot to say to the big-mouths later.

"Oh," said Flash, "you know. People talk. They don't mean any harm though. They just haven't got anything better to do."

"Haven't you?" I asked, taking his hand and putting it where I wanted it.

"Oh Silver," he said, putting down his bottle of "my name," "Silver, as long as I've got you I don't care."

9

MARYNA

The year of my arrival in the Skeerpoort district was the same as my mother's death: 1942. I was twenty-seven years of age, a qualified nurse and social worker, with a B.A. degree in sociology, and my Nursing Sister's Diploma from the General Hospital in Johannesburg, where I had continued my post-graduate studies, preparing myself for an eventual M.A. Unfortunately we had had the double tragedy of my younger sister's accident and my mother's death. Her long series of operations and the cost of my mother's treatment had left us in uncomfortable circumstances, and I felt that the two of us had drained enough from our father, and that it was time that we were struck from the nest, as it were. I assured father that we were well able to care for ourselves, and that he could concentrate on his own life for a time now.

Maria bravely stood by me, although the thought of coming up to the Transvaal, where I could find work easily, must have terrified the poor girl. She never ventured out of doors without a silk scarf covering her features, and I don't blame her, because, although the surgeons had done all that was possible, she had a barely adequate face, and she knew it. There was no way whereby I could be diplomatic about it either, because she knew what people looked like, and she had access to mirrors. She knew that she didn't quite look like a human being. The scars were too many, the plastic surgery too obvious, and cosmetics made her face only a doll's mask, it had to be applied so thickly, as she sometimes did when it was inevitable that she should be seen with her face uncovered. Generally, though, she avoided people and occasions.

She had worked very hard at getting her wasted vocal chords back into usable condition, and once these had been developed by the therapists, we were amazed to find that there had been no permanent damage. The problem had been entirely psychological, part of her withdrawal after the accident. She just had not wanted to talk. It had been necessary for her to spend those six years without speech. There, in the silent world, dumb and expressionless, hidden behind bandages, a natural healing had taken place anyway, in spite of the withdrawal of her mind making things difficult for her rehabilitation.

Speech therapy had done wonders for her, and I sometimes suspect that in her mind, those six years, she must have used words, and so kept herself familiar with them. It was only a matter of a few months from her first ability to speak, to a quite reasonable form of talking. At the start of her treatment at the therapy clinic in Kimberley, she had been inclined to stutter painfully, and I had been afraid that she would not be able to cure that condition. It was, as a rule, a lifelong symptom of the sort of shock that had driven her to silence in the first place. The doctors said that we would just have to accept it, but, without telling me, Maria spent all her hours of solitude practising. When she was in bed or walking in Kimberley's beautiful acres of parkland in Belgrave, properly scarfed against prying eyes, she would repeat words over-and-over again, especially the difficult ones. Instead of just an hour a day at therapy, she would spend as much as twelve hours at her own efforts, recapturing her ability to speak.

Once there had been a time when she had spoken with great distinction, and as a young girl she had won many competitions. She had set out to recapture that one talent that the accident had robbed her of. The damage had only been in her mind, because her physical needs of speech had been relatively intact. So, by herself, and using all her guts, she had cured her stammer, and had developed her voice to its once-upon-a-time grace and melodiousness. It was never to be strong enough for the parade ground, but then, she would never need to be anything but gentle, ever again.

On arriving in Johannesburg I went for an interview to the social welfare people, going over to Pretoria by train, because that was where the offices were, it being a national department, located in the Administrative Capital. I left Maria at home, in the little boarding house near the station, promising that I would look out for something that she could do as well.

I had always wanted to go to one of the smaller, older, more historical villages in the Transvaal. Their sense of tranquility, and the promise of a peaceful life, appealed to my mood. I also wanted to continue my studies, as I had always been a natural learner of things. To absorb knowledge of any sort had never been any trouble for me. I had enjoyed every day of my school years as well as my university studies. Those years I had spent qualifying as a nursing sister were also, for me, quite invaluable, and I enjoyed my hospital work as well. Had things been normal I might just have gone on from there to a study of medicine, but I was never really interested enough in just treatment alone.

The sociological facets of life fascinated me, and I wanted to work in this field, assisted by the smattering of medicine that I had learned. In fact, I was more than qualified to be a senior district nurse, and I applied for that type of post, asking for work in a village rather than a city. As applications were usually the other way round, country girls wishing to make careers for themselves in the cities, there was no difficulty at all in finding a position for me. As things were, I could choose, and I decided on Skeerpoort because it was within 35 miles of three cities, two major towns, and a number of smaller settlements, all of them interesting enough in their own way, and the setting of many a great battle during the two Boer wars. Talking of settings; Skeerpoort was an extremely charming little Victorian village nestled between the Magaliesberg mountains and a range of hills known as the Schurveberge, which means "coarse mountains." They were thus named because of the rough-weathered dolomite of which they were composed, needle sharp and like knives along the edges, which had caused them to be described in "The Times History of the Boer War," London, as "The most rugged and inhospitable terrain of the entire war." But that was only up on the hills. Down in the valleys the earth was rich, deep, and wonderfully fertile. With two rivers, the Magalies and the Skeerpoort, to feed the irrigation furrows, the setting was quite idyllic. There was a train service to Magaliesburg and Pretoria twice a week, and a good school, as well as two churches. There were two trading stores, those of a man called Calitz and an Indian named

Moosa. It was a friendly rivalry, because there was enough trade to keep the two families in quite reasonable comfort. There was a post office with a telegraphic service, and, in 1942, a farm party line gave the few who wanted to subscribe access to the outside world by what can only be called a public telephone. To the lonely, to the gossips, to the foolish, and the frail, such party lines provided unconscious company, new sources of stories for hushed spreading, reasons for argument, and for venting inner hatreds on an outside world. It was a human, beautiful village that had, potentially, all the factors I needed to make both my work and my studies rich and rewarding.

I didn't know all this when I chose the village as the site for my career. I just looked at the map, found everything favourable, and made my decision on the spot. I am, I must say, inclined to actions that are at times more impulsive than wise. The emotional moment has always been my favourite, rather than the carefully considered decision. This is why I have so often landed in the shit. But, I must say, over the years people have learnt to understand me and even, on occasion, to like me. I will admit that my impulses have caused a number of people to bless the day they met me, but an equal number have wished that I would just go away, disappear.

That's an occupational hazard with social workers. We are inclined to pry into people's affairs. We want to know why children for instance, are under-nourished, or why a mother is unable to look after a child, or why a well-paid father's son is dressed in rags? What caused certain scars, is another of our little questions, and why isn't this child in hospital? My interest, however, isn't just in children. I had a deep and tender feeling for all the privileged as well as the under-privileged ones, of all races, and Skeerpoort had Indians, Bantu people, and those of mixed blood called Coloureds, and whites, all, rich or poor, with troubles of their own. Generally, the labourers lived in conditions that were shameful, exploited, and they existed from hand to mouth. Their medical needs were not at all well catered for, and living as they did, their lives stretched out before them in a rather hopeless way, without much to live for or aspire to. This was in 1942, during the war, and conditions were to deteriorate even more before the awakening of international conscience after the war, when the problem was tackled by the government on a national-interest basis. Even so, many years were to go by before conditions were even tolerable. Some never even reached that small standard. Rich fields, indeed, for a person interested in the subject of sociology. In this little village were all the components of the international disaster of that time.

I had to pay several visits to Pretoria, as officialdom moves slowly in the matter of appointments, pension funds, medical aid schemes, medical examinations, and I had to be subjected to other interviews to determine my fitness for the work, the provision of transportation, the requirements for stocking the clinic, and all the other thousand-and-one things that had to be settled before I could don my uniform and go to work. Maria had to stay in the boarding house near the station, and when I saw that I was still a few weeks from actually taking up my appointment we packed our suitcases and moved over to Pretoria, making the daily train trip unnecessary. I had told Maria of my intention of working in a very small community, and she had agreed wholeheartedly, because of her shyness and fear of crowds.

One day, when I got to the hotel after a particularly trying day, for I was now at the "transportation . . . selection and care of" stage, she was missing. In Pretoria all official offices close at 4.30 p.m. rain or shine, war or peace, National or United Party, and I usually got to our room at 4.45, because, when an office closes at 4.30, work usually stops at 4.00 to give people a chance to pack their brief-cases and fold up their re-usable sandwich papers. I wondered where she could have got to, because up to then I had had the impression that she spent her days waiting for me to get home. Finally she arrived.

"Where the hell have you been?" I asked, but not angrily, although the words may seem to be a little brusque, it was just my way.

"Out," she said. "I went for a walk this morning, Ryna," which is what she calls me when she's feeling relaxed. It was a good sign, because she had very few enjoyable days, not that I could blame her, poor little bitch, all buggered up as she was.

"I did something very difficult today," she said. "It was almost impossible to do, but I managed to do it. I kicked myself right in the arse, like you did the day mother died."

I was most surprised, but I saw in her eyes that she had gone through what must possibly have been the best day of her life, so I shut up tight, only showing by the interest in my eyes that I wanted to know more.

"Yes," she laughed. "Right up the arse. It hurt too, with this big heel." She took off her old-fashioned wedge-heeled shoe, and passed it to me.

"We'll have it gilded," she said. "This is independence day for me, and for you. Sorry it's September, and not the 4th of July. Ryna, I went for a walk this morning up Beatrix Street. I came to the park opposite the hospital there, and I went inside, to sit at one of the benches. I got to the only vacant bench when some young soldiers in hospital blues came up on crutches. I couldn't sit down, because they were tired too, from walking. I had my scarf over my face, of course. They couldn't see that there was anything wrong with me. One of the boys had only holes cut in his bandages, for the eyes, nose, and mouth, and underneath I could see his smile, because we were all embarrassed. So I sat down on the grass, and as I did so I felt this heel get me right in the arse, and I thought to myself, 'thank you God,' and I jammed it further, really kicking myself. You see Ryna, these boys had been wounded in the war. 'I like sitting on the grass,' I said. 'You boys sit on the bench.' So they all sat down. The one with the bandages all over his face said, 'Are you an Indian, lady, what's with the purdah bit? With the hankie over your face you look like a bint I once had in Cairo.' 'Yes,' said one of the others, who only had one leg, 'what's the problem?'

"So I told them. I told them about the accident and the operations that hadn't worked, and how horrible I looked, and the one with the bandaged face leaned over and asked me to take off my scarf, talking very gently. So, I took it off, and the others were very quiet when they saw my face. I know they were shocked, but the boy with the bandages over his face said, very quietly, 'I wish they fix me up as well as that. I'd be quite happy with that. That Jerry grenade sure made a mess of me.' He asked me what I did for a living, and I realised that he was serious. You know, Ryna, it had never occurred to me that I could be independent. I'd always seen myself as sort of your sidekick, with my face hidden by a surgical mask such as they wear in operating theatres. Suddenly, with my heel right up my bum, kicking, I asked them if they thought I could get a job as a learner-nurse in the military hospital. So they called me 'Miss Frankenstein 1942' and escorted me over to the administration department of the hospital, where they had a long talk with the man in charge, a Doctor Grové, a very sweet middle-aged man. He looked at me, because the boys hadn't allowed me to put my scarf back on, and said, quite frankly, as he saw my scars, 'Jesus, what a bloody mess that car must have made of you. But this isn't bad, you know, it's quite good work, they really did their best. The boys tell me you want a job here. We're short of staff, you can start whenever you like, trainee-nurse. You'll have to live in, be on call, 24 hours a day. Pay poor. Food dreadful. Working conditions and hours, horrible and too long. Okay?' I felt like kissing him. I'm to report in tomorrow morning to sign all the papers and I start work the day after. See what I mean by independence day? Isn't it wonderful? Isn't it?"

Her poor twisted scar-tissued face was radiant. There was even a sort of beauty to it. I can well imagine her discovery of herself that day, that she had been given work, the first step to an identity. The boys had kidded her all the way back to the hospital gate afterwards. And at the gate they let her put her scarf on again, making her promise that she would remove it whenever she came into the hospital grounds. They approved its use outside in the streets, though, and greeted her, saying goodbye to her by using her new nickname, of which she seemed to be over-proud. I thought the humour behind it was a little too black. But I never heard her use her nickname with anything but pride after that. I even remember, one day, she introduced herself to one of the Skeerpoort people, when she was spending one of her rare weekends with me.

"I am," she said to a startled Calitz, "I am Frankie van der Kolff."

So, she was settled in work that, I could see, was of vital interest to her and the people she would be working with, and, as she said, it was independence day for all of us. There we were, on our own feet, and I could carry on with the work that I wanted to do. We had truly struck ourselves from the nest.

Therefore I arrived in Skeerpoort with a clear and almost, let me admit, sparkling conscience. I knew that Maria would be all right. I had gone and spoken to Doctor Grové and he had assured me that he would take a personal interest in her rehabilitation as well. He was a kindly man, good in his heart, and I knew that he could be trusted with her welfare, and that she would do her job well, to her own good. And there I was, with no further excuse for not putting my guts into my work, no alibi for laziness. As I have gone through life I have come across these false reasonings so many times, and they have always seemed so pathetic to me. People saying that they never had the breaks, that this factor, and that one, the raising of children, the caring for a husband or the providing for a wife had made it impossible for them to do anything with their own lives, and therefore, with their own immortal souls, for the two are indivisible, in my opinion.

I have this confession with regard to Maria. I had viewed with horror my own over-generosity in taking her off my already sorely over-taxed father's hands. People often indulge in these idiotic acts of generosity, all the while knowing that they are being fools and that they are allowing people to take advantage of them instead of standing on their own feet and having guts of their own. I have never been able to see anyone floundering, even if I knew perfectly well that they would be able to make the shore by themselves. I am an interferer, a professional social worker, always trying to do the welcome, or the unwelcome, but whatever I do must be done or I'll feel bad about not doing my duty. That is the nature of my work, and this is no time to start making complaints.

Maria had come with me all compliant and even eagerly, and I had brought her along, because she was my sister, and if I could do anything for humanity I must at least be of service to her, my own flesh and blood, so horribly scarred. In spite of my over-protectiveness, she had had the courage, that afternoon, to take all the frankness that had been flung at her by the seemingly unsympathetic manner of the soldiers and Doctor Grové, who, I think, had been a little too demanding in the testing of her guts.

They had, with their "Miss Frankenstein 1942" and "Jesus Christ" gone just a little over what I would have called the limits of good taste. But it had worked. They, and my sister, had experienced battle in an arena of disaster that was not within the bounds of my own knowledge, so I cannot, in all honesty, criticise something that I do not understand all that well. I had been willing to treat her, handling her with kid gloves and the occasional kick, but she had gone beyond me, and relieved me of a responsibility that, I say to my own shame, I quite frankly had not really coveted. Duties are always in their way, chains. One must never accept them if they can be avoided with honour. And yet, in the case of my own sister, I had been willing, although I was horrified at my willingness, to sacrifice a great deal of my life. I saw myself do-gooding my own precious years out of existence, and I had wondered who the hell I thought I was, some bloody martyr or other?

I'm no saint and I don't want to be anything but a living human being, with my own identity, subservient only to the ones of my choice, should they require it or not, because love is the subservience, love of a man, in my case, also in my case, love of my fellow man. I say it quite without shame. I don't ever trust a first or any other reaction that isn't based on what is in my heart. Once it's there, I go.

I was free when I arrived in Skeerpoort that September day in 1942. It was lovely, and misty, as I got to the village in the new Ford that the administration had bought for me, my new licence to drive in my pocket, and all my confidence in myself intact. I was happy because I had had all my chains cut off from me by my sister's braveness, and breathless with excitement as I drove, imagining my new life, which was all that I had been working for. At this point, it is usual for people who talk about their lives to say something like "but alas, little did I know of the disillusionments that lay in store for me, the unhappy years that were to follow." Let me at once take all such anticipations out of these memories. I was, from that moment, in complete control of my life, and any unhappiness that I experienced after that was caused by me only.

No one stood in my way, all the world was as friendly as could be, the officials in Pretoria, although frustratingly tardy at times, never questioned any decision or requisition of mine, and my freedom to operate in my own way was never in question. Do you know how terrifying it can be, when, for the first time in your life, you have to take the responsibilities of all of your actions?

Skeerpoort, from the lowliest farm labourer to the Cilliers family who lived in the "Great House" as it was called, welcomed me, and gave me every possible encouragement in my work. It was also very frustrating. I would, for instance, call upon Jock Travis the farrier, who was by the time of my arrival, Travis Transportation Company, and I would tell him what a swine he was to let his black mechanics and drivers live in such horrible hovels.

"All right," he would say. "So you draw up the plans and get in the builders and do it the way you think it must be done, with lavatories and showers, the bloody lot, only get off my back and go see what Calitz the shopkeeper has in his backyard for his kaffirs, okay?"

Then I would go to Calitz and tell him that I'd had a complaint about the conditions his black people lived under, and he would assure me that, within that very month, the condition would be rectified. I had arrived there as a crusader, determined to stir up shit to the greatest extent, and all I found were people who were perfectly willing to be reasonable about everything I had to say. It can be very frustrating, when you want to be a militant fighter, to find that everyone you come across is prepared to be reasonable about things, even Moosa, the Indian, who employed quite a number of coloured people. It took the wind right out of my overenthusiastic sails, and I was quite prepared to furl them.

I had other work to do. There was the matter of my M.A. As I was now, in every sense of the word, a field worker, I could go in to my old lecturers and professors, and, with my Nursing Sister's Diploma and all my experience in hospitals, plus my official appointment as a District Welfare Officer and Nurse, an unusual appointment for those days, I had their admiration and respect, and I was able to start working on my thesis without delay. I chose, as my subject, the relationships between the various racial groups of a small Transvaal village, and my observations of those relationships over three years, because I was in no hurry to finish my hundred-or-so pages on the subject.

I learned economics from a gentle person, Bertie Theron, an attorney of uncertain talent, who lived in the village. He was more than happy to return knowledge in exchange for my company, during the evenings when there wasn't much to do, and I wrote a correspondence course on economics and mercantile law in my first year there, which qualified me to speak not just from a sociological point of view. I was now entering what was then a new science, that of socio-economics which since then has become an everyday thing in Africa. But I was one of the first to correlate the relationship between the social and economic factors determining the living conditions of the people who coexisted in my village, as I began to think of Skeerpoort. How very amazing it was to me to find, after almost a year there, that there was something in the village directly connected with my sphere of activities, that I knew nothing about.

I had, of course, in the first few days of arriving in Skeerpoort, called at the Great House. There I had been welcomed and been given tea by a lady called Bettina Cilliers. Lovely tea, most elegantly served, silver, bone china, and little cinnamon-sugar biscuits just warm from the oven. A tiny feast, most well done, as if they had been expecting me. They could not have been because social workers never make appointments, they take by surprise, before the crap can be cleaned up and the skeletons hidden in the cupboard. It was obviously a very elegantly run home, and the quarters of the black people adjoining the poplar drive which, after a mile, led to the front door, appeared to be most adequate. Little neat cottages, each in its own vegetable and flower garden, even a little ostentatious for the time. Obviously with inside sewerage served by a septic tank system, and I could see the power lines from the farm's central generating plant running to the little cottages as well. Obviously a farmer who believed in good labour relations.

Dawid Cilliers was, of course, very wise, because what he had to offer in the way of creature comforts gave him a choice of the best labour that the district had to offer. Having come to know him, that sounds as if I am critical, accusing him, perhaps slyly, of doing good things only for his own material benefit. This assumption would be wrong.

I had called at their home and was entertained most elegantly, and I was completely satisfied that there was no need for me to look for skeletons-in-the-cupboard or bed-bugs, here. So, without even meeting her husband I took my leave of Bettina Cilliers. A nervous looking lady, most gracious at the age of forty-two. My twenty-seven years longed for such an elegant future as that. She had a certain dignity, but I did notice a lack of calm. There was no reason for such a person, in such gracious circumstances, to be anything but serene, but she was nervous, jittery, and I, no probing, suspicious detective, only a prying, gullible social worker, put it down to my unexpected call, and perhaps a tiff with the servants, or the time of the month.

There being nothing for me to do but to assure her of my best services at all times of the day or night, I left. She made no gesture of assuring me that we would meet again. In fact, I drove away feeling that I had been told, in my own language, "You have come prying, looking for dung, you've found nothing, you may leave now, and don't bother us again." To top it all off, as I drove through the white-washed gateway, I felt upon my tongue-tip the fragrance of cinnamon and sugar in the most delicate balance, a tastebud-experience to remember, and to envy in a home where it seemed to be an everyday occurrence to concoct such fragrantly delicate luxuries. I had had only two of the silver tray's warm biscuits (set upon the silver tray: first, a delicate petit-point cloth of intricate design, then, upon that, a warm Wedgwood, and thereon, a linen-paper in an antique design, to absorb any lingering butter, and only then, casually heaped, the biscuits, square, perforated every quarter of an inch), but I remember still the soft, delicate sweetness, gobbled up by me, because I had thought that they would be the first of many.

Quite a time was to pass before I was again to enter that house, and by then, its biscuits were no longer of interest to me. The village had kept its secret well. I thought that I was the one to be welcomed, by their behaviour. I went nowhere without being fussed over, and oh yes, I was the great success. The perfect social welfare officer, the greatest of district nurses. And all the hospitality and willingness? I don't know, perhaps it was real, perhaps sham. I shall never really know. Who can ever penetrate a village?

Do you know what a village is? It is like an ant-heap. It has a character, a heart, muscles and sinews of its own. Eugene Marais said that an ant-heap is a single being, its components separate, but one being. So the elements of a village are also part of a single being. In a village there's very seldom one complete inhabitant, a person who is apart, separate. Always, he is involved with the whole, the design of the village, its pattern. So they made quite sure that I became part of their pattern of life, before they let slip to me that, far away, where the tunnels closed, there was a forbidden entrance behind which they were sheltering their own inimitable secret. How clever of them, to make me one of the ant-heap, in tune with its existence, before revealing to me, slowly, that it had a flaw. It was their flaw, and it belonged to them, and they made very sure that I was one of them before I was led to the curtain that concealed what I think of, to this very day as their beautiful secret, with its awful, horrible, tragic overtones.

Let me attempt an objective description of my discovery of the secret of Skeerpoort. There, see, it's impossible, I ask you, have you ever, now, the Secret of Skeerpoort, yet, like a penny bloody horrible. Yes, that's cleared the air a little, like the swear-words in the mess tent of the officers of the Black Watch, at Magersfontein, after the great Colonel Cameron Clack had had his breathing stopped that day, when a Boer bullet had caught him in the chest, and he had said his last words to his adjutant: "Oh Willie," he said to Major William McDougall. "Oh Willie, they got me. Fuck it." By the way, what is this rubbish about Lord Nelson not having said, "Kiss me, Hardy" when he lay paralysed, on the deck of the Victory at Trafalgar. The great British heroes have always been a little queer. Nelson was no mystic, and he would never have used a phrase like "Kismet, Hardy" to denote the end. He was too much of a practical queer for that. Don't take Africa from Rhodes either, because of his affair with Leander Starr Jameson, his male-secretary-mistress, in whose arms he lay, dying, saying, "Darling boy, please tell me that they will never change the name of Rhodesia." So, in spite of his little peccadillo with Lady Hamilton, I must admit that the idea of Nelson as a queer intrigues me more than the theories of the apologists and explainers of his last words.

The great Colonel Cameron Clack, at Magersfontein, saying, "Fuck it, Willie" on the other hand, was most certainly not making an invitation to a penetration of his anus. He was referring, angrily, to fate, and life, and death, in general, as befits a scholar, a soldier, and a gentleman.

A little while ago, an old gentleman of Skeerpoort, one Groenewald, mentioned to me that the biggest queer of them all was "that old sodomist, Winston Churchill." Now, I must say that this Mr. Groenewald was pro-Nazi during the war, and I have no idea why he never made the Smuts concentration camp at Koffiefontein. The Smuts government probably thought that no one could possibly be as anti-British and pro-Nazi as Mr. Groenewald said he was, so they must have let him off, because of his enormous eccentricity.

If Ezra Pound had only been 10% more mad during World War Two in Italy, he would never have had to spend all those years behind asylum bars in America after the war. As a lunatic, Pound was a failure, because he had put all his available lunacy into his poems, which were a moderate success. But I go beyond myself. English III at the University of the Witwatersrand, although difficult to negotiate for a girl from Kimberley, certainly does not qualify one to comment. There is, among certain authors, even a current theory that a professorship at any university automatically disqualifies you from making any comment whatsoever. So, here in Skeerpoort, the reaction against the academic reaches out, and touches even me. I should dearly love, now that I have my M.A., to become eligible for my Doctorate in the Humanities, and to the phoney intellectuals, we scholars can only speak in the words of the great Cameron Clack, when he said his last gasping, obscene, wonderful words.

One night, to be serious, I was spending some quiet hours with the very Reverend Doctor George Webb, spiritual head of the declining Methodists of the parish of Skeerpoort. I had established, in my first two years there, a certain rapport with the man. He was an extremely charming gentleman, always conscious of being a sinner, and like Bertie Theron the attorney, he was forever thinking up ways to seduce me. All I ever wanted a man to tell me was that he loved me, and he would find me more than willing, if he were attractive in his spirit, as both he and Bertie were. But they resorted to all the subterfuges of the seducers, and in being dishonest with me, they lost the balm that I may have been able to provide for them. I have ever been a most direct person.

I lost my innocence, but retained my hymen, when I was fifteen, to a cousin who had confessed that he loved me so much that he had spent his whole month's pocket money on three contraceptives. (Does one spell French letter with a capital F, or will the French object? I don't know. If anybody ever called it an Afrikaans letter I will be furious, unless they use a lowercase "a" to start off with. I mean, the capital "F" makes it so *officially* national.) However, I was so touched by my little cousin, who was a year younger than I was, in the first throes of his bursting knackers, loving and desiring me to the extent of spending his whole month's allowance of half-a-crown, that I willingly allowed him to use his beautiful rubbers on me, penetrating me gently with his adolescent little penis, although I was at that time already big-breasted and ripe. It was no trial for me, rather a deep pleasure.

I received very much from my cousin, more than just pleasure (I had no knowledge of the evil pleasures of incest). There was something lasting starting up between us. I never really lost my hymen, there was never blood, and only slight amounts of pain. Once, I spoke about it when I consulted a gynecologist, and upon examination, he found that I had never been ruptured, but in my adolescence I had been gradually stretched.

I was most fortunate, in my puberty, in finding a doctor who understood my willing nature. I had thought myself pregnant, because my cousin could afford only three contraceptives a month, and, at the age of fourteen, that is sufficient for only one of thirty nights, so we did take a few chances, foolishly, because we didn't know anything more than need, and wanting. Even when I was not particularly ready, the mere fact of the enormity of his need would soften me as soon as I knew of it, and I would comply, and, within a short while, became a part of his desires. That was in 1930. Nine years later in 1939, after having known each other for all that time, we had grown in intimacy, and knowledge, each of the other's spirit. Then when I was twenty-four years of age and already on the verge of my diploma as a nursing sister, he had joined the South African Forces and had gone to the desert war in the north. He had survived until Mersa Matruh, when a German tank had rolled over his red-crossed hospital tent where he had almost recovered from a leg fractured by a trench mortar. So that was the end of him, and the end of nine years of my life. The family had been conscious of our close relationship, but they had regarded it merely as a fondness.

As I said, once I had thought myself pregnant. That was when I was sixteen years of age, and a doctor, seeing that moralities would not help a person of my kind, had given me certain advice and a few prescriptions, with the result that my post office savings book was drawn to a point of emptiness by precautionary requirements which I had to purchase, and my cousin had been able to save his half-crown a month, which was sufficient for two matinee performances (at sixpence each) at the Plaza in Kimberley, opposite Piet Louverdis's cafe, and two tickey chocolates. We had been first cousins, and it had, strictly, been a case of incest, but we never gave that a thought. We did, at times, speak of marriage, and the fact that the family would forbid it, but only in terms of "one day, when we can, we will go away together." It was that sort of impractical thing.

From him, in my eagerness to know everything, I learned all the swear-words I use so easily now, words that he could not use to communicate with me in the last years of his life, because everything that was written from the Saharan war was censored by an officer from his own unit. Conscious of this scrutiny, he was most correct in all his final correspondence to me. I was never fooled; beneath all the words like "devotion" and "longing" and, occasionally "desirable" I heard his young voice singing the real words of sex that we had used, when we had been young, and entranced by the splendours of each other.

People wonder why I have never married. Let me confess, I have been married twice, in the way the coloureds take common-law wives, without benefit of clergy, each time for many years. I have no certificates of proof. I don't need them, because the memories belong to me, and I have nothing to prove to anyone, because what is mine is mine alone, and also, half of it is the property of that mouldering spirit at Mersa Matruh where the hospital once stood beneath the date palms, and the other one I will tell you about, later.

They say, in the Middle East: "Cursed is he who destroys a date palm or an olive tree." I curse that Wehrmacht driver, every day of my life, but not because his tank went over the trunk of an olive or of a date palm. I wonder if he survived the war. I hope he did live through the whole thing, and went home afterwards. I hope he remembers the day he went over a white tent, under the date palms and the olives, a white tent with a big red cross painted on it. I hope he remembers it. If he lived he will, and if he survived there is no need to wish him any evil. He will have it all right inside of him, and he will know of it. If you hear my voice on the winds that blow northwards, tank commander, hear me wishing for you a very, very long life, with all your memories.

Oh hell, I'm probably just being bitter. My cousin and I would probably not even have married. It can even be that he was in the hospital ward because of a gonorrhoea that he had picked up in Addis Ababa or Khartoum. I forgive him. Of course I must stop picking over old bones.

Well, that is over with now. Sometime, I knew, I had to tell of it, and there it is. Not as many-paged and sweet a story as it is in my mind. Told a little coarsely, and with too much bitterness. Nobody really cares if I miss out Berlin when I visit Europe. Time has healed all the troubles, and we are friends now, are we not? Yes, we are. I am a scientist, a socio-economist, a Doctor of the Humanities; I destroy all my achievements by bringing to life an over-active memory, because sometimes I can't sleep at night.

One would think that such a person would also have the abilities of an unusual perceptiveness, not so? But I was blind to the secret of Skeerpoort until, one night, having spoken of many things, the Reverend George Webb asked me: "What is your attitude towards Daan?"

"Daan?" I asked.

"Daan," he said. "The twenty-two-year-old. In the Great House. The one they keep on the silver chain? What are you going to do about him, the whole village is wondering?"

"What," I asked, "is your attitude. What is your advice?" I knew that something had been kept from me, so I pretended I knew all about it.

"I have my ideas," I added, "but you've known about it for so much longer, and much of it is a mystery to me. So why don't you tell me everything you know, and give me the benefit of your many years of experience with the subject?"

Well, let me confess, George Webb, the man, was a dreadfully poor seducer, and he never managed to get me, although he came close a few times because of my capacity for pity. But as the Reverend Doctor Webb he was good, he knew immediately that I was only pretending.

"So," he said, "they've kept it from you. But you had to know some time, and that's why I've let it slip tonight, deliberately. Here's the story, but, if you ever tell that you know of it, I shall deny, at the peril of my soul, that I was the one who told you of it. I'm telling you only because you will eventually go beyond the shield, and penetrate all the defences. You're such a person. It intrigues me that I am the one to break the silence. Am I telling you because I feel that I am the right person to tell you, the most objective of the village opinions, or am I the weakest person here? Did you penetrate my shield of secrecy first, because I am the least of the trustworthy ones, the biggest gossip, the great mouth, the talker, the fool, the biggest of the sinners, the weakest of all the shields of the tribe?"

He was certainly in a dialectic mood, even patriarchal, almost Ishmaelitic in his disillusionment with his loose mouth. Had the poor fool kissed me then I would have been his for many a month, because I find a *human being* quite irresistible. But he had forgotten all the ambitions of his crotch in the quiet desire to be the greatest of the gossips: The one who had finally broken down to my probing.

I had never pried where I wasn't wanted. I had no idea that there was anything more than the usual tensions of village life beneath the surface. My amazement at this hidden facet of the town was complete, and the whole matter was, even on that first evening, disconcerting to me. I had no desire to scratch, unkindly, beneath these surfaces. I didn't want a village scandal bigger than myself. My nocturnal conversations with the Reverend Doctor Webb, Bertie Theron, and Doctor Cloete, married but quite randy, whose visits to my little cottage, at night, were the subject of quite a lot of talk, especially from the widow Watson. The one, I understand, who allows "Jock Travis the Transportation" as he is called, to slither through her shuttered windows and into her bed only when it is after midnight, when all the sharp eyes of the coloured and black people have been dimmed by alcohol or lust so that they are unable to recognise its counterpart in the white people's acts.

Here now, was a new scandal. It was told to me in fits and starts by the poor Reverend Doctor Webb, the one whom the coloured women of the town refer to affectionately as "old Holy Moses." Apparently he had quite a reputation for his fondness for coloured women, having been kicked out of Rhodesia for sleeping with some of his charges while running a missionary school there. The same thing happened in Tanganyika. He had never been tempted to marry any of the girls, seduction seemed to be enough for him. I found, on further study and evaluation of the available gossip, that he had a peculiar prostitutional trait, in that he would have intercourse only on condition that he could pay for it. I often wonder if the boxes of chocolates he regularly sent me, to my cottage, by messenger, brown-paper-wrapped, marked "contents, educational books" were a form of payment, in advance, for favours that the poor man hoped to receive? How much better would it not have been for him, to say to me, in all seriousness: "The sight of you makes me want to have you, so for heaven's sake, go away or come to my bed." That is the sort of honesty to which I could react, even love. But the poor old twit strangled himself in his own bullshit, and in the end his devious, devout mind defeated his desires.

Skeerpoort is a Victorian village, with lacework iron gates, wooden trellises, vines, rambling roses, fretwork, antimacassars on the chairs, iron tracery over the rooftops, and hothouses in case of the black frost, and it also has the sweetness of people who are good, because the soil is good, and black. It is the colour of soil that has been cared for, and all the colours in-between, because of the colours of the crops. Like all the Victorian villages in the world, it had its great and gruesome secret which, once I knew of it, was pretty ordinary to a person like myself who had lived and grown up, and studied, on the fringes of the medical world of the early thirties, as well as the war years.

The Reverend Doctor Webb told me about Daan, the village idiot, and I could do no more than accept it. "Of course," I thought, "all Victorian villages must have a village idiot, and at last, after more than a year, he has come to light." The Reverend then told me more than was necessary about Daan Cilliers, enough, in fact, to suggest to me that this was the one case that lay very clearly within the sphere and scope of my activities, and that I would have to do something about it. It was very difficult for me to know how to proceed. Obviously, the parents did not want the child to get mixed up with any form of officialdom, and if I interfered I would clearly not be welcome. And yet, I felt that if I were able to help in any way, it would be my duty to take a hand in the matter, I was, after all, next to Doctor Cloete, the person most qualified to be of assistance. That was the way I thought, brash with the knowledge of my academic qualifications and practical knowledge.

I thought the best way would be by contacting the father, and the road to him lay through Doctor Cloete, who had been a frequent visitor to my cottage. As district nurse and welfare officer he had to see me frequently, and as we were both usually busy by day, the affairs of my clinic were as a rule discussed at night. I often felt his hand linger on my arm or back for what appeared to be a little too long, but, although it was obvious that he was another potential lover if I wished to indulge, I had no real desire for an involved relationship at that stage. Having lain dormant for so long, I needed more than a slight suggestion of willingness to re-awaken me.

"So you've found out about Daan?" said Doctor Cloete, "I'm sorry you did."

"Why, Doctor Cloete, surely that poor boy's plight is directly my concern?"

"No," he said, being quite firm. "It is none of your business at all. Medically, there's absolutely nothing that we, you or I, can do for him. And it would only be a cause of distress to his parents if you re-opened the case officially. You would have to resurrect him in the government files, you know, and that could get a lot of people into trouble."

"What do you mean, resurrect, Doctor?"

"Officially, we killed him off when he was nine years of age, that was twelve years ago, and as far as the official records are concerned, he's stone dead."

Then Doctor Cloete told me of the incident, a dozen years previously, when they had faked all the papers between them and put an end to all official prying into Daan's fate from the government point of view. I thought the story quite a delight, in view of the characters involved, but it still did not solve my problem. I had to become involved with Daan Cilliers in some way, but I had no idea as to how I should proceed. I sensed almost instinctively that the entire village was fearful of my long-expected action, and that they were all waiting to see what I would do. I knew that any step I took had better be in the right direction, or these people would lose faith in me. All the initial success of my work hung by the delicate thread of my ability to solve the problem of my own involvement. I had to be careful. I had never been on thinner ice.

Doctor Cloete told me about many of the medical aspects of Daan's case. I was particularly interested in the physiotherapeutic machines that had been built up to provide exercise for the little boy's body in his growing years. Now, Doctor Cloete said, Daan was at a self-locomotory stage, built up by pure habit and muscular reaction, which made it possible for him to move about with difficulty, in the halting, staggering way typical of people suffering from cerebral palsy, in the special piece of back garden that had been constructed for him. A new room had also been built, by his father, who, using the experience gained by carefully watching the boy's needs during the years of his growth, made him as comfortable as it was possible for him to be. With his new talent of walking (new in the relative sense, of course, it had taken many years of devotion and effort to develop this property in him), he was able to take a lot of exercise, unfortunately chained, in case he should lose himself or even stray off his pathways. The chain also satisfied an obscure law which contented the more stupid people of the village. Walls of brick had been built too, but only as a surround. His walking was guided by the chain suspended from a wire above him, which supported him in an upright position, while the motor reactions of walking took over. His father had made many beautiful objects, all of wood, in case his sense of feel was strong enough to distinguish between shapes and textures. We found out later that that had been the case, and that these objects had added a valuable tactile dimension to his dark life.

I now understood the nervousness of the mother on the day of my first, and only, visit to the farm. I could guess with what trepidation she must have watched my arrival, from her bedroom window, and the courage it must have taken to face me. There is, when something is wrong in a family, however innocent they may be of wrong-doing, a fear of social workers, of the intrusion of officialdom in their private affairs. People protect their shame as fervently as they shelter their loves. In the light of what Doctor Cloete had told me I was more than ever determined to attempt to make contact with this fascinating case, and to do what I could to be of help. Again, I knew that the right person to contact would be the father, away from the farm if possible, without his wife knowing of it, because she was obviously frail, no matter how dignified, and it would be wrong to distress her.

I awaited a chance to talk to Dawid Cilliers but he, in his turn, seemed to avoid me like the mastitis in his favourite cow's udder. Although I was a member of the Dutch Reformed Church, I even went so far as to attend the Methodist service, and was welcomed, from the pulpit, by the Reverend Doctor George Webb, as if I had become converted. For a moment he really made me feel like the returned lost sheep, until I reminded myself that he was wearing the sheep's clothing, the old wolf. But this didn't help at all, as Dawid Cilliers's wife was there too, and he didn't mind being friendly to me in a crowd, where he felt safe from my prying. I had to be patient. I knew that any precipitous action on my part would be foolish, and to no avail. So I awaited my chance, very carefully, with all the patience I could muster over the months that he, equally carefully, avoided me.

It became a sort of silly game between the two of us. Some of his lifelong habits had to be abandoned. He never again came for his mail at the post office exactly at 10 a.m. every Saturday. He staggered the hours of his visits to the shop, and, whenever one of his labourers needed attention at the clinic, someone else would drive the vehicle that served as ambulance and station wagon on their farm.

"If it means so much to him to avoid me," I eventually told Doctor Cloete, "tell him that he can stop upsetting his routine. If he needs my help I'm here, at any hour of the day or night, tell him that."

"Do you mean it?" asked Doctor Cloete. "You've been quite persistent, haven't you?"

"So much so that it's stopped being anything but childish," I said.

"I'm pleased you think so. He does too. Remember, he has nothing against you at all, he's just not of a mind to talk about his son or to re-open all sorts of doors that have been shut for such a long time. Surely you understand?"

"Of course I do," I said. "If I'm to be the villain of the piece, cast as the prying busy-body, I have no interest at all. I have far too much work here, helping people who are really in need of my services, to mope over losing one prospective case. Very well, let them withhold him from me."

"You mustn't be hurt by it. He really wasn't trying to be rude."

"He may not have tried very hard, but he certainly succeeded," I huffed.

Because, really, it had apparently stopped being serious with him, it was a rude game he was playing. Knowing that I would never deliberately speak to him in the company of others, he made sure that there were people about whenever he came into the village for mail, shopping, petrol for his vehicles, or parcels at the station. Always, without fail, he had had someone with him, someone who was watching every action of mine on behalf of the entire village, later to report that I had slipped up again, or at least that is what I thought. So I gave up, and that was the tactic that worked.

One night, just after supper, there was a knock at my door. When I opened it I recognised Dawid Cilliers, alone, attempting a smile.

"I should like to speak with you," he said.

He had a peculiar, almost archaic, perhaps, even, a foreigner's way of speaking. Then I remembered that he was an Afrikaner Methodist, speaking two languages, and that their usages must inevitably become a little mixed in his mind. I invited him to come in and he entered my little hallway.

"Have you eaten?" I asked, trying to be polite.

"No," he said, to my surprise. "But I haven't come to impose. I'll eat when I get home. It will all be prepared and waiting for me."

"You eat late at the Great House," I said, for want of anything to say.

"I haven't come to discuss the feeding habits of the Cilliers family," he said with a smile. "We're actually very ordinary people. I have come here to apologise to you."

"Apologise? What have you done?" I pretended.

"Nothing," he said. "And that's what I have come to apologise for. I have done nothing to welcome you to the village, or to put you at your ease. You are a stranger here, doing wonderful work, and I've behaved like a complete pig towards you. I must beg of you to forgive me."

"You've done nothing," I said. "You've merely avoided me, because you thought that I would pry into your private affairs. You had every right to do so. I'm only sorry that you're so completely wrong about my motives."

"What are your motives?" he asked.

"I was fascinated, curious, when I heard about your son. I have had a lot of training in hospitals, among people who could not care for themselves. I once spent several months in physiotherapy. I thought it my duty to offer my help, if it were ever needed."

"And if it's not needed?" he asked bluntly.

"That would be for you to decide, together with Doctor Cloete. He's perfectly well qualified, certainly better than I am. And please don't think that I will ever open a case-book or file on your son. I regard this conversation as privileged, much as a doctor or lawyer would."

"And I regard this conversation as a privilege," he said. "Don't you ever ask someone to sit down, or offer some coffee?"

So I made him comfortable in the best of the two old leather chairs that I had found in Moosa's store-room. They had been in an awful state but with upholstery studs of brass and some dubbin they had polished up beautifully.

They were the first of my luxury things.

"This is a good chair," he said. "It welcomes. It has warmth, a pleasant manner."

"You talk about it as if it were alive," I said.

"I like to think that all the things of the world can feel something," he said. "People take dumb and inanimate things for granted. When you've brought up someone like my son for twenty-three years, you start thinking like St. Francis, that stones and leaves and trees have their own personalities, and that they can feel. I like to think that even an object like a chair can respond to being loved, and that it sometimes likes a little praise, because it does its work so well."

"You're being surprisingly frank about your son, after all the running away and the secrecy," I said. "What made you change?"

"Doctor Cloete told me you'd given up, and that you were available whenever we needed you. That made me realise that you were concerned not only for our son, but that you were worried about us as well."

"That's true," I answered, glad of his insight. "Often the presence of such a patient in a house can cause, well, certain frictions. Very often the guardians are more in need of care and comfort than the patient."

"That's about the case," he said. "You will know, from your conversations with Doctor Cloete, what the position is in our home. Oh, don't feel bad about knowing, he broke no confidences, I gave him permission to speak quite freely to you. You see, I wanted you to know why I was avoiding you, and the way things are in my personal life is one of the reasons."

"I would like to know all the reasons," I said. "After all eighteen months have gone by since my arrival here."

He moved his tall, blond frame, lean and sharply chiselled, very well kept for a man of more than forty years of age.

"May I smoke a cigarette, can I offer you one?" he asked.

I nodded and he settled down into a position that seemed quite relaxed, very comfortable.

"My God," he said, "this is a comfortable chair. I could spend my life in it."

"Then take it," I said.

That's the sort of bloody stupid thing I always do, quite without reason. Giving things I treasure away just because people say that they like it.

"I'd prefer your forgiveness for my rudeness," he said. "But I won't dream of taking your chair."

I heard this with some relief, but I knew that he would want to come back, to sit in that chair again, and that, one day, I would insist on his taking it for his own.

"All right," I said. "Forgiveness; take all the forgiving you want. I know how difficult it must have been for you to come here tonight."

"No," he said. "Once I realised what a boorish clod I'd been, it was the easiest thing in the world. Now I'm here, speaking to you, being quite frank about the things in my house, I feel better. I suppose there are few things as good for you as a friendly talk with someone who looks on you as a human being. You do, don't you?"

"Yes," I said, "I do look on you as a human being."

"I suppose I ask questions like that because I've lived so long in an unnatural world that just simply chatting with someone is a rare delight."

He certainly seemed to mean it, about enjoying a little chat, because it was eleven o'clock before he made any move at all, just sat in the red leather chair, smoking cigarette after cigarette, with me occasionally joining him. I made coffee three times, and let him talk, because he needed that more than anything in the world. The last time, I used a few tots of the brandy that I had in the kitchen cupboard, for sauces and the occasional tot when I was tired, and he seemed to enjoy that even more. He was a chain smoker, and I had to clean out my diminutive little porcelain ashtray three times, with the coffee making, so in the end I gave him a polish tin lid to put out his cigarette ends. I didn't mind doing things for him, but he insisted on a bigger container.

It isn't necessary for me to try to fool anyone by being too subtle about what was happening. After all, we had been conscious of each other for eighteen months, and for six months I had virtually had the poor man in a state of siege. I was very nearly thirty, and life had seemed to pass me by, there being nothing of romantic interest in the village, with the exception of the poor attempts at seduction by the doctor, the attorney, and the minister. I had become very conscious of my prey's good looks, and I knew what calibre of man he was by the things he did for his people and his village. His was the best of the farms, his labourers the happiest, best fed and educated, living in the best accommodations. Doctor Cloete had told me of the gadgets that he had constructed for Daan, the special way in which he had cared for the unfortunate young man. I knew also about the separate bedrooms, and the guilt complexes that were ravaging his wife Bettina. It surprised me that a man like Dawid could not solve that problem, because he had a great deal of what I call native wisdom in his spiritual arsenal. Certainly he was extremely attractive physically, and I had been conscious of all of these qualities for some months now, so it was wonderful for me to have him spend an evening with me, in my house. When he left he said that it had been a lovely evening for him, that's what he said: "This has been a lovely evening for me." So I said that I was always at home, every evening, and if ever he wanted to call in and have a chat, I would be only too happy to get out the lid of the Cobra polish tin for his cigarette ends.

By the time he had reached the garden gate, ten yards away, I knew that I was hopelessly in love with him. So I did what I had to do, I ran after him, and reached him as he turned to wave goodnight. He was most gentle, as he took my arm and led me back to the house. "I love you too," he said.

What had happened is that, over the months that I had been pursuing him and he had been trying to get out from under my constant gaze, we had become over-conscious of each other. As I have already pointed out, I had an almost exact and complete knowledge of the sort of person he was, his daily routines, and the sort of life he led, as well as the things he liked doing, and others that he didn't. He had, through escaping from me, learnt everything about me. I was still, although very nearly thirty, not an unattractive woman. I just needed some sort of explosion to wake me up again. And it had happened.

He had a strong, wonderful, tender way of making love, and a good smell of the fields and tobacco about him. That first time was very nearly like an explosion for both of us. I wanted it to go on and on into eternity, of course, and so did he, but we needed each other too urgently to be patient, and within a very few minutes we had done and lay separated, spent by the force of our need. It was a short self-conscious consummation. We had both achieved an orgasm to finalise things but I was terribly in need of more, a continuance until dawn at least. I knew that that would never do. It was a small community. Fortunately, they were used to seeing people in my house at all hours, but it would be wrong for Dawid's car to remain parked there throughout the night. That would make things too public. And, there was his wife Bettina. I knew that I had not taken anything that was still hers, because she had rejected him so many years ago, but hers was a reaction of something bordering on mental illness, and I had no wish to become involved with anything that might hurt a sick person. My need and desire and love were all there, I felt it all over me just looking at him, but we had to be careful, and I told him so.

"You must go now, my love," I said. "Go quickly, before anything is noticed. This is the last time we must be together in this bed. We must be just as careful with our loving, to keep it to ourselves, as you have been with Daan. You do see that, don't you?"

"I don't know," he said. "Wouldn't it be better if everyone knew? I know they'll gossip behind our backs for a while, but after that everyone will accept it for the natural thing it is, and we will be able to live it out openly. I'm not ashamed you know. Everybody knows that my wife and I don't share the same bed any more, so it won't be too much of a scandal. People will understand, I think."

"No Dawid, I want it to be a private thing, only ours, no one else must ever know about it. That's the way I want it to be, please Dawid."

"It's important to you then, the privacy?" he asked.

"Yes Dawid, I don't want to be talked about. And you've had enough of it too. But what I'm most afraid of is that it will reach Bettina's ears one day. She has also been enough of a subject for village loose talk. I don't want any of the wonderful things that will happen between us to be public, just part of the old village scandal. We'll make a plan."

"Yes love," said Dawid. "We'll make a plan, and all right, it will be something that only you and I will ever know about."

"You must go now, my love," I said.

Strange, if he had been just one of my visitors sitting in the chair in my lounge talking, he could have stayed till dawn, night after night, even with the curtains drawn. But now, when we had made our first love, those innocences could no longer happen, so I kept pushing at him, quietly, and saying: "You must go now, you must go now." I held him back, saying it, and pushed him away from me. Then he kissed me, and went.

10

MARIA

When I reported at the hospital the day after I met Doctor Grové, in September 1942, I had no idea as to what would happen to me. First of all, I had to go to the recruiting officer, and then I was signed on as an army nurse, in effect. I was given a uniform and Doctor Grové gave me special permission to wear a scarf over my face.

"You are on your honour," he said, "to take it off as soon as you can. You'll be working with people who have been shot all to hell, and we want them to see what can be done."

"But won't it frighten them," I asked, "to see what can be done? I mean, if I'm an example of the best there is, then they won't have much to look forward to, Christ doctor, just look at me."

"You're fine," he said. "You're human. That's all they want. Nobody minds being ugly, especially if he's a man. But next time you're out in the street look around you. Look at the way some potentially beautiful people have crippled themselves by things like obesity, carelessness, dirt, ah—a thousand different things. Do you really think that you're uglier than some of them? If you do, you're over-reacting."

"Of course I am, doctor. I was beautiful once, you know, really beautiful."

"Look here, after what's happened to you, be grateful that you can react to anything at all. You must have survived by a miracle. Now you have a chance to be useful, and I don't want to hear one more sound of self-pity coming from you. You'll be in the wards from now on, as soon as you're in your uniform. There you'll see for yourself how badly people can really be hurt, and continue living. Nobody has to talk like this to those men in the beds of the military hospital. They have their own guts. We don't talk them into it. The moment they realise they still have the gift of life they push on through. I know a man who had half his penis shot off, a Sergeant Weideman, and we had to trim a little more off it, because the ends had been frayed. That was only one of his many wounds. He was filled with bits of steel. But it was the penis wound that worried him most until he realised that, in spite of its new size it still worked. Now, he's happy as a lark, 'I can't wait,' he says, 'to get out there among the bint to try out old shorty.' Now that's the kind of guts you're going to be working with. It isn't just a matter of half a loaf being better than none. Those fellows are grateful because they can walk past the bakery again."

That's the sort of man Doctor Grové was. Straight as they come, and not afraid to call a spade a spade. But, if he was frank, it was nothing to what I would come across in the wards. The boys I'd met in the park were there too, and soon my new name "Frankie" was all over the hospital. Just to see what it was all about I once went to a film starring Boris Karloff as the Frankenstein Monster. It frightened me, do you know that? It actually frightened me. I couldn't believe it, but somebody in Hollywood had dreamt up something that was, oh, three times as bad as I was, at least. I was so proud of being able to get up out of my seat, and being frightened, actually afraid of the face of someone else; a face that had been worked upon.

Something I found out very early on was that the boys in the wards liked me to join them in ganging up against the officers. Officers were in a different part of the building, and the men were in the big wards. They all ate the same food and, as I liked telling "my boys," the officers had the same bedpan problems. Another thing they enjoyed very much was when I used dirty language, the same as they did. They had, for years, been living in a man's world, where dirty words were just sounds. "Fucking" had nothing at all to do, nine-tenths of the time, with sexual intercourse. It was just a sound, something to make a sentence sound perhaps a little stronger. They liked it and, of course, with my sister Maryna being one of the most foul-mouthed people in the world, I had learnt a great many expletives that not even the soldiers had known about. One of the delights of my use of language was a fair knowledge of the researches into the fourteenth-to-seventeenth century cusswords that had been brought to light by John Massingham, so I made free use of phrases like go "swive thyself" or "watch out buster, or you will be roundly Rogered."

A whole generation of crippled ex-soldiers came home after their convalescence, with swear-words that testified to a certain cultural status among their mistresses. I have always been happiest when I was able to use language roughly, after my accident, that is. My sister's adolescent and university-bred coarseness of speech fell at first on horrified, then accepting, and then delightedly studious ears. Why Maryna was coarse was, she said, if you were a worker in the fields of sociology and nursing, your vocabulary didn't have a chance of staying pure. At least, that was her excuse.

I made friends with the patients. There were so many of them, so much worse off than I would ever be. The luxury of feeling sorry for others who had been damaged, almost beyond life, many of them certainly just on the verges of barely adequate repair, was something that I never had thought I would ever again experience. Whenever I entered the gate of the hospital I would remove my scarf-mask from my face. It would have been totally wrong for me to have worn it in the wards and corridors. Medically, I had been healed. The art of cosmetic surgery was still in its infancy in Pretoria, and some of the great advances that had been made in other countries were only then in their final stages of development, ready, as it were, for export. We were short-staffed in those days, and we worked long, hard hours. Usually a day or night shift of a full twelve hours at a stretch, but it was not too much for me. I rarely ventured out of the hospital grounds, because I felt that I had no business walking about outside among normal people. Here in the wards, the men who had lost faces, ears, eyes, legs, arms, testicles and penises, toes, feet, noses and buttocks, whole shoulders, half stomachs, bladders, lungs and pieces of liver, these and the toothless, the ones without tongues, those who needed new intestines or rectums, they were my kind, I thought. Among them I was not only comfortable, I was needed. How many volumes of corn have been written about the need to be needed, and yet I assure you that it is one of the basic necessities of my life, for which I will sacrifice anything, do anything, become anything. This isn't being pathetic or self-pitying because of my face, it's, I think at least, something that always was in me. I know it is in Maryna, my foul-mouthed sister (whom I intend, one day, shocking out of her head in that department).

Probably it was a family thing, because I know my parents gave their whole lives to us. I don't think they ever had any of it to themselves, and then of course, my mother had to go and die when she was barely fifty, leaving my father completely bereft, because he had been devoted to her, and she to him. I wonder if that word, "devoted," is perhaps not the operative word in our case, Maryna's and mine, that we had inherited from our parents. They had wanted a third daughter, who was to be called Marietjie, and the three of us would then have formed the trilogy of names as mentioned in one of their favourite Afrikaans songs. It is called "Kom Dans Klaradyn" and it is a beautiful song for a family to sing around a piano.

My whole life was centered in the hospital. I was always afraid, out in the street, that some person would grab hold of my scarf, or that it would come loose. I had nightmares, many a time, of that happening. I would be walking, quite fast, to go to the shop and to get what I wanted, when something like that would happen and I would suddenly become the focal centre of the whole street full of people, and there would be a hushed silence. Even the trucks and motor cycles would suddenly be quiet, and there I would be, standing, my scarred, out-of-shape face revealed to the whole world. Faces of all sorts, good ones, pretty ones, and ugly ones would all stare at me, black, brown, yellow, pink, and even the raw-blotched albinos, but I would be the ugliest face that they had ever seen. And one by one (not because they were cruel but because they were embarrassed), they would start giggling, out of sheer nervous reaction, until the whole street would be laughing at me, even the bells on the city hall tower. Then I would try to run, but my feet would not be able to move, so I would sink down on the pavement, and assume the foetal position, curled into a tight ball, and my dry throat would try to scream, but no sound would come out of it. So I would wake up many a night, in my bed, rolled into a tight little ball of fear.

How different it was when it actually happened to me one day, in spite of all my precautions. A motor car had come, the wrong way, up a one-way street, and a black cyclist, swerving, had steered into a crowded pavement. I was also involved in those who clutched about wildly for support, and my scarf had been ripped from my face. So there it was, the nightmare situation for which so many of my dreams had prepared me. I was perfectly willing to roll up into the womb on the pavement as soon as I heard the first giggle. But people just glanced at me, those who could be bothered, and I searched about for my scarf, but it was in the hand of the coloured woman whose clutching-for-balance fingers had ripped it from my face. She looked at me. There wasn't any shock or laughter in her face, only an accepting softness, as she said: "Here's-a scarf madam, an' I'm sorry, hey, let me show madam where there's a cloak-room here in the big Stuttafords Building, just-around-a corner." And she took my arm and led me, white-faced to Stuttafords cloak-room, which had mirrors. She was, of course not allowed in there herself, being just a little too dark-complexioned to pass for a Spaniard or an Italian. Her nose was also a little too flat. And then she had that funny way of talking, that always amuses me. They know it too, these coloureds, and they deliberately talk a little more broadly than is necessary when they know that it will make you laugh. That's the way they are, anything for a laugh. Except work. They are the worst workers in the world. If you don't believe me, ask anyone from the Cape.

So much for my worst dream becoming reality and ending up in a slightly silly, almost bitter bit of stupid local labour-politics. Maryna is the one for talking about whites, blacks, and coloureds and all the inter-racial tensions and so forth, it really isn't a part of my world at all. When you have been in the shit to the extent that I have been, and also my patients, then you seem to be excused the usual political small-talk that goes on, or any of the practical things like the price of bread and sugar. People seem to think that a more semi-philosophical sort of conversation is called for in the presence of the physically handicapped or unsightly, as if our presence, or perhaps our scars, are a reason for indulging in conversations concerning what they call "the deeper things of life." Try to remember that I grew up in an age when a very ordinary cliché was considered either a philosophical wisdom or a sign of wit. There's still a lot of it about but not as much as when I was a young woman. I am now talking of 1942/43, when I was nearing my nineteenth year.

My experience with hospitals over nearly seven years had given me a distinct edge over the other trainees, and within a year I had achieved, along with my night, or, should I say, off-duty courses, my matriculation, several promotions, and, far ahead of my time but because of my vast practical experience, a rank of second lieutenant. I was never considered fit for overseas duty, but by that time regular flights of ambulance aircraft came down from North Africa, and later Sicily and Italy, to keep us as busy as we could be. The hastily done patchwork of base and field hospitals kept us supplied with a seemingly endless line of patients for surgery, convalescence, physiotherapy and discharge, either on their feet or feet first to the mortuary. Unfortunately, we lost a lot of patients, but some of them really should have been allowed to die on the battlefields. I think they would have preferred it that way. I had had unusual experiences of patchwork surgery, so I know what pain there was connected with the continuous operations the men had to go through. I have always thought that any doctor should first allow himself to be operated on, even if he allows only a minor bit of surgery like an appendectomy, a tonsillectomy, or a haemorrhoidectomy, which Maryna refers to as "having your arsehole out." Then they would know, from these minor operations, how much it really hurts to have one of the big ones. Knowing about their pain I was more sympathetic, loving even. And my particular talent was seeing them through when they went over the line. They liked me to sing sad songs for them too, the ones who were going to make it. They particularly liked the Australian one that went:

"Play a didgeree-doo-boo,
Play a didgeree-doo,
Keep playing it till I shoot through, boo,
Play a didgeree-doo."

Funny, I had always thought that a didgeree-doo was a drunkard's way of saying "dirge," so I was of the opinion that the words meant "play a dirge, boo," "boo" being buddy or mate. But no, a "didgeree-doo" is an aboriginal musical instrument. It does make a plaintive sound, though.

A lot of the Australian things went over very well, because there were a number of English and New Zealand and Australian patients in our hospitals too, and they liked to hear me sing the sad parts of Waltzing Matilda, for instance, especially the part where the jolly swagman tells the lawman, "You'll never take me alive, said he" and I would let my voice go very low, and give the fellows goose-flesh with

"And his ghost can be heard,

As he wanders through the billabong,
Singing, you'll come a-waltzing Matilda, with me."

I must have, at least, had a reasonable voice, because, often at night, my ward would be the envy of the whole hospital because of the soft, sentimental songs of the old days, and even the songs of that time, echoing through the corridors of pain caused by the people of Mr. C.P. Snow's Corridors of Power. The patients would like to softly add their voices, until it sounded like a haunting sort of choir, far away, and the patients in the other wards would take a little heart.

My ward was the worst one, where the ones in danger of the terminal experience were mostly sent, and, let me tell you, I sent a lot of them back to the general treatment wards, because of their guts. It amazes me to think of it today, of all the men who went out of that hospital, into life, who fixed themselves up when nothing in the world could be done for them. They were, so often, alive only because their hearts were still beating, and the only thing that we could really do for them was to shoot them full of pain-killers to ease them through as humanely as possible, but so many of them just would not give up the ghost, they clung, fought, in the face of the most horribly stacked cards, and they lived, on and on, day after day, a moment at a time, until we had to admit that they had beaten the odds.

I saw it so often, really, men who could no longer live, taking life and holding onto it with both hands, until they could go home, patched up, maimed, but alive and full of guts. The rest of the hospital, hearing the big choral act from the terminal ward, got a bit upset. Once, a lady colonel came in and found us, after lights out, singing, of all the macabre choices, "Swing low, sweet chariot, coming for to carry me home." She was so shocked that she felt she had to object.

"Lieutenant," she said huffily, "these patients are in need of rest. This is a hospital ward, not a music hall, you know."

The patients fell silent, not wanting to get me into trouble, but one of them, Lefty Lesser, a tall big nice bugger with a Stalin moustache, let off one of his snorting, melodious, two-tone farts that he had been practising for years.

"I'm sorry, Colonel," I said, and looked over at Lefty Lesser with his Stalin moustache, shaking my head to let him know that he must not get the colonel angry.

"That wasn't you, Lootenant," yelled Lesser, "it wasn't for you to say you're sorry. It was me that farted, and it's for me to say I'm sorry. But I won't."

He then let out another long wind which he blended with his voice to form the opening note of yet another "Swing low, sweet chariot."

There was nothing the colonel could do, except report me to Doctor Grové, who was by that time a Brigadier General. He out-ranked her, but she was responsible for the nurses, so we had a meeting, the three of us. Doctor, or Brigadier General Grové shat on me properly for nearly ten minutes, then asked the colonel if that was what she had had in mind. When she said yes, Doctor Grové dismissed her and promoted me to full lieutenant. "And," he said, "don't sing quite so loudly or so late for the next couple of weeks. The lady colonel has been posted up north to be in charge of the nurses at the base hospital at Bari in Italy. When she's been there a few months you'll see a difference in her."

I was kept on duty in that terminal ward at my own request. And mine were the ministrations that sent many a young lost man back to surgery for another go. As the war grew in Europe, more real base hospitals were established there, and, in time, only long-term patients requiring years of surgery and physiotherapeutic treatment came in. The terminals were now allowed to end their days in the "foreign fields" of Rupert Brooke, for which they had given their lives. I still think that that was the best way, to be buried amongst their mates, where they had known the exhilaration, the pleasures, the comradeship, and the pain of war. So my terminal ward became just another of the long-term treatment wards, and we weren't allowed to sing after hours, but you could never stop a fellow like Lefty Lesser from singing, and long after lights out he would join me, on his crutches in the duty sister's room, and we would shut the door and hum a few songs so that the other patients could go to sleep in silence. Lefty was an enormous man, and he had been very badly wounded: Left leg and arm amputated at knee and elbow, use of testicles also lost, whole left side badly lacerated, left lung pierced, left ear torn off, loss of hearing on left side. Miraculously, he had both eyes intact. He must have turned his head when the shell exploded. His healing had taken more than a year, and a few more operations were needed to trim off the results of hasty, lifesaving emergency surgery. He always complained of the loss of both testicles and the retention of both eyes. "I'd have given up one of each, gladly," he said. "It's hell not to be a man no more." I looked up his case history on his card. It was true that he would never be able to have children again, but his scrotum had been saved, and, although the testes were no longer fertile or capable of ejaculation his looks, genitally speaking, were normal. I explained all this to him.

"Ah," he said, "so what's the use of a pair of wind balls, shooting dust from the Western Desert? I don't mind so much that I won't have no more children, I've left plenty around and about, even in Naples, and, long ago, in Durban, and I think there must be a couple of brown ones in Mtubatuba. That part of it, about having children doesn't worry me. But, you know, women are funny about the seeds, they notice when you can't, and they laugh at you behind your back, and call you a windball, you know?"

"Yes," I said. "I know. I know you're afraid of things that just won't ever happen to you. You're a beautiful man and women will go crazy for you the moment you're out of here, and none of that nonsense now."

"If only I knew," he said. "If only there was some way to tell. Then, maybe, if it ever happens to me, I won't be afraid, or self-conscious, and I'll, you know, maybe stay up, instead of going all slack, because I'm scared of making a mess."

"You'll be fine," I said. "Really Lefty, you're a very attractive man. There's more than enough of you left to make any woman happy. Really, I wouldn't bullshit you."

Lefty looked at me with grateful eyes. We had this conversation many a time, in my duty room, late at night, when the rest of the men in the ward were sleeping. Only a very few times would one of them call me for a bedpan or some pain-killing pills, or a fresh glass of water. Often, when one of them could not sleep, I would sit by his bed in the half-light of the night and hold his hand, or stroke his hair. And very often one of them would tell me I was beautiful. I won't dwell on that or make a big thing of it. I just say that very often one of them would tell me that I was beautiful in the half-light of the hospital night. Only Lefty Lesser, of all the patients ever said it to me in the full light of the night sister's duty room, one morning about two a.m.

"You know, Frankie," he said. "You know, you're a very beautiful girl."

"I bet you say that to all the monsters, you lovely shit," I answered.

I always use words like that when I'm too embarrassed to do anything else, or say something. I haven't any taste, I suppose, when it comes to how to take a compliment gracefully, Or maybe it's just bitterness. Lefty thought that he had hurt me. He was sitting on the edge of my desk, his one leg on the ground. He reached down and pulled me off my chair. Then he pulled me close to him. He held me as close as he could, and I put my arms around him, while he kissed me all over my scarred face.

"You know, Frankie," he repeated. "You're very beautiful."

"Thank you, Lefty," I said. "Thank you. That was lovely of you. To say that."

"It wasn't just words, Frankie," said Lefty. "I mean it."

"It's nice of you, to say, and to do, and thank·you for the kisses," I said.

"No," he said. "I mean it, see." He slipped his good arm from around me and started to fondle my breasts. "I don't just mean beautiful, with words."

I was startled, but pleased, because the light was on in the office, and I could feel him pressing himself to me. There was a physical reaction. His penis was in the erect state, and the reaction was for me. Oh hell yes I know that he could not have had a woman for at least a year, and I don't know if a man without the ability to ejaculate can have nocturnal emissions, or at least its sensory equivalent, but that hard-on was mine, in bright electric light. My scarf was in the drawer of my desk, and I did a quick strip-tease, stripping both him and me, while I did the casbah-purdah thing with my face, tying the scarf around me, so that he could see me at least from the neck down, where the most successful surgery had taken place, under my clothes where I thought no man would ever see the remnants of my beauty.

Lefty played along with this act for a while. We were both naked on the resting cot in the little room just off my office, and the light was full on. I don't know what God had given Lefty his wisdom, or his guts, or just his extraordinary randiness that night, but when I put out my hand to put out the bedside lamp, he stopped me. Then, while he was slowly entering me, because he had to go easily with me, there being a painful obstruction called a hymen that no amount of masturbation by fantasy had ever ruptured, he removed the scarf from my face, and as the pain flowed likc quick-silver through my groin, he kissed me, all over my hurt face, my eyelids and mouth, the stitched, doll's cheeks that I had thought was composed of dead tissue, and my, and his need, gave me a tactile sense. I felt those wise lips on my dead cheeks. I hesitate to use the word "love," instead I say "need," because I don't want anybody to think that I have such an enormous opinion of myself that I would ever use the word "love" in connection with what must, in modern terms, have been just a quickie with the duty nurse in the rest-room. I can only say that I thank God for Lefty Lesser being randy, or sentimental, or corny, or Socrates and Sartre that night. All of them, I think, even if he can't even spell half of "philosophy," he could *do* all of it. And diplomacy as well. And humanity and understanding. Oh, he was a wonderful man, Lefty Lesser, with his one lung and missing balls. That night he knew that the orgasm which he had feared unattainable was possible. He had never imagined that he would ever experience it again. He knew that he could now go out into the world, as the dawn began to break and I had to hurry him back to his bed before the day staff were due to take over. Orgasm had been experienced, by both of us, several times, the sheets and the pillows were soaked with my reactions of the night, lying warm-wetly beneath our bodies, but he knew that it could be done, that climax was not only a possibility, but a fact. And he was pleasantly surprised to find that *he* could also experience an orgasm, and share in the pleasure that he was so very keen on giving. Because the warmth and the wetness had come from me, and his deepest satisfaction had been in my pleasure; and mine, in just knowing that a man could keep the light on, and make love to me, looking at my awful face, and feel enough pity or tenderness or love or wisdom or just be randy enough to want me, and to go through with it.

I will never question what caused the erection of Lefty Lesser that night, but I am grateful that it happened as it did, with a real, whole man, all man. Without balls and with his whole left side shot away, Lefty Lesser was all that a man could ever be to a woman.

As I hurried him, on his crutches, to his bed, and tucked him in, kissing him with the desperation of parting forever from a loved one, because I thought that he would never again be like that, that daylight would bring a more sober evaluation of my totally absent charms, I felt as a woman should feel after she has said "good night darling" to her man, and I felt that all the other women in the world had very good reason to be envious of me. The solitary hours of lonely and embittered masturbation were over for both of us. We knew that we could, if we had to make it in the world that lay beyond the hospital gates.

I wonder if Lefty remembers me, if he remembers the nights that we spent on the rest-cot (because Lefty wasn't a one-shot man). That's not meant to be funny. I know he couldn't, will never again, ejaculate into a woman, but for the months before his discharge (again, there is a fear of double entendre. Have you noticed that it always happens that way, for instance, when someone has died in a family, don't you hear yourself using phrases like, "I'm scared to death" or "I died laughing" at the funeral wake, with horror). His manufactured testicles, with their plastic-cosmetic little softnesses, were unimportant, just lumps of factory-made prostheses for the belles of the outside world. But in spite of his inability to make even the slightest opaque droplet, he filled me with his warmth.

So, I cured a patient, because that was all that Lefty needed to get him out of the hospital and into the world at large, and the last thing in the world that I wanted was a Lefty out of hospital, but he had to go, and so in a way, had I, also, one day, to face the world. Thank heaven my time to go had not yet arrived, while Lefty was up and raring to go.

That was a time of being in heaven for me, my very first man. He had 20–20 vision, and he wanted the lights on while he loved me. I never met his like again as long as I lived. I loved more, because I fell in love with more beautiful men, and, being surfeited, I lost the meaning of that word "beautiful." Lefty used to mouth it after me, as I did the rounds of the ward, until I blushed through my scar-tissue because I was always conscious of him as he lay there, looking so bloody helpless, remembering the incredible cavortings of which he was capable during the night-hours of our love; and I was conscious of his lips making the "you're beautiful" movement. I lost all that, but what I lost, most of all, was the way he meant it. I had, long afterwards, a greater, more tender, and more lasting love than Lefty. But it was Lefty who taught me what it was all about when a man put on the light and said to a woman, "you're beautiful." I may have cured a patient, and sent him out into the great big world beyond, conscious of his ability to generate and experience orgasm. But let me tell you that I was also cured by that patient, who would always insist on the light being on. It didn't matter how embarrassed I would be by the things I found myself doing to him, and him to me, things that I would have liked to do in the darkness, but he would not let it be so, "because," as he said, and God forgive me this sin of pride in repeating it, "because you're so beautiful."

Funny, he never used another word, always just beautiful, and I wondered if his schooling had been lacking in terms of vocabulary-training, or if he had never heard that many words are the same in meaning as "beautiful." I would use some on him. Look them up in Roget if you wish: lovely, desirable, glamorous, gorgeous, pretty, wonderful, thousands of other words of praise to the person you love, but he never used any other than just that one. And I thought, "All right, so he isn't educated, so what?"

I never realised that it was all deliberate, that he had done so as part of my cure. On the day he left the hospital, on his crutches, to be taken by military transport to the railway station, and from there, by rail warrant, to Villiersdorp, a village in the Cape, a thousand miles away, where he would be met by his people, who would drive him to the family wine farm. On that day, at the gate, when I wanted to cling to him like a pip of a yellow cling peach from Kakamas, he turned my face in his hand, looked at it, and kissed me very softly on the lips, now so full of love's life. Then he broke open the Pandora's box, kicking it to bits there at the gate, so that all of its treasures lay at my feet.

"You're beautiful," he said. "I know there's a thousand other words. A million other things to say between people like us, who feel for each other the way we feel for each other. And I don't know what I feel. You must allow me that honesty. But you know that I do feel, and I know you do as well. Don't let's fall in love with love. Don't let's use that, or any of the other words. But I promise you, and this is on my oath, I will never again as long as I live, no matter who I am with, I will never again call anyone or even anything, no person, tree, flower, mountain or sea will I ever call beautiful. It's my word for you. And if ever I hear the word, or read it, or want to use it, I'll think of you. That's a promise."

So that was Lefty's gift to me, the speechless one at the gate who was so taken up by his words that I couldn't even say anything to him, just moo at him with cow-eyes full of tears, silly bitch that I was, selfish, thinking only of myself, never giving a thought to the fact that the young bugger was going out into the world, with only the confidence of an erection between himself and what was facing him. He needed something of me too, and I couldn't speak for anyone but myself, and what was I but an awful looking bloody cow with a nice pair of tits, one real, one cosmetic, and a good line of sparse pubic hair, with a passable figure topped off by a dreadful face?

How could I tell him that I was capable of speaking for all womankind, and that, when he fell in love, he was not the one who had to be proved worthy in the bridal bed, but that it would be the responsibility of his new wife. I knew that there would be a wife. I prayed for him that it would be the right one, so lovely that he could break his vow even to me and call her "beautiful," with my blessing.

Let me get back to reality. Why do I, whenever I love, become a throwback to Victorian sentimentality, why can't I just look at the fact, and it is a fact, that it's all just theory and you do the right thing by it or you go for a shit yourself? We speak too many words.

Lefty had the right idea. "Beautiful," that was his word. I think he may have used that line on a dozen different women, now that I remember the twinkle in his eye. But it is all right, I don't mind, as long as he didn't ever let me know that he had used the one word he had promised would be mine forever, on anyone else. That was the end of Lefty for me. I would receive letters from him for quite a few years afterwards, but, such is the nature of things, that even I had gone on to other matters of the heart not too long after he had left for Villiersdorp. He had set a precedent. I could have sex, and in 1945, when the war ended, I had had an endless line of affairs with my patients, so much so that I had been dubbed "Frankie the Nympho" by my superior officers and fellow nurses. My name, by the end of the war, was as much a mess as you can imagine. But I had been called the most glorious array of names by my lovely patients. I knew that, with the end of the war, the procession of new patients, embittered and panicky about their eventual re-absorption into public or private life would come to a trickling end, but this didn't worry me. The military wards of World War II would continue to need me for many years after the surrenders had been accepted, and my own surrenders were quite inevitable for the foreseeable future.

While the entire world was trying to do its thing at the United Nations, talking about peace, I saw the outbreak of warring factions in the Middle and Far East as something in which we had to become involved, eventually. I had no belief in world peace, and no desire for it, because, horrible as it may sound to you, peace meant whole men, without fears, and only a real nut-case would have anything to do with a thing like me. On the other hand, if the bombs and mortars had done their work well, I, the military nurse, would be assured of an endless supply of willing experimenters, who, in the soft light of the hospital's post-midnight wards, would look at me in the quiet, cosmetic darkness, that made all the scars look smoother, and tell me I was lovely.

Yes, I admit, I took advantage of these poor broken bodies, made limp by war, even to the extent of going down on them at dawn when pressure of urine caused their erections. They knew the word for it, the ex-prisoners-of-war, because the Germans had a word for it. The German guards used to steal into the huts quietly, at dawn, with cane rods, and when a man was lying on his back with a urine erection, they would cut at it with the sharp edges of their sticks, to fracture a boneless desire. They called it a "water stand," eine wasserschtend, and made it a hell for the fellows, so that they were afraid to drink any water for hours before they went to bed. That, by the way, is my contribution to the list of Nazi War Crimes. It is original research, and was told to me one morning after I had found a young man, Eric, groaning in his bed, with an erection tenting his blankets, appearing to be warding off the attacks of Stuka dive bombers from his stiff dick. I put my head under the blankets, after putting the death screen around the bed. Nobody could see what I was doing. I committed fellatio on him. He woke up, all warm and coming, and held my face in his hands in the lovely light of just-before-sun-up, and looked at me with all the love in the world. I knew then what fear of a dawn erection could mean to an ex-prisoner-of-war, and watched out for that fear. Many a time I soothed away the panic with my hands and some rubbing cream or my lips, as they wished. I was an instrument, to be played on as needed, and any melody, classic or modern was all right by me, as long as I could be of service, and thus be serviced. Now that I look back on that particular phase of my life, and all the things I did, I sometimes wonder if I should feel ashamed of myself. Somehow, I never do.

I know that it's pathetic to make love to people who can't protect themselves, who are swollen by months without a woman, in hospital wards from Udine to Pretoria, with stops at Bari, Brindisi, Wadi Halfa, Kisumu, Khartoum, all along the way from Cape to Cairo. I know that there, some place, is a cause for a sort of shame, but I don't feel it. I have only a pride in giving happiness to all those lovely men, who needed me so very desperately, in so very many ways.

It's something that may happen again when a great war comes along, and the maimed will again rise up for me. Exhaustion, even when I was totally happy with my patients, came ever so often, even if it was only that my vocal chords had run out on me with a case of laryngitis. They taught me the songs of wartime, and I knew the lot. So filthy that even I was, at times, a little more shocked than delighted by this new facet of my education. There were some really great ones, like "Salome, standing there with her arse all bare," and the noble poetry of "She can run, jump, fight, fuck, wheel a barrow, push a truck," with the monumental enormity of her pubic fur: "hair on her belly like the branches on a tree." Oh, I think "Salome" was their favourite, although there were some other great ones like:

The captain's daughter Mabel,
Whenever she was able,
She'd give the crew,
A jolly good screw,
Upon the kitchen table.

I remember, on the same licentious craft, there was a nasty, tricky little cabin boy, most selfish with his dreadful little anus, ah yes:

A filthy little nipper,
Who stuffed his arse,
With broken glass,
And circumcised the skipper.

I could go on for hours, but that's enough to give you some idea of the songs we sang during the early hours of the evening. My patients, especially the new ones, delighted in hearing their filthy words coming from the pure lips of the great cripple-faced Florence Nightingale whom they called Frankie after their favourite monster, from the same producers who gave you the unforgettable, epic, collapsing steering wheel in the chest, with the incredible, spectacular, impact-explosive petrol tank.

You like this world of mine, don't you? I did too. It was a fairyland spectacular, with no holds barred. Anything that I could do to give the fellows a little pleasure, to make them ready for their eventual pass to the world of ordinary people, or to eternity, was all right, nobody minded. Even if the story went right up to the General that "Lieutenant van der Kolff was up to the most spectacular sexual tricks" in her ward, the General would merely say, according to what I overheard in the staff showers: "If they enjoy it, and she enjoys it, it's a mutual therapy, so just let it go. This is no peace-time ward." Hell yes, I enjoyed it. They were my years of revelation, when I was the belle of the ball, and by ball I mean testicle, singular or plural, depending on their nearness to the grenade or mortar. Sometimes that great umpire in the sky had even no-balled them. (I don't think I should try to be deliberately funny, do you? Seems a bit forced, even for me. But I never pretended to have good taste in these matters, did I?) As I said, I sometimes got tired, and, forty miles away, was the village of Skeerpoort, where my sister Maryna was social and district nurse, getting degree after degree and becoming more wise about helping people to get the best out of their lives. She was a remarkable, lovely person, of the sweetest disposition, able to smile away any really bad thing, or cure it with a salve, a pill, or a kick in the arse. She had a way of telling which of these panaceas or shocks would be most effective in any crisis. Right, she was a little on the coarse side from time to time, but that's hardly something to even mention in this part of the twentieth century. I could never understand why she didn't take a husband. She would have made a wonderful wife and mother, and, with it all, she stayed beautiful. As I said, there was a time when she seemed to be all academic, a devoted student, going for M.A's and Doctorates; she was bookworm, fool, wasting her lovely lips, ripe breasts, and probably fantastic labia in the exacting pursuits of greater knowledge. It seemed such a shame. She actually appeared to be drying out. I visited her every two or three months, never quite regularly, and usually, at the beginning, quite unexpectedly, because the telephone to Skeerpoort, then as now, more than thirty years later, has never been a match for a little kaffir with a cleft stick.

Suddenly, during one of my visits, I noticed that my presence was a little resented. You know the feeling you get when people appear to want to know when you will be leaving? I had the distinct feeling that I shouldn't stay all the long-weekend I had off, that I should go, as soon as possible. I'm good on these feelings, never really wrong, so I was able to tell Maryna, within two hours of my arrival on the Saturday morning, that I only had the one day off, and that I had to be back in Pretoria late that same afternoon. I'm also good at seeing when people are immensely relieved, and she was. So much so that she arranged a lift for me with a local farmer, Dawid Cilliers, that same afternoon. She would also go along, to be with me for a little while longer, and to buy a few things in Pretoria.

I met the man Cilliers that day. He was the one with the retarded, spastic man-child in his backyard, of whom I had heard. Maryna had been asking me for any information that came my way as a result of the great part that physiotherapy played in my work of rehabilitating the war wounded, and I was able to give her quite a lot of information regarding the latest machines and the addresses of their manufacturers. It appeared that this man Cilliers was devoted to the retarded, paralysed child, or young man, in his backyard, that was his son, and would do anything in his power to help the poor creature. Cilliers seemed to be a very nice man, a little on the old side, certainly past forty, but charming in a forced, old-world squire-ish sort of landowner way, if you see what I mean. You know, I nearly said not "my type" until I realised suddenly that all the men in the world were my type, if they wanted to be. I don't think I would ever be able to say "no" to any man who needed me in any way. I have made sacred the "beautiful" of Lefty because he had opened the door and switched on the light. But, let's face it, Lefty had gone away, leaving the door open, and I'd walked through into the new ballrooms, reception rooms, places to eat, sleep, and dream. Make of it what you will, I'll never regret being the "great whore of ward twenty-two."

But about Maryna, she gave me to understand that her studies for, at that time, her Master's degree, gave her very little time off, and she said that she would appreciate it if I would let her know when to expect me. The telephone was a pain, yes, but an urgent express reply-paid telegram would always reach her, provided it was sent on Wednesday to reach her by Saturday. That was also thirty years ago, and the same thing still applies now, in 1976, in the small towns of the entire Johannesburg/Krugersdorp and Pretoria district. A strange matter this, considering that party lines have caused rifles to be cleaned, and females to spit at each other at the post offices. One would think that the Ministry of Health and Hygiene would insist that the Ministry of Posts, Telegraphs and Pensions would pull up their socks and do something about it, as only in post offices near Pretoria will you find the notice, prominently displayed in all parts to which the public has access, "Moenie spoeg nie—Do not spit." That's by the way, my sister was telling me, "moenie onverwags kom nie—do not come unexpectedly."

She was very clever about the man Dawid Cilliers, making me sit in the middle, there being only the one seat in the little 3/4 ton truck. She was studious in her behaviour, and I had no trouble at all seeing that her complexion had heightened, her hair shone as it had not for many years, not since the war had started, and that her eyes sparkled. There were also traces of exquisite cosmetics, especially a perfume that would drive a whole ward of my fellows stone mad and randy. Little extra traces that one notices, like the farmer's pressed pants and shiny shoes, his newly laundered shirt, and a scarf about his neck. His brushed hair, and the smell of after-shave-lotion, at four in the afternoon. Who the hell did they think they were bullshitting, as they drove me back to the hospital that Saturday afternoon?

I was a little hurt, although jealousy was no longer a part of my personality, but I had also become very good at what they were trying to do, that was, to hide my feelings. I had had so much practice by that time that Maryna and her new-found Dawid must have thought that I didn't ever want to see my sister again, or, rather, that I didn't really care whether I did or not. As I got out of the little truck at the gate to the hospital Maryna came with me.

"I see," she said, "that you don't wear your scarf over your face any more. That's very good. I'm proud of you."

"Yes," I said. "Actually, I usually wear it when I go out of the hospital grounds. I took it off when I got to your gate this morning, and I forgot it there. Keep it for me, will you? And, Maryna, when you'd like to see me again, please, you send the telegram."

So, I thought, in my funny possessive way, that I'd got my own back on her, as I turned and walked away to the great double doors of the hospital, without even saying "thanks" to her or the Cilliers man. But she got her revenge because, two days later, when the post offices had started up again after the weekend, there was a "most urgent" telegram, paid double rates, in my correspondence tray on my desk in the duty room. It was one of those stupid telegrams written by a person who had no sense of the expense of sending such messages. It read: "Darling I want you to visit me today and tomorrow and any day that you have the time so please let me know the moment you are off duty for long enough to get here or if you only have an hour or two to spare let me know when they will be and I will be there to meet you your loving sister forever Maryna." I could not let her beat me like that, so I sent her an equally stupid telegram, also double rates, urgent, express, that read: "My dearest Maryna please forgive me for being a silly fool I only want you to be happy and I do not want you to be worried about me because I really am fine and I think I am as happy as you are if you see what I mean your loving sister Maria."

That is the way in which we told each other that men had come into our lives. Strange that I should have been worried about her. Such warmth needed a catalyst, someone to make it flourish and be meaningful. Her worry about my own personal life was understandable. People had always been worried about me.

Although farming was supposed to be a seven-day-a-week occupation, most of the farmers I knew had organised their lives around drinks with their male friends in the pub on Saturdays with perhaps a few games of billiards thrown in. Then sex on Saturday evening, church on Sunday morning, and sleep on Sunday afternoons, after the big feast-meal at midday. The rest of the week meant really hard work for the successful farmers, loafing about on the porch for the bad ones. There was no doubt that Dawid Cilliers was good at his work, his was one of the model farms of the area, a real pleasure to drive past. People would stop and look at his fields and the herds of cattle and sheep. So he did not have a lot of time for Maryna in the course of his everyday life, and I certainly did not want to interfere or be in their way.

The morals of the situation meant nothing to me. We had, it seemed, each gone her own way and we kept our lives private from each other, only occasionally hinting, as we did through the exchange of telegrams, that our lives were, at that time, being lived satisfactorily. I had a deep sense of pride in the things that I had been able to do with my life, that had, at one time, seemed to be not worth living. I was more than happy, because I was independent, unfettered by pity, and free in a way that I had never thought possible.

The years went by, the end of the war came and there was a future of long convalescences for the men who had been very badly hurt. Many of them came back for further operations as new surgical techniques became known all over the world. It wasn't a case of experimentation so much as that many operations, unknown till then, came into being on a do-or-die basis. The surgeons at the great military hospitals simply had to go in there and do something or the patients would have been lost anyway. With every week's overseas mail there came news of new methods, techniques and procedures in the fields of surgery and physiotherapy. I can say, with a certain sense of shyness, that I believe that my particular brand of physiotherapy did as much good as the pills and injections that I dispensed throughout my long nights.

Once again, because I did not want to take up any of Maryna's time, I withdrew to my ward. There was work for me that I found pleasurable, fascinating and rewarding. The work I was doing was healing me also, and many of the scars on my spirit were made healthy tissue again by the peculiar and hardly, well, decent way of life that I had made for myself. I cured many of my patients in the way I had fixed up Lefty, most of them maimed men who were afraid of facing the outside world. All they needed was the little push that I was able to provide. It wasn't all that satisfactory of course, once the novelty had worn off and the encounters grew reasonably numerous.

People are never satisfied, and now that I had started thinking of myself as a person I wanted more. I longed for someone to tell me, truthfully, that he loved me. Many of the lads used phrases like "you're a love, Frankie" to get over that hurdle, knowing in their hearts that I would spot a lot of untrue junk the moment they said it, because there was a hardness to me during the business-like hours of the day, when I spoke their language, that warned them not to take any liberties with the truth when I was around. In the age of the over-sentimental, before the use of the word "objective" had quite made it to the southern hemisphere, these boys knew that any enchanted garden stuff that they might be tempted to fling at me would find its way right down their throats or up their anuses in a minute.

But I had been to the films and I'd seen the buckets of slop that were being poured over the international audiences by the treacly-millions of gallons. It was that sort of over-dramatised, melodramatic, super-gooey time when the current language was the sort of thing that last year's hit screenplays had been made of. I knew that the sort of talk that went on between the people who had to speak those stupid, shallow words had been made up by writers who had split their tongues in half and put them in both cheeks, that it was the worst possible stuff, turned out by the most dishonest group of people that had ever gathered together in one place in the world's history, nothing excluded, but yet I wanted some of it for myself. Cheap, nasty, horrible, I know, but I wanted it. I think because I needed the option to experience it, and then to reject it, but it was never offered to me so I never had the chance to say my "no thank you's."

Then there was my future. I could see that it would be all hospitals. Beds at night, people who were in agony, seeking any kind of comfort. Nurses are as a rule busy, crisp, efficient, cool-headed. I wasn't, in spite of my reasonable rank of acting captain when the war ended and the long years of convalescence stretched ahead for a large proportion of my patients. I wasn't really a good nurse, in the accepted sense of the word. I was a foul-mouthed singer of dirty songs with young men who had gone to war and had come back shot to bits, fearful of the awesome world that lay in wait for them. I was the holder of the hands that were left, the soft stroker of brows, or any other part that needed stroking. This wasn't really good nursing. I became too involved with my patients, and in doing so I went to certain lengths of unethical behaviour, a thought that has always worried me.

When the Americans dropped the atom bombs on Hiroshima and Nagasaki, our men had been diverted from the European theatre of war and troop-ships were actually sailing eastwards from Suez to go and give a hand. Then, all of a sudden, the war was over, and a hideous thought came into my head.

"Oh shit," I thought, "now there won't be any more patients." That was an awful thing to think, while people were dancing around Church Square and kissing soldiers, I was disappointed that it was all going to end. I asked many soldiers, afterwards, professionals who had stayed on in the army after the war was over, whether they too had felt that way about the peace, whether there had been any sense of disappointment for them, but the answer was always the same. "Not bloody likely," they would say. "Once you've had those guys shooting at you, to kill, and you've come through it, you're a very happy man when you hear that peace has been declared." Not one of them ever wanted to go through it again. And all of them, without exception, told me about how afraid they had been.

There was a brief interval of war, a little later, when, with the trouble in Korea, Pretoria sent a squadron of Sabre Jets to fight on the American side, but whatever happened to the casualties, none of them ever reached my ward. I was now strictly in charge of convalescence. The exercise and physiotherapy people would spend hour upon hour with my patients, and I would make such encouraging remarks as occurred to me, but the old dramas of life and death struggling against each other every hour of the day and night were, for the most part, things of the past.

A few patients struggled along, refusing to die, for a number of years after the war, losing the battle finally, unable to take the pain or the hopelessness any longer. These men had by then become friends, with deep feelings of friendship that went far beyond the temporary relief of sex, and I had to buy a black hat and a veil, a black skirt, blouse, and stockings, gloves and shoes, because I started getting into the habit of going to their funerals.

There were hundreds of patients all over the military hospital, and most of them had been, for a time, in my section. When they were finally even partially mobile, whether ambulatory on their feet, crutches, or wheel chairs, they would come over to my duty room at all hours of the day or night looking for a bit of chat, or whatever. They liked to sing the old dirty songs, and often, in my hours between duties, I would stroll across to the green-grassed park opposite the hospital, where they lay about in groups, or sat on the white-painted benches in their hospital blues. Somebody would be sent off to a nearby bottle store for some beer, and we would sit chatting, singing, and drinking beer until it was time to get back for supper.

Discipline was not too strict, because these men were in very serious trouble anyway, so it wasn't a good thing to be too hard and military about things. I enjoyed those post-war years, when the convalescents relaxed their over-strained bodies and prepared themselves for the future. No one hurried them, we didn't want to have them feel that the war was over and their jobs were done so they had to fuck off now, nothing like that. We wanted them to feel well enough to go. At least, that was my attitude. I would wait until a fellow would come up to me and say: "Listen Frankie, don't you think it's time I got off my arse and pissed off the hell out of here?" Even then, I would say: "You're almost ready, just a few more weeks to make quite sure and then we'll let you know." And it was with a genuine regret that I allowed them to escape from me. I had become like an old hen and it was hard for me to see them struggling off into the traffic.

Every week or so there were people to drive to the station, to be seen off on trains to far places, some never to be heard from again, real friends by now, because of the length of the convalescent periods, in some cases as much as twenty years. There were funerals to attend, because many of the Pretoria and Johannesburg men, and the others from the dozen or so reef towns, within thirty miles of the hospital, didn't quite make it, so they were readmitted and we let them back in the old wards where they could die amongst people who had not forgotten what they were dying for.

A lot of them would ask to be buried in their home towns, without fuss, but others wanted the full military thing, in the cemetery at Voortrekkerhoogte, with the last post and a volley fired over the flag-draped coffin.

I went to all the funerals of my friends. I never bought great big bunches of flowers, just a sprig or two, depending on the season, a little something that I made up myself and added to the grand wreaths that others had sent. I always wrote, on my card "with love from Frankie." That was the best I could do. In my mind I heard their mock-solemn voices singing the old, sad songs of the war years, and the filthy ones, when the coffins were let down, and I always lingered on a bit after everybody had left, saying a few dirty words, just anything that came into my head, to help them shoot through. Many of the fellows would come in for after-care or check-ups, because there were lots of legal things to attend to after the war as well. Pensions for the disabled were worked on a pro-rata basis which meant evaluating the chances of recovery as well as the sort of work that they would be able to do. Naturally there were many who were all set on never working again, hanging onto their disabilities for dear life, wanting their full disability pensions to stretch into infinity, but they were a minority. Generally they wanted to get back to useful work as soon as it was possible for them to shake a leg or flex a muscle.

The shell-shock cases from the psychiatric department were the most difficult ones to judge. They would remain registered as out-patients, coming in for regular treatment, some of them drooling at the mouth, for a quarter of a century after the war had ended, drawing their disability pensions, when we knew perfectly well that they had been cured years ago. But there was nothing that could be done for them or about them. They had chosen shell-shock, faked and prolonged, as a life style, and that was that, an awful waste of what could have been good, solid men, mewling and puking and shitting their pants, quite unnecessarily, just to get a little free pension money, barely enough to keep them in any sort of comfort.

The officials could never take a hard line with these men, and we all had to keep our mouths shut. "It may just be genuine, but we don't know quite enough to be a hundred per cent sure," was the official line. Thank heaven I didn't have much to do with such people. When they went out of my ward they had their self-respect and their ambition, most of them, and the ones who would dwell on their war experiences as their only conversation would have been like that anyway, whether they had been wounded or not.

I suppose that the war had been the highlight of the lives of so many people, that it isn't strange that armchair soldiers are a fact of everyday life and conversation for twenty-five years after the peace treaties. In these post-war years the Americans and the Germans had made fantastic strides in cosmetic surgery and physiotherapy, two subjects that were in my particular field of interest. Great new exercise machines that turned the wasted flabby flesh into working muscle arrived by the Dakota-load. Virtually every week or two something new was added to the things that the men could do to strengthen broken backs and necks, spinal injuries, paralysed limbs and immobile arms, legs, fingers, hands, toes, feet and ankles, all the joints that could be made active again by the use of one or other machine, and men whose recovery would normally have taken many years were speeded on their way to complete mobility within a very short time. Others only regained the use of their limbs partially, but to a greater degree than had been foreseen. It was truly a time when miracles of guts and inventiveness gave new life where the chances had been very slender.

It was the most rewarding thing, I remember, to see a man who had been bedridden for a number of years, slowly recovering, going through all the stages, from stretcher to wheel-chair to crutches. One of the most touching days of my entire life was the day that Charlie Kruger, who had always needed a bedpan, propelled himself to the toilets, went inside, on his crutches, and stayed ten minutes. I got worried about him and went to the toilets. I knocked at the closed door and called out: "Charlie, are you all right?" There was a little silence, and then a delighted yell from inside.

"All right?" he asked triumphantly. "Am I all right? Why by-Jesus I've just wiped my own arse. How's that for being all right?" Such little miracles made my life rewarding, worth living, for all those years. I knew, naturally, that I would not be able to stay on in that job permanently. But the army seemed reluctant to let me go.

After the death of my great friend General Grové his successor, a Brigadier Vlok, treated me with great understanding and kindness. I sometimes suspect that I had been left to him in General Grové's will, as a legacy of the great days. One day he even asked me to put myself in the hands of the surgeons again, for one more go at getting my face to look pretty, but by that time I had become used to myself as I was, and I didn't really want to take the chance. With plastic surgery involving a great deal of scar tissue, of which most of my face was composed, the danger of the already impaired blood circulation being even more damaged was always present, and I could just possibly come away with skin grafts that did not take, or with the blood circulation stopped. In any case, I had grown used to my ugly old face, and I wore it without worrying too much. My job rarely took me outside, and I could always wear a reasonably opaque veil so as not to frighten children in the streets.

A lot of men had made love to me, and I had felt needed and wanted both as a person and as a woman. It had all been my choice, and I wasn't too miserable, except that my patients kept dwindling over the years, and there was less and less to do, but always enough to justify keeping me in my job.

A peace-time army was also being built up, with twenty thousand or so men joining for a year of military training every January. In addition, there was the regular permanent force, and accidents do happen to people in training for the violences of war. Not so many serious ones though, very few of the "permanents" of my hey-day, just a fracture here and there, or a bit of perforated intestine or muscle, a burn, or a bit of shrapnel in the bum.

And a lot of overturned cars on Saturday nights, chasing home before the expiry time of their passes, a few fatalities, a few drunken accidents, some assaults, and, very occasionally, from one of the borders, a mysterious patient who could not be questioned but who talked freely about the terrorism that was building up. Nothing that looked like a war from the hospital point of view, though.

The physiotherapy machines that were brought in by the hospital authorities during those years were of particular interest to Dawid Cilliers, and often he and Maryna would come through from Skeerpoort to inspect the latest exercisers and other inventions from England, America, Germany, Japan and Italy. He would have long conversations with Brigadier Vlok and other officers about cure-percentages and effectiveness. He was tremendously knowledgeable, and often he would go into the workshops to suggest a modification that he had found useful. He and Maryna became quite familiar figures in the hospital, sometimes calling as often as twice a month. I knew that these physiotherapeutic study sessions of his were also excuses to see my sister in private, either before or after they had been to the hospital, and, knowing by now the circumstances of his marriage, I had no moral judgements to make. Their lives were their own, and they were entitled to some of it, for themselves. Once, Maryna asked me what I thought about things.

"You don't ever mention anything, Maria," (she could never get herself to call me Frankie) she would say. "You *are* my little sister, you know, and I have no secrets from you. Surely you know what's going on between Dawid and me, that we love each other? Are you disappointed, or hurt, do you think I'm making a mistake? I'd like us to talk about it sometime. It's lonely without someone to chastise, criticise, perhaps approve."

"It's none of my business," I answered. "But I think he's very nice. I've never thought of marriage as a certificate either. And I'm the last one to criticise or make any comment at all. I haven't been all that angelic myself."

Well, God forgive me again, because that was just blatant bragging, as if I wanted to be quite sure that Maryna would make no mistake about it. I had had my fair share of men, and nobody need feel sorry for me.

11

MINA

From that day when he took his first steps Baas Daan started to show that he was not just a carrot, like everybody called him. A carrot can't walk, not even two steps. So I never again want to hear anybody saying that he is sommer a vegetable, or I will get the hell-in. Suddenly, the poor little bugger could start to learn to walk, and all the things they said about him were proved to be a lot of nonsense. He could walk and if a man can walk he can do a lot of other things as well.

Baas Daan seemed to be trying. I could see it, somewhere, underneath him, he was trying to get out of the thing that was keeping him imprisoned. His face started getting what you call expression. It was the same face, and only the eyes moved around, but now that I knew he would be able to walk one day I also knew that there was a real person behind those eyes. And all the stories that he couldn't feel anything was rubbish. I knew all along that there was nothing really wrong with him, because if a person can suck at a breast and swallow the milk he is already a person.

It's a big pity that Missus Bettina never tried to feed the poor little bugger. If she had she would have felt a lot better about him, maybe she would never have told the Oubaas to make his bed in another room, away from her, and maybe all the other things wouldn't have happened.

Baas Daan first took a few steps when he was fourteen years old, and after that the Oumiesies Bettina, Oubaas Dawid, Doctor Cloete and me, walked with him every day, trying for hour after hour to get him to walk again. It was quite a few weeks before it happened. Every day we would first put his feet in the flat pedals that went just like a man walking, like dragging flat feet. And every day he would be in this machine for a long time, like we were trying to make him do things sort of automatic. Then we would take him out of that machine, and he would be put into another one, that didn't move the feet, and his feet would drag along the ground.

This went on for a long time after the first little walk, like I said, a few weeks, and then, one day, when we had transferred him over to the machine without the flat pedals, and we gave it a push to make it move, he walked with it again. Still on flat feet, like he couldn't lift them off the ground at all, but that was all right, because we didn't have a walking machine that lifted the feet, only one that moved flat. Now he was shuffling.

I think that day he took nearly fourteen steps before his feet started dragging again, and we were all very excited, everybody was, except Missus Bettina, who would not allow me to talk about the Kleinbasie and his exercises. I tried it the first time, and got shut up for my trouble, so I didn't tell her, only the Oubaas who phoned Doctor Cloete and told him.

The next afternoon they were both there, and again the Kleinbasie walked, and I knew that he was over his walking trouble now. We had managed to bring the life that had been hidden deep inside his legs to the outside, and now he would be able to walk, all it needed was patience, and I've got lots of that, more than any person I know about. So, for years, I walked him day after day in his machines, because the Oubaas was very busy with the farm and he just did not have time every day. The Oubaas knew that he could trust me to work hard with the Kleinbasie's walking and all the other exercises with the machines.

Some of the machines came by aeroplane all the way from Italy or London, places like that. Some of them you just strap in the Kleinbasie and you plug him and the whole machine into the electric on the wall, and you switch on, and the whole thing moves, and gives you a lot of exercise all over the body, it's better than running five miles, the exercise you get from a machine like that, the way it throws you all around, with your arms moving and your fists closing and opening and your fingers stretching and your neck turning this way and that way and up and down. It also exercised the legs and the ankles and the feet. No, that was another machine, also electric, that did the bottom part of the body, from the waist down.

For hours and hours, every day, the Kleinbasie would get his exercise. If he didn't get his exercise, Doctor Cloete told me, he would grow up to be a big fat blob, like a jelly-fish that spreads all over, and he would die. But I knew I could keep him alive because the machines gave him all the big exercises that you get from running or chopping wood or digging in the garden.

So he grew up a nice strong boy, and I rubbed every inch of fat off his body, and years before the electric machines the Oubaas had built other ones that were just as good. It was because we had faith in the Kleinbasie that we kept him alive, when others would have called his case hopeless and let him die. That is how it went over the years.

What made the Oubaas do all that he did I don't know, because he is a farmer, and he knows how silly it is to keep a bad calf in the herd, so I don't know about him. I wanted a baby to feed because mine had died and my breasts were big and hurting me. Once you have had a child at your breast it is yours also, and you will fight for it like any animal will fight for its little ones. You will do all you can for that child, all of your life, to make sure that, even if it had only a one per cent chance of being a person one day, like Baas Daan was when he was a baby, he will be given a full go at the chance. I always say, a chance is a chance, it's better than no chance at all, so take it if you can, because you won't get anything more from life.

So the years made him well, as well as it was possible for a person to get who can't see or hear, and who could only make noises like the grunting of a pig. He started walking, and, even in his sleep, we could sometimes see his feet jerking about, like a dog dreaming it is chasing rabbits. This was another of the miracles of those years, because I could swear that the Kleinbasie was dreaming that he was walking. This meant that there were things going on in his head, something that had never seemed possible before, because we all thought that there was nothing in his head anyway, with no way for it to get in, through the eyes and the ears. There were other signs too, that a change was happening in his head.

One day I went to the funeral of my uncle Piet Stolp, who had died of old age when he was seventy, and my auntie Kate was there, being the widow. She didn't think seventy was so old that you had to go and die of old age, but my uncle Piet Stolp had always been a very headstrong man and you couldn't tell him anything. If he thought that seventy was the right time to die of old age he would do so. He found it in the Bible, you know, the allotted span of three score years and ten, and nothing would make him wait another couple of years.

Anyway, there he was dead of old age and I was standing by his widow, being the nearest woman relative she had, with the bottle of smelling salts. This is a bottle of strong smelling salts you buy at the chemist and you use it when people are at funerals. Just as the coffin is going down in the grave and everybody is singing their hearts out the nearest woman relative of the widow takes the smelling salts out of her handbag, then, when the widow looks like she is going to faint, you open the bottle and wave it about under her nose. That way she doesn't faint, because the smelling salts fixes up fainting at funerals.

After I had come back from the funeral with my bottle of smelling salts in my handbag I took a sniff at it and Jesus Christ it was strong stuff. It also is so strong that it makes water come out of your eyes if you hold it there long enough, but it is wrong to hold it too long because before the tears come you feel like you want to choke, so you have to cough. Any case, you don't ever have to make tears with smelling salts at a funeral for coloured people because they cry very easily at such times, because that's the right thing to do.

It gave me the idea to see if Baas Daan (I must stop calling him the Kleinbasie now, because he's a big man) could smell really strong stuff. We had never tried him with anything like smelling salts, so when I took the top off the bottle and waved it under his nose, just like I had done at the funeral, that afternoon, under my auntie Katie's nose, Baas Daan pulled his head away as if he didn't like the sort of burning smell that was going up his nose. The next day when the Oubaas got home I told him about it, and showed him. He phoned Doctor Cloete who came around straight away and I did it again. They both stood looking at Baas Daan with big eyes, because they felt like a pair of fools, specially the blerrie doctor who should have tried it years ago, and now they had a simple black woman who showed them how to make sure that a man like Baas Daan can smell like other people.

So we knew that he could smell, definite. All the years me and Missus Bettina had worried about his food and the stuff we should put in his room, and she had planted stuff with nice smells all over the garden, and the food she had made for him was lovely, with all sorts of nice herbs and gentle spices. Not the burning curries that Adam Long likes so much, but more the quiet tasting stuff, like a few drops of wine and a pinch of thyme, you know.

Our trouble was that we had never had a real go at anything really strong, so that we could see if it burned his mouth or made his nose sore, like smelling salts, but now it was started, so we did a whole lot of tests. Without Missus Bettina knowing I put some soft cooked red chillies in his soup one day, and when he had finished eating I could see that there was trouble with his mouth, the way he kept on licking his burning lips and the way he liked the drinking pot of cold iced milk I put to his mouth. He drank the whole lot down, with the Oubaas and the doctor watching. I tell you, if Missus Bettina had ever found out what we were up to she would have knocked hell out of us. She didn't like anything to be said about Baas Daan to her, but she didn't like people to do anything to him either.

Baas Daan had to be cleaned, and fed, and exercised, and put to bed. That was all so far as the Oumiesies was concerned. I think the doctor and the Oubaas were both scared of her. After we had given him the chillies to eat they told me not to talk about it to anyone. The doctor said that Baas Daan was improving steadily over the years, and that he still had a chance. Things were happening all over the world, and one day it would be safe to take him to one of the big hospitals where they could study his case and see what they could do to help him. I thought that was all blerrie nonsense, because it was as plain as the hand before your face that Baas Daan was going to be all right, given time, and the exercises, and the right food. I had no worries.

Doctor Cloete said many a time, that he had written to a lot of doctors all over the world about Baas Daan, but they all said they had never heard of a case like him, and the only way they could maybe help was if the patient was brought to them so that they could make all sorts of tests to see just what the trouble was. Any blerrie fool could tell you what the trouble was. He was deaf and dumb and blind, and he didn't want to know anybody's troubles. But he had started to like walking, so he was walking, and he had found out that food could be strong or weak, and smells could make you feel like choking. All new things because we'd never tried them out before.

I was happy the way things were. We didn't have to go buggering around all over the world just to parade Baas Daan before a lot of doctors who couldn't even speak our language, English and Afrikaans and Tswana is our language, and what does a Italian know about our stuff, and the germs that we got here, that they haven't got in Italy. I mean, it stands to reason, Baas Daan got his sickness here in Skeerpoort, and we got our own doctor here who knows every germ in the district. What can a doctor in Italy do for him that Doctor Cloete can't, hey?

I couldn't talk like this to them, and I didn't want to tell Adam Long about it, because he's got his own problems lately, in his left shoulder, he says it feels like a needle. I asked Doctor Cloete about it and he says if Adam Long picks up his arm and it feels like a needle in the joint then he's got rematics, and the best thing for rematics and artritis is to drink a couple of Bayer aspirins or even a Aspro or two, but not too many or they will make you sick.

I told Adam Long about what the doctor said but Adam Long looked at me like I was stone mad and he said to me: "Don't talk shit man. You know what aspirins and Aspro costs, don't you, almost as much as a blerrie bottle of wine man. No, if it's the rematics I'll just stay with it until I'm used to it, and I'm not cutting down on my wine." I told Doctor Cloete about this and he said the wine was bad for people.

Sometime in the war, I think it was between 1943 and 1944, Oubaas Dawid used to go a lot to Pretoria, to the soldiers' hospital there, and he always used to go with Nurse Maryna van der Kolff, because her sister worked there; the one with the dead face that was in the motor car accident near Kimberley that night that all the children and the two teachers got killed. It was in the newspapers and they still talk about it.

At the hospital Oubaas Dawid got lots of ideas for new machines and they all came to us, and we tried everything. It was all electric but we got Escom power on the big lines from Pretoria, so the whole farm had all the electrics that it wanted, and even the engines that pumped water to the orchards and washing out the milking sheds was all electric. We even made up some new swear-words, like, in the old days, we would say "your granny's poes man" if we wanted to swear at somebody in a really nasty way, but with Escom power all over, we used to say "your granny's electric poes."

But that time there was a electric machine for everything and people called electric-shins came from Pretoria and put wires all over the house. Our old electric, with the engine in the genner-ayter room was just for electric lights, but suddenly all the hot water came from the taps without fire, and the slow combustion stove went to the scrap-yard. There was everything electric, and new electric stoves and pressing irons in the kitchen, and a fridge that just worked without parafien. All of the new machines that came by the passenger train to Skeerpoort was also electric, and I just put Baas Daan on them, and strap him in, and switch on, like I said.

So there was me looking after him, and I could see that he was doing very well. I knew all that there was to know about him, and I could see that he was getting more right in his body, with smelling and feeling things, and tasting, and lots of other little ways. He was getting to look right. He was not keeping his mouth open so much. He kept it closed for a long time. And a whole day would go by without his head falling on his chest or his shoulder.

But the fingers and the toes, too, were feeling out, like sending messages, and I put the round and the other shapes of wood that the Oubaas had made for him to play with in his hands, and he would hold them, and touch them and his fingers would go over them and feel them out, so I knew that he was beginning to come out of that fright that they had given him, and that it had taken a hell of a lot of time and a moer of a lot of hard work, but his body was going to be O.K.

Steadily, he had been coming right, every year we could see something new that was happening to him. But there were some things that I never told his father or the doctor. These were the things that were none of their business. If I had told them about these things they would have taken a lot of him away from me, and that was something that I did not want. As the problems came up, I tried all sorts of things until I knew how to handle them.

You must know, I suppose, that as the years went by I still had to clean him after he went to the toilet, even if he managed to go by himself. I tried for many years to train him to clean himself, after he was a big man. I didn't mind because for me he never became a big man while he needed me to look after him. He was always my baby. I never thought to myself, like Silver once said: "Ag man, he's just a big grown-up baby really." I never thought like that. He was just a baby to me. While he needed me to clean him up and feed him.

And this is the sort of thing that I never spoke of to the Oubaas or to the doctor, because I knew that the moment I told them that there was some sort of problem they would become a pair of blerrie busy-bodies and start getting in a lot of people that I don't want in the house, because they don't know how to look after a person like Baas Daan. You know why? I'll tell you. Because there isn't a place in the whole world where you can go to learn how to look after a patient like Baas Daan. Because there isn't anybody else like him in the world to learn from.

I have heard Doctor Cloete talk to the Oubaas, and I know that Baas Daan is the only one of his kind in the whole world. So there he was. He had these fingers that were looking for things to feel, and sometimes he would feel the stones, the sand, and the leaves of the trees, because he was allowing himself to come out into the world. I know that he always had feelings in his fingers, even after he went away from the world the day he was buggered up, and I know this because when a baby is hungry he will do things with his little fingers and his tongue on the tit, so I always knew he was all right, but I never told them, because they had broken him.

I didn't want anybody to know more about Baas Daan than they needed to know because their world had made him sore, and I didn't want him to be buggered around any more. I told them all the things that meant that they would buy stuff for him, like a new kind of bunny blanket, and where in the magazines you could buy cotton, or what was best for the skin, and all that stuff. I even told them that he could smell and taste, so that they could be extra careful about getting for him the nicest food and the most sweet-smelling stuff so that those things could be part of his poor blerrie life. But there was a lot of stuff that I told them buggerall about.

They don't fool me, the Oubaas and the Doctor and Missus Bettina. They must have known what was going on there in the back room, the new one that the Oubaas had built after Baas Daan could walk, the one with the wire and the two rows of plants that had all those beautiful smells, it was like taking a walk in heaven, if you closed your eyes and walked there. People who can build such things can also see that Baas Daan was a grown-up man, and they knew that he was still being washed and powdered, and his body rubbed, by a black girl called Mina, in the room that they had built for him so that he never hurt himself. But I wasn't going to tell them anything, and if they had ever had the cheek to ask me about those things, I swear to God I would have told them to bugger off and mind their own business.

I didn't mind what happened, because he was just a baby to me, but a lot of people would have thought that it was a wrong thing, with a black girl doing what I had to do to a big white man, every four hours. I mean, look, you see, he had a big pair, that I had watched grow, and he had the other thing too, the same size as a real man's, and sometimes it looked like it wanted to do what God meant it for, you know, so, I used cold water there, and I never warmed my hands or the cloth when I worked with him there, with the cream or the powder. I always did it quickly too, and I never looked except to see if there was anything wrong.

Sometimes it would become big, but I didn't take any notice, and sometimes he would have his hand there, you know, holding it, but I never punished him for that, because I reckoned if he had something to hang onto then it was all right, because he didn't have a lot from his life. I sometimes wondered if I shouldn't just fix him up, you know, but I couldn't do it, because he was my own child by then, and we black people don't do things like that, even if you do. I was afraid, also, of what God would do to me. Because he couldn't say "no thank you" or "yes please" so it would have been like sort of raping him, and I didn't want that on my mind.

He couldn't do anything much for himself, in those big grown-up years, when he was going from seventeen to thirty, but he could walk, and he walked a lot, all hours of the day or night, with the little silver chain tied to his leather wrist-guard that the Oubaas had made for him. He knew when it was day or night, I know that, because most nights he slept through, and he never passed water or dirtied his bed, because I had had him house-trained like a little dog for many years already, but I never slipped up, and every night and day of his life I was with him, every four hours, except the day that Adam Long and I got married, and that other time when I got so sick that Nurse Maryna and Doctor Cloete gave me a injection so that I fell asleep for two days.

That time Baas Daan was already a big man, and Missus Bettina and Oubaas Dawid looked after him, so I was angry, but I wasn't worried. But those were the only two times that I was not with him every four hours of the day and night.

Sometimes he walked at night, and I wonder if he had found out that he was a person, with a spirit. And on those nights I wondered if he had found out that his spirit could be troubled so that he walked at night, like other worried people.

I used to take a lot of bullshit from people in the location, and the other servants in the house, because they also knew that I was looking after a white man who was grown-up altogether, with all his, I mean, things. I know that some time after he was fourteen years old he had started, you know, doing it, and it was dried on his blankets and things; but I couldn't wash it myself because then that sharp-eyed bitch Silver Adams, the wash-girl, would know something had happened. I only hope she never inspected anything and just chucked the bundles of laundry into the wash bin. Anyway, I would never allow the kitchen people or the farm servants to talk about Baas Daan, but there were a lot of Hotnots in the town who didn't care because they didn't work at the big farm, so they asked me questions, sometimes, but I always shut up like I didn't know what they were talking about. And some of them gave me a hard time with their questions, but I didn't care, because I had my work, and Adam Long.

Now-and-then, when they got to be too full of rubbish, and cheeky, I would say: "Adam Long won't like this," and they would laugh like they didn't care, but they would also stop their nonsense. Because nobody buggers Adam Long around, and Adam Long doesn't like people to bugger me around either. And, Jesuschrist, when he hits you between the eyes you go down, man. But let me tell you that while Baas Daan was growing to be a full size man, and the years afterward, everybody in the village had a new thing to talk about: That a black girl was touching a white man's thing every day, several times. Thank God it's not the sort of thing white people talk about in their houses, only in the lavatory at Baas Fritz Smit's bar, so the white people of the Great House never got to know about that sort of talk, or there would have been a lot of trouble for me.

But look, man, the poor bugger was blind, and stone deaf, and he'd only just started walking properly, so you must see, surely, that there was no harm in it. He didn't even know what he had between his legs, except it must have felt nice to him, but he didn't know what to imagine in his mind, if he had one, so that he could, you know, pull it. Maybe he did and maybe he didn't. It sometimes just spills over, after passing water, and it's sometimes a dream. I don't know if he had anything to dream about, to make him, you know, shoot. I also don't know what the Roman Catholic priests do, and it's none of my business anyway.

Here was this poor bugger, who didn't know anything about buggerall, and every now-and-then you could see that he wanted something, and he didn't even know what it was. I just kept quiet about it, because he was still my baby, and I didn't want them to take him away from me, and if ever anybody had talked about it there would have been trouble. Thank God only the coloured people talked, among themselves, and it never ever got to the ears of the Reverend Doctor George Webb, although he has no business calling himself a doctor, he's worth buggerall, except for preaching and praying. But if I ever had any trouble from him I would have given him a threat, all right, the bugger, old ten bob.

The village had been trained to keep their mouths shut and off Baas Daan, and that, I think, is why there was no trouble about me being his nursemaid and still looking after him like a wet-nurse now that he was a grown-up man. One day I asked Adam Long what he thought, was there a chance that Baas Daan knew what was up down there. But Adam Long says that it's none of my business and none of his, and if he hears I've been trying out things on the poor Basie he'll fetch me such a clout I will never forget it as long as I live.

12

BETTINA

It is 1946. Not only is the war over, but the men are all back. From our village, thank God, few remained behind on the field of battle. Young Jakob Bekker who was to have farmed in the Kloof would not be back. Now that he is dead in North Africa his younger brother Phillippus will take his place. The farm will go on, as the family will. Harry Willemse, from over near the dam, has been missing since 1944, and he is now presumed dead, somewhere in Italy. All the others who baled out of his aircraft, near Bologna, were taken prisoner. His parachute had opened, but after descending into the young olive grove, he had disappeared and was never seen again. But he had three brothers. One had been slightly wounded. They had a large farm at Hartbeesthoek, enough land for ten brothers, so there would be many post-war wives, and children conceived and born on the Willemse farm and the large family would set an empty place for a few years only, on old year's eve, and even that slight habit, redolent of forgetfulness rather than remembrance, would die out. The family, however, would survive into the future, and be happy and prosperous. On the main road to Hekpoort, Alex Brink had come back from the war with a bullet path through both optic nerves, behind the eyes, in front of the brain. Except that he was irreparably blind for the rest of his life, nothing had changed, not even the charm with which he spoke to ladies. That comes of being curious while you are in a tank, and opening the turret to take a peek.

We were not a particularly distinguished area, as you can see, in respect of life given on the battlefields of North Africa and

Europe. Statistically, we were far below the national average, but I am certain that no inhabitant of our area feels any guilt at all. The farms would go on producing crops and babies, and the families would survive into the coming generations.

I am now forty-six years of age, and although I have lived the most sheltered life possible for a woman of my time, when I look into the mirror I see an old woman. I wonder why all these lines have appeared, covering my face and neck, leaving me with the complexion of a dried-up salt-lake in winter, with much of its texture as well. When I bath, I see my two perfect, girlish breasts, and I am often tempted to take a razor and cut them off so that they will no longer accuse me with their impertinent forwardnesses.

I sit here, thinking, wondering if I have deserved the punishment that I have meted out to myself. After all, it was only a moment, and not a very enjoyable one at that. It was a mistake that I had recognised virtually immediately. As a result, I have denied myself the pleasure of my husband's body and of his company. He had always been willing enough to be my husband in all respects, and he had told me so often enough. The rejection had been all mine. The punishment of myself had been justified in my own eyes every time I had looked at my poor son. But my self-chastisement need not have hurt my husband.

And yet there was no other way. I could not have given of myself, to him, without experiencing the pleasures of his loving. So there was no way out for me. I had given him his freedom, and to this day I have no idea as to whether he has taken advantage of it. He has often been away from the farm, sometimes for a whole weekend, but always for perfectly plausible reasons. Another thing: I did not think that I had the right to question him, I never spoke to him much, anyway. I was curious, and jealous, because I had never stopped loving him. My punishment for my crimes was my self-denial.

I have read much of this new science of psychiatry, thinking that I would find some wisdom that would explain the harshness of my conduct towards myself, but it has only strengthened my knowledge of the guilt I feel. I need no analyst to tell me that I have a guilt complex and that before I rid myself of it I will never return to the world of normal people. How can I rid myself of a guilt complex that, in its expression, is the only way I have of telling my people how sorry I am for what I have done to them? I would rather die than feel free of this guilt.

My husband has discussed this matter with doctors, never telling them my name or that it was his wife who was being discussed, so he tells me, and he has begged me, many a time, to stop now, that the punishment I have meted out to myself has to come to an end, and that he would never refer to the trouble again. That, I am afraid, will not help at all, because references to the trouble have invaded our home to the extent of complete dominance. At least, that is how it seems to me.

Now, after my once-reasonable beauty has fled from my face, and Dawid can only see an over-wrinkled woman of forty-six still wallowing in her own guilt, I can understand that he may not want to speak to me too often, because, in any case, I reject his attempts at trying to make conversation with me. Still, in spite of my surly attitudes, he remains kind and courteous, with never a blunt word, except his own particular kind of gentle bluntness. This must be the worst confession of being an ogre ever, but I cannot help my attitudes.

I know that I have become bitter, and that I have wasted my own life. There is no excuse for a waste of life, one would say, until one goes to Daan's place in the thyme and frangipani avenue, where the strange thing that is my son, my own complete creation, shuffles about so pathetically that I could scream and scream and scream. But I am a straight-laced lady, and I keep myself private from all those who attempt to read even the slightest emotion in my face. My crime is my own business, and I have judged myself. I will serve out my sentence to the end. There is not the slightest chance in the world that I will ever grant myself an amnesty.

Life has to go on, I grant you that, and it may be a valid opinion that I am punishing myself too harshly. This is not the case at all, I am alive, but I have allowed myself only the minimums of living, in order that I live as closely to Daan as possible, in his world. I have, for instance, all his life, created for him the loveliest of fragrances, and lately the doctor has assured me that he has a good sense of smell. So I have allowed myself to open some of the perfumes that Dawid often buys for me when he goes to the city. And I have allowed myself to share them with Daan, whereas, in the beginning, I would only give them to him on his night-clothes and pillow-slips. It is a great delight for me to know that there is a part of his world that he can know and enjoy, and that all my experiments with food, plants, herbs, shrubs, flowers and the like have, over the years, made their impact on his senses, as his mind came out of its self-imposed prison.

He had been, in the light of what I know now, in a state of hysteria resulting from being treated so murderously the day I tried to destroy him and this had caused his withdrawal. There had been physical damage as well, and he would be a spastic for all his life, as far as we knew, because no doctor had ever invented the kind of surgery that would be needed to cure him in that respect. It was impossible to evaluate the results of the other more subtle injuries, caused by the episode which had shocked him to the extent that he had withdrawn from life, in complete terror, with his still-thinking mind. He had not wanted his brain to work, so he had allowed himself to inhabit a world akin to catatonia, in which he had lived for many years. There was no real dramatic moment when he emerged out of it again. Over the years healing consciousness allowed gradual, almost imperceptible improvements, as if it were afraid that my sudden revelation of personality would again be met with violence, injury, and pain. I like to think that my flavours and perfumes helped to bring him back to the world with their gentleness and the love that had gone into them.

Now he is twenty-five years of age, and the war is over. I sit here, often, pretending to myself that he had known all the lovely and sinful years of his youth. Then, I pretend, he had gone away to war, and that he was now a little shell-shocked, and all we had to do would be to care for him and love him, and the shock would disappear. The great doctors would find miraculous cures for the brain in bondage, for the unseeing eyes, and for the broken ears.

Often, just to keep me a little sane, I have indulged in these day-dreams, fantasies of hope I call them. But I know by the terrors of the nights that my brain is also deteriorating, not just my beauty, and although I have dreadful things to relate, of the moments when I know that I am going away from this world into the horrible world of the lunatic, yet I make no attempt to bring myself, as it were, to my senses.

I had murdered, for a long time, my son's brain, and it would be only right if I too were to suffer a like punishment. I feel a necessity to destroy my eyes and to pierce my ears, but then I will no longer be able to do the few small things for him that I am able to. It is wonderful to know that I have a use in his life. If taking my own sight and hearing would be of any help to him I would not hesitate to sacrifice them gladly for his sake. But it seems to me, at the moment, that it would be a little silly to deprive him of my cooking, and my sense of perfume, that are probably the only pleasures he has in life.

Now that he is in his middle-twenties, a grown man, I often wonder if I should repeat the sexual experiment that I had attempted when he had been an infant, when I had tried, by kissing him, to bring him to an erection of his private part. But I know that I cannot do it. Now, as I turn back the pages and read the faded words on that yellowed page, written so many years ago, I know that I lack the daring to again repeat the kind of immorality of which I was capable then.

I suppose I was fresh with courage then, even a youthfulness, but I have, with the years, become dried out, and I should hate my wrinkled, cracked lips to be the first to pleasure him there. Apart from that there is the matter of incest, to which I gave little heed when he was an infant. But now that he is an adult, and beautiful to look at, handsome as his father, he probably has the same physical features genitally as his father had when we had engaged in that disastrous coupling twenty-six years ago. The thought is just too much for me, and it brings up phantoms and spirits of dead things that have never lived, and I am in terror.

Let me tell you of these terrors. My nights have been lonely now, since Daan is no longer a child in the nursery next to my bedroom. His father built a special place for him some years ago, and we have laid out its garden-walk to fit in with his new way of walking.

The new sergeant at the police station at Thornhill, called Karner, had come to my husband during his first month of duty. He had heard of our son from old Sergeant Hendricks, who had retired after a lifetime on the Hill. The new man was able enough in his devotion to duty, but he was, thank heaven, no stickler to the letter of the law, or Daan would have been in danger of removal. My husband had, many years after, heard of the official "death" that Doctor Cloete, Bertie Theron and the Reverend Doctor Webb had arranged with Sergeant Hendricks, and he had told me about it.

When we had heard that a new man was to take Hendricks's place, I was terrified that the whole thing would be re-opened and that Daan would once again be in official existence. There was a sort of thrill to it also. The mind that is becoming disturbed grasps at straws, and these straws are not always harbingers of sanity. The thought that my son had a chance of living again, even if only in the official records of the country in which he lived, gave me a strange feeling of resurrection for him, as if he was going to be a little like Lazarus, and that he was being given a chance to live again by the change of constabulary on Thornhill. So there was that masochistic aspect too: that he would be uncovered, the official grave opened and the unofficially dead body exhumed to walk again in the corridors of the Union Buildings in Pretoria, where the records are kept. He would exist again, if only in a file that some clerk would be carrying about between the dusty shelves of the population archives. That was one face of the coin.

The other was the aspect of fear: that he would be interfered with again from the official point of view. Since the days of the good Sergeant Hendricks, whom I had easily chased from my home with a broomstick of stout poplar picked from our own grove, the village had changed. We now had a district nurse who was also our registered social worker. A person of some tact, since she had left us alone after a preliminary call. I have always been afraid of social workers; people tell me that they are inclined to pry, to open cupboards that had better remain closed. She worked in close liaison with Doctor Cloete, and he had reported to me that he had her assurance that she would not scratch in our affairs.

I believe that it had been more than a year before she had discovered that Daan even existed, and that only because the number one enemy of the village gossips, the Reverend Doctor Webb, had been unable to restrain himself from revealing the secret. I had felt better about it being out in the open as far as she was concerned, because Daan's case fell directly within her sphere of responsibility, and I was grateful that she had allowed the matter to rest in our hands. Knowing, however, that officialdom was about, in modern transportation, first with the arrival of the social worker, and later, when Sergeant Karner took up his duties, I had some bad dreams. The fear of Daan's imminent discovery was something that I could control during the hours of daylight, but the nights were another matter. Although Karner had also promised to let the matter rest in our hands, the terrors of near discovery and the imaginary disasters stalked through my conscious fantasies, at night, as well as my uncontrollable dreams.

These poor, innocent, well-meaning people became ogres in my night-time travels in the worlds of fear, and it was with difficulty that I managed to be polite to them whenever we met in the village. They represented officialdom and the long corridors of nightmares, they and my son, always being dragged off, by them, into some enormous vista without end or horizon. Long black plains ringed by white hills and the most leaden of grey skies, with no hope of arrival, ever, at any place at all. Just a ceaseless dragging of my son over these enormous vistas of the mind to places of torment that lay far beyond comprehension by even my over-active imagination.

I am sure that both Sergeant Karner and the Van der Kolff woman must have been quite charming. Her one visit to me when we had taken tea on the porch had gone well enough, and she was obviously a person of some background, although she had appeared to control her speech with just a little difficulty, as if her natural way of self-expression were a little inhibited. But I seem to have that effect on people. They may be full of natural good spirits and in relaxed mood when, should I appear among them, something of the gaiety of life goes out of their normal conversation.

I know what it is. My whole adult life, since the birth of my son, has been unsmiling. It is something that has only recently struck me. No one has seen me smile for all those years, and the muscles that cause people to smile have probably become as atrophied as my son's brain must be by this time.

I keep telling myself, lately, that it would be only polite of me to invite the social worker to my home again, for tea, but something prevents me from doing so, and I must confess here that it is not a good thing to judge a person as I have done to her. She must be completely innocent of being a threat to my home. I even have her assurance, diplomatically conveyed by our family doctor, that she would leave us alone, with our secret intact. And yet I feel her presence as a vague sort of threat in my waking hours, and as a direct one in my dreams.

I am afraid of these people. Their capacity to do good is equalled only by the harm that can come of their good deeds. But she has, in her own way, managed an indirect infiltration into these affairs, by means of my husband, and his great interest in physiotherapy. He had always been determined that Daan's body would not waste away, and that, if possible, he would be made to walk and to perform other tasks that normal bodies are capable of. So he had consulted the Van der Kolff woman, and found that she had a sister working in the military hospital in Pretoria, who knew of most of the new advances in this science. They had often gone to Pretoria together, where my husband spent many hours in the company of a General Grové, who was head of the hospital. There he had learned of all of the newest techniques for exercising dormant muscles and tendons. He had ordered many of the new machines from the Continent, and he was proud of the fact that his experience with Daan, and mine, had been listened to by the military doctors, who had commended him for the good advice that he had been able to give them. On occasion, he had spent some time at the hospital, helping to design new modifications, and building them, in order to bring some of the more antiquated equipment up to date. Apart from the wisdom in his natural manner, and his tremendous spiritual strength, my husband had the advantage of willing, strong and skilful hands.

These things happened during the war, and my husband retained his interest in the soldiers at the hospital for many years after the end of hostilities. At least once or twice a week he would go to Pretoria, usually on Saturdays, to do our shopping. I had long since allowed him to take my lists and to telephone the appropriate orders that would re-stock our shelves. These he would pick up, and also go to the market place to study new trends in packaging and transportation of farm produce, because he was one of those people who would not allow any activity in which he was engaged to become out-of-date.

Saturday was his study day, and often he would stay over in Pretoria for the night as well, in order to complete some project on which he was busy at the hospital, or one of the other clinics in which he had an interest at the time. I often wondered how he found time to do all the things in which he had an interest.

His mind raced far ahead of mine. Once, I allowed him a look into my private world of the Eastern Meditative Religions, and I was amazed at his knowledge of the subject. He even had some books in his room, which I of course never entered, which he gave me to read. I would not, however, allow any further discussion on the subject, as I felt that the reasons for my interest had very little to do with religion as such. My only purpose in studying these books had been to allow me to shut myself from the world, so that I might join Daan in his prison.

Often, I think I saw my husband looking at me over the dinner table with despair, in the days before my total withdrawal, when we still took our meals together. The despair was because, as he put it, "The life that we once had a chance of sharing, there isn't much left of it, you know Bettina." He had said this with a fair amount of urgency in his voice, as if he had a real need to penetrate my defences, my walls of guilt. As I write that, I think of how close the word "guilt" is to "gilt," it is difficult to make them sound like different words, but there is such an enormous world of difference between them. How I would have loved to be gilt and golden to my man, instead of the guilty, prematurely-aged woman who shared his table.

I knew that, when he spoke of the little time that was left of our lives, he was referring to the way I looked. There was nothing to speak of left of my face, and the useless, firm breasts would have looked grotesque to any man who had to see my face and torso in one point of view. That was during the war, about 1942, I think.

"I have told you, Dawid," I answered him, "that you must make a life for yourself without my physical presence. But now that is also an antiquated request, because I find, more and more, with each passing year, that my mind is also withdrawing."

"But don't you want to come back to the world?" he asked. "There's so much to live for, and we're only in our early forties. It's what Doctor Cloete calls the prime of a man's life, and it's even better for a woman. Why don't we try, just once more, to bring about a new life for ourselves? Those old matters are dead and buried and they need never concern us again. Why can't we try?"

"No," I said, "I couldn't. It would be impossible. Please Dawid, I don't ever think of my life in those terms any more. You're opening wounds that have bled enough."

"One night," he said. "One night, don't be surprised if I come to your bedroom and rape you, just to show you how wrong you are. I'm sure I can wake you up again. I'm sure there's still some feeling for me, somewhere in you."

We were sitting at opposite ends of the long yellow-wood table. We always ate by candlelight, and he was ever courteous to me, so I was amazed at his suggestion. My reaction was quite uncontrolled.

"I love you, Dawid," I told him, "more than Daan or God. But if you ever touch me in that way I'll kill you. There's none of that left in me, or for me. I have denied myself the pleasure. It is my atonement. It is all I have, my nun-hood. Please respect it, because if I have a soul at all, my restraint is a very large part of it. Can't you see, Dawid, I may not feel pleasure again, I have forfeited the right to it, and it's something that I have done by myself. It is my only possession, can't you see?"

He sat back in his chair, not at all shocked, and closed his eyes. "I'll try," he said.

You may think that it is easy for a natural spinster, straight-laced and without feeling, to deny a husband of Dawid's attractions. I was not a straight-laced person. I only appeared to be one. I was, in my mind, for all the years of my chastity, a woman like any other, and I experienced all the desires of any normal person. I believe, even more than the normal desires, because mine were tempered, made finer by guilt.

It was not easy to go to bed at certain times of the month, when my sexual needs were at their most urgent, knowing that a wonderful husband was needing me only a few yards away, down the corridor, in his own bed. I pictured him in his bed, remembered him as he had made love to me in the golden days of our marriage, his kindness, his gentleness, his quiet consideration for all my needs. I remembered every detail of his body and every movement he had made, torturing myself with a desperate hurt. But I would not touch myself to obtain release, and I would drive these sweetest desires from my mind by replacing their images with that of Daan in his worst days.

There were the uncontrollable dreams over which I could exercise no discipline. These took the form of my actually having intercourse, usually with the sort of monster that inhabited my nightmares as well. Here, in these sleep-ridden nocturnal adventures, my mind and body, having been released into the realms of gross fantasy by exhaustion and sleep, found a kind of physical life that was unbelievable in its variety, monstrous and evil. These ogres lurked, genuinely, beneath my so-called straight-laced spinsterish exterior. They were part of my life, and if they existed deep down in me, where I could not reach them or exorcize them, there was nothing I could do except pray that they would stay where they were; too far down to do any real harm to those around me. About myself and my own immortal soul I had long since despaired. The awful experiences of my sexual dreams, the heinous privates of the fiends who gave me such thrilling pleasures as they penetrated me with their vile, diseased lusts and emissions, were part of me, I could not deny them. Somewhere in me, in my soul, these things lived. They were my foul husbands, my half-decomposed lovers. I tried to banish them from me. I read every word in the Bible and prayed incessantly. I hurt myself down there where they took their ghastly will of me, so that I would be conscious only of pain, squeezing my breasts until the great bruises, left by my fingers, bled. I tried to abuse myself so that my ghoul-lovers would find only ruins to ravish, but nothing helped, and one night as I hurt myself again and again, I found, to my extreme horror, that I was in the throes of a great and memorable orgasm that tore through me like electricity, making me heave with enormous, uncontrollable spasms that did not want to end no matter how I hurt myself to make it all stop.

At last I lay exhausted. I had read enough to know immediately what had happened to me: In torturing myself for all those years, self-denial and pain had become part of the needs of my subconscious, which is one of the many conditions of masochism. My chastity had been penetrated in my nocturnal wanderings in the evil worlds of fantasy, and I had experienced the rapes of my demons, being awakened by orgasms which quickly died away, with the coming of consciousness, that caused the horrors to leave me. But in trying to hurt myself I had made pain a sensuous thing, and it had taken root so deeply in my personality that I had become a true masochist in the sensual context, able to achieve orgasm through inflicting pain on myself.

Years of torture were to follow this discovery. I was tempted, in the kitchen, to plunge my hands into the boiling fats and oils, to sit on the electric hot-plate, to clasp the elements of the electric fire in my bare hands. I could never go outside without being tempted to slam the door over my fingers, or to twist my ankle on the porch steps. I longed for the tractor to drive over me, the plough-shares to sever my feet, the threshing machine to consume my hands and arms. Even the sight of an ordinary needle for sewing, darning, or knitting made me want to inflict strange tortures on and into myself. But, fortunately, I knew what was wrong with me, so I was able to recognise these awful temptations for what they were. The memory of that dreadful pleasure stayed with me for many years, and probably will for the rest of my life. I continue to hurt myself, but to a degree only. After all, if I could deny myself the delight of Dawid's golden love it was easy to deny myself the orgasms of pain. I was never to achieve any control over my dreams, and I did experience the advances of rapists that came to me when I was in my deepest sleep, but they and their attentions, in retrospect, were so totally loathsome to think about afterwards, that I never failed to recall all the details so that I could purify myself by nausea.

All of these matters were for my own personal experience, to be confided only to my journal. I know of masturbation, and I had practised it guiltily as a lusty schoolgirl. The reason why I have put down, in a fair amount of the most utterly distasteful detail, the elements of my sex life after I had denied myself to my husband, is to make it absolutely clear that no trace of pleasure in sex after that was ever searched out by my own conscious actions. Everything that has happened to me, in that connection, was without my consent and quite against my will. There is nothing in the world that would have flattered me more had the appellation of "dried-up old sinister" been a true and accurate description of the state of my body. I do not wish to over-state the point that I am making here; but you must try to understand the extent of my penance. I find, lately, that I am making perhaps too much use of expressions that properly belong to the Catholic faith. Although I have read the *Lives of the Saints*, a favourite book in our village, and of their self-sacrifices, I must make it quite clear that no such motive lay behind my actions. I am no martyr, not even to myself, and I do not lay claim to sainthood. Even though I would physically seem to have made of myself a martyr it was mere punishment; therefore, spiritually, I am not a saint. No, I am no such thing.

The temptations of St. Anthony or of Christ were completely

different to the horrors of my mind. These things are in me, not superimposed by evil as in their case. They are part of me, welling up from the dark pools of filth that are down in me. True, I did not want to be tainted to this extent, I never deliberately welcomed such things in my life, because the word "purity" has always meant a lot to me. But a pig can't help it if he is a natural wallower in filth, and the dung beetle must roll his little ball homewards. The jackals will feed on carrion and the hyena will consume whatever is foul. There are seed-eating birds and there are the evil vultures. It is no one's fault that they are as they are. What remains is for me to accept that I am as I was made, a spreader of unhappiness and corruption. I had taken a good seed into the soil of my womb and turned it into a bad fruit, and my husband is a good enough farmer to tend to this devastated harvest of his loins. He has worked hard, persevered where any other sensible person would have given up, and finally, now, in his twenty-sixth year, my son walks, breathes in perfume, tastes flavours, and feels pain and, I think, pleasure.

With that word the evil rises up in me as I think of pleasure, this time his, my son's. Is there no way for me to know that he can experience pleasure? I have seen him handle the textures of objects, and their shapes. At times I have seen his hand rub at his privates, as if they were irritated by something. But I cannot speak of it to his nurse, I cannot question her, it would not be seemly to do so. Sometimes I believe it is time for my husband to do something about that black girl who sees our grown-up son with such intimacy, but then I decide to leave it alone until it becomes an issue. It is not for me to say. Perhaps she is able to accept things better than I.

In any case, she has seen him grow, from day to day, and he has been past puberty for almost twelve years now, so it would seem to be fruitless to attempt any action in the matter at this late stage. We have left it, all of us, until it was too late to do anything. Now would be no time to take the actions of twelve years ago. It nags at me, though, the thought that he may have seed that is fertile, and enough feelings for pleasure. I can hardly restrain myself from going to his room at night, ostensibly to wash him, but to see to what extent I may be able to stimulate him. I push it from my mind, with all sorts of excuses, making myself mad with curiosity in the process, or is it desire?

The things that I have written in this journal, recently, make of incest almost a Sunday School Picnic pastime, especially as I have so much justification for indulging in it for my son's sake. Does my son feel pleasure? It would be so wonderful for me to find out, to know, in my heart, that his life is not just all pain or nothingness. I want to ask my husband about it, or Mina, but it does not seem proper to say anything about such an extremely delicate matter, and it might stir up all sorts of mischief. Imagine the social worker girl getting to hear of it, or the police sergeant. What will they do? It must surely be illegal, Mina is not a registered nurse. ls it possible to get her to be registered, to make it legal? Does she know what she is doing when she cleans him? Does she know why I cannot come into his room any more, when she has him naked? What are my true feelings in the matter. Is it curiosity, concern, or lust? I have no pretensions about myself, and all the dishonesties are going away from me.

It is curiosity *and* lust, why fool myself? I have not seen his privates since his thirteenth year, when he was equipped with a small and pointed appendage, and a little wrinkled scrotum, the two testicles that had been hardly visible. What is it like there today, with the blonde hair of his father, curling about like that of some mythological faun, tendrils of the purest, finest spun gold, is it? And I am concerned. Will he ever find a use for what God has given him, is it of use? How can I find out? Is there no way, except to make myself even more horrible, in my own eyes, than I am now? And are these phrases merely excuses for lust, for a desire to add incest to all my other crimes? I frankly do not know. Two, or three years ago, when I still had a lot of control over myself, I would have known. But I know that I don't have that control now, that something in me is bending before the storms that rage about my spirit.

I sit for hours with my head in my hands, just holding it up, as Daan's head used to be held up by a round leather harness with holes, brass-studded, to allow the skin to breathe and to perspire. My head is bursting with anxieties and guilts I cannot name, and my monsters await the nights. Mina used to bathe Daan every four hours, and change him, every night. It was such a solace to me that she was there, and often I would accept that she was watching over me too, but just not saying anything about it. Those nights, when the terrors came, I would lie waiting for her soft footsteps, her whispered murmurings as she nursed my son towards his adulthood. I wonder if she ever knew that her soft steps and sweet words and songs were mine also, not just Daan's? She did a double job, but I was always too shy to tell her that my head had also lain on her breast, and that my ears had heard the quiet, gentle soothing voice that my son's dead ears were unable to hear.

How I long to be able to tell her that the lovely little noises that she had made in the night had not been wasted on deaf ears. But you never know with people like Mina. You tell them something like that and they shy away like frightened horses, as if you have put a finger into a pool of liquid gold, and disturbed it.

I have come to know Mina over the years, and I think I know what she will say and do if ever I bring up the subject of Daan's genitalia. I think she will not answer, and I think she will look me in the eye, unflinchingiy, which, for her tribe, would be about the rudest thing that she could ever do. And she will insult me even further by thinking that I do not know that a Balobedu does not look anyone he has ever respected in the eye.

So it may perhaps be better to leave things as they are. There is another servant in the house, more coloured than black, called Silver. She has been faithful to us for many years, and, having more white blood in her than Mina, it has often been possible to communicate with her in some way, and I feel that she will readily discuss all sorts of personal things should I want to, but I have no desire to do so. She doesn't appear to have Mina's dignity, and I would not like to know her too well. With Mina it is different, I feel, of course I do, that she is Daan's second mother, but that is one of those things that you do not speak of to a Balobedu, one of the tribe of the great rain queen Modjadji, she-who-is-forever-young. Why, even the mighty Zulus feel uncomfortable in the presence of one of the Balobedu, and no Shangaan, no matter how great he has been in battle, has ever set foot in the sacred stockade, or looked at the holy cycad forest.

Now I have the most urgent longing to go to Mina, and to tell her to come to me too, in the night, to see if I am well. I wonder if she will despise me if I do. I will tell her that I have a strange new habit; that I throw the blankets from me, and that I will catch cold and die, and ask her if she would mind just peeping in on me, to see if I am properly covered.

So desperate am I, that I am thinking of doing such an undignified thing. But my mind is leaving me, and I need someone to care for me. I can't ask Dawid, he would sit up next to my bed all night, and attempt to hold my hand, and it would be too wonderful for me. I must deny. I must not feel pleasure. The comfort of Mina's concern, yes, I could go that far as a self-indulgence, but not any pleasure.

So, these years, my own hands have been hurting me. The dreadful scars that I have inflicted upon myself, all the hurt, bruised flesh, lumped and ugly, have bled and festered, and the time has come when I am unable to look at myself in the mirror and see the dreadfully wrinkled face above the bruised and scarred body, with the lovely pink-nippled breasts pointing upwards.

But, while these scars were hurting, I knew that other wounds, of a more durable nature, were opening up somewhere inside me, near to my soul.

13

MARYNA

One day Dawid confessed to me that a strange thing had happened to him, that worried him greatly and that he was ashamed of it. He knew that one cannot be blamed for every thought that goes through one's head, but he was afraid of such things. He had wished, without wanting to, that his wife Bettina would die now, and leave us a little chance of life together.

"And I feel terrible about it," he said. "You and I have been in love for seven years now, and I have never felt ashamed of anything that we have done."

We had first loved each other in 1944, and the year was 1951. Dawid was fifty-one, as old as the twentieth century, and I was thirty-six. I had never thought of myself as a mother, for some reason. I would have liked to have had a baby, but the bitterness of my first love's death had removed thoughts of normality from my mind and my maternal instincts had been held in abeyance for so long that I was, in any case, getting a bit too long in the tooth for motherhood.

As a social worker I believed in letting nature take its course, and there were women who were natural mothers, who could only be truly fulfilled as human beings, by having children, while others did not take exactly the opposite view, but it wasn't such a driving force for them. Not all people are the same, but most women wanted children at some or other stage of their lives, and I was no exception. But to have a baby out of wedlock, in Skeerpoort, in 1951, was out of the question. I had to have my job, because it gave me a reason to be there, near Dawid, which was where I had to be. Near him, for the rest of my life. That was my only need. Strange how we, in the village, all thought of Bettina as being a living corpse, like her son.

I never dared to say anything at all of that to Dawid, and I had kept my promise and stayed out of Daan's life, letting him live and letting them care for him as they wished. The only alternative was a lunatic asylum, in any case, there being no other institution available for his singular case. Being spastic, there was nothing that could be done for him, except physiotherapy, and in that department he certainly had the best possible care. There were, at that time, a few institutions for spastic children, and great advances had been made in their treatment, but, according to the doctors whom I had consulted privately, the problem was Daan's deafness and blindness as well, there being no proper communicative channel through which a definite analysis and diagnosis could be made.

Neuro-surgery was still in its infancy and, as a treatment for spastic conditions, unheard of. I told Dawid all of the medical facts that I could get hold of, but of my own reactions I said nothing. It shocked me, the day he told me of his thought that Bettina would be better off out of the way. He had very seldom mentioned her in my presence, just telling me that she had withdrawn from life because of a deep-seated guilt. Apparently she had felt herself responsible for the condition of her son, as mothers will, and her feelings of inadequacy as a mother had, to a certain extent, caused her to become perhaps a little mentally unbalanced. I don't really know. Adequate medical care for the problems of the Great House could be arranged by Doctor Cloete, and I felt that, in view of my relationship with Dawid, I had better stay in the background on that terrain.

"You know, Dawid," I said. "It's a very common thing. The death-wish. You shouldn't worry yourself about it. People have those thoughts about the ones they love most, lots of times. It doesn't mean anything, it's just one of those thoughts that come up in your mind from time to time, and you can't suppress it because you don't know what's in your mind every moment, anyway."

"No," he said, and I could see that he was deeply troubled. "It isn't like that at all. I know that the thing you're talking about is normal and natural and most people have these little unbidden things coming up in their thoughts. But mine wasn't like that at all. It was a real thought, that I had originated, starting in my conscious mind as I saw her there, last night, at the other end of the table. I wanted to look up and see you, not there, far away, but with your place set next to me, so that I could see you close to me and talk to you."

"You were just a little lonely," I assured him. "Don't let it worry you."

"Of course I was lonely, Ryna," he said. He also called me Ryna now that he had heard my sister Maria use it as my name. "I'm always lonely when I'm away from you. I'm fifty-one years of age, in love, and I know that there's only twenty or thirty years left. That's not a lot of time, when you love someone as much as I love you. It's very short. Even if I live to be a hundred, the time left will always feel short to me. I can't have enough of you. I wish they hurry up and invent something that will give me more life, so that we can be together for longer. I want to stay with you, and marry you."

"Yes, my love," I said. "And that's why you had that thought at the table then, because you're impatient. You mustn't let it trouble you."

"It wasn't just a thought," he said. "It was, well, a murder in my mind. I looked at her, there, on the other side of the table, behind the candelabrum and I wished that she was dead. I looked at her, without any feeling of shame or of sadness. There was no love either, all that is gone. Then I found myself wondering why she didn't die. It was a lapse, without manners. I had, for a moment, lost control of my mind. She looked up and saw the look in my face. She noticed."

"What do you mean, she noticed? Surely you didn't say anything?"

"No," he answered. "I didn't say anything. I just sat there looking at her, and she must have felt my eyes on her, because she looked up and at me. And I know that she noticed, before I was able to change my eyes and face. So now she knows that I don't want her there any more, because what she saw in my eyes was different to what had always been there. She had always seen love, or understanding, or even a little anger, or sympathy in my eyes. But what she has seen now is something else. I don't know how perceptive she is, if she can pin-point the feeling, but she knows that I don't want her around any more."

"Dawid," I said. "I don't want you, ever, to think such things again. You hear? I don't want you to do anything to her. Oh I know it will be easy to have her committed to an insane asylum, or to divorce her, or just to ignore her and take me to your house. But I don't want you to do it. There's been enough unhappiness in that house, and I don't ever want to do anything to hurt Bettina even more than she has hurt herself by going away from you. She must never know about us, and you must never make her feel unwelcome in your home again. Promise me that."

"I can't," he said. "She knows. I don't want to talk to her about it anyway. She doesn't talk to me any more. And she's grown old, you know. She looks a hundred years of age, like someone who can't live another day. But she's wild in her eyes, and strange, and it's been like this now, in there, inside her, for about ten years. I can't get through to her and I can't talk to her. She just sits there, going through the words and motions of being mistress of the Great House to the servants, so that they won't notice anything wrong with her. But she doesn't even give me that little courtesy. Merely a nod to signify that she is ready to hear grace said. Grace, I ask you? What a word to use at a table like that. The servants get the only words that she ever speaks. Even the shopping lists are written out and delivered to me, no longer discussed. Can you wonder that I want her away, when you could be there, warm and living?"

"Dawid," I said. "I'll only ask you once more. Don't ever do anything to hurt Bettina. It could never make us happy. Come to me, at any time of the day or night. Make our love a public thing if you wish, only don't let her get to know about it. I never want to hurt her. It's unreasonable, I know, after what she has done to you I should want to murder her, with you looking on, but I have a feeling about this, that anything we do to her would be wrong, even if we're in the right, doing it. Please Dawid, please, I beg of you."

He promised, of course. Dawid would have promised me the moon if it was his. And I was very happy to notice that he didn't take me up on making our affair (well of course it was a bloody affair, damn it, so no need to start looking for other words) public property.

We had taken an apartment in Pretoria, in a quiet suburb in the east, and over the years I had furnished it for him. He had excuses of all sorts for being in the city for hours and sometimes days at a time, and I regulated my time accordingly. Although my work was supposed to be a 24-hour-a-day business, I was very seldom needed now, as the little community had dwindled. Many people had gone to the cities. There had been a few years of drought and the smaller farmers had gone bankrupt, or had moved elsewhere. Dawid's strong boreholes in the hills had left him unaffected, and his farm continued to flourish.

My services as a district nurse had virtually come to an end with the appointment of an assistant, and welfare work wasn't something for which you had to be on call all the time, not in Skeerpoort anyway. In the cities, of course, things were different, but my case-histories were well-established and the patterns of sociology had established themselves firmly on my graphs and reports. Very seldom was there a deviation from the norm, and all my statistical graphs kept going up in a very slight incline, the way Pretoria liked it.

Dawid and I had had our own way of life together, and very many hours of complete happiness. He was a bold, virile lover, in spite of his middle-age, and when he had overcome his shyness with me he was able to express his needs and desires in the sweet, graphic, uncouth, gentle language that I loved. And, you know, it's funny. They used to call me old "vuilbek" van der Kolff in the old days, at the hospital and the university. It means old "dirty-mouth" because I used such frank language and so many swear-words. But with Dawid I was never able to be dirty mouthed, I loved him too much. I was too sentimental about him. So, whenever I used a little swear-word, or a big one, in passion, or in pain, I would do so shyly, like a virgin. Things got so bad that I once spoke very sharply to my sister Maria when she was in a particularly foul mood and swearing like a trooper. "Listen to her," said Maria to Dawid, "old vuilbek herself, telling me not to use any bloody fucking dirty language." Later, Dawid wanted to know what on earth Maria had meant by her outburst, but I had lied, putting it down to a temper. I had lied about something else to him too, once, and he had believed me. It has been troubling me for some time now, but it's such an old lie, and so many girls tell it, that I think I will be forgiven it, one day in heaven, because it made him happy. After our first night together, that had been like a huge explosion for both of us, he had asked me, one day, if I'd been a virgin when he had taken me that night.

"You didn't take me," I said. "I gave myself, remember?"

"Yes, and then I took what you gave. But it was tight and

virginal. Was it your first time? It doesn't really matter, but I'd like to know."

So I told him a sort of truth, that was a lie. "The sheet took a lot of cleaning, the next day, darling," I told him.

And that is why he believed, all the years of our love, that he had been the only man in my life. I had been careful to tell Maria not to drop a hint of anything she'd known of my past, but she pretended complete innocence of any knowledge at all, the lying little bitch, because she'd caught my cousin and me, in bed, one day when she was eleven.

I had come home from university, on vacation, twenty years of age and the envy of my little sister who had such a long way to go. Anyway, we'd all been so embarrassed that we'd never mentioned the subject again. But I'm sure it's not the sort of thing you forget, catching your sister with her bare bum winking at the moon, at two in the morning, with her own cousin. But she pretended, the sweet thing, to have forgotten all about it. And so Dawid never knew better, or worse. I'm sure it made him happy, although he never said so.

Our relationship was like a sailor's marriage, or that of a fisherman who only came into port for a few hours every week, sometimes for a whole weekend, before sailing again. At least, that's the way I thought of it, because it made the nights away from him seem more bearable, pretending that there was an ocean at the other end of the Magalies mountains, and that he was sailing there, the skipper of course, gathering in some rich sea harvest.

I've never been the complaining type, and I was almost ecstatic about our little apartment, with its rich, lovely old furniture that we had searched for, piece by piece, over the years. The first thing I had moved in was his favourite red leather chair that he had taken a fancy to that first night in Skeerpoort. It was one of the things that made him happy. I have such a long list of the simple things that made Dawid Cilliers happy. I believe it would take a whole exercise book to list them all. He was a man who was most easy to please. I would call him "my love" and he would ask me to repeat it. I'd do so, and he'd say "again, please if you will." That particular little game would keep him relaxed and smiling, looking at me, for a half hour at a time.

Sometimes, when he was troubled, he would make me repeat phrases of need over and over again, as if he couldn't believe his luck, or whatever he called knowing me. This almost childlike need would be wonderful for me too, and the years sped away, far too quickly, and both of us, as I've already said, wished that there was some way for us to put a brake on time.

We did not speak much about the son Daan. Somehow Dawid must have been a little embarrassed at the thought of the grown man in his house, only six years younger than I. Medical things had been taken care of by Doctor Cloete, who had aged quickly after the death of his wife. He seemed to be just hanging on, for some reason he didn't even know about. I think that he and his wife had found a rapport again in their older years, and the little longings that he had expressed towards me in his fifties were replaced by grave courtesies about ten years later. Then, in the year 1952, his wife died, still a youngish person in early middle-age, and he was left widowed at just over sixty. As I have said, many years had passed since he had tried to seduce me, during those first months of my stay in Skeerpoort.

Old Bertie Theron and the Reverend Doctor Webb had discovered chess. At least, that was their reason for not calling at my place in the evenings any more. This made me wonder how much the people of the village knew of Dawid and me. All my potential lovers had, almost overnight, deserted me for other innocent pursuits. I didn't care, for myself, who knew. I just did not want a public scandal for Dawid's sake.

I wonder if I have been successful in hiding my feelings towards him on those occasions when we had to be in the same gatherings; a church function, a political rally, a travelling entertainment, or a dinner. There were the occasional dances too, organised by the people of the village in aid of things like new tennis courts for the school, or a project to renovate the Dutch Reformed Church. The two rival churches had come to expect the entire village to contribute to their causes, and, as the fortunes of the Methodists declined with the dwindling of the English-speaking church-going population, it became quite common for a Methodist function to be attended by more members of the Dutch Reformed Church than Methodists. Eventually, only a few Methodists were left, a matter of eight or so, and some of them not regular church-goers. It became a habit of theirs to congregate in the tiny personal chapel that the Paulsons had built on their farm a century ago.

Dawid had re-decorated and painted it, and he had installed

a gracious little pulpit of his own design and making, so simple that it took one's breath away as it stood, just a box of yellow-wood really, with the golden heavy crib-beams from an old stable forming a cross against the rough white plaster walls. It was an enormous contrast to the ornate woodwork of his pulpit in the main church, and I asked him about it.

"It's very easy to explain," he told me. "When I built that over-ornamented one in the main church, as well as the almost Baroque one that I gave to the Dutch Reformed Church, I had looked upon God and heaven as very complicated things. Life was complicated for me, in those early days of my childhood as well as the first years of my marriage to Bettina. The prospect of having a life of my own was something that seemed impossible, difficult ever to achieve. Try to understand: my son had been born and had become what he is, except that he can walk now. But I saw only a life of caring for him ahead of me. Bettina had withdrawn from me, first with her body, and then with her mind. Nothing existed for her except the need to suffer along with Daan. My own life was in a mess. I am not the sort of person who withdraws from contracts, even if they are broken by the other side. And I don't believe in kicking sick women like Bettina out into the world of mental institutions or hospitals where she wouldn't be able to survive. So there I was, making pulpits as complicated as my life.

"Now, I have made three pulpits, one for each phase of my life. The one standing in the Dutch Reformed Church was the first, and I think it was a subconscious thing really, that I made for the holy place of my childhood and youth. You know I went to the Dutch Reformed Church for my first twenty years. I was christened there, at the old stone font. And I experienced the first of the religious ecstasies there. When you're a child and your parents have been reasonably wise about God you do experience such things, you know, as a little boy, in the mystical presence of God."

This surprised me very much, because I had never thought of Dawid as a boy. He had always been the strong one, and he'd been forty-four years of age when he had first held me in his arms. I had almost written down the phrase "I had first held him in my arms," because I had, in my work, always been the protective one. Now, it suddenly came to me that he had always had his arms around me, that I had never, in all the years of our loving, held him to me. I had luxuriated selfishly in his arms, never even wondering if I could console him, sometimes, if the world ever got to be too much for him. But I had never thought of him as a boy, and I was fascinated by finding, in my mind, a new dimension to him. He had been a boy, once. A baby at his mother's breast, a young lad with scuffed boots and with his shirt-tail hanging out. He had suffered the lonely agonies of the nights of longing of boyhood. It had never occurred to me. I had always been satisfied with the strong, middle-aged man who worked his soil so well and who made love so wonderfully.

Suddenly, I was able, in the hours of his absence, to walk along the path where he had strolled as a child, where he had kicked a stone or a bullybeef tin. The birds must have been the same. He had heard these songs also. I went to the church and looked at his pulpit, then at the walls, the floor and the windows. I had found out from him where they had always sat, and I went there, for a few moments, whenever I passed the church, looking up at the great decorative ceiling that some Victorian plasterer had made on the spot. Slowly, by asking him carefully selected questions, I was able to piece together a patchwork of his boyhood, even to his little sexual desires, and, with the coming of his puberty, the down-like growth of hair and the first little pointed erection. So, in my mind, his boyhood grew in me, and I was able to love, for the first time, a complete, three-dimensional person. The village that had been his playground took on a wonder for me that it has never lost.

That day, when he had told me of his first church, was memorable also because I found that he, the rough one, was a most devout person. I had always thought that he had taken me, and my love, as a thing of nature, and he had done so, it is true, but he had also needed to examine very closely the demands that it had made, and was making, on his spirit. I had never given this part of love a second thought. My own feeling had been that my life was mine, to do with as I wished, and that there were no external considerations except the feelings of consideration for Bettina, whom, I felt, life had harmed enough.

"You know, Ryna," said Dawid, still talking of his pulpits. "When I married Bettina I became a Methodist. And then I had to make a pulpit for her church as well. It wasn't to God, it was to her. And I made it after she had withdrawn her body from me, when I was still deeply in love with her. It was a sublimation of sorts, that pulpit. I made it of the most beautiful woods that I could find. Most of the polishing was done with the palm of my hand, working it to a soft sheen that a cloth could never achieve, like a sculpture. It was a transference of my sense of touch to another object, because the feel of wood can be as sensuous as the feel of a woman's breast, if you know wood. We who work with woods for the pleasure of it can never be understood by any but the very finest of carpenters.

"So that was my second pulpit, a complicated, intricate piece of work, that suited the state of mind I was in. And now, I've done my third one, the little farm chapel. And it's my pulpit to you. I'm not going to explain it, but I want you to know that it's for you. When you pass by there, go in, sometimes, and look at it."

It was to be many years before I knew all the things that that little pulpit, with its simple, rough cross, against the bagged raw plaster, had to say. But on that day, when he told me that it was for me, I asked him how he managed to express his relationship with me, which was surely irreligious, with so strong a statement as a pulpit and cross, but he wouldn't tell me how.

"You'll find out for yourself, Ryna," he said. "Don't let's explore all the things and mysteries in one day. I can tell you, though, that I don't know if it is right or wrong, the way I feel about you. I have built a shrine to you, and people have the right to build shrines. Usually when the ones that they have loved are dead. But I've done it while you're alive. And when I'm in church there, with my living-dead wife beside me, I look at the clean, strong lines, the simple and uncomplicated shapes of my design, and I feel you there, warm, in me, like a religion. But I don't want to desert the God of all those years. I tell you, religion has given me some of the strength that I needed. I can't be flippant about you. Loving each other as we do is an enormous thing for me, not just the expression of a simple need. I can do without that sort of undisciplined lovemaking, I don't need it. If I have to be a monk then I will be a monk. The physical demands are nothing, I can cope with them quite easily. I've been tempted, yes, and regularly. And I've given way to the temptation at times. I don't pretend to be a monk or a saint. A man who has a few drinks doesn't have to be an alcoholic, and a man who never takes a drink can be enslaved, a total alcoholic. But with you, it's not just the body alone, it's the spirit as well. I think I worship you, and I don't want it to be wrong. I need to feel that whatever lies outside of our spheres of perception approves of us and the thing that's between us. I don't know about God, and I don't know about His approval. Those are things I don't think about without knowing that the human mind and its present knowledge isn't adequate. Am I irreligious, a heathen, an adulterer, the picture of the unrepentant sinner? I don't think so. I feel pure and fine when I've been with you, and uncomplicated, as if God and I are, in a way, close together. I find purity in you. I don't know, Ryna. I believe in you, that you are as necessary for my spirit as God is. That takes me out of the church, where I've found strength for so many years, and I go to other places where the pantheists and pagans are, but I have no sense, ever, of excommunication or of a spiritual disapproval. I don't feel as if I've been kicked out of God's congregation, but that I have been allowed to go beyond the pulpit, into the pages of the Bible, where God dwells serenely alongside some of the most original sinners in the history of sin. So with you I am in the company of David, Solomon, and the Magdalene, and all those others whose sins made them glorious to God and understandable to human beings. I like the Catholics, and I feel that one should at some time or another, in life, descend from the harshness of the other doctrines to the humanity of Catholicism, which is a religion that only pretends to strictness, it never really practises it. Their saints are so humble, so human, so prone to temptation, so terribly depressed when they cannot resist it. I like them. But, it's not my job to talk to you about these things. Reverend Webb is the right man, although, when I sometimes try to mention matters of this kind, he is inclined to change the subject, as if I've embarrassed him."

In this way, speaking slowly, searching for words, Dawid would open his heart to me. I felt, instinctively, that he needed to say things to a woman, that it was a need that had to be satisfied. The talk, in the evening by the fireside, of things that had nothing to do with crops, eating, groceries, and bank balances.

There was a life in him, being lived spiritually, for which he had not had an outlet. It was a private world of his own, that he had, it seemed, always been eager to share, but he had found no one who would walk alongside him on these paths of speculation. So he related it to his experience of me, and made me a factor in it. I was pleased to know that there was some part of him, a very important segment of his life, that had never been shared by any other person, and that it was in that mansion of his spirit that he had housed me. I didn't always understand what he was trying to say, in spite of my degrees. I had been made a doctor of philosophy because of my studies and work in the social sciences, with a dusty-dry academic thesis of some five hundred pages to prove something, I don't know what. I am now ashamed of those years of study when I learned nothing of any importance, really, and all the work of co-efficients and correlations that took me so many nights to put into the form of graphs is now done by computer within moments.

So our monuments become dust, or conceits barely remembered. No one except Dawid ever knew that I had one day gone to Pretoria and had taken part in a ceremony that entitled me to be called Doctor. In Skeerpoort I was always Nurse van der Kolff to the coloureds, and Sister Maryna to the children. I don't know what the adults called me behind my back. To my face I was simply "Miss." The day I was capped I told Dawid about it, insisting that he keep it a secret. That evening he took me to dinner at Holzen's, which is one of the world's great restaurants, and we danced until long after all the other people had gone home. Mr. Holzen didn't mind, because we were happy in his place. It was a very daring thing to do, to go out together in the evening, where we could be seen. Dawid was a well-known farmer, and gossip could easily penetrate his life, and hurt it. But he had known that, in spite of my seemingly uncaring attitude, it had been a milestone in my life that had been worthy of dancing and champagne. And he was right, there are occasions when one is entitled to be just a little proud of achieving something. Even if it is meaningless, it is also, usually, the result of a great deal of hard work and self-discipline. Honours can come from others, but the worthwhile ones are very few. It is not a public thing.

Dawid and I were together for seventeen years. That is a long time to be one man's mistress, and an equally long time for a man to have only one mistress. Because of that length of time, I believe that our relationship was something more, for both of us, than just an affair. It had been marriage of sorts, one that could never be made official, or blessed by the church. But I am happy about it. It was a secret, that's true. I believe that only my sister Maria and one other person ever knew about it. I tried once to discuss it with Maria but she felt that it was none of her business, merely suggesting to me that she was happy about my being contented with life, and that she had found satisfactions of her own. I never learned what they were.

For a social worker I am a curiously non-prying type, and I felt that as Maria respected my privacy with an almost excessive courtesy, I would do the same for her, merely assuring her that if she ever fell on her bum I would be there to help soften the blow, and that I expected the same help from her if I should ever need it.

Those seventeen years might sound like a very long time, but, for me, they were done and over like a quick dream. I never tired of seeing Dawid, nor he of me. We were always impatient to be together, not just because of sex but for the whole of being together, the quietness and gentleness of it. I suppose it was a port-in-the-storm affair for both of us, but that only made it better: All the world around us seeming to be disintegrating in war and political upheavals; our country continually under verbal attacks and threats, our lives influenced by the world changing around us, and no way of living on in the homes of our great-grandfathers with honour, and no place to go. But I may not go into the politicians' area here. I'm not a political person, nor a racist. I am my own person, and I will fight for those whom life has short-measured, for whatever reason. It was inevitable that a sociologist would run into politics, head on, and I won sometimes, and other days I lost, but I never stopped trying, and that is all I am going to say on that subject.

I never brought my frustrations to Dawid, and he made a point of keeping whatever complaints he had against life to himself as well. We had other things to talk about. But one night in 1956, after we had made love, I tried to put my head on his chest, as I always did, and he moved away from me. I asked him a question, I remember, it was something silly. I got a little silly after a lovemaking, always, because I was so happy: "How would you like me to be a magic-maker, then I could turn myself into a horsey and you would ride me all the time?" He didn't seem to hear me, and I looked at him curiously.

It was an effort for him, but he tried to get out of bed. There was perspiration all over his face and body. Then he asked me for one of his vitamin tablets, that he kept in his jacket. His voice was strained, as if he was in great pain, and he collapsed on the bed, backwards.

I had seen too many heart attacks in my time not to recognise this one. The nitro-glycerine tablets were in his pocket, in a little box which he had marked "multivitamin tablets," to fool me, I suppose. I put one under his tongue and positioned his head to clear his breathing, but his heart and lungs had stopped working. There was no pulse, no heart-beat that I could hear, so I struck him a firm, sharp blow over his heart. All this must have taken about fifteen seconds or even less. After the blow I listened to his chest again, and his heart had started to beat again, not very steadily, not well at all, but beating.

There was no doubt in my mind that he had suffered a major coronary occlusion, very nearly fatal, and that it had not been the first. Dawid had always seemed a healthy man, he had never complained, once, about any ailment, and he was only fifty-six years of age. Young for a man who had looked after himself. He just wasn't the type to get heart attacks. And yet, there he was, virtually flattened.

His heart was gaining strength again, and the pain must have subsided with the nitro-glycerine pill that he had dissolved under his tongue. There was a telephone at the bedside, never used, because we had never called anyone during all the years we had shared the apartment. But now I knew why it had been installed, and why there were three telephone numbers written on the little pill box. They were the office, home, and emergency telephone numbers of a prominent Pretoria cardiologist, a Doctor de Koonig. Dawid had me get through to him, and he spoke to the doctor himself.

"Doctor," he said. "Dawid Cilliers here, it's happened again. At the apartment. Can you come over?"

He handed me the receiver, but it had gone dead. The doctor must have known the address, and this plan must have been discussed between them. It was the sort of thing that Dawid would do; plan ahead for the possible emergency, to spare me. I wanted to know everything, but I knew that this was not the time for asking questions, or to upset him in any way. He had to be kept as quiet as possible, with no disturbance at all. It made me particularly helpless, because I knew that he would need someone like me for the next few days, to take over intensive care.

"He doesn't know about us," he said. "I don't want him to. He'll be here in about ten minutes. You will have to go now."

"Yes," I said. "I'll go. But keep your hand on this light switch, I'll be across the road. I can be with you within thirty seconds. I'll leave the door off the latch. Switch off the light if you feel any worse. Particularly if the pain starts up again, or anything that causes you anxiety. Then I must come to care for you. The doctor will have you moved out of here to an intensive care unit. Don't argue. Go. It's not a secret any more. I know now. I won't be able to see you until tomorrow, when I'll arrange to visit the I.C.U. at the hospital. You'll see me, but we won't talk unless it's completely safe. After that, we'll see what's best."

I was speaking very hurriedly, and all this didn't take more than a minute or two, so there was enough time left to make him comfortable and to kiss him, perhaps, I thought, for the last time, an awesome shuddering thought it was, almost too much for me to take.

I had become used to our "arrangement." Years of habitual meeting, virtually at the same time, always at the same place, and the pain of leaving each other had conditioned my life with Dawid. Suddenly, in 1956, when I was forty-one, confidently entering middle age, not suspecting that there was any possibility of the coming years being lonely, my whole world was turned inside-out and upside-down. The familiar arrangements were no longer applicable, the movements of love had to be adapted and revised. Everything that had been sure had now, in a moment, been made uncertain.

I went outside and stood in a doorway opposite, staring at the light in our window, on the first floor, wondering how Dawid was feeling. I knew that only the most urgent of symptoms would make him switch off the light to summon me, that he would hang on until the doctor came, for his dear life, and that he would try not to worry me. Those were very long minutes, and I was severely tempted, a thousand times in no longer than ten minutes, to throw caution to the winds and to rush over the road and to hold him to me, and to make sure that his heart continued beating, even if it meant that the doctor would find out about us. But he didn't want it like that, and I knew that if I disregarded his instruction, Dawid would perhaps not be angry but he would certainly be upset, probably for my sake, because he never really thought of himself.

I had once, long ago, told him that I wanted our relationship to be a private matter, and he had respected that wish, made so many years ago and certainly no longer important to me, in the arrangements that he had made with his cardiologist in case of an emergency situation developing at the apartment. These were all matters that could be discussed at a later date. The doctor would certainly know that Dawid had had a woman in the apartment, and that it was an intimate arrangement. I had not bothered to hide anything as I went out, and I was standing in only my dressing gown across the road, waiting so impatiently for the doctor, who finally arrived.

His car stopped at the front door, directly in the "no parking" area, and he ran into the building and up the one flight of stairs. I waited impatiently for the arrival of the ambulance that would take Dawid to an intensive care unit, but it did not come, so I assumed the worst, that Dawid had died with the light switch in his hand, or that he was too ill to be moved..And I died the usual thousand deaths, shivering out there in the warm night.

After a half hour the window of our apartment opened and the doctor put his head out and looked across at me. He made a calling motion with his hand and I crossed the street, went into the building and up the stairs, and entered the apartment. Dawid was sitting up, looking tired, but the pastiness had gone. Because of my social work and my many papers on socio-medical matters, which have no place in this reminiscence, Doctor de Koonig knew of me, and we had, on occasion, spoken briefly.

"You never leave the patient, Doctor van der Kolff," he said. "That is the first rule in any crisis involving the heart; never leave the patient alone."

"I know," I said. "But he would have been upset had I insisted on staying."

"Remember, Doctor," he said, and he wasn't really angry with me, or making a fuss, just being nice, but truthful. "Remember, Doctor, that when he is going through an incident of this nature, he is most upset anyway. To be left alone is to bring up all kinds of fears, terrors even. We don't want that."

"I've told him about us, everything," said Dawid, from the bed, in a surprisingly strong voice. "He felt that it was necessary for him to know."

"It's more than necessary, it's completely essential, if you two are going to spend any amount of time at all in each other's company in future. Doctor van der Kolff is perhaps the most ideal of companions for you. She's a trained nursing sister and she knows all the emergency procedures. She saved your life with that blow to the chest, starting up your heart after it had stopped beating, and she knows of other procedures if that fails. She can become your heart and your lungs and keep you going until I arrive. What's between you is your own business. I can only say that I'm happy for you Dawid, and for you Doctor. Of course, you need never fear that this will go any further."

"You didn't have to say that," I said. "But thank you. And now, if I'm going to have to watch over him while he is with me, I think I need a little bit of case history, diagnosis, prognosis, the lot, please."

"Very firm woman this," said Dawid. "You'd better tell her, Doctor."

"This is the third of these incidents," said Doctor de Koonig. "The first was eight months ago, the second three months later, and now the third. This seems to have been the worst, the other two were minor coronary occlusions, although the second one was quite painful, it couldn't have been anything like tonight's. This was a big one and it's likely that it did some damage. However, his apparent recovery makes things look much brighter, but I'll have to have him in the I.C.U. tonight as well as the whole of tomorrow, perhaps even longer. I'll see then, about further treatment. You may communicate with me. I have the patient's permission to tell you everything. It was foolish of him not to tell you in the first place."

"What about his wife?" I said. "Somebody will have to tell her."

"I've already telephoned," said the doctor. "She was . . . well, funny, strange, as if she didn't really care. She asked me what his condition was, and I told her that we were doing tests. She then told me to keep her informed of the results of the tests, if I wished. Well, yes, that's what she said, 'if you wish,' just like that. No pretence of caring at all. Does she know, about you?"

"No," I said. "I'm certain she doesn't. She may suspect that there's someone, but she doesn't know, not for sure, isn't that so, Dawid?"

"I doubt if she has given it a thought," said Dawid. "She's withdrawn herself completely from the world. I doubt if the news of my death would be of much meaning to her. She's just not in the world any longer. Not with me, at any rate."

Doctor Cloete, whose wife had died in 1952, had survived her by only four years, and he had been the general practitioner who had referred Dawid to Doctor de Koonig for specialist treatment after his first attack eight months previously. It had been one of his last duties as a doctor, and he had died within a few days of the incident, still in his early sixties but too lonely to continue life all on his own. He had had his lusts, and his pleasures, but his heart had been with his wife and son. The boy had gone through medical school and his father had lived to see him graduate. He had not been to his father's funeral, because he had been away on a hiking trip through the lake country of Scotland, where he has been studying for his post-graduate degree of Bachelor of Surgery at the Royal College of Surgeons, at Edinburgh, at the time of his father's death.

On hearing that his father had died the young Doctor Cloete had come back, not having distinguished himself in the field of surgery. He had been a good medical student but as a learner-surgeon he had been the despair of his tutors. He had recognised his failings as being a part of his personality, and, quite happily, he had left Scotland to return and settle in the little village, taking over his father's practice, and, strangely enough, the post of district surgeon, which called for little or no surgery as such.

These developments finally relieved me of all medical responsibilities and I was able to continue my sociological investigations and work, while my assistant and all the clinical apparatus were taken over by the young Doctor Cloete. These are the reasons why I told Doctor de Koonig not to bother about phoning Bettina Cilliers, as it needed a more personal contact by a doctor to explain whatever needed to be said to her, with great patience. He did as I asked and told me that the young doctor would go, in the morning, to see Bettina, and to tell her the latest news of her husband's condition. It was then that the ambulance arrived, and Dawid was taken away on a stretcher, to a modern nursing home that was equipped with the latest monitoring equipment, where a check could be kept on his heart-beat, continuously for twenty-four hours of the day.

I could not go along without causing comment at the nursing home. Only the next day could I accompany Doctor de Koonig, as an investigating sociologist, in a fairly official capacity. Nursing sisters are a gullible lot, and there was no difficulty persuading those lovely ladies in charge of the patients of the intensive care unit that I was indeed Doctor van der Kolff, and that I was on a research project involving the ever-increasing menace of coronary thrombosis in modern society.

I was given the run of the place, and I was able to speak to the patients who were well enough for conversation, but Dawid knew that I was hovering about like a mother hen, and taking no chances, even though he was getting the best care and treatment possible anywhere in the world. Bettina never came to visit, and Doctor de Koonig transmitted daily bulletins to her by means of the young Doctor Cloete.

The subject of Bettina was most trying to me. My thoughts were of an evil nature, amoral, perhaps even indecent. I knew that I was the real Mrs. Dawid Cilliers, in spite of the lack of a marriage certificate. I was hovering about him, concerned for his welfare, while she sat, withdrawn, and, so I thought, blamed the crippled child on her husband's seed. I was going into middle age, Dawid was preparing for death, and I would be left, lonely and longing, with only memories. I knew that if I had the chance, if only Bettina would die, that Dawid would live longer, and that even the patient in the backyard, their son, would receive at least trained medical care.

Dawid had felt bad about his death-wish, involuntary and innocent, regarding Bettina, but I now felt a bitterness at her insistence on living. I had always thought that Dawid, so strong, healthy, so careful of his diet and his general health, would live to be a hundred, and I with him. In the back of my mind I had also been waiting for Bettina to die, unconsciously, so that we could at last marry and be together every moment of the day. It had never entered my head that Dawid would be the first to die, leaving Bettina in her corner and me in mine. Dawid was the strong one. It just wasn't on the cards. I don't know. How could this have happened? We were going to keep ourselves well, so that we would have active bodies and minds until a very old age, always in love. And now, there was this sudden disastrous knowledge. He had had three, not one, but three heart attacks within eight months. He should have been quiet, resting, not driving around to Pretoria at least twice a week to see me and make violent love to me. I blush now when I think of the demands that I had made on his body, I was going into middle age. Forty is what is called middle age, and I was there. My youth was gone, but I was more than just demanding, I must have seemed insatiable to him. But I had never noticed. No strain, no fatigue, just occasionally, he would say that he had forgotten to take his multivitamin tablet, that, he told me, he took because he wasn't all that fond of vegetables. It never struck me that he seemed to make a habit of forgetting his vitamins, or that he took them, quite often, after we had made love, exhaustingly. That was when the pains must have come into his chest. He just took the tablet, and the pain would go away. And then, that night in 1956, when the pain was more severe, the heart slowed and stopped until I thumped it back to life again.

Now there was a whole new set of problems. I told Dawid that the continual driving to Pretoria was out of the question, even dangerous. He had to stay quiet and not be subjected to any stress whatsoever. I knew that my body had been shocked, by the fear of what was happening to Dawid, into complete chastity. I just would not be able to make love to him again unless I was a hundred per cent sure of his recovery. That did not seem to be a possibility. I knew what diseased hearts were and how they acted. I knew, more or less, when or why they stopped beating permanently. My terror was absolute, because I knew too much. Three in eight months, not good, not very promising.

The patient had to be cared for very carefully, if not constantly. The patient was a strong-willed man, belonging to the group of patients who could not be easily controlled. He would not lie down, or stop smoking. He would go down with all flags flying.

The other thing I knew was that, if his body spoke to me in its own way, in the language that I had learned so well, then mine would answer back. Dawid had already experienced one self-imposed nunship in his life with the physical withdrawal of Bettina. He would not make himself responsible for another. What he had found in me, he would want to keep. That was why he had told me nothing of his first two attacks, knowing that I would fuss over him and insist that he did not make himself tired, or indulge in anything that could be a strain, and so overload his heart. I knew that he was going to be difficult, if not impossible, to control.

He was in intensive care for two days, and then he was moved to a private ward, where I could spend hours with him. I admit that the day and night nurses must have been more than just suspicious of our relationship, but we were never caught out. I was always demure with my notebook in my hand as they burst into the doors without knocking, hoping to catch us out. There would be a time for physical contact later. Just looking at Dawid made my heart beat faster. The strong smile of welcome he gave me whenever I arrived was enough to give me a thrombosis-feeling, so that I was sometimes afraid that I might have the same effect on him. But it seemed silly to discuss the matter. Girlish. And there's nothing sillier in life than a girlish forty-year-old.

There was no reason for me to see Dawid professionally except for the occasional drive to Pretoria to visit the physiotherapists, and even that excuse must have been wearing a little thin. And I also wondered whether the sharp-eyes in the village, forever on the lookout for something over which they could make a little mischief, might not have noticed how often Dawid and I had been away from the village at the same time. If anyone did notice, or work out any statistic, it was never communicated to anyone I knew, and I was unaware of any scandal that could have connected Dawid and me.

It was, however, obvious to me that a new scheme of things would have to be worked out, and I was sorry for the loss of our little "home," as we called the apartment. We had done wonderful things there, with ourselves and our lives, and it was awful to feel that it was all over. A set of rooms is only an arrangement of cube-spaces, but they can be made magical in a moment by what is brought into them. Quite apart from the material things, just the matters that concern the spirit and the air around can leave their mark tangibly on the breath of wind that floats out from it into the world. It had a good feel to it, that little apartment, and while I was planning its disposal, and trying to think of how I would change our lives around so that we would be watchful of his health and still be able to see each other occasionally, Dawid was in the hospital talking to Doctor de Koonig, laying down his own laws and making his own plans without asking my advice. He knew what I would have said to his plans.

Doctor de Koonig ran into me, as if by accident, a day or two later, at the hospital, and invited me to tea in his rooms. I went along gladly, eager to hear his news. He was in an awful quandary, so much so that I pitied him. He just did not know how to say what had to be said; also, he did not really want to say it, because he was a shy man.

"Doctor," he said, using my formal title, "I have to tell you something that dismays me and that will shock you. Dawid Cilliers is hell bent on destroying every medical fact I believe in. He refuses to give up smoking, he won't hear of abstinence of any sort, not even, er, with you, and he insists that he is well enough to drive his car to Cape Town and back. I don't know what to do. He's right, you know, he's not the sort of man you can tie down, and to release him from medical discipline will also harm him. He tells me, if you will forgive me for repeating it, that he will under no circumstances give up even one moment in your company. He wishes to continue to see you exactly as before, and to indulge in exactly, those are his words, exactly the same activities with, er, this is a little difficult, with the same frequency and, if you will again pardon me, the same enthusiasm."

"Perhaps if I spoke to him, Doctor. That might help. I won't pretend that I'm not delighted by what you have to say, but I am, as you can see, very deeply concerned, and I know that what he proposes to do is to die fighting. There is very little of bravado in that. If he has said it he means it. But I think that a compromise can be worked out. He is an intelligent man. I can't let him be upset, for instance, letting him just wait while I don't turn up. That will never do. But I think that we will be able to work out something."

So Doctor de Koonig left the matter in my hands in the meantime and when Dawid was discharged he allowed young Doctor Cloete to drive him home for a short convalescence. Fortunately, Doctor de Koonig was one of the progressive cardiologists who got their patients out of bed and sitting up as soon as possible, within two days of the attack, so Dawid at least was not confined to bed, which would have driven him mad.

All our fears were quite unfounded. Dawid became a model patient and did everything the doctor said, with one proviso; that he could go on seeing me. The doctor realised that I was a necessary factor in the quality of Dawid's life, and he blushingly told me to "take it easy." I have often noticed that men who are ill appear to be more sexually orientated than those who are in good health. I asked Dawid about it, because the subject had become an obsession with him, and I had to be very careful not to strain his heart again, but he told me that it was possibly just being in bed and having a lovely woman to look after you; that was natural enough and sufficient explanation for him.

We had worked out a way for him to get to town, to our little apartment. He refused, under any circumstances, to give it up and had even signed a long term lease renewal. One of his workers would drive him to a parking garage in the centre of the city, and would wait there for his return. Dawid would walk to the taxi rank in the next block and be driven out to our little "home," as he chose to call it.

He recovered well enough, and I took frequent blood-pressure and pulse readings, over many hours, which Doctor de Koonig found valuable as a record of his recovery. There had been some damage to his heart, but he could, with care and the cooperation of the people with whom he came into daily contact, live for many years. He was encouraged to take moderate exercise after a few months, and within a year, he was, to all appearances, well again.

The three attacks had been purely a matter of neglect on the part of the patient, and Doctor de Koonig, who had once despaired of Dawid's life, now gave him every chance of, as he said, "many more years of happy and useful life." Dawid had spoken to him about his chain-smoking habits, and de Koonig had told him that smoking would rob him of some years. That was a statistical fact, and no getting around it. One day, after we had made love, he playing the passive role which he rather enjoyed, I searched for his cigarettes. I had always lit a cigarette for him after lovemaking. It was a little ritual, one of our personal things. He told me that he had stopped, because it meant more years with me.

I repeat these nice things he said to me, not out of any sense of conceit or pride, but because this is how he was, and such things that made me feel good, came easily from his mouth. Although he was approaching his sixties, he remained a strong and robust person, with a leanness in his late maturity that was not just part of his body, but of his whole personality. He had trimmed life down to its essentials, and he didn't speak much. He never said things like "I love you" anymore, and I wondered why. But I couldn't ask him, and it wasn't necessary in any case. I soon learnt that, in coming to me, being with me for a while, and leaving with reluctance, he was saying thousands of words without speaking one. There was an ascetic, monk-like poverty to his richness. He would bring me the first leaf of autumn, which I still have, pressed in my old school "Golden Treasury." He would find a pebble and leave it on the lounge table for me to discover another time. And the words he used were lean too, and polished, like sentences by Eliot.

He never spoke of the big philosophical things any more, the huge questions of life and death and the reasons for existence and love that had once been such favourite topics of conversation for him.

In those years, when he was getting strong again, his growing health seemed to be a part of his soul, and with him I discovered a whole new world that made him even more precious to me.

He would frame, with his thumb and forefinger, a little piece of leather or the Khelim on the floor, and marvel at its beauties. He would do the same to various little parts of my body, speaking of my textures as if I were a sort of abstract painting. But gradually I too saw the world in detail, and the mountains and canyons of a pebble, and the universe of a flower. It wasn't a world of the mind. I don't want to give that impression because it would be unfair to Dawid.

It was a true physical world, in which we made love physically as well, with our bodies reaching out to each other, and taking what the other had to give. "Had" is the right word, in the imperative sense. There was no other way for us, to go anywhere, than by way of each other. We had to give, and we didn't care at all about taking. But, in giving, we were taking all that there was in the world. Together we discovered the spiritual things of the physical world, and it was so much better than abstract concepts, which we both understood but had little time for. Dawid had worked far too closely to the soil ever to encase his spirit in an intellectual ivory tower. His ecstasies came from within him. That is perhaps why he never drank much. He would have an occasional glass of wine with food, or a beer for thirst, or a whisky for relaxation, but it was never a habit with him, "because," he said, "I'm half drunk all the time anyway. I like things, even if my life has certain unwelcome miseries I still like being alive. Yes I know that Daan is a trouble, and Bettina, but it has knocked me, and I keep fighting back. I suppose I'm a happy punch-drunk boxer by now, but I appreciate things. If you want to describe me, you'll have to call me an appreciator. That's what I'll call myself from now on."

He had a tenderness for me that I found heart-breaking. At sixty an extreme gentleness was always in his eyes, and his skin had become transparent, like the softest folds beneath a woman's breasts, his wrinkles were deeply etched, but they gave his face its full strength. There was, always, a feeling that he was near to tears, and often, when we would sit quietly and listen to music, the adagio passages from Dvorak and Beethoven, Tchaikowsky, and the little refrains of Chopin, would cause tears to stream down his cheeks. He was ashamed of his tears. They weren't manly, he would say, and I found that the only fault in him, that he thought his tears should be hidden from me.

I woke up one morning, in the big double brass bed in our apartment, but I knew that the sun was up and I didn't want to open my eyes too suddenly. I was always afraid of lights that were too blinding. I felt a shadow fall between my eyes and the sun, and his voice said, "you can open them now." He had been looking at my face for more than an hour, he told me, and he had known the moment of my waking. This is what I mean when I say that he had trimmed life, and love, down to the essentials of existence, the core of personality, I like to call it. He had become the complete man, in all ways.

But I speak too long of pleasant things. If I am to be honest in my memories then I must tell of the matter that has caused me a great deal of anguish. I had always thought of myself as a person of some sensitivity and intelligence, able to conquer my fantasies and fears with a fair degree of success, which takes some doing in this century. I had never considered myself to be an ill-adjusted person or a problem personality, but in one respect I was monstrous: I loathed and detested Bettina Cilliers with a fantastic intensity. I would sometimes for hours lie alone in bed and dream that she was dead. I would make up daydreams of weapons so secret that they could strike from far off, killing her instantly and leaving her with all the symptoms of, for instance, a stroke. I never allowed her a heart attack, deep down in my subconscious that was reserved for Dawid and me. I wished her dead, deliberately and consciously, for many hours of my life.

Once, I even invented a way of killing her. I would drive to the Great House and tell her that I was doing a research project, and would she allow me to draw a little blood from her veins. It was for a nutritional study, the effects of diet on the blood; very social-welfare-alibi-conscious I was, in my scheme. I had a syringe in the old case that had been my companion in the days when I had been the district nurse. I had kept all my old-fashioned things. I would open the case and take out the blood-test syringe, slowly, I would withdraw the plunger, before putting the needle point into her vein, and then I would depress the plunger, shooting a stream of air into her blood-stream, killing her, painfully. That would leave the symptoms of a heart attack, but I didn't mind that. Only my fantasy weapons left her heart undamaged. The real weapon, the one that could actually kill her, would leave a heart attack symptom, and I would have committed a perfect murder.

Now, don't let me pretend that this was just a matter of thinking. One day I took my old case with me, on the seat of the car, and I drove out towards the Cilliers farm, knowing that Dawid was away at a cattle auction at Hekpoort. I drove through the big white gates with their lovely wrought-iron tracery and rode slowly towards the Great House. Then, on the road, I saw the coloured woman called Silver, and she waved me down.

"There's nobody at the house now, madam," she said. "The Oumiesies is in her room and she don't talk to nobody no more, and the Oubaas has gone to Hekpoort for the auction of old Harry Walters. He mos died a few weeks ago, and now they selling off all his cattle and goed."

"That's all right, Silver," I said. "I was just looking at how beautiful the farm is. Don't you go telling them about it, will you?"

"Of course not madam. The Oumiesies get into a hell of a temper if she hears about strange people on the farm, and I get hell from her because I am the only one she talk to, because I do her room."

I made a U-turn and drove away slowly, shaking, wondering if I would have gone through with it. And I sometimes wonder what Dawid, with his new, diamond-sharp mind, would have made of me, committing a murder because of my love for him. Often, after that day, I would dream of her screaming death, and wake up glad, with the feeling that she was out of the way and that I was in the Great House with Dawid, as it had happened in my dream. Then I would look around and see that I was in the bedroom of my cottage in Skeerpoort, alone. It would take a while for me to orientate myself to my surroundings, the hate and the murder, and the release for Dawid and me, having been very strong in my dream.

Dawid had sent me the title deeds to the cottage where I lived, as a gift. I had had no idea that he had been my landlord all of these years. I had always paid the rent at old Bertie Theron's office, and it had never occurred to me to buy it. I suppose because I had other more grandiose ambitions in my subconscious mind: The Great House, and Dawid and I, together.

And now that I have remembered everything, and put it down, it is time for me to tell you also of the second day of December, 1961, when Dawid died. That was very blunt. Shockingly so. I could have worked towards it slowly, preparing for the moment. But life didn't do that to me. It was a most undiplomatic way of death. Sudden. Without warning, because we had forgotten the warnings of five years ago completely. He had recovered, he was well, there wasn't a muscle that wasn't in perfect shape. True, he was sixty-one, but there wasn't a healthier looking man in the district. And, because of the secrecy of our affair, and the fact that no one in the village knew of it, I was informed of his death in the most shocking way, by the butcher, from whom I was buying meat. I asked for fresh chops, and he said: "These are fresher than Dawid Cilliers by four hours. Strange that, a big strong man yesterday, the picture of health, and now, a corpse, all alone in his bedroom, waiting for the undertakers, it makes you think, don't it, Nurse van der Kolff, yes, it makes you wonder when your own time is going to come, Mister Cilliers going off like that, in the middle of the night." He rambled on, as was his way, and I stood, numb with shock at what he was saying. When he turned his back to work at his chopping block I was tempted to run, screaming. The sudden flow of adrenaline to the outposts of my body had made me ice-cold, and my heart was beating furiously, with a strange, light, almost fainting feeling about my head, I stood there, listening to what he had to say, not hearing anything any more, the words "my love, my love, my love" endlessly running on through my head, as if I couldn't think of any other words to say to him, wherever he may be.

I so desperately, at that moment, needed to think that there was a form of life after death. But I didn't believe it. I envied the whole world who received that solace from their faith, but it wasn't mine, and I couldn't, even in that extremity, adopt it. I don't know how long I stood there, in that butcher's shop, that morning, or how I managed to get home. I remember that I phoned the young Doctor Cloete, and that he had been out at the farm for most of the night. The servant, Mina, had phoned him at midnight, to tell him to come quickly, because there was "something terrible wrong with the Oubaas. He's lying in the yard, where the Kleinbasie walks, and he's in pain, and he can't move. He says come quickly." But by the time that Doctor Cloete had arrived at the Great House, Dawid had passed away. It had been a massive thrombosis. No treatment could possibly have helped.

Of course, I blamed myself, I should have been with him, all the time, in spite of gossip, in spite of hatred from Bettina. I should have been there, and I would have beaten that clot through his heart, no matter how big it had been. I was a little mad for the rest of that day. I knew that I would be expected to attend his funeral, but I wasn't at all sure if I could bear it. I knew that it would be a miracle if I didn't break down. It wasn't my job to weep, even; officially I would attend as a comforter.

I went to the little chapel that contained "my" altar that evening. I was surprised to see that the candelabra had been lit. I opened the door and saw the new, strange square shape of yellow-wood. It was Dawid's coffin. Later I learned that, in a personal affidavit to his will, he had specifically requested to be buried from the little farm chapel, and that his funeral should be as simple and quiet an affair as possible, with the body in an open coffin for the sake of those who wished to pay their last respects.

I know why Dawid, a simple person who had hated false ceremony, had asked for this. His own coloured and black people, who had worked for and with him through all the years, would want to say their goodbyes in their own way. And it would have been an insult to them had they not been allowed to view the remains. They wanted it so, and they would come dressed in their best clothes, as a further mark of respect. Also, the day of the burial had to be a holiday on the farm, and they would be allowed an ox, and some sheep, and there would be bread and cakes, so that they could make the parting memorable, with a feast of food and drink.

They were there that evening, singing softly in the little space inside the chapel, taking turns at their viewing, mumbling respectful farewells. I went inside, and sat in one of the pews, just to be near him. I knew that any real reaction on my part would cause comment later, so I kept my feelings in the background.

It wasn't very difficult, as I had been shocked to a point of numbness.

Old Bertie Theron came by, and, surprisingly, stared at the dead face for a long time, weeping copiously. Only afterwards, when he had turned away from the coffin, did he notice me. Again, surprisingly, he came over to me and pressed my arm in a wordless gesture of comfort that had me fighting to control myself. I don't know what old Bertie Theron knew, but it was something. Enough to enable him to make a significant, telling gesture.

They buried Dawid the next day, in the farmyard, next to the cattle kraal. I could not cry, as I had broken during the night, and there were no tears left for the ceremony, thank God.

14

BERTRAND THERON

I was sixty-three years of age, two years older than Dawid Cilliers, on the day that he died. Our dear friend, Doctor Anton Cloete, had also, by that time, passed away, to be replaced by his quite pleasant son, and now there were only the Reverend Webb and I to carry on the work of caring for a family that had kept us alive by acts of kindness and understanding, if not of outright charity, by the giving or commissioning of work, some of it fabricated especially, in a world that would have been too hostile for us. We would never have survived without Dawid Cilliers. There just wasn't enough work in Skeerpoort for me to make a living, and, as for the Reverend Doctor Webb, there had never been much of a reason for him to exist in our midst. He was poor as a preacher, and dreadful as an example. It is possible that he was weaker than I, unbelievable as that may sound.

I make no judgement, because I am not the magisterial type. I knew, early in life, that my bright dream of a career in law, in the cause of justice, was just so much silly starry-eyed nonsense. There was no law worth talking about, anywhere in the world, and justice was peculiarly absent from all the aspects of the world's courts. I could never have had the lack of faith in my fellow man to become a man of the law. I could not plead the truth of a skilful lie, or the demerits of a clumsy truth.

I wasn't clever enough to be a lawyer, or a judge. For all my professional degrees, I have never done anything dishonest, except the day we declared Daan Cilliers "dead" officially.

I know that in confessing that I have never done anything dishonest, I display a pathetic misunderstanding and misuse of my professional qualifications. But there it is. I am an honest man, in spite of my education.

Dawid Cilliers gave me the work of keeping his affairs in order. To do that I went to the trouble of taking an extra degree, that of Bachelor of Commerce; it was no trouble, as I had plenty of time on my hands. I was, I know, quite overpaid. Dawid Cilliers was a generous man with those who served him even adequately well, and my service was devoted. I had, in my arsenal, a complete set of precedents, in international law, that could be used if the law ever tried to separate young Daan from his parents. I had conducted correspondence to all parts of the world, and had myself pored over thousands of books in the legal libraries. If ever it was attempted to remove the boy from his parents, I had a whole case mapped out that had to succeed in any court. Dawid Cilliers knew of this and he appeared to be especially grateful, because I had done it unasked. It was a volume of nearly a thousand pages, and, had it ever come to court, I was quite prepared to handle the case myself, so confident was I of my efforts. I know that it must have taken a load off Dawid Cilliers's mind, to be sure that there was an impenetrable line of defence, that would have demolished any application to the contrary. It was one of the small ways in which I could repay the tremendous generosity that I had been favoured with under his kind patronage.

He owned a great deal of the village. He was not an acquisitive type, but as people, with the passing of time, sold up their small uneconomical, often badly-run farms and businesses, Dawid Cilliers purchased them, and continued farming the area. He once told me that he didn't like the idea of "Ghost Towns," as they are called. He was prepared to pay for the future of the village.

Now that it is a beautiful, rural, river-fronted real estate proposition with all the potential of such properties in the over-crowded seventies, his vision and confidence appear to have been justified. He and his wife, while he had been alive, and she lucid, had made a will leaving the bulk of their property and its income to the care of Daan. I had also a small part in the will, and my offices and home, which stood on property owned by Dawid Cilliers, would be mine to do with as I wished, for the rest of my life.

I had made provision for my own death many years ago, and, with the approval of my patron, I had chosen one of the less offensive firms of Pretoria attorneys to take over the affairs of the estate in case of my demise. So all that is, as they say, quite sewn up and watertight, and nothing can go wrong with my affairs or those of the family. I had been instructed to draw up a plan for a fair distribution of the income from the estate to a large number of black and coloured workers, in the form of a pension fund, which I had managed to have officially registered without too much trouble, so even his black people will be comfortably off after they have become too old to continue working. I did not know if any other person in the country had ever done such a thing, but I was proud to be associated with him in such a unique act of generosity.

I had also drawn up a document in which he had specified that, in the event of the death of their son while unable to attend to his own affairs because of his lifelong ailment, I, or the successors appointed by me, would give the Cilliers estate to the National Society for the Care of Cripples, as a recreational and rehabilitational institution. In all these matters, Doctor Maryna van der Kolff would be in charge of the practical details and medical requirements.

I had already given Maryna the title deeds to the rented cottage that Dawid Cilliers had purchased on her behalf, and another rested in my office safe: The deeds of transfer to a newly surveyed twenty-one morgen, specifically subdivided again after its initial incorporation into the greater Cilliers estate, now again separated from the whole, a piece of land on which the farm chapel stood. This he had also bequeathed to Maryna. It was from this chapel that we buried him.

I had found her there on the night of his death. He lay, in his best Sunday suit, with not a wrinkle furrowing his face, perfectly at peace with the universe and seeming, from the expression on his still features, quite willing to go back to the earth to which he had contributed so much. Now life had finished with this good man, or he had finished with it. I don't think that he had wanted to die, or that he had died without regret. I don't think that he had accepted his end. It is my belief that he had wanted more years. He had not used much of his life, or the material things that had been his. His life had been one of service, and only in the office of the local accountant and attorney will you find the records of the services that had been rendered to the community by a man of his calibre. He had held small ten per cent interests in a number of businesses that he had, at times, financed in order to keep them going during bad times. Travis Transportation, Geraldo's Crushers, Jackson's Sand Works, supplying crushed stone and building sand to construction projects thirty miles away in Johannesburg and Pretoria, and all the growth points in-between, were all businesses that he had at one time or another saved by injections of capital.

He had rendered them a greater service than that by also teaching them to work together as a local group of independent firms inter-dependent on each other for their real prosperity. The sand was difficult to sell, so was the crushed stone, and their transportation difficult and inefficient, until Travis Transportation bought a concrete-mix truck, and the stone and sand firms combined with Henderson's Building Supplies, from whom they purchased the cement for the pre-mix concrete, which was delivered on site.

This was a business that flourished, but, most importantly, it kept the people concerned in Skeerpoort, as there was plenty of contractual work on roads, bridges, and public as well as private ventures within the viable delivery radius. By conceiving, financing and organising such ventures, Dawid Cilliers made sure the village was able to grow. He kept it together with his good sense and the judicious use of his wealth.

He had also purchased a great many of the smaller farms as their owners had left either through being unable to make a living from the land, in which case they had been bad farmers, or through thinking that life in the cities had more security and pleasure to offer, in which case they had been fools. Dawid Cilliers let them go, and wisely so. He bought their land at the best prices, but he kept the farms producing and the homes in reasonable condition until others came to my office, attracted by the peaceful beauty of the village, asking for a piece of nice farmland with something of a house.

I would take my instructions from Dawid Cilliers, carefully vetting the prospective buyers, a job that had been left to me. What was involved in these transactions was not just their financial status, as more than just money had been required, I was, then, on the lookout for people who appeared to be in need of a place to anchor, to throw down roots. These I would help, and, although the population of the village changed, to a certain extent, its exterior factors remained unharmed while a healthy growth in its interior, its spirit, made new and fascinating branches.

Dawid Cilliers had spoken to me, very seriously, one night as we sat, having a small drink in the corner of Fritz Smit's bar.

"A village," he said, "is a living thing. It is a complete thing, like a person or a tree, and it is capable of bearing bad and good fruit, like people, or trees."

There had been no bitterness in his face as he had spoken of the bad fruit, indirectly referring to his son, only an acceptance of things as they were.

"Those of us who work with the affairs of a village have a lot to do with its pruning and shaping. I don't want us to change Skeerpoort too much, so I don't want to encourage the investor or the speculator. I want to encourage farmers. Even if they have always lived in the city, you'll always see a farmer, recognise him, by the way in which he will crouch and let the soil run through his fingers, by his interest in the kraal manure and the compost heap, or by the feeling he has for the water furrows. Watch out for them Bertie, don't let them get away. They're a rare lot, and, if this is their village, they'll find it. Don't advertise. They'll arrive, over the years. Until then, we keep the fields working as part of the Cilliers farm. I don't want or need any more money, so the profit motivation can be secondary, but these things will in any case show their own profits in all sorts of ways, financially as well. When you see a citizen of Skeerpoort for the first time, you'll know him, I think, because you're that sort of man. Secure him for us. In that way we can be sure that our village will grow internally. I'd like to leave it a better place than it was when I came here. Now, a lot of the early weed-growth has been eliminated by nature alone, without our help, and I've secured every bit of land that's ever come on the market. And you're to continue with this work, and I want you to appoint successors whom you respect, who will carry on after the two of us have gone to ground."

People who take over my affairs will find this deposition in the file marked "Dawid Cilliers, Personal," as distinct from all the other dozens of files in the cabinet in my office that is devoted entirely to the many matters to which I have attended in his behalf. The question might arise in their minds: What is a deposition of this nature doing in a business file? Surely this is a personal matter which cannot be of any earthly interest to the executors of the estates concerned? Well, that is true, but I have never been an especially good lawyer, and the presence of a document of this nature in my private files is just another example of the fact that I am inefficient in court and hare-brained in my office. Not that you will find any evidence of poor work on my part, everything that I have done for the Cilliers family or the village is in perfect order, and completely up to date, with no loose ends, ready for the most stringent audit.

But you, who will take over my affairs, will also be handling the affairs of the Cilliers family, because the two are indivisible. I do not want you to stomp into these matters with hob-nailed boots, rather, wear a pair of soft slippers. And do not read these papers, the contents of all these files, in your office. Take them home, and take a few months over going through them, while you enjoy a nice liqueur whisky or an old brandy, and, if you smoke, a cigar. I do not know who you will be, but I have chosen the firm for which you will work, and no doubt you will be newly qualified. There are only two filing cabinets, one for the Cilliers family, and the other for the village. You will find that the two are inextricably bound together by a strange marriage of money and love, rather like a "marriage of convenience" that worked, in spite of its original motives.

I have never married because I have always been too timid and uncertain of myself in the company of others, especially women, and I have had to content myself with fantasies of love. I have never had to restrain my libido, so there have been no problems with my sex life. A while ago I fell in love with a social worker of rare qualities, but I must have made some mistake in my handling of the matter, because, although she remained my friend, she would not become my lover or wife. So my life has been my lovely little office, and the work that people have been kind enough to manufacture for me. My court cases have always been referred to your firm, and I have not seen the inside of a court of law these fifty-five years since my graduation in 1920. I leave no children, and my inheritance is slight. You will see, from the last will and testament in my own file, that I leave all my possessions to the Cilliers Trust, as I believe that Dawid Cilliers was wise in the disposal of his estate.

Take these files home (and this is an instruction), and leaf through them as an art collector will page through a folio of his prize etchings and drawings after dinner, over coffee, liqueurs and cigars. These documents are all that is left of my life, and in them you will discover the vital facts needed to perpetuate the life of a village. If I have communicated to you the things that

Dawid Cilliers thought of and dreamed of for Skeerpoort, then I know that you will not allow its affairs to go awry ever, and that you will, in your turn, appoint successors of taste and feeling to guard over the fortunes of the village.

There has been evil here as well, and people have been cheats and liars. These are all matters that, at some stage, have passed through my hands, and they were all referred to your firm for negotiation, settlement, or court action, as your senior partners thought fit.

My attempts at argument, or the application of the letter of the law, have always been quite pathetic, and I was always a poor negotiator. I could only do things that were right according to my conscience, and you will find, in my records, the accounts and vouchers, correspondence and contracts, of an honest man. I beg your pardon for writing my own epitaph, but I doubt if anyone else would want to be burdened with that out-of-fashion duty, so freely indulged in during the first years of my life, by squire and commoner alike, now fallen into disuse, as have people like me. For God's sake, I beg you, look after our earth.

Memorandum: From the desk of Frank Hamilton Senior, founder and senior partner of Hamilton, Frazer, Du Toit and Partners, Attorneys at Law, to Frank Hamilton Junior, junior partner:

You will read the attached deposition by the late Bertrand Theron, one-time attorney and accountant for the village of Skeerpoort, district Pretoria, and its environs, and faithfully interpret and put into effect all the instructions, material or spiritual, actual or implied, contained therein. Please report to me, in writing, at least once per month, what you have done in respect of these favours and instructions, in order that we may discuss the matter further. It is a subject in which I have an abiding interest.

I can almost say that Bertrand Theron has been part of my conscience for many years, and I would like to be kept up-to-date on all facts of the brief. I would also ask you to consult your Bible, Isaiah, chapter 40, verses 6 and 7, in order to set for you the relevant atmosphere of this assignment: "The voice said, Cry. And he said, What shall I cry? All flesh is grass, and all the goodliness thereof is as the flower of the field. The grass withereth, the flower fadeth: because the spirit of the Lord bloweth upon it: surely the people is grass."

Bear these words in mind when dealing with this matter, and much that now would appear to be extraneous matter to you will assume its correct perspective and relevance. Our late client, colleague and friend, Mr. Theron, was worthy of our envy, and we accept his brief with misgivings, as we are not sure of our ability to do it justice.

I should like you, also, to pay visits to the village regularly, in order to familiarise yourself with its people and problems. You may find that such visits will stimulate a great deal of business for our firm, which I would like you to handle, and report on, to me, personally.

Remember also, as you carry out these instructions, the words of Thomas à Kempis: "Opto magis sentire compuntionem quam scire eius definitionem" ("I had rather feel compunction, than understand the definition thereof"), and those of Cicero: "id quod est praestantissimum maximeque optabile omnibus sanis et bonis et beatis, cum dignitate otium" ("The thing which is the most outstanding and the most desirable to all healthy and good and beautiful persons, is comfort with honour"). Then there is the voice of Gregory VII, who died in the year 1085, saying: "Dilexi iustitiam et odi iniquitatem, propterea morior in exilio" ("I have loved justice and hated iniquity, therefore I die in exile").

As you know, I am due for retirement soon, but I will continue to take an active interest in the affairs of the firm. This particular Skeerpoort Portfolio, as I call it, is part of my legacy to you. As I have said, I have always maintained and handled Mr. Theron's assignments and I know that he respected the integrity of our firm. You will see, from his notes, what an intense personal love he had for his work, and this factor contains a lesson for all of us. I will of course, after retirement, continue to be curious as to the fortunes of the village, and I hope that your efforts there will be as successful as ours have been in the past.

I would deem it a personal favour if you would visit Bertrand Theron's grave, and arrange for an appropriate tombstone, with his suggested epitaph engraved in Graeco-Roman script, to be erected, and the grave maintained, at our expense.

You will notice that his instructions, which he refers to as a deposition, with typical modesty, is dated 1961, eight years before his death in 1969, only a few months ago, in the spring. It was therefore written also as a memorial to his long association with his patron, Mr. Dawid Cilliers, whose unexpected death in 1961 was such a shock to all of the people of the village.

I should therefore appreciate your making a photocopy of this document. Please send it to his surviving family. I believe there is an invalid son, undergoing therapy. He may be interested in the high opinion in which his father was generally held by all who did business with him.

Finally, I realise that I am putting a great deal of work onto your shoulders, already overburdened with your duties here and your continuing studies, and had you not been my son I would have hesitated to do so. I ask you to accept that, in giving you this assignment, I do you honour.

15

BETTINA

It was unfair of Dawid to go first. I had tried everything in my power, short of the actual fact of suicide, to precede him. He wanted to be buried from the poor little farm chapel, so sparsely furnished. I suppose it appealed to his spartan sense. He never was a man for luxury, and thank heaven for that because I never did much to improve his comfort. It wasn't deliberate, it just never entered my mind. Very few things have entered my mind in the past fifty years.

I have shut out everything. I live within myself now, raging with great fires, but invisible ones. You would never know, by looking at me, I mean the exterior me, just what a dreadful slut I am. You know that I once had gonorrhoea? Don't you? Where have you been? If you haven't had it at least seven times you're not fit to be called a sailor's girl.

I wanted to die first. It was unfair of Dawid. He should have waited. I am now seventy years of age, and the ten years without Dawid have been a nightmare. I had never, in the old days, known what his presence in the house had meant to me. It was something that I had taken for granted, only after he went did I realise that I was all alone in the Great House, with my defective ghost, that dreadful seed-fruit of my womb and my infections, my horror and my hatred, my love. I was suddenly, dreadfully, all alone.

Mina never came into my part of the house any more. She stayed with Daan, and the kitchen was as far as she ventured. I had often wanted to call her to me, clutch her to me, my sister-mother, black caretaker of my son's needs. I didn't do it because I thought that she would despise me.

I am so lonely now, now that Dawid's footsteps are no longer heard in the corridors of the house at night. I would welcome any human being who cares to come and visit me, because my mind is peopled with things that I have created in my awesome loneliness during the years of hatred of myself, and I cannot bear these creatures that I made to keep me company.

Dawid should have waited, not only for me to go, but for Daan as well. Then he could have married someone else and made a new life. He went without having had anything of his life for himself. We used it all up, the soil and I, and Daan, so there was nothing for him. And he died in such a lonely way, in the avenue of frangipani and thyme that I had made for Daan.

He was sitting there, late in the night, with Daan's things around him, when he died. There wasn't anyone to help him. They called me but the fact that my husband was dying was just one more of the horrors; after all, I was no stranger to agony, it was nothing to get excited about. I had no interest in Dawid's well-being. Why, he was a healthy man. Tell him to blow his nose three times and go to bed. No meat and no red wine. The sleep would make him feel better.

Now he is at the side of the kraal, where the cattle come in the evening, and I want to go to him. For ten years I have wanted to go to him, but the Reverend Webb, who is seeing me more frequently now that I am not so firm in my resolve to be lonely any more, tells me that I may not commit any more sins of a mortal nature. God knows what I am supposed to do with this utterly useless thing that is me, and the feeling of consciousness that they describe as life.

If only I could feed some of this into Daan, in some way, cut off little bits of myself and make nice dishes out of it, so that he may eat the flesh that gave him life. But no, it won't give him any life at all; the spirit not residing in the flesh, nor permanent anywhere within the human body.

I just saw that. I called myself "human." What an awful mistake to make at my age. This mind was bright once, as a summer sky, so good and heavenly. So clean and starched like a layette of the finest linen in the chest at the foot of the bed. That was the sort of purity that I once had and took for granted.

Now the demons have been at me, and I have been fouled

with the scum of scurvy feculence and the awesome corruption of my phantoms, and their touch. Oh yes, I have felt them and their seed. They are no longer ghosts who come to make me love their putrescence, no, they are real now, in the night, and, if I am not careful, they slip in during the daytime as well. So I have become the slattern of my own creations, obscene and corrupt beyond any tainted carrion that festers on this earth.

The good, kind old Reverend Doctor Webb tries so hard to struggle with the furies in my mind, they who are busy taking over my entire body as well, they who tell me to fabricate obscenities with my flesh. They who are my mentors, advising me that corruption is the ultimate purity. The poor preacher, he doesn't know what to make of me sometimes. I am quite the mad dog, who should really be destroyed.

The other day, thinking to drag him down to my depths, I waited for a particularly pious moment, and, with superb timing, as he was praying for my immortal soul, on his knees, I was unbuttoning my blouse, pulling it away from me, so that, when he opened his eyes after the prayer, he looked right into my bosom, still haughty and proudly pointing to the sky. I asked him if he would care for a taste of damnation, just to see the point of view of the other side, but I had completely emasculated him by my little joke, and he had left in a state of disarray, quite forgetting his prayer book, which I subsequently tore into tiny pieces, the whole work of doing so taking almost a full two days, working eighteen hours a day. It must have been a fulsome sight for his old eyes though. They were still as beautiful as they have always been, although they are prettier now by far, because they have a background of decaying, bruised, and wrinkled flesh, which I created as their setting, to show them off better to my vile lovers, the brutes and beasts who ravish and torture me when night falls, and during the day as well, sometimes, when my inattentiveness allows them in.

They have entered me, as men will, and they are all masculine, but totally, and all their beings would pierce me there and make their slow, corrupt way to my brain, where they would prompt my hands to the obscene acts that so delighted them. I hurt myself to the point of repleteness, but never allowed the orgasm to take over my spirit. I was not so vile as to allow that. When it did occur it was because I had been asleep, and I have long ago stopped feeling guilty for the things I have done in my sleep.

There have been thousands of irresistible, hypnotic hours, when the maniacal full-moon braying of the jackals in the hills joined with my quiet hysterias. Oh yes, I have brayed and laughed, highly pitched my voice at the full moon, and, indeed, in all its phases. But I was a quiet lunatic, never one to upset the servants or the neighbours. That would never do. Black, dingy and unkempt was my mind, all the hours of some of my nights, and I must write quickly now in this journal, that Dawid never read, as the time for writing is almost over. Dawid will not read it, it's too late, the worms are at him now in Hamlet's glorious, ready convocation, eager to reduce, down beneath the manure in the kraal-yard, where the cattle droppings form his sweet-loathsome carpet, he who should have been wrapped in silk and carried to heaven by the hands of hosts of angels, he.

I have been the malignancy, the filthy cancer of his life, and I survived. There is a thought for you, the man died, the disease lived. I can't even say that I killed him, because I didn't. I wish that I could have made some contribution to his life, apart from the drooling thing in the yard, that has started walking, so they say.

They bring me samples of my son's food now, the servants. They are well trained, and I am not needed to look after anything now. There is a black man called Port who tends the perfumed walk, as well as the rest of the garden, and there is Mina, who will not let anything go wrong.

I wonder what will happen to me after I am dead? I believe that they will bury me next to Dawid, as I had asked, long ago, when we had made our joint will. I suppose that that is what will happen, but I don't really care. I have other company. Although my body may join that of Dawid in the kraalyard, my soul can never go where he has gone. I wonder if you can be lonely in heaven? I will not be lonely, not where I am going. My demons are waiting for me there as well, and we will engage in our revolting practices until the day of the resurrection, when the graves will open, and the Kingdom will be proclaimed. And all the graves will give up their dead except mine.

I will refuse to go through all this again. If there is an eternity, I don't want any of it. Oblivion is my wish. But with people like the Reverend Doctor Webb about, there doesn't seem to be much of a chance for me. I know that Dawid doesn't want me at his side through eternity, anyway. But he will just have to put up with it. It is not my fault that he gave away his life, wasted it. I wanted him to let me go, but he preferred me to stay.

There was no fairness to his hatred. I saw it, one day, a few years before he died, in his eyes. We were sitting at the dinner table. Those were the days when I still went to the dining-room for my meals. I had been lost in a thought. I know exactly what it was, a speculation, "is corruption the result of sin, or its cause?" I had entertained myself, with fair hideousness, with this little hypothetical unimportance, quite lost in the speculative arousals implicit in its charming simplicity, when I looked up and saw Dawid looking at me. My eyes must have been dead, because thoughts of corruption always killed my senses of sight and sound, so that I joined Daan in the tactile world alone, where I could feel pain, and the demons at me. I must try not to be so disjointed. Daan is spastic, he can use the disjointed phrase. I must be lucid, like water. Dawid was looking at me. A look of hatred, it was. Plainly, clearly saying, "why don't you die?" I saw that, and it's no use pretending otherwise.

Can you pretend still, Dawid? Are you in a state of suspended animation, like an Egyptian magician or a dervish, waiting for me to grow older and die, while you wait patiently, not ageing? I wonder if they will let me open your grave, so that I can see if the worms are in truth at you. Wouldn't it be lovely to know that, when they bury me next to you, you will step out of your coffin and say: "And now ladies and gentlemen, for my next trick . . ." I would like that. I would applaud from within my box, because I know that our being together throughout eternity is, now, just a hypocritical nonsense that you couldn't be bothered to change, and that I will leave as it is, as an instruction in the will, so that I don't have to explain my reasons for changing it. In any case, if you hated me so much, you were perfectly at liberty to alter it yourself, Dawid, and there is no reason for you to hate me, you know, because I gave you your freedom, I even offered to take Daan away with me, to a strange place where nobody would have known about us, and you could have married again, or you could have had a mistress. I told you that I wouldn't mind. I would have, but you were not to know that. I told you it would be all right, so there was no reason for you to sit there at the other end of the table, with your wise-owl eyes suddenly gone cold, and to look at me with the sharpness of a jackal, with that knife-look that asked me to go away and die. That hurt me.

It wasn't necessary to wait for me to die, no matter what you wanted to do after my death. I was already dead. Only if you had flaunted your actions before my nose would I have asked you, perhaps politely, not to dishonour what we had once been. But that look told me that all the love you ever had for me had died. I will take that look with me to the grave.

I will never know if you took my advice and organised satisfaction for yourself, but I hope so, and, if you did, I can only say that you did it with consideration for which I thank you, dead as you are.

Of course, your death will never match mine, because mine has been drawn out for fifty years, all of them lived in utter horror. You have had it served in silver, your death. Mine has been a shabby, overdone affair, and I am sick to death of dying, but the foul things of the hours of consciousness will not let me go, they find me too amusing a mistress for their loathsome pleasures, in which I indulge so odiously. There has been an inversion in my life, and the repulsive nightmares have become day-things as well, now that the winter is here, and I am too tired of their onslaughts to make further attempts at repelling them. I am worn and ravaged by the obscenities that I have allowed the demons to command of me, but I am unable to die. I want to, have wanted to, but there is no death for me.

I have summoned the new doctor, also a Cloete, to me, and I have ordered him to place the appropriate poisons in my pill-box, and to instruct me in their correct dosages, under cover of medication, so that I will not know which dose will cause the destruction of my flesh. Russian roulette with poison and aspirin. I cannot take my own life with absolute deliberation, but I will make a game of it, if I can. There is to be no easy way out for me, I can see that, and, for persons like me, suicide has always been the easy way out, and I have never done it, because I cannot take that soft path under any circumstances.

So, it will have to be the slow way, because the doctor is a young fool, who will not kill me. He says it will not be ethical. I ask, is it ethical to let me live? I can see his point. He is also not one to take the easy way out, and the young fool is probably in for a life of suffering. The next time I see him, I will suggest that he mixes potions for both of us, by which course of action he will save himself much suffering.

I think the time has come to take up this pen for the last time, so that I may write up the last sheets of the ledger, and then lock this journal away, while I still enjoy a few moments of being lucid.

I am hurt, you know. I think that I have paid, now, for what I did to my son and my husband. I look at myself in the mirror, and there isn't a square inch of my body that has not been bruised and scarred in some way during the past twelve years, I think it is, since I have become addicted to the pains that I was able to inflict upon myself, as a way of saying how sorry I was. They also drove me to a point of extreme pleasure, so that I could stop the pain and thereby frustrate the orgasm. At times I went too far, inflicting pain that would not stop when commanded to do so, and I was then wracked by the spasms of satisfaction as I flailed myself to make it as painful as possible which, I found to my horror, only increased my pleasure. This happened once, when I did not know what my reactions would be, and other times, when I did, because I would be in a semi-comatose state, without resistance, as my brain was under other commands that I could not help but obey. I allowed them to take command, because I knew that they would allow me to experience satisfactions, which of course I wanted, because of my revulsion for pleasure. They knew that in my self-gratification there would be hidden a deeper guilt, and that, having had some pleasure from my pain, I would be merciless with my mind after I had exhausted the body's capabilities for suffering.

Portrait of a Lady. I sit at my little escritoire, all gilt, writing in the lovely journal that my late husband had given me, its two little locks undone, writing in my best cursive italics that the nuns had taught me when I was a boarder at the convent in Parktown, where I had been taught all the graces. I am sitting in a graceful chair, not too soft, perfectly at ease, my quill pen gliding gracefully over the page, writing tasteful things: Perhaps, copying recipes for my grandchildren, or my own sweet memories of the happy years of my marriage with my strong and handsome husband. He who could be very naughty at times. Still the gracious lady, I write of the joy with which we received every child as a gift from heaven, and how sweet they were. Of the lovely things they said and the little funny things they did as they grew up. I tell of the expeditions to the great city of Johannesburg, when we would hire a suite at the Carlton Hotel, with its beautiful wrought-iron balconies and Victorian-velvety interiors, the lovely old furniture and the elegant silverware. We would go shopping at Ansteys and Mannies, where the prettiest new fashions were to be had, while the men went to their tailors in Exploration Buildings to be measured for new shirts and suits.

In the evenings we would have a table at Chez Sabaudi's, with his menu of a hundred exotic items, and we would return to our suite tired but happy, to be served hot toddies by the Italian steward in the red-and-gilt uniform. You know, my husband never said a harsh word to me in all the fifty years that we were together.

And there the dream-bubble bursts, bringing me back to reality, because he didn't. I know that that look he once allowed me to glimpse, when he asked me to die, with his eyes, I know that was no imaginary thing on my part. But that was all. He was, even after that, as if he knew that he had hurt me, the thorough gentleman, all kindness and consideration. They told me that he had suffered a number of heart attacks prior to his death, but I knew nothing of them.

I had never needed a doctor and neither had he. What little ailments we had could easily be remedied by the full range of Lennon's medicine that we kept in the kitchen. There was never any need for anything else. We were healthy. So it is hardly surprising, and you must not think badly of me, that I did not believe that he had died, and, even now, it is difficult for me to accept that he is indeed dead.

I am the dead one, not Dawid. Surely they are lying. Surely. I had worked out a speech, that I wanted to memorise and repeat to him, very carefully, telling him exactly why he could not have access to my body; that it was a source of putrefaction, and that he should find himself a clean woman who would bear him undamaged sons. I was a mutilating force, far beneath his requirements.

And I have hurt myself, and my life, sufficiently. I feel, now, that the cupboard is empty, the well dry, the light out. This is a feeling that has been creeping over me in these past few weeks. I notice the smell of perfumes, fleetingly, again, as if I deserve them. Can you understand this? I have a new feeling. The account has been settled. Whatever is outstanding has been written off. There isn't any more. My creditors, the greedy twins, guilt and sorrow, have given up. They have bled me dry, and you can't get water from what you have turned into stone. The pressing on my skull is gone, and I slept last night with the light turned off. They tried to reach me, but they didn't get anywhere near me, and I feared them, yes, but it was my fear that frightened me, not anything that they did.

I have read this rather peculiar document, and I don't know what to do with it. Shall I, perhaps, be more explicit about those monsters of mine, and what they had me to do, or shall I just lock up these pages, and leave them, to be found when someone forces the lock? Or, shall I destroy all that I have set down here? That would surely be dishonest to myself. Perhaps, in the future, somewhere, someone will know that I paid, fully, for my mistakes, and even the ghost of Bertie Theron, careful as he was with accounts, will have to admit that at my end the books had been balanced, finally.

So, with a certain amount of peace in my soul, not really caring what is going on around me, I go through the motions of living, even imagining a fantasy world in which all went well for Dawid and me. I know exactly what is happening to me. I have insulted my body, and my brain, to the extent of extreme damage.

This euphoric state will become more and more pronounced, and I will become, in a few months' time, an amiable idiot, comparable to someone who has had a pre-frontal lobotomy. There are such surgeons now, who tamper with the brain, and the personality. I devoutly hope and pray that Daan never ends up under one of their knives. But Daan is now a man of fifty, and no longer my responsibility. I have not struck him from the nest, that is true. He may have the nest, and I will take only this corner, of which he is not even aware, as I deteriorate.

All is in order, I know, and the will that Dawid and I made is quite good; there are provisions in its clauses to ensure that our wealth will pay for the care of Daan, and for all our other people.

I will call Mina in here today, while I am still able and lucid, and I will ask her to look in on me, also, just to see that I have not become incontinent. I have certain instructions for her with regard to the final things that are to be done about me, and she is the only one I can trust. No man must ever see my unclothed body, no undertaker or his assistant, no doctor or coroner, no policeman.

I know what it is that has entered my life now, replacing the awful phantoms of the past years of self-abasement and flagellation: It is death. It will take some time to come, months, perhaps, although I hope only weeks, or mercifully, days. There is no reason why things should not be made easy for me now. I have paid. Really. I do not owe any more. I will close this little journal now, and hide away the key, as well as those to the escritoire-drawer, in my little box of precious things, that I have not opened for so many years. Someone will find it, and read the words herein. Pray for me, please.

16

MINA

The Oumiesies Bettina called me in by her room one day late in 1970 and she told me all sorts of things, and I was sorry for her, because I knew all the stuff she was trying to say. She was mad. I knew for a long time that she was mad, but I didn't tell anybody, because you don't just walk about any old how and tell people, "listen, my madam is blerrie off her head, man." That's the surest way I can think of to lose your job.

We was two old women, and I was also going a little bit off my head anyway, like all the old people do. I don't mind, you know. Because I know us old people go like that. Missus Bettina was four years older than me, so I was only sixty-six going on sixty-seven, and she was seventy going on seventy-one. So she wasn't so much older than me, but I was not as mad as she was.

I was sore and old from all the work that I had to do, because for so many years I had to do the extra work of the washing of the bedsheets, in the new elektric washing machine, for Baas Daan and the Oumiesies Bettina. I couldn't let that yellow bitch Silver do it, because once or twice is enough for her to see, but when it is every day, then you must keep your people private, and Missus Bettina and Baas Daan, they were my people, and I didn't want that yellow-mouth kitchen-coloured-cow to see what was happening to my people.

Baas Dawid, before he died, told old Mister Bertie Theron all I had to do to get money for things, and there was a Mister Hamilton, a lawyer from Pretoria, a young man who was very nice, who used to come and sit every Wednesday afternoon in old Mister Bertie Theron's office after 1969, when he died, and this Mister Hamilton, he took over all the books and everything, and he came every Wednesday, and any money I wanted for things for the house, I only had to ask, so I got all sorts of things to help me with my work. There was also old Mister Andries Burger, the manager of the farm, and all I had to do was ask, and they got me everything I wanted. I ran the place.

It's only right too, because a kitchen-hotnot like Silver Adams, with her big mouth, was okay for just ordinary work, but my work was special, and I looked after my Basie Daan, and the Oumiesies Bettina, like they was my own family.

You see, I didn't mind, in the beginning, for Silver to know that the Kleinbaas, while he was still a young man, sometimes left seeds to dry all over his bedsheets. That was natural, as every kaffir in Africa knows. White people let kaffirs wash their sheets all the time, millions of sheets, with their seeds on, dried like too much starch.

Hell man, I'm sorry I say kaffir, because now you must use words like black people, or Bantus, or Africans, and all kinds of names like that, that keeps changing all the time, so you don't know what you are any more, so if you don't mind, man, I'm a old woman, and I will just stay a kaffir, till I die. The young people can call themselves anything they like, but I will go on in my own way, because all this blerrie rubbish can cause your head to be too full, and I am growing old, and it is time for my head to start emptying, so that when I die one day, all the troubles will be out of it.

But I won't let my people down. Baas Daan and the Oumiesies Bettina; I will look after them all my life, and I know I must not die before them, because then there will be no one to look after them, and they will be put out into the madhouses, where it is horrible to die.

So I will wait, and look after them, even if it takes another thirty years. I suppose, with Baas Daan, if he lives another thirty years, he will be eighty, and that will make me almost a hundred. You know, my grandmother is still alive, and her mother too, and granny is now eighty or ninety years old, because she was with the Cilliers people in the time of the Boer War, and my great-grandmother, she must be a hundred at least, because she remembers the Kaffir Wars, and that was a long time before the Boer War. So we live a long time, I think it is mainly because we know how to sit down and empty ourselves very slowly, in the sunshine, as we move around the huts, and we don't try to work, because it is the young people's job to look after us, and we don't care about tomorrow, because something will always happen. People eat too much anyway, and you don't need too much food to sit in the sun.

But it's different with white people. They keep right on worrying, even when they are over eighty. You know, when you are over eighty your head must already be half empty, man, or you're in trouble, because when you get to eighty-five, that's it man. There must be nothing left of the worries and troubles, no tomorrows, so you can sit in the sun and do a properjob of remembering buggerall and being scared of nothing, just good dreams, is all you want then.

I don't know how long Baas Daan will go on. When there is heart trouble in the family, like with his father, Baas Dawid, and like with his great-grandfather, and all the women, then the heart trouble is also in the children from the day that they are born. Except Baas Daan, he didn't work too much, and we had to make him do his exercises, so I don't think he had a lot of worries. Young Doctor Cloete has got a lot of machinery, and he puts it all over Baas Daan, like elektric things, that write on pieces of paper, what it says in the heart, blerrie nonsense if you ask me, and he says Baas Daan has got a heart that is one hundred per cent first class, Pretoria, German, best-kind. So if he tries to live longer than me, he will have to get over eighty, because I think I am good for a hundred, and I don't think he's got a chance, so maybe everything will be all right, because even seventy is good enough for a white man, and some, like Oubaas Dawid, he even settled for sixty.

So it happened one day that Oumiesies Bettina asked me to come to her room, and Silver Adams, who was the kitchen-girl then, because she was getting on and she was good with the special food that Baas Daan had to be fed, I must admit, she called me and told me the Oumiesies wanted me, as if I was in some sort of trouble, because the Oumiesies never talked any more, she just sat by her window, dressed to her neck, and with tight cuffs and collars, and small shoes, so all you ever saw was her face and her hands. They were very old, they looked like what was left of my great-grandmother's tits, and she is at least a hundred or a hundred and twenty, anyway, she's blerrie old, and her tits used to hang by her stomach, flat, but they are all shrunken up now, and they pulled up to half their size, all full of lines and wrinkles, like the Oumiesies Bettina's face and hands.

The Oumiesies told me then, that day, that she knew that she was getting too old. I can't talk like her so I must just say more-or-less, like I talk, what she said, about how she knew that the things that were inside her head, down where the bottom of the brains are, were giving her a very hard time, and she was afraid. All the years she was afraid of all sorts of other things that had been right down in there, but they were going away now.

She knew about the bedsheets. Her own, I mean, because she knew that I came in every morning, to bring her coffee, and took her sheets away, before the other house girls could see them, specially Silver Adams with her big yellow mouth. The bedsheets always had blood on them, in the mornings, for a long time. I can't remember exackly, but it was about ten or twelve years, I think. I never wanted the other people to see what her bedsheets looked like, because I didn't know what it was all about. Maybe it was a bleeding disease. I don't know. I knew it was private.

Also, sometimes, there was that other stuff, all dried up with the blood, you know, like there had been a man, or, like you know. Well, if I got to say it, it was like she had played with herself, or like she had dreamed a naughty dream, like all women do, sometimes, when they can't help it. I mean, it's only natural, man.

Well, the Oumiesies wanted to thank me for keeping it private, all that, and I didn't want to talk about such things, because I was afraid she would also start saying all kinds of "thank you's" to me. And I don't want that, because I did all my work because it was my work that I wanted to do, and the minute people start talking about it, and saying "thank you" and such nonsense, then it spoils it for me, so I didn't let her, I just said, before she could talk too much, "that's okay madam." So she must have thought I was a blerrie old fool and not worth wasting words on, so she shut up about that part of it. She was right, it's not worth wasting words on me.

Baas Dawid always knew that, when he was alive, you don't have to talk to me, much. There's special ways of talking out things like "thank you" and those words are very ugly, when you think how nice it is when you look at a man who is your boss, and his eyes say all the things, about you. That's the nice way.

People who talk, and call me nice names with their words, they are almost always stupid, or rubbish. The Oumiesies wasn't rubbish, but she was mad, so I didn't let her talk too much, because I didn't want her to make a fool of herself.

The things that had caused the blood and other things on her bedsheets, they were leaving her head, with all the troubles of the fifty years of Baas Daan, and now she was doing the right thing and making her head empty, so that she could try to think of nice things. She was going to be a baby again, like seventy years ago, and I know all about such things, because it sometimes happens with black people as well, that when they are very old but not very healthy, a few years, or months before they die, they become babies again, and they must be looked after like babies.

The Oumiesies was asking me, and not wasting words, to look after her as well as Baas Daan, so now I was going to have two babies, and a lot of work, that would keep me healthy and busy. There wasn't any blood on her sheets any more, so the things that had once made her bleed were gone, they had been like the things in the Book of the Saints, which is our favourite book, that old Holy Moses, sorry, I mean the Reverend Doctor Webb reads for us on Saturdays at the special story meeting as we call it. Those things were gone from the head of the Oumiesies, so now I could let the other kaffirs wash her sheets, unless she became a baby too quickly again, because that would have to be private again.

Baas Daan's sheets had to be washed every day, sometimes three times, because of the things that he did with himself. I had tried to stop it, for many years. I had even flicked my finger to hurt him when he started, so that he would go soft, but it wasn't any good. You know, they always tell the Christian people that it is a bad thing to play with yourself, because you will shoot all the marrow out of your bones, and you will lose your teeth, and you will swell up and die, or, if you are a girl, you will get ugly babies, and all such sorts of things. They even say that you will shoot your brains out, when your marrow is all used up, and you will dry up in your head and die.

And you know, I once also took a lot of notice of those things, that the converted kaffirs said. I was also a converted kaffir, just like them, because I liked going to church, because it was like a bioscope, when old Reverend Doctor Webb got going, he could tell a good story, specially when he got older and didn't worry too much about what he said, although I didn't think he should swear with children in the church, in the morning service.

Anyway, I asked my great-grandmother about what happens when a man plays with himself, and she said that when she was young, before the missionaries came, you didn't get any diseases from it, and the young men used to play a game, to see who could get it to fly over the highest branches, and who could do the most, and all sorts of other games, and that the young men would sleep in the same huts with the young girls, and it was all right to play with each other, as long as you obeyed the rule "aikona pagati" which means "not inside," because then you would have to pay the lobola cattle to her father, and take her to your own hut so that she could be your wife. Of course, if you had made a contract with her father, and you broke her in, then you had to pay when she got a baby because that meant that she was all right. That was another law.

Well, as you can see, I didn't worry much after my great-grandmother told me of the old days, and the young men playing with themselves, so I stopped worrying, because Baas Daan didn't have much of a life, and I thought to myself, if the poor little bugger can get some fun this way, then I will let him. So I stopped flicking my finger at him there, and I also stopped putting cold cloths there, when I washed him, and if it came up, then it was all right, so I left it alone. I swear to God, I never touched it for any other reason than to wash him and put on Johnson's Baby Powder.

That was something I did all his life, because it is good for a person. I used it myself, and Adam Long always liked it. We are two old people now, and they say that old people must stop after a certain age, but Adam Long hasn't stopped, and I don't want him to. I know that he has other girls, who are younger than me, but I don't mind, just as long as he gives me my share.

I don't want to tell a lot of lies, because I'm getting on a bit in life. Baas Daan is a very beautiful-looking man, like one of those statues you see in the books. He is fifty, but he still does all his exercises every day, and he seems to like it. The dentists have not had to pull one tooth out of his mouth. They come every three months. And he is a perfick man, like you think of the ancient ones, who were all like gold, that the old legends are about, that the witch-doctor tells you about, the one at Hekpoort, who can remove frogs from your insides by just giving you some stuff to drink, when he throws the bones. That is how Baas Daan is, with muscles, like Tarzan of the Apes, that I once saw in a bioscope at the church hall, when we had a bazaar, and he wasn't Baas Tarzan at all, but another baas called a akter by the name of Baas Johnny Wise Miller, who was only pretending for the photos. Well he was just like Baas Daan, except Baas Daan is not so tall.

So, let me now tell you, to be honest, that when Baas Daan used to get that way, I buggered off quickly, and the next time I saw Adam Long, he was in for a hard session. So, maybe I'm also bragging, so since when is bragging such a big sin? All his life as a grown man, I had to wash out Baas Daan's sheets. I don't know how many times a day, because he didn't have anything else to do, until the day of the little wireless.

Let me tell you about this, because it is very nice. You know, in about 1960, it was possible for us kaffirs to afford wireless sets. They were very small, and they catched a station called Radio Bantu right out of the air. I think they called them tram sisters, with ef em. I don't know what it means, but I got a little one, that cost more than forty rand, for Christmas, the year that Baas Dawid died. He was already dead early in December, but he had bought the presents for the kaffirs, and mine was the radio. He gave me a lot of things, but that was the nicest thing, and I got it after he was dead, from the Xmas tree, Xmas eve. There was a note in it, to Moosa, the Indian at the shop, that said I could get all the batteries I wanted, on the account. I played it softly all the time, whenever it was on, even when I was sleeping, and Adam Long liked it too, and he played it also, specially when we, you know, did it.

One day I had it in the room with Baas Daan, and I was busy washing him, and when I turned him, to do his backside, his ear got close to it, so he moved his ear closer, and he took the radio in his good hand, and he held it to his ear, and I swear to God he was listening to the radio. But he didn't hear other things, like sharp noises, or voices shouting. He had to have the radio next to his ear, and so he could hear things, because he would not let me take the radio away from him, that first time. He was like a child with a new toy, and he wanted my Philips tram sister ef em. I let him keep it, and, let me tell you, Adam Long was blerrie annoyed, because he liked to keep it on all the time, because Radio Bantu was blerrie good hey, and it made us happy to listen to everything in the world, but specially the music, with the old songs of our people, and the new Kwelas and the Rock and Roll, and all, and how you must buy Colgate, and Vim, and F.G. Coffee. You learn a lot from ef em. Like Philips don't just make the radios, they make bicycles also. Baas Philips must be a very rich man. They say his factory is in Johannesburg.

Anyway, I went, early the next day, to the farm manager, Mister Andries Burger, and I asked him to get young Doctor Cloete out to the farm as soon as possible, because there was news about Baas Daan. When the doctor arrived I told him the whole thing, and showed him Baas Daan with the little Philips, so he did a lot of tests that day, and he told me that Baas Daan could hear things, but they had to be right in his ears, or his ears had to be pressed up to them, because it was the wibrayshins, like the trilling of a kitaar string, that went into his head, and made his ears hear, something like that, if I make myself clear.

Anyhow, he bought a set from Pretoria, with a big loudspeaker, and put it in Baas Daan's room. You know, it was a special room, and if the door was closed you couldn't hear a thing outside. It was what you call sound-proof. Oubaas Dawid had built it, with quilted leather cushions all over the walls as well as the floor, so that you had no place to get hurt on, or sharp corners, or things to trip you and make you fall. Baas Daan put his head next to the big loudspeaker, and he played the set all day long and all night as well.

But then a lot of other people arrived and they started doing all sorts of things with things that looked like ear muffs, and machines that screamed. So they put a lot of new stuff in his room, special stuff for people like him, so that he could listen to music. But I remembered all they had said about the kitaar strings, and the way they thrummed, and I wondered to myself if he could hear me if I talked to him. So I tried it one day, when it was quiet. I switched off his music, and I put his head against my bare chest, that didn't have tits worth talking about any more, so it wasn't, you know, like that, and I spoke to him in a low voice, with his ear pressed flat against my chest, and he said "mamma." He was almost fifty. I didn't tell anybody about it, because I wanted to teach him some more first, and then I wanted to brag about it. I mean, it's only natural, to want to show off a little.

The next few months I did all the sounds that you do when you teach a baby to talk, and he started picking it all up. But he would not do it by himself, only when his head was pressed up against my chest, then he would start singing with me, and saying little words of a baby, but I knew it was wonderful and not a thing for pity. I wanted him to talk better, before I showed him off to the world.

The Oumiesies was going down all this time, and there wasn't anything that the other people could do for her. There was almost nothing left of her brain, and her body needed to be looked after like that of a baby, as she was going that way now, very quickly. Already, she was wearing nappies again, and growing smaller every day, like a person who was shrinking. One day I had found her, and I knew all the signs. The spit on the cushion, her half-open mouth, her eyes with sleep-crusts in the corners. And I knew also that she had done what children do before they learn to control themselves. So I had another baby to care for.

I often think about it. That it was strange. When the boy started to grow out of being a baby, the mother was going back to being one. Blerrie funny hey, the way life sometimes works. But it was all the same to me. I had to get the rubber sheet out of the storeroom again, and fix it so that it would protect the mattress. I bought some nappies again, from Moosa's store, and washed them myself, in the elektric washing machine. Nobody knew, because the house girl only came in at six o'clock in the morning, and by that time I had cleaned up everything, and powdered her, with Johnson's Baby Powder. I also put a nice scent on her pillow, from one of the dozens of bottles in her drawer by the make-up mirror, I think you call it a dreskas, or a dressing table, or something like that.

But the state of her body was terrible, you know, I was so shocked, I just looked at it for a long time, when I took off her nightie, and got the hot water, to sponge her down. She had marks all over, where the blood on her bed-clothes had come from, for all those years when I hid the stains from the other servants. It was horrible. There was not a place on her, except for her tits, excuse me, breasts, is what white people have. Anyway, they were still perfect, like a virgin girl's. No sag at all, and no wrinkles, but the rest of her was in a terrible state. She must have done it with her finger-nails. I remember now, she used to keep her finger-nails long. That must have been what she used.

Now her nails were short, like they had been made like a man's, so that she could not scratch anything. A lot of the body was full of bruises, still, that would never go away. She must have come out of herself as she saw that I was looking at her body, and I knew then what she had meant when she had told me that no man, no doctor or even an undertaker, must ever see her body naked, no matter what happened.

She was whispering to me, that she wanted to die, but nobody would help her.

The poor old soul was seventy, and she was a baby again. Her brain was gone, she just whispered something to me, about paying, and no more installments. You see how mad she was? I knew what she wanted me to do, all right. You had to think carefully before you could allow a poor soul like that just to carry on suffering. But, you know, to take a person's life is a horrible thing to do, and you must be sure that you are really being kind. You don't want to do anything that just takes a load off your shoulders, because then you are not being kind, you are just being lazy. So you must be very sure about it, because you must put your cap on right in the mirror, so that you look smart when people see you in the house. You must always be able to look at your own face in the mirror, because if you can't, you are in real trouble.

To care for the Oumiesies again, like a baby, was a lot of trouble, especially because I had to hide her from everybody, even the doctor. She still allowed me to dress her, and I would put her in an easy chair by the window, at the little desk where she used to write in her little book.

I got a slate and some crayons, all the bright colours, and I would sit by her, and take her hand, and we would draw colours on the slate. She seemed to like that, and I could leave her alone with her crayons for hours. One day she even drew all over the walls, so that I had to wash them off. It didn't matter, really, because it was her room. When she did it again I let her, and I didn't wash it off, because if she was a baby and she wanted all those beautiful bright colours on the walls, I did not see that it was any of my business to wash it off.

All this time I was wondering if she was having just a living death, or if I should let her go on. It looked to me as if she wasn't hurting herself any more. So that meant that she wasn't in a lot of pain. Now, we, who look after sick people, we know that our job is to put an end to their suffering, if they seem to be having a hard time, that is too much to bear. But I got used to seeing the way that her body was scarred, and I made up my mind and changed it a dozen times without knowing what to do. She was being a baby girl again, and the devil had left her alone, for many months, while I was trying to make up my mind.

So, often I had been quite sure of myself; I had to put the poor woman out of her misery, then, just as often I wasn't so sure any more, and if there is one thing that I know, you need not be sure about any of your own things, there you can take all the chances you like, because it is your own bum you will be falling on, but, when you play about with other people, and their feelings and their lives, you must be blerrie sure, or you will have the problem with the mirror. So, as I kept on being uncertain, I left things alone, and after a while, I started liking my baby girl. I would go to her at night, after I had finished with Baas Daan, and I would get right onto the bed with her, and take her in my arms, and put her head on my breast, where she would fall asleep with a little smile on her face, something that nobody had seen for fifty years, since that dreadful day, you remember?

Now, you will think to yourself, here is a dirty kaffir woman in bed with a old white woman who is too sick to say no, and she is holding this poor old white woman's head to her tits, like the poor old white woman is a baby. That is a bit blerrie cheeky, hey, isn't it, she thinks a hell of a lot of herself, that black bitch, doesn't she, hey?

Well, let me tell you it wasn't like that at all. We who care for sick people, we know all about what they need, and sometimes the things they need can be blerrie peculiar, jong, I'm telling you. I've never been sure about Baas Daan, if I did the right thing for him. I know that he could have used a woman, because he was almost always ready for one, many times a day, and it wouldn't have hurt me to let him do what he needed to do. He didn't know anything about black or white, or sin, or about it not being right, in our country, for people of different colours to, you know, do it together. Also, it was against the blerrie law, man, you could go to jail if the cops catch you. But nobody would ever have found out about me and Baas Daan, because we were left alone.

I don't know, I couldn't do it. I will admit that I wanted to, sometimes, I think, because of the way I climbed Adam Long's frame afterwards, and there was another white man that I also fixed up sometimes, because he was lonely and I was sorry for him, and he always wanted to give me ten bob, that I always put in the collection plate at church, folded across, just like when he gave it to me. I often wonder what he thought, when he saw the same ten bob note in the collection plate, that same Sunday.

It wasn't also just that I was sorry for him, but because, after I was fifty, I still looked all right, because I'd had lots of good food and not many worries, and I got so, sometimes, that I couldn't wait for Adam Long to come home that weekend. That was before Adam Long stopped working and started on his pension, because Baas Billie-over-the-hill, where he worked as foreman, had also made a pension thing, for his kaffirs, because he didn't want to feel bad, and he had liked Oubaas Dawid's ideas, that Nurse van der Kolff talked about to everybody.

I still wonder if I shouldn't have fixed up Baas Daan. It wouldn't have cost me anything. Or maybe I should have got one of my young cousins to come, sometimes, at night. But they wouldn't have, because all over the district people thought that Baas Daan was mad, and that if he ever got loose there would be murder and rape. People felt sorry for him, but they were also pleased about the chain, which held him to his path.

Sometimes, naughty children would stand on each other's shoulders, and peep over the wall, to try to see him walking down his sweet-smelling bushes that Flash Port looked after, but I saw them once, and I followed them to their house, and I waited till their grandfather had taken off his heavy leather belt, with the Boy Scout buckle, and he had dondered them until their arses were red through the black skins. He had to, because I ruled the people there, and if they didn't behave themselves I could get them in trouble because the white people liked me, and I had Adam Long, who doesn't allow anybody to bugger me around.

Baas Daan was used by parents to frighten naughty children, if they were rude, or didn't eat all their porridge, or didn't go to bed and sleep when they were told. So I don't think I could have got any other girl, prettier than me, to fix up Baas Daan because they would have been too scared. You must remember that he wasn't able to help the snot or spit from dribbling, if I wasn't there to wipe it right away, and he also had a way of making funny noises that would have, excuse me, scared the shit out of you if you weren't used to them. But I could have fixed him up. And that would have given him a lot more of his years, because, if it had been all right with God, it would have been all right by me, but I will never know, so it's maybe better that I didn't.

He seemed to enjoy himself all right, you know, when he did for himself, he seemed to manage okay. The other thing, pressing his head up against my chest, so that he could hear things, like he was using my chest for a soundbox, was a very good thing and he kept right on at it, learning words from me, so we even got so far that, if you knew the song really well, you would reckernise it from the way he could sing it. It was the music, I think, that he liked the most, and I would sing a lot of songs for him, stuff that I had half-forgotten I ever knew, and he would hum the little tunes, not too good, but okay, for him.

In that way he would go to sleep, with my arms leaving him, while I tucked him into bed, and he didn't go to himself so much any more, which I thought was a good thing, as he was getting a bit too old to be still, as Adam Long would say, "bashing his Bishop," or "throttelling his turkey." Then, when Baas Daan was asleep, with the music in the little thing in his ear, playing, so that only he could hear it, I had to go to my other child, in the big bedroom, where I would take a big dish of warm water, and sponge her down, and put on a new night-gown and a fresh nappie. She smiled more and more, every time, as the months went by, but she didn't talk much. I would hold her in my arms, also, and sing little songs to her.

One night, she held me. I had always held her, but that night her arms went around me, and I knew she needed me a lot, so I stayed, pressing her to my chest. I could feel her arms holding me, not relaxed, but holding me, fast, as if she was afraid that I would go away, and she whispered a word that sounded like "mamma" to me, although it could not have been. I sang songs to her, the same ones that Baas Daan liked, and I stroked her hair, also white, just like her son's hair, in the same way, you know, softly. Then she fell asleep, and the tight little arms relaxed from about my waist, but I stayed there, that night, not wanting to move, in case I disturbed her sleep.

After a while, she stopped breathing, but I held her in my arms until I was quite sure that she was gone. Then, while she was still soft, and I could move her arms easily, I took all the nice things that she had made, long ago, for her burial, and I dressed her very carefully, so that no man would ever again see her naked, because that's how she wanted it. It was raining, that night, and the telephones didn't work, so I waited for the morning, because it wasn't urgent.

17

MARIA

Twenty-five years after the end of the war saw the end of my usefulness in the convalescent wards. With every year the number of patients had dwindled, and all sorts of strange cases were being put into my beds, even young men who had picked up a bit of trouble with drugs, drunkenness, and a few rather strange sex injuries, which I took to be signs of the times. In the sixties the world was going through a funny phase. Everybody, all over the place, but especially in organisations like the United Nations, was saying that they wanted peace, but they were all fighting one another.

It all seemed stupid to me, but our country was peaceful enough in 1971, with just a little nonsense here and there. I know a lot of soldiers were dying in other parts of the world, like Vietnam and the Middle East, and so on, and people were being killed in the streets and the universities in the United States and Ireland. Some horrors were happening in Europe too, and in our part of the world the Portuguese were fighting in the north of Mocambique, the Rhodesians were holding out against sanctions, and there was trouble in West Africa as well as in Angola and the Congo and Nigeria and a lot of other places. But in the south, things were peaceful enough.

Peace is something that you see happening in the military hospitals. You could judge the trouble your country was in by the sort of case you got, and, for me, the whole thing was beginning to be a bit of a bore. I had been with heroes, in my time, and these fresh-faced little boys needed pretty nurses to look after their healing appendectomy scars and the fractures caused by their drunken driving. I had never been a general-hospital type of nurse where commonplace diseases, deaths and injuries made up the working day.

I was a war nurse, and I was out-of-place in peacetime. My superior officers also found me to be a bit of a nuisance, as I presented something of a problem with my ugly face. The old days when I was "Frankie," were gone, and I was now Major van der Kolff. I had been promoted, quite regularly, over the years, and they couldn't do much more for me. From the rank of Lieutenant Colonel and on you were expected to appear in public, and that would never do in my case. I had outlived my usefulness to the army, and there was only one thing to do, and that was to resign gracefully.

Fortunately, just at that time, my sister Maryna came to see me and told me of a job that was mine if I wanted it. I knew of the case, having met the patient's father, Dawid Cilliers, now ten years dead, who had once been my sister's paramour, I think will be a nice way of saying it. I know that it had been a very long relationship, and an important one, but she did not speak much about it except to mention his name sometimes in an unguarded moment.

As for the job, the pay was excellent, the living quarters quite lovely, and the work was not at all taxing: I was to take care of a man of fifty who had been involved in an accident as a child, and who had grown up as a spastic, nearly deaf, sensitive only to vibrations, able to make a few sub-normal sounds approximating the speech of a one-year-old, blind, with typical paraplegic movement patterns of his left arm, side and leg, as well as his right leg, and with an almost normal movement of his right arm. An extremely conscientious and devoted black staff formed a squad of willing assistants and physiotherapists, and the setting was quiet, rural, and beautiful.

I made a decision on the spot, and told Ryna that I would ask for an immediate release from the army. My senior officers demurred a bit, out of pure tact, but finally decided that, if I wished, I could be paid out the many months of leave that were due to me in lieu of notice, and that I would be paid a full pension, in view of my rank and many years of devoted service, even if it meant bending the rules a little.

I was quite wealthy in my own right, because I had never spent much of my quite generous pay, and with all the benefits due to me after twenty-nine years of service, since 1942, I was due to enter a comfortable retirement. With the opportunity of well-paid, light work, I would be able to keep myself reasonably active, and, to tell the truth, I had been getting just a little tired of my army job.

As a major there had seemed to be a huge increase in paper work, and very little nursing. I really had very little interest in the new generation of patients and neither did they have any in me, with full justification. On the day after my resignation, I left the hospital for the last time. There was nothing sad about it, because there wasn't anyone left who remembered the old days. I tried singing, under my breath,

"You'll never take me alive, said he,
And his ghost can be heard,
As he wanders through the billabong,
Singing, you'll come a-waltzing Matilda with me."

I had a little car, a Mini, which was big enough for me, and good in traffic. The boys in physiotherapy had taught me to drive many years ago, and I had often, after the death of Dawid Cilliers, driven out to Skeerpoort when I had had a Saturday or Sunday off, to visit Ryna, who was now again happy to see me, for a reason that I found sad: Because my presence wasn't interrupting anything any more. Life had given her quite a nice hand, not too many aces, and she played it well. I don't know how she felt about the game, whether she thought that she had won or lost. I know that, with all the negative factors considered, I think I'm in credit, and that, in spite of my ugly face, I've had more happiness, tenderness, and even, perhaps, love, than millions of women more beautiful than I.

It was with no sense of loss that I drove the thirty-five miles to Skeerpoort that day, with my very few, rather pathetic possessions packed in only two medium suitcases and a tea-box. I had never been mean, it had just not been necessary to buy too many things. I'd been perfectly happy with the army-issue uniforms, and there were no other things to buy, except, sometimes, a little perfume, just for the sake of being silly, and a few underthings. I had tried experimenting with pancake make-up and other cosmetics, and, although there had been a little improvement, I'm afraid that the structure of my face, the underlying form-giving bone and muscle had been too extensively damaged. Therefore, the surgeons were not able to do any really effective cosmetic surgery. Prostheses made of foam rubber and plastic could be applied, with spectacles, like masks, and they were quite realistic. So good that candlelight would hide them from even close scrutiny, but, of course, these things had to be taken off when you go to bed, and it is there that you like to look your best, isn't it? It was the old case of being able to fool some of the people some of the time, and so on.

I had, by the sheerest luck, come across the one employer who would not mind my appearance, outside of military life, because he was blind. I knew that my face would not matter much to the black and coloured people, their acceptance of such phenomena as me always amazed me. They were the ones who never stared or made rude remarks after you had turned the corner. It is not that people want to be rude, they are just embarrassed, and they hide it by behaving badly, for which they are usually ashamed, later, when they're alone. I have only found this kind of thing happening with groups, in any case. Human beings who are alone are much better than when they are with friends. Alone, they don't have to say or do anything, and their reactions are honest. In groups they must impress each other by being funny, or witty, or wise, and they generally fail.

Not that I am wise, not by half I'm not, it's just that, in my nearly thirty years as a nurse in military hospitals I have come across a hell of a lot of the basic things like guts, or fear, and there had been a number of wise ones too, like my first lover, Lefty Lesser, who knew exactly when and how to do and say the right things. I am very happy for him. He had eventually learned to walk again, with a false leg, and they had strapped an extension of an arm onto the stump he had on his left side. He became, in time, a big man in the earth-moving business, and his was a household name in our country, like Roberts, Liebenberg, Schlesinger, Anstey and Robinson, more or less in that bracket, just below the huge ones like Wessels and Oppenheimer. I often saw his picture in the paper, after he had given up full-time farming. The family vineyards had remained in his possession, but he used it only as a place of relaxation. Once he had found that he was able to make it in the big world, in business as well as being able to live the fullest social life, he had plunged in and had made a great success of his life, and I was proud of him.

Quite a few of my patients became reasonably well-known in high media-exposure occupations like politics and the arts, as well as journalism, and many of them would remain my friends for all of their lifetimes. Through the passing years I had been invited to dozens of weddings and christenings, and, although I was quite often tempted to go, I never did, because you don't frighten brides or children. Still, I was often sought out by these former lovers and patients, who would bring their wives to meet me, and we would all have drinks, and discreetly, the husband and I would refer to those great old days in the ward, and hum songs that would sound innocent enough, the wives never dreaming just how filthy the unsung words were.

It was no embittered old lady who drove out to Skeerpoort that day to start a new life, certainly not a shy old woman who felt that she had to hide away from the world. Daan Cilliers was just another patient who needed help, and if I could be of service, and live a pleasant life, then I didn't want anything else.

But, before we get to Skeerpoort, I must close off my remembrances of my life with men in those in-between years, because there is something about which I have been dishonest, and I must tell you everything, so that the decks are clear. I want the Skeerpoort episode to be clean, without any skeletons in the cupboard. Confessions of vices are inclined to be dreary, especially when they involve sex, and I find Krafft-Ebing's book, for instance, alternately boring and funny. Especially that chap who was discharged from jail after serving a few years for bestiality, and who immediately bought himself another pig with his prison earnings. I think that's funny, but I have a weird sense of humour, and maybe I know too many army songs. If you have been singing words like,

"Hey jig-a-jig-a-jig,
Fuck a little pig,
Mush-mush . . ."

for twenty-seven years in a row then Krafft-Ebing becomes old hat, and you laugh because your whole system is attuned to collapsing with laughter at certain sounds.

Well, I too had my sick-kick, or, rather, I provided a certain gentleman, not a military man, with a certain awful sexual release. You know, there are people who come their cookies when they go it with old women of ninety, the more wrinkled the better, and those really sick types who go for anything that looks diseased, or the chaps who can only get a release out of the racial thing, white with black or the other way round, and the million-

and-one other types and stages of sexual deviation. I mistrust the word "deviation" because it means differing from normal, and I have found that there is more deviation than norm in today's world, so the old-fashioned types who practise the "missionary style" are perhaps the weirdos nowadays.

My particular deviation was practised with a handsome man of fifty-five, very well dressed and with an obvious good education and an affluent manner, who picked me up in a bar lounge one day. Not a scruffy place, but one of the best. I had been to an afternoon show and I'd decided to don my veil and go into the Culemborg for a nice tot of whisky as a stop-over on my way back to the hospital. Lots of my patients had smuggled booze into the ward, and I had often joined them, so I was a reasonably well-salted lady.

This gentleman, who introduced himself as James Singer, asked if he might join me at my table, as the lounge was reasonably full and I was sitting, alone, at a table for five. He then proceeded to, as they say, "chat me up" with some rather strange remarks about my beauty, so, because I had my back to the body of the lounge, I thought I would give him the fright, or the lesson, of his life. When my drink arrived, and he had gallantly paid for it as well as his own, and had added the right amount of ice and soda, just the way I liked it, I threw back my veil and lifted my glass.

"Well, here's how," I said.

I had expected that his hair would stand on end, and that he would make up some story about excusing him because he had to go to the loo, or that he had to make a telephone call, and then disappear, but he didn't even lift an eyebrow, he merely said:

"Cheers, Miss van der Kolff, or do you prefer to be called 'Major'?"

"How the hell do you know my name?" I asked.

"I've known you for some time," he answered. "I followed you in here deliberately today. You work at the military hospital, and you've been there since the war. A lot of people speak very well of you, and I've come across a few of them, from time to time. I saw you coming in, and I wanted to say 'hello' to you, so here I am. Do you mind?"

"Not at all," I answered. "I'm rather flattered to know that you were being nice about my appearance. You obviously must have known about my disfigurement?"

"I don't find you at all disfigured," he said. "And I meant it when I called you beautiful."

"Oh," I said. "You mean, you're one of those beauty-is-only-skin-deep diplomats. It's the soul inside that really matters, that's where real beauty is found, and all that shit?"

"I don't think you have a right to do that to me," he answered, looking a little hurt. "After all, even if I was only being polite, that's not such a crime, is it? No, let me finish. If I want to call you beautiful, that's my business, and if I want to say that I've always admired you from a distance, then that's my business too. I don't have to explain myself, I didn't have to follow you in here, you know? It was all voluntary, nobody forced me."

"All right," I said. "So what do you want? Are you an advertising man looking for the 'before' part of the 'before and after' ad?"

"I really don't see why you should be rude to me," said Mr. Singer. "All I did was buy you a drink, no strings attached, unless you'd like to join me for dinner at Holzen's?"

"How in the name of God did you know that I can't resist Holzen's creamed cucumber salad?" I asked.

"I think I know everything about you."

"Then you must have gone to all that trouble for some reason."

"Yes," he said, "there is a reason, but at the moment it's the wrong time to talk about it. Come, let's have a few drinks, and I'll take you to dinner in the full knowledge that the attraction is Herr Holzen's creamed cucumber salad, in your case."

"And in yours?" I asked, "what is the attraction for you?"

"Your company," he answered, "and please try to be nice to me. I really haven't done anything wrong."

I capitulated, and we had a wonderful dinner at Holzen's, with exquisite wines, fresh oysters from Knysna, prawns from Mocambique, and a guinea-fowl tender as a baby chicken, then Crêpes Suzette with a ten-year-old K.W.V. brandy, and coffee so thick you could stand a spoon up in it. I ate, also, three bowls of creamed cucumber salad, and Mr. Holzen, knowing me for many years now, had a double portion packed in a special bowl, covered with foil on which he taped a spray of fern and a carnation, which he asked me to take home, "for tomorrow, and keep ze bowl, compliments of ze house."

At the end of the evening I was pleasantly tiddley, and when James Singer suggested music, more coffee, and an even older brandy at his home, I accepted, never dreaming that the man was going to try and seduce me, which was exactly what he did, and he wasn't being polite either.

"I've got to have you," he said.

"But why?" I asked. "You're handsome, successful, a lovely penthouse, you have obvious taste and an eye for lovely things."

"Because I've got to have you. I don't know why, either, but I long to have you, quite unbearably."

"Okay," I said. "But don't blame it on me."

"Blame what on you?" he asked.

"Whatever happens," I said.

We went to bed, and he left a little light on, reminding me for a moment of Lefty Lesser in the nurses' rest room. James Singer loved me very kindly, and gently, with a lot of passion, which grew all the time. But I could only sense the passion, he didn't vent it on me. It was as if he was holding back, afraid of himself. The second time, early the next morning, after we had slept together, I again felt that strange tightness and restraint, so I told him to let go.

"Come, darling," I whispered in his ear, "let it all go, so you can relax again, don't be afraid, I know what's happening, and I like it, so go ahead, do what you really want to do."

He took me at my word, and fell upon me with an enthusiastic, incredible gusto. I was only forty at the time, and able to take a lot of physical activity, but that man, fifteen years older than I, exhausted me. It lasted a very short time, because of his intense excitement, and, after the excessive finish, we both lay exhausted, spread out on the big double bed. After a while, when he had got his breath back, he kissed me on the lips, and the eyes and ears, and murmured "thank you, darling, thank you, thank you."

He disappeared from my life about five years later, and during that time, when we made love every ten days or so, always after a dinner at Holzen's, he confessed to me, by degrees, so that it would not come as a shock to me, that it was the sight of my damaged face that excited him sexually, to a far greater degree than any other woman had ever made him react.

It took about a year for him to say it. But I knew it right from the start, the second time, that first night. I'm a good sex therapist, and I sometimes enjoy my work as much as my patients. This man, James Singer, had offered me any amount of money and security if I would join him, but I didn't want to be dependent on a mutilation-addictive sex-nut, because it seemed to me a little dangerous. I imagined that the time would come when he would like to be responsible, personally, for some of the scars and disfigurements that caused him to become so excited. I spoke to a psychiatrist about it, because we had some of them in the army as well, and they didn't cost anything. Being a sort of colleague I could be quite frank about things, and they didn't have to mince words either. The psychiatrist told me that I had, indeed, been playing with fire, and that we would hear of Singer again, and so we did.

About two years after he had disappeared from his apartment, his art collection, furniture, and all his effects were put up for auction by Jimmy Bernardi, the auctioneer. I made some enquiries, but Bernardi wasn't the sort of man to betray a confidence, so I could not find out what had happened to Singer. The auction catalogue had stated, simply, that the items on sale were from the "Collection of a Gentleman."

A year after that there had been a sensational case at the old Bailey, in London. A man called Jacques Sangier had appeared, charged with carrying a false French passport, but that was the tiniest of the offences on the charge sheet. He had also murdered a prostitute, and was suspected of the killing of several others, by violent, sadistic mutilation, in the words of the prosecutor, "too horrible to describe, of a degree of grossness as to be unbelievable, fiendish and vile." A picture had been published, and it was of my gentle old lover. But let me tell you, I shudder at the narrow escape I had had. I suppose there wasn't anything more that he could think of doing. His aberration had been with disfigurement of the face, above the reasonably unblemished body, and mine wasn't too bad, below the collarbones.

So, there it is, I had slept with and made love to a real nut, and I'd enjoyed his aberration, as it expressed itself on my body. It seems an awful thing to say, but I did it willingly, happily, and it gave me many moments of intensive physical gratification. And the fact that he was handsome, distinguished, and good company, also made a great difference. But what I liked most of all, was that he never took me for granted, and he was always courteous, and, afterwards, grateful.

That's about all for Pretoria, so now we can go on to Skeerpoort with a reasonably clear conscience, not having anything to hide any longer. When I arrived at the village, they told me that

Maryna was waiting for me at what they called the "Great House." It all sounded very grand to me, and I felt a sort of Scarlett O'Hara going home to Tara feeling, but, because of the patient that was waiting for me in the yard, it was also mixed in with overtones and under-currents of Manderley and a waiting Mrs. de Winter.

Two lovely old Colonial style white gates, with wrought-iron work, led into a drive of beautiful poplars growing next to furrows in which ran streams of clear mountain water. After about a mile the drive widened and I saw the house, also Victorian, with its wooden fretwork trellises and porch decorations, and the wrought-iron lace-work in the roof and the turrets. It had obviously been kept and cared for with great love, because there wasn't a blemish. I learned later that, during the Boer War the British had used it as an officers' billet, so it had been left undamaged by their usual scorched-earth policy, because, fortunately, they had been driven from it to the Magaliesberg fortresses before they could set it alight.

There, that first morning at Skeerpoort, I met Daan Cilliers, and I must say that I was amazed. He was obviously a man of late middle age, but he was built like a Greek God, in spite of his white hair. I didn't quite agree with the chain, although I could see the reason for it. Safety precautions and sops to the community can be carried too far, and it's sometimes a good thing for a patient to learn, through painful experience, if necessary, that should he exceed the limits in a certain direction, he could hurt himself.

I had had lots of experience with patients of Daan Cilliers's type; quite a number had been wounded to become much like him. Although the diagnoses would of course never match, he had many external similarities to patients that I had treated. Much of the physiotherapeutic treatment that had been routine in my previous place of work had been introduced into this case as well, because of the father's visits to the military hospital with my sister, and, generally, there didn't seem to be a lot of difficulty waiting for me.

I could see, immediately, that the old woman Mina who had wet-nursed him as a baby and had cared for him ever since, would have to be handled with some delicacy. She obviously thought of me as some sort of intruder, even a usurper of her position, so I determined to dispose of that problem first, to our mutual advantage. Maryna had told me that Mina had spent fifty years of her life in attending to his needs, every four hours. For a woman of her age that was ridiculous, and yet I knew that such habits die hard.

I was set up in the master bedroom, in which his mother, Bettina, had died only thirty-six hours ago, but death had become such a part of my life that I didn't give the matter a second thought. I was grateful for the comfort, because it certainly was a lovely room, and the only alternative would have been the late father's room, which for some reason was verboten to me, or one of the smaller, less comfortable guest rooms.

I didn't mind the ghosts of suffering that places always have, because I had lived in hospital quarters for twenty-eight years, and I was used to them. They do exist though. The things that happen in a house become part of it, oh hell yes.

To solve the problem of Mina, I knew that I had to go about it cautiously, because black women can be super-sensitive, and, in trying to be kind to them, it is very easy to give them that unwanted, useless feeling, and they start getting the idea that they are being edged out of their jobs, which can often be equated to being moved out of their lives. But she was going on seventy, and it was time for her to start taking it easy, and she knew that. I think she may have resented a younger woman more than she did me.

I have come across these resentments among patients and their nurses and doctors before. It is a kind of possessiveness that really clutches at a patient, sometimes detrimentally so. However, this one was easy to solve. I knew, by her talk, that Mina missed her "Oumiesies Bettina" dreadfully, speaking of her with the tenderness that you usually put in your voice only when you are telling someone of a lost child, and I attacked from that front. She had been the one who had done the supervision over the cooking, and I set about learning that department's ins-and-outs as soon as possible. That kept me busy for the first week. I insisted on Mina telling me if she needed anything at all. It was extremely difficult to win her confidence, but one day she needed batteries for her radio, and she asked me to get some from the Indian Moosa, because I was going to the village in any case, for provisions. On an impulse I bought Mina a large slab chocolate, and I gave her this, saying: "I hope you also like chocolates, Mina, because I haven't met a nurse yet who doesn't. It's a habit with us. I think because we need the strength it gives us to stay awake at night, while the rest of the world is sleeping."

"Thank you, missus," she said. "Yes, I like chocolates, too much."

"Don't call me missus," I said. "We are both nurses. Just call me 'nurse,' that's the best name you can give me."

After that she called me Nurse Maria, which I liked, and the name spread all over the village. After nearly thirty years of being "Frankie" I was Maria again, and I enjoyed it very much; it seemed to go with my new profession.

After that, the ice was broken. It wasn't a matter of the chocolate. All blacks, or nearly all, love sweets of any kind, and they can never really afford them. I know that Mina need only have asked, or even mentioned her liking for chocolates, and a storeroom full would have been provided by her now-deceased employers, and their successors, because the debt owing to her was enormous, unrepayable, and the more so because she didn't want anything more than to continue serving Daan. After having gained her reluctant confidence, I got it completely by appearing, with her, at some of the four-hourly intervals during the night.

At first, she seemed surprised to see me, especially in the early hours of the morning, about two a.m., when all white people are either drunk, making love, or asleep; certainly not sitting in the moonlight in Bettina's frangipani avenue, watching the door of a patient. This happened many times, until one day, she said:

"You don't have to sit here at night, Nurse Maria, I will come, every four hours. You can sleep. I don't mind. It is how I have always lived."

"It's the way I've also lived," I said. "I won't ever keep you away from your patient. But I am also used to being with mine at this time of the morning. So you mustn't chase me away, that won't be nice."

"Then you can have your mornings at two o'clock," she said, "we will both come."

After that, a few more weeks went by, and, one weekend, when I knew that there would be a big combined wedding and christening, of one of her family, I told her that it was high time she stayed at a party all the time, and that I would attend to Daan. "And don't come in till six o'clock in the morning," I said. "I've always liked the night shift, and I'll stay with him, because I like the music."

"You know what to do, if he wants to go to the lavatory, and afterwards?" asked Mina.

"I've done it at least a million times," I told her, "and none of my patients ever got bedsores."

"All right then, Nurse Maria," she said. "Just this one night then, but it will be funny, after all these years."

"We will talk of that another time," I said. "You and I both know that the time will come when you must sit at the side of the hut, and move with the sun, as my time will also come. But not yet. I think we both have too much to do first, so, you will have to wait for a while longer, before the side of the hut can have you. But all that is for another time, you go and enjoy yourself, you hear?"

She went off to the party, and I stayed the night with Daan. I knew the signs, when he wanted to relieve himself, and I loosened his chain, and led him gently by the hand. It was difficult for him, getting used to this new kind of human supportive balance, but, when we came back to his room he had improved perceptibly, and I knew that there was a lot that could still be done. I then removed his old-fashioned night-shirt, and sponged down his body with soft lukewarm water and Pears soap, and, as was to be expected, while I was cleansing his genitalia he immediately reacted.

I wondered what to do in his case. I would certainly relieve him, because that is the job of a nurse and a doctor, to relieve the patient's symptoms, should he be uncomfortable. His hand was at it, but I didn't want that. It had been probably his only form of relief ever, and, although I had nothing against it, I didn't want him to live and die without ever knowing what sex was about. I thought of using my hands, and a soft lotion, but I knew what I should really do, so I did it.

I removed my clothes and lay down next to him, putting my arms about him. It struck me that he had probably never been kissed, so I did it quickly, softly, gently, on his lips, and his eyes, his neck and ears, and his cheeks, and I put my breast to his mouth, between his lips, and, as he kissed it, his body found mine, but, before I could teach him any further, he had done, and he lay back from me, gasping, in the crook of my arm, with a confused look on his face. I pressed his head to my breast, and held him there, while he slept. After a while I also fell asleep, and did not wake up till it was morning, with the sun bright overhead, when I put on my clothes and went outside. Mina was in the kitchen.

"I came home at half past four," she said. "And I couldn't see you anywhere. There was no light in your room. So I knew you were in there, with the music, so I came here, and made coffee, and I waited until you came, and now you have come."

"Mina," I asked. "Has Baas Daan ever experienced a woman?"

"No," she said. "I have thought about helping him, but it would be against the law, and I'm not sure that God will like it, because I am more like his mother, and I'm old, but it would have been wrong, even in my younger days, because of his mother and his father, it was their work, that part of taking care of him, and honest to God, Nurse Maria, I never knew what to do, and I still don't. Tell me then, has he, now, experienced a woman?"

"No," I said, "not yet, not fully, but I think that he can, and I think that it is right for him. I am another kind of nurse, Mina, and I have worked with the walking dead, so you must try to understand me. You can see my face. But let me tell you, many men have needed me, and, if ever I could help a man that had been hurt, in any way, and if ever I could give such a man a richer life, or just any kind of living, I would do so. That is the kind of nurse I am. And if our Baas Daan can feel some of the things with his body, that nature wants that body to experience, then I will help him. Let me be honest with you too, Mina. He's beautiful, our Baas Daan, and if I look at him, and he is like that, ready, then I am ready for him also, so it isn't just service, it is my need too, and I can see nothing wrong with two people needing each other. It is a way of speaking, Mina, of saying to him, 'look here, feel, you are not alone, there are others of your kind in the world.' If he can't speak in one way, then we must get him to in any other way there is, because it must be very lonely there, where he lives."

"I have heard all that you have said," answered Mina, as she gave me a cup of coffee, "and it is not for me to say 'yes' or 'no,' but if you are asking me what I say, then I will tell you. Are you asking me?"

"Yes," I said. "Of course I'm asking you. You're also his mother."

"Well," said Mina, clasping both her hands around her mug of coffee, and kneeling down on the sheepskin rug in front of the stove, "I think it is a very strange kind of betrothal, this, with the girl asking the black foster-mother for her white son, who does not know much about such things, and I have never heard of it happening to a Balobedu, although we are ruled by a woman, the Rain Queen, Modjadji, but, even with us being a matriarchal tribe, I have never heard of such a thing, so it is a new thing. I say 'yes.' "

"Then," I said, "I will take the night shift from now on, and you will work in the daylight only, which is the right thing for a woman of your age."

"You are not so much younger than I am," she answered. "After forty, a difference of twenty or thirty years is nothing. But all right, I will try this way of yours, and see if I can sleep at night. It will make my man, Adam Long, happy, and I am doing it for him too, because he is also getting old, and sometimes, when I am with Baas Daan, Adam Long wants me, and I am not there, and then I see Baas Daan, and I want Adam Long before I do something stupid, and I run back to the huts, but Adam Long is gone, and he only comes back in the morning. It's been a bugger sometimes, Nurse Maria."

"It will be all right from now on," I said.

"You were talking about the way people can say things to other people in other kinds of ways," said Mina. "Now I will let you in on a secret. You know, Doctor Cloete helped me to fix up the music, and the ear things. Well, the ears are different. There is only one of the little plugs that goes in the ear, and he likes it best in the right side ear, and that is the ear that I press against my chest. And now I will tell you that secret. He can learn to talk, because, one day, he said 'mamma,' a few months ago, and he is learning to sing. Come, I will show you, so that you can also help with his school-work, because I am sure that if we both work, we can teach him to talk."

I was, as you can imagine, quite thunderstruck. I knew that he could experience pleasure from the vibrations of music, which is a very primitive form of hearing, but I had no idea that there had been attempts at reproducing sounds, that he had heard speech and tried an imitation with his own voice. This opened a completely new field of investigation. I knew that even in the late sixties, only a very limited number of cases could be helped by surgery, but, as I had arrived at the military hospital in the midst of the golden age of physiotherapy, and in my way, had helped Daan to retain the body of a man, so I had now arrived on the scene as his personal nurse in the middle of the greatest revolution in specialised types of surgery that the world had ever known.

Within three years the whole scene had changed, and operations, unheard of only months ago, were already becoming commonplace. The fact that Daan was able to distinguish speech patterns through his right ear, by the chest vibrations of his teacher, and that he was attempting a reproductive process with his own vocal chords, meant that there was a chance at last, after all the years of waiting. There was a distinct possibility that surgery could restore some measure of hearing to what was not a dead ear, but rather, a very badly damaged one.

Mina demonstrated to me what progress she had made, and I was delighted to hear Daan's attempts at following her with efforts which were the vaguest of imitations, and yet, something that was similar, not just random noises. I had worked with crippled people for many years, but I think that my learning of the possibility of establishing an auditory form of communication with this patient was, perhaps, among my very best days. I mean, it was so totally unexpected. Here we had thought that his hearing had been through vibrations of the skull only, a very coarse mechanism for transmitting the infinite subtleties of sound, and Mina had discovered, by pure perseverance, that Daan had some hearing left in his right ear; as I've said, very badly damaged, but not destroyed.

There are three small bones in the middle ear, the Malleus, the Incus and the Stapes. They make contact with each other and form a sound-conducting chain from the ear-drum to the inner ear. This is the mechanism that is necessary for sound to be conducted, and, if the chain is broken, hearing is disrupted, because the vibrations caused by the waves of sound cannot be adequately conducted. The smallest joint in the whole body is between the Incus and the Stapes, and the disruption of this joint, as a result of his injury, was the most reasonable explanation for Daan's lack of hearing. A primitive operation that could repair certain displacements or injuries to this little joint had been reasonably commonplace for some years, and young Doctor Cloete told me that he had already investigated the possibility of surgery in Daan's case and he had been told that nothing could be done for him.

More dramatic was the fact that a new surgical procedure had lately become possible in the case of certain patients who could not be helped by the available early methods. Previously, a cut was made behind the ear and through it the surgeon could reach the middle ear and there he could reposition the displaced Incus, which is often found lying loose in the middle ear cavity, making it useless as a sound vibration conductor. When it is repositioned to make contact with the other two bones it regains its function and the sound conducting chain is re-formed. Usually, deafness due to head injury could be repaired by this operation, but there are far worse forms of damage.

In the case of Daan's utterly useless left ear, the damage had been too severe, the injuries to his inner ear could not be put right by any means because they had been too extensive for any operation to be of help, but, in the early seventies a Doctor Markham of Johannesburg had returned from a study trip to the United States and Britain with a new surgical technique for a far more serious condition: deafness caused by serious fracture of the Stapes, which had been regarded as an inoperable condition, as this kind of bone just cannot be set to knit again. The whole thing was too delicate, the joints too fragile, and to attempt the knitting process was quite out of the question. So, instead of attempting to repair the broken little bone, a futile gesture, the new procedure was to remove it entirely and to replace it with a prosthesis in miniature: a little piston that, in its coarse form could be of stainless steel but in its new and highly refined form, which was usually successful, was made of the miracle Teflon, the same stuff that allows you to fry eggs without using fat or oil if your pan has a coating of it. This little piston is about half the length of a pin, about four millimetres, and it is a marvel of miniaturisation. It has a loop on the one end, and this is hooked around the Incus, and the other end is fixed onto the footplate of the Stapes, and this, once again, forms a chain that will transmit sound.

I knew a number of surgeons in Pretoria, and they contacted Doctor Markham, who, as a favour, drove out one Wednesday with a car-load of testing devices.

Johannesburg's surgeons, as a rule, do not have anything to do with their patients on Wednesday afternoons. That, by tradition, is their "little Saturday," or golf-day. Fortunately, for us,

Doctor Markham had pulled a muscle in his shoulder, and, not having any appointments, he drove out to consult with Doctor Cloete and me.

We told him of everything we knew, and called in Mina, who described her experiments with Daan's hearing in detail, and Doctor Markham was suitably impressed by her obvious devotion to her patient. I had briefed him, and he did her the honour of calling her "nurse." We had to be very diplomatic with her, as she would have been horrified at any suggestion that Daan would have to be cut by a surgeon's knife. She was as interested as all of us in Daan's reactions to the dozens of tests that the doctor performed on the patient that afternoon.

I was in an awful state of tension. I just couldn't wait, and everything seemed to be going so slowly that I could hardly restrain myself from telling them to pull their fingers out of their arses and get going. I had been in my new job with Daan for almost a month at that stage, and I had become most attached to my patient. He seemed to need a break-out of his sound-and-light-deficient world with an urgent desperation, and I wanted it for him too. He was, physically, very beautiful. Others, I think, without my background of caring for the worst cases imaginable, would have found him unpleasant in the extreme, as he did not have much muscular control, especially over his facial expressions, which, with his sightless eyes would have made him look somewhat of a fright to ordinary people.

But I found him beautiful, especially his drive to escape from the prison of his disabilities. Somewhere, deep down in his spirit, was the thing they call guts. He didn't know what fighting meant, or how to do it, but it was there, a natural part of the personality that was struggling to get out into the world. There were other, personal factors, that made it necessary that I should be able to communicate with him, but I think it would be better if I did not mention them now, as they would only cloud the issue. In any case, they are probably medically irrelevant and I am trying to be the professional nurse here.

I therefore restrained my impatience and assisted as much as I could. Doctor Markham, like all medical men who knew what they are about, was a most conceited man, and I liked him for it. No false modesty for a man who could do the things his hands were capable of, he was the best and he knew it. Time and again I have found this to be the case: The modest man usually has all the reasons in the world to be self-effacing, at least, this is the case in the medical world, but people tell me that it is true of all the other professions and activities as well, even religions, where pride in one's achievements is especially frowned on by the rather peculiar bureaucracies of the ecclesiastical world.

Doctor Markham was capable of taking infinite pains. He was a man for detail and there was nothing slipshod about his procedures. He knew that the testing programme would take a long time, many hours of painstaking attention to readings on dials and squiggles made by instruments. He would check and recheck, and he had a perpetual worried look on his face, which rather disconcerted me, as I thought that I had been wrong, and that there was no hope for Daan at all. He kept at it though, and, late that afternoon, as the sun was setting, he asked Doctor Cloete and me to help him with the packing up of his equipment. I was so impatient, I could have screamed. Would the bloody man tell us what he had found? Surely he could see the anxiety in my face? And Doctor Cloete himself was also showing signs of unusual strain, as if his patience had been just a little taxed by this strange worried-looking surgeon. I knew that Markham was the best, there wasn't any other surgeon in the country to touch him, and, as he had just come back from the world of Britain, Europe and the United States, bringing with him all the world's available techniques and procedures, we had to fix all our hopes for Daan's hearing on him, because that was where the line ended.

But he would not be hurried. After he had, with our help, repacked all his equipment in their foam rubber containers, we went to the porch for coffee and biscuits. Doctor Markham appeared to be struggling with himself, as if he wanted to say something. He did not touch his coffee, although he nibbled at one of our home-made biscuits and pronounced it "absolutely delicious." Finally, when he spoke, it was to tell us something that had nothing at all to do with the case, and his reluctance to speak of his findings was making me cross my legs in anxiety, as if I needed to pass water.

"I'm a creature of habit," he said. "And you notice that I have had no water or coffee for the past three hours. This is my way of making myself thirsty on a Wednesday afternoon. Every week, at this time, just on six p.m. I relax with, first a cold beer, and then a large glass of whisky. I pack the glass to the brim with ice, then I add sixty per cent of whisky to forty per cent of water. That is how I like it. I wonder if you would allow me to . . ."

But he wasn't allowed to finish because Mina called from the door, where she had been hovering: "Right away master, justa second." Within thirty seconds the silver tray, stein glasses and a selection of four kinds of beer was served by James the kitchen steward. A few moments later she brought the whisky, ice, and water. I noticed that she had seen fit to serve a forty-year-old Glenlivet, rather than allow Doctor Markham a choice. This, I must say, was typical of the sort of hospitality that any visitor to the Great House could expect, as had been stipulated in Dawid Cilliers's will: The house was to carry on functioning exactly as it had during his lifetime. Finally Doctor Markham, after frowning deeply for a while, started talking.

"It's impossible for me to say anything right now," he said. "I must cross-check all of this afternoon's findings. There's something, and I can improve whatever it is, so you don't have to worry on that score. Now we need better X-rays. The ones you have here, from your late father's records, Doctor Cloete, are not quite adequate. They were made by a mobile unit more suitable for searching out tuberculosis than the delicate sort of thing we are looking for here. I only know that there are for instance, advanced types of hearing aids that can help him, but that's only a last resort. His left ear is gone, you're quite right there, but his right is certainly active, although to a limited degree only. But that, in itself, is full of hope. There's life there. And, by the way, he can also smell but only with his right nostril, the tiny, hair-like nerves that are responsible for his olfactory experiences have been damaged, also beyond repair, on the left side of his face. That's the trouble with these nerves, once they've been inactive for a while they die, and you can never get them right again. But, you know, he's been using his right ear all his life. Those random noises, like a little piglet grunting, which Nurse Mina described as the sounds he made during most of his life, were a form of communication. If we had a child like that today we could do something for him right away. Even if we could never restore hearing, we would use those noises as a basis for teaching him to communicate. But what has happened here is that we have a patient who has been waiting for surgery to catch up with his condition, and now is it going to be possible to do something for him. At the worst, we will be able to improve his hearing to three or four times what it is now. At best I hope to give him a normal ear potentially capable of all the discrimination and audio-selectiveness of the usual human audio-system. Your problem will be in teaching him how to use it to the fullest advantage, and nurse, while you wait I suggest you attend the speech clinic at the university immediately, and get hold of the proper advice and equipment. There's a lot to be done, and the sooner we start the better. I want him at the hospital on Sunday evening. We will go through a further day of diagnostic procedures, mainly by X-ray, on Monday. And then, I think I'll probably go in there on Wednesday, a week from today. This is an absolutely delicious whisky."

18

DAAN

I began to feel what I think might have been a sense of time. Through the years my life became more of living and less of just being. I do admit that there is very little left, of the progress that I must have made, in my memory. When one day is much like the other, and the progress that is being made is so infinitely slow, then there really isn't anything that is worth remembering. I am told that life usually has its mileposts, clear beacons, the highlights of living, and these separate the many thousands of dull days, or just ordinary days, so that your memories are reasonably well marked by these unusual occurrences. But nothing happened to me for such long periods that it is one lengthy blur in my mind. My first experiences with my tactile senses were of smell and taste, and that, apart from my painful progress towards walking, was just about the lot for me. I don't recall much of it. I know the exercises hurt a bit, but I got used to that, and there was the incident when Mina shone a torch into my eyes to make me shed tears on the day my father died.

When I entered the golden age of puberty, I discovered my genitals. Before the age of about thirteen I had probably experienced the usual pleasures of little boys who experimented, sexually, with themselves, but, although the doctors tell me that this must have been the case with me as well, I must honestly confess that I do not remember any of those experiences before puberty. I had also been in a self-induced state of shock for most of that time, and my emergence into the world, dark and quiet though it was, had been very cautious. My mind probably did not want to come back to the world. The memories of horror that are stored in the subconscious mind go right back to birth, and, some experts maintain, even to the intra-uterine phase before birth.

My own awakening to an enormous experience was when, one day, or it might have been one night, I was fondling my penis and it stiffened under my exploring fingers. There was nothing new in this. It was something that had been happening to me for a number of years, I don't know how many, but it had been a long time. At that time, though, when I entered the age of puberty, my habitual exploring had increased in frequency, and I was doing it more out of habit than because of any understanding. There was a form of sensation down there, not unpleasant, like a warm tickling, not more. But, on the day I was telling you of, my fingers found a new kind of motion, and, although my arm was getting tired, and my fingers were over-tense, I did not stop, for some reason that I could not fathom. It was quite beyond my understanding, and totally uncontrolled. There was no conscious sexual experimentation on my part. I had not, like other boys, grown up with friends who discussed these things among themselves. I was ignorant of the fact that it was supposed to be a pleasure, so it felt more like a pain to me, and when it grew unbearable I stopped, because I was getting afraid.

I had never heard of or seen any of the things that usually stimulate boys of my age. I had no idea of the concept of "girl" or "legs" or "breasts." Nor did I know of any reason for the existence of myself or of my various appendages. It was nicer to fondle my genitals than it was to suck my thumb, that's about all I knew. The first day, I frustrated myself because of fear. It seemed that something was happening that may be in process of becoming a hurt, it had that kind of intensity. I took my hands away, but my genitalia insisted on remaining in the erect, tight state, with my testicles virtually drawn up inside me. Strange spasms shook my body, like the involuntary pinching movements of the buttocks and anus when one completes a voiding or the passing of water. This was as far as my experience went in the erogenous field, although I will admit to a certain fondness for sucking my thumb in those early years, as well as feeling pleasure when my anus was being cleaned with warm, soapy water. I also remember, at times, fingering my anus, and even inserting my finger into it. A doctor has recently discussed this matter with me, because I was, for a while, concerned at these memories.

"You must remember," he said, "that your tactile senses were enormously developed, far more so than with other people. You had no idea of morals, modern or Victorian, and you had no understanding of what was happening to you. So, in those years, you were bi-sexual. Of course you couldn't know, and there had been no way of telling you what the mores of society were, and its norms. You were the full reactor to any erogenous experience. You must not feel guilty at breaking any law, because you had not been aware of the existence of the laws, anyway, and, in terms of today's world, those laws of your thirteenth year are now obsolete in any case."

Well, I don't know, I accept what people tell me, because there are very few things that I feel like arguing about. I'm not vegetable, it's just that it is going to take me a long time to catch up with the world, and I would rather spend it learning than in a useless postulation of my own views. For the moment, I am a listener, and, because I have been asked to, I am writing down as near as possible a description of my world as I am able to manage with the limited means at my command. I have a little understanding of language, and the way it works, and I have been very busy working up a large vocabulary, but it seems that there are no words that can adequately describe the life I led for all that time, because people don't make up words to describe things that they haven't experienced.

I attempted to stop my genitalia from irritating me, that time, but there was nothing I could do. I tried pressing it all down, and pulling at the testicles, so that they would drop again, but nothing happened, everything stayed up, and I remember wondering if I was going to feel pain to a greater degree, because it was the nearest thing to pain in the sum of my experiences at that time. This fight went on for a long time, until the sensitivity became almost unbearable, but I continued with it, because I was getting used to the various textures that were now ranging from the coarseness of my scrotum to the almost polished silken feel of the glans. After a while I was more than getting used to it, I found, rather, that it was acceptable, to be pursued, like a good flavour, or a nice perfume, only more intriguing. The sensations heightened, and I found that my hand had, of its own accord, started a certain motion which was quite unfamiliar to me. This continued, and became harder, firmer, and quicker, until I reached the point of extreme excruciation, a pleasure-pain that had me gasping for breath, my head in a state of throbbing tightness, and then I experienced a sharpening of the spasms. I could feel the wetness of the ejaculation on my hands, but I had no idea of what it could have been.

I remember thinking that I had passed water, but it didn't feel the same to my fingers, and, when it dried, it became crusty. The texture was, in its wet state, like that of the liquid that came out of the open places that sometimes appeared on my outside after I had done something that had caused me pain, what I now know to be bumps, abrasions, or scratches, and the liquid, blood. So, when it dried, I felt that I had caused myself some kind of sensation of the same family as pain. But it had passed, not like the pains that usually stayed for a long time. And this pain had been something that I wanted more of.

Now, looking back, I wonder if there is a sort of built-in instinct to preserve one's own privacy, quite apart from the conscious. I believe there must be something like that, because I don't remember ever fondling myself when I knew that Mina was with me. I couldn't control the erections, to be sure, they arrived at all times, whether I was alone or not, and I enjoyed them in the early days before Mina flicked at the glans with her finger in order to inhibit me. Later she also used cold water to bathe me there, and that was unpleasant, though effective.

But there were many times when I was alone, especially in the place where I went to void my bowels or to pass water at the end of my perfumed walk, and I would often find myself ready there. In this way I became a masturbator. I have told about it at some length, and I should like to bring a close to the subject, because I feel that I am invading my own privacy, but the doctors tell me that everything I have to say will be of value in a proper study of my case history, and that these sometimes seemingly irrelevant details can have great meaning and could even formulate methods of treatment for those who are, in some way, ill in their minds or their bodies, which are concepts that are not quite clear to me.

Well, if I must continue, I will, because "shame" is also a word that has no meaning for me. I will, if need be, masturbate continuously before an audience, because, you see, although I know what the words "shame" and "audience" mean, they are not real things to me. I have not been taught in the same way as you would teach the average seven-year-old. I became, from puberty onwards, an inveterate and incessant masturbator. At least, that's how it seems to be. I even dreamt, while sleeping, that I was doing it. I don't suppose it was all that much, really, but it's all that I remember as outstandingly different from what I now call "a long time," also an abstract concept.

I believe that my educators have certain things in store for me, like history, of which I already know a smattering, and arithmetic, as well as mathematics, if I wished, and biology, which, as it is described to me, appears worthwhile. Anyhow, masturbation is an off-shoot of biology. Maria tells me that that is what is called a pun, and that some people laugh at puns, but I don't really know about that sort of laughter, yet, although I have laughed, at other moments, when Maria has tickled me. I'm not sure that I like it, but she seems to.

That first day, when I ejaculated and thought that I had bled on my hands, started a long series of experiments, with my hands, some of them painful and others pleasurable, as I explored my body, looking for other points of what I had begun to know as areas of reaction, desirable and to be sought after. I found a number of erogenous zones on my body, where stroking myself appeared to be pleasurable, but I didn't persist with any of them. My penis appeared to be quite sufficient, and all the others were, I suppose, just fill-ins. I think I am beginning to understand what Maria means by a pun, but I still don't think it's funny enough to laugh at; only tickling and happiness makes me laugh, but "happiness" is an enormous concept, and it will take too long for me to explain it now.

These tactile senses gave me my major life-experience until I was nearly fifty, when I discovered music. I had been aware only of my own voice, which I tried to use in a way that would give me pleasure, something to which I could react. It must be some kind of built-in creativeness that will make a person with my disabilities indulge in a method of using his voice to create little vibratory patterns which would take the place of the audio-world of the normal. I grunted, belched, hummed, made high-pitched squeaks or low rumbles, that must have been horrible to hear, but I must have liked them, or I would not have indulged in them so endlessly.

Then, one day, my ear turned and found a cold thing while Mina was washing me. I heard music for the first time, softly, too gently to make me afraid, only a little pulse beat really, with vibrations high and low, but music. Mina's hand had tried to take my music away from my ear, but I would not let her, it was mine, and I clung to it very strongly. Mina didn't, she says, wrestle me for it. If I wanted it she was more than pleased to let me have it. I put the apparatus to my other ear, where the dullness had always been, but it was not the same, so I put it back where it had been the best, and it stayed there.

I had learnt to listen, and then, when I rested my head against Mina's breast one time, she pressed it to her more firmly, and she said words. I knew that it was like the music. She said one word over and over again, and I could hear it quite well, although it was far away and funny, like a little tickle. She did this many times, and she also sang to me, like the sounds of the voices on the music that I held to my ear, and I tried to make the same sort of sounds, until, one day, I made a noise that was like "mamma" to me. I also attempted to repeat the singing, which was like the music, and other little words like "num-num," the usual vocabulary of the infant, and the usual songs. I believe I managed reasonably well. At least, Mina tells me that I was a marvellous student, or, as she says, "blerrie good school-child." I must have experienced many months of pleasure after that, because I had Mina with her words and songs, as well as the music, which had been made better for me, louder somehow, and clearer. And I had my own body, which I had used for pleasure for the thirty-six years since my first experience of sex, when I was fourteen.

These were highlight times, of course, and I felt that I was able to walk a little better as well. Until then my gait had been very painful, and extremely slow. But, with the growing of my fund of living experiences, I must have come to understand, even if only subconsciously, the meaning of an activity like walking, and felt the first small glimmerings of what I now like to think of as my emergent personality.

These were huge happenings but none were bigger than the time when I felt new hands bathing and cleansing me after I had been to the lavatory at the end of the perfumed walk. I had already become conscious of the fact that a new person had replaced one of the old ones. There was another smell to her, and a different way of holding my arms when I did my walking and other exercises. This person soaped and sponged me down, and I felt fingers on my genitals, bare, not covered with cloth as Mina's had always done. Immediately I became erect, and, a few moments later, my body unclothed, was lying next to a body like mine in some ways, only softer, and I felt arms about me. A hand guided my lips to a lovely, soft form, a breast, which had a firm, hard nipple, but larger, more tender than those on my chest, and I felt it entering my mouth, so I sucked at it, like a thumb, and I liked it. Lips fluttered across my face, and met my lips, and my erection felt a swollen, silk-haired softness. My thighs and loins went into spasm, and I ejaculated without having touched myself. The soft, indescribably warm arms and body lay with me as I fell asleep, and when I woke up it was gone, so I thought that I had had one of those experiences that happen sometimes when I sleep, that are called dreams.

Soon after that a lot of other people came to my room, and tied all sorts of things to my head, and I was probed and pushed about, and my head was turned this way and that, with things stuck into my ears and up my nose. Then a day or two must have gone by with nothing exciting happening to me, and I was made to walk a long way. I got into a motor car, and sat in it for what seemed to be a very long time. I did not know what to do in a car when I needed to make water, so I held it in for a long time, until I couldn't any longer, then I opened my pants and pulled out my penis, because it was hurting, and I didn't know what to do. But the car suddenly stopped and the new hands helped me to get out, and I passed water standing up, which is the right way. I had often been in motor cars, because, I now know, my father liked to drive me around the farm, as a variation of experience for me, so the motion was familiar to me, although it had not happened in a long time. I had never been in a motor car for more than a half hour previously, so this was a rather protracted trip, and I wished it would end, because I didn't find it pleasant, although it was a different thing.

I was taken to a place that felt and smelt differently also, and put into a bed, with things holding me down, which I did not like, and people put me on other things that rode about, and turned me to cold surfaces, and hard ones, and soft rounded ones. My new person, the one who had caused me such an intense pleasure before by being with me, stayed with me all the time, and I was less afraid because of her presence. I knew fear. It was an old companion, although I have only recently learned its name. In the presence of this new person, as with Mina, there was no fear in me.

I don't want to hurt Mina, but this new person felt nicer to me, so that my body reacted. I suppose I had become used to Mina, and the new person was a different experience, and made the world consist of one more being for me. Mina did not come on that trip, nor was she there when they wheeled me into other corridors and rooms, and pushed needles into me. They were tiny pains, though, and I let them be, because the new person was holding my face in her hands, so I was not as afraid as I would have been had she not been there. I went to sleep, and I do not remember much of anything after that, because they had drugged me.

I know now that my right ear had been operated on by Doctor Markham and, when I woke I was aware of a great deal of noise in the world. The days of silence were over, and I could start learning to use my ear for real pleasure, and my voice for communication. Only a few days after that I was taken home again, and allowed to go to my familiar room.

There, a great variety of noises had been made for me, all coming from an apparatus that was held over my ear by a piece of leather-covered steel and immediately, my education began. I still had to exercise my limbs for at least two hours daily, but the rest of the exercises were by means of sounds now.

I was awed by the beauty of the music, and by the loveliness of the voices of Mina and Maria. My education was during the conscious hours as well as the hours of sleep, "subliminal absorption" I believe it's called, below the level of consciousness, which worked for twenty-four hours per day by means of long-playing tapes. I think that I was the best and most eager student that Maria could ever have had. I emerged from my cocoon of silence with a demented determination streaking across the sky like some mad Mercurius, intent on absorbing every message of every moment of every day, in case something escaped and I lost an experience.

While I was working with the primitive playback equipment, Maria and her colleagues in the physiotherapeutic world were outfitting a complete sound, speech and language laboratory in what had once been the nursery, and, when it had been completed and she had learnt all of its technicalities, I was taken there for most of the day. I was, it has been said, the best student ever, and within six months I had mastered the first thousand words of basic English. "Mastered" is perhaps a silly word. Let us say, I had "learnt" them, memorised them parrot fashion, and that I was, very slowly to my mind, getting an idea of what language meant. I was able to use simple sentences, and I had assimilated enough to have orientated myself to certain speech patterns.

The abstract world had been introduced to me, and I knew what things like "pleasure" and "sadness" meant. To me they were very simple, because everything was a pleasure except when I did not know where Maria was. I had come out of the silence into a world that I had, at first, found to be excessively noisy, so much so that I sometimes closed my ear with my fingertip, to shut out some of the noise, but, soon, I learnt that one could listen to a dozen sounds at once, and know what each means, what its origin was, and what it meant to me personally. Once this processing of sound, by the brain, became second nature, I was no longer disturbed by it, and I was continually delighted by just listening to the sounds of the farm around me.

Music continued to be a lovely experience, but I was not allowed too much of it, and Maria would allow it only as a relaxation. Her theory was that I had too much to catch up on to sit listening to songs or orchestras all day long, and she was quite right. The speech therapy laboratory that she had set up fascinated me, as it taught me to use my voice correctly, measuring vibrations, and learning how they should be used to their best effect. It seemed to be a lengthy process to me, but within a very short time I was talking to her and Mina, in little broken phrases, certainly, but the start had been made, and from there on there was no looking back for me.

I now experienced the new sensation of mental tiredness, being quite exhausted some days, by the continuous effort. Then, one night, after Maria had cleaned me and was drying me, I became, as usual, erect, and she, as usual, took no notice. She had never again undressed and lain beside me, and I longed desperately for her to do so. I do not know what prompted me, but, instead of allowing her to dress me again, and remaining docile while she did it, I reached out with my good hand, the one that had the arm working just as I wanted it to. I took hold of her neck and pulled her towards me until I was pressing her cheek to my chest, then I put my arm around her and held her whole body to mine, and turned, so that I could touch her again, all the way down to her feet, with my body. She lay there a long time, like that, and I thought, she must now take away the clothes, and let us be naked. I didn't yet know those words, or their order of saying, but I felt it as I am saying it now. She must have understood, and agreed, because she removed her clothes and lay down next to me, this time holding me to her breasts, and I again felt for and sucked at her breast, while fires of an immense desire burned at me. Then, she rolled under me, forcing me to lie on top of her, and my spasms started again. She made certain movements with her legs, and she kissed me, and I felt her hand guiding me until I entered her, and, as I pressed downwards at her with my loins I again experienced an enormous orgasm, my first real one. There had never been another like it, only because there cannot possibly be, it would be unbearable.

She allowed me to relax again, in her arms, but I was too excited to sleep. My hands explored her body, all over, and she allowed it. This was my first physical knowledge of a woman, and it remains as one of the most wonderful things that has ever happened to me. That first time, when I had ejaculated prematurely, I had had no idea of the existence of a warmer interior woman, which could be penetrated, and I had, in any case, fallen asleep, as had been my habit after most of my nocturnal sexual experiences.

Now, she was a whole new universe to me, as my first experience of music had been once the connection that had conducted the sound-waves had been established. I had always enjoyed my tactile senses, and I had explored textures and shapes for their own sake, but my hands discovering the body of Maria was an experience of pure joy such as the poets sing of.

I have heard a great deal of talk recently, about the soul of man, and the spirit of things, and of spiritual things. I find it all a little confusing. While I had no body worth speaking of and no sight or hearing, that was the area of my spiritual experience as well. I could only relate to those things that I had known, touched, smelt and tasted. There was no other world, no sublime soul that allowed me at least a spiritual existence. There was only the physical, and those things of the soul of which I had knowledge had all been recreated, in spirit, from actual bodily experiences. My imagination could take the world which I could grasp into new dimensions, that is true, and I could think of things related to the things I had known, in new ways, even beyond the realms of possibility. But I had been anchored only to my understanding as a molecular being. And I have a theory, born of my awakening consciousness with Maria that night, that a man creates his own soul, and that until you have done so, you don't have one. To be sure, if you wish, you may give it or dedicate it to God or Satan, but you have to make it first. I didn't have a soul until Maria came to me that day. Slowly, as she took charge of my healing, she helped me to make myself. And I am my soul. I don't like to think of it in any other way.

I asked Maria, some years later, when I could talk, why she had not allowed our love-making sooner.

"The very first time we slept all night together," she said, "I was a nurse. I had been trained that the job of a nurse is to relieve a patient's suffering. I had always carried this instruction a bit too far, using my body as a medical thing, a therapeutic object, not always approved by my colleagues. Anyway, this has been my way of doing things, and my body, used like that, has given me joy and it has also taken away a lot of pain, mostly in people's spirits, although physical frustration can also be painful. Now I want you to understand this, Daan. That night I had been a nurse, and I was helping to relieve your suffering. Then, as I looked at you and helped you, especially during the days before your operation, I realised that I wasn't just your nurse any more. It was the first time that I had ever loved a man who couldn't tell me 'no,' and that made it an entirely different thing. That would have meant that the medicine was taking the patient, which is wrong, you understand? It's as wrong as morphine, or any other drug. Oh I realise that I'm just a habit, and an easy one to kick, be rid of, but, Daan, I had to give you the chance. So, when you put out your arm, and held me to you, I knew, by the way you did it, that you were telling me that you needed me. I felt a communication that was far beyond that, and if I misread you, I'm sorry, but I felt that you wanted me, in particular. Not that you'd had much of a choice of women, but that didn't matter to me. I just wanted to feel your need of me. That is what was important, and that is what I was waiting for, you bloody idiot, until I could scream with frustration, because I had to leave you many times before you did it."

These were things that happened in 1970, the year of my mother's death. Since then, six years have passed, and during that time I have pursued my studies with great diligence, so that I am now able to converse about many different things. The prosthesis implant in my ear was completely successful, and Doctor Markham was relieved, because he had never operated on someone with such a long-standing injury. He has, since, operated on a man of seventy-five, with ninety per cent success, and I am happy that my case proved something to the world of medicine, which is a field I would like to know more of.

I know it is too late for me to ever become anything but an interested bystander, but my fascination is such that I have made the subject my favourite hobby reading. I still work on my speech every day, taping my voice, comparing it to the master guide tapes, working on all the nuances of accent and implication, as well as attempting to speak with the lovely distinctive clarity of Maria's voice.

She has, herself, in teaching me, been taking a refresher course in speech herself, and we have made it a mutual effort. I don't know if she is just being kind to me, or even only diplomatic, but I like it when she tells me that she also needs the things I need. It is one of those things that help to make up a man's soul.

She was once, her sister Maryna tells me, a girl who had had a great future, on the stage, and she had been injured in a motor car accident that had robbed her of the ability to speak for six years. Maria would never talk about herself, but Maryna told me of the long years of suffering, and of the hard work that it had taken to repair her injuries. I had never noticed anything wrong. She felt wonderful to me, and I didn't need or want any other woman in my life, ever again. In fact, the concept "other woman" is incomprehensible to me, because Maria is much more than a woman to me. With this in mind I had begged that I sleep with her every night, and she had agreed.

I once spent a night in her big double bed in the master bedroom of the house, and I insisted on moving in with her, so that we could be together all the time.

There were all sorts of moral difficulties, such as scandal in the village, and a shocked Reverend Doctor Webb, but such things were out of my sphere of knowledge or caring, and I merely refused to be denied the pleasure of her company for even a moment more than was absolutely necessary. I even wanted to go with her to the lavatory when she passed water, and I wanted also, to hold my hand there to learn how it happened, because she told me it was different with women. I was curious about everything, and I spent hours exploring her with my fingers to find out just how she was built and what made her so wonderful. One day, when I was working in the sound laboratory, I was conscious of her talking with her sister, Maryna, in the bedroom next door:

"You'll have to do something to make it legal," said Maryna. "The whole bloody village is talking."

"What do you expect?" asked Maria. "I can't marry him, it would be taking advantage of the poor man. What if he ever finds out what I look like. Can you imagine?"

"That's bullshit," said Maryna. "And you know it. You're a damn sight better looking than he is, with his . . ."

Suddenly they were quiet, as if they had realised that I might be able to make out what they were saying because Maria knew that, with my one working ear, I had acute sound perception and that it was directional. I pretended not to have heard a thing, because I did not want to distress Maria any further than the obvious anguish that had been trembling in her voice. That night, I kept telling her that she was beautiful.

"More beautiful than what?" she asked, trying to be hard on herself, because she knew that I had no basis for comparison.

"Than the first early morning song of the mocking-bird," I said.

I had been aware of sounds and learning to speak for three years, and it was then 1973. We had been lovers for most of that time, and I had discovered the fact of love. I suppose I'd learned of it from the many books that she had read me, and the hundreds of stories and poems on the speech laboratory tapes, so I think I knew what love was. And even if I didn't really, it was marvellous to be able to tell her of the romantic things that I had studied, and that I loved her. She would never allow me to go into that matter. It was a forbidden, closed subject. I would tell her that I loved her, and she would say:

"You'll have to do a lot more studying, and find out many more things than you know, before you say something like that."

"But don't you love me? You speak as if you do. And it's what I want, that we should be in love. Surely you love me, Maria?"

"Yes," she would say. "I do."

"Well then, why can't I be in love with you? Surely it's a mutual thing? And why can you love me, but you won't let me say that I love you?" I asked.

"Because I have done all my home-work," she answered,

"and I know all about being in love. Don't be in such a hurry. And, instead of talking so much, why don't we do something about it?"

In that way I lived through a certain amount of frustration of the mind but it was more important to her than she would actually say, because I heard trouble in her voice, and pain as well as fear, so I allowed things to slide. Once she had said to me:

"There's something you must know about me, before we make love again. You have, today, learnt about the word 'beautiful,' and how some people are ugly and some are beautiful. Now you must realise that, by all the standards of the normal world, I am what is called ugly."

This was so idiotic to me that I could not take it as seriously as she would have liked, but I did take notice of the trembling in her voice, and that was all. If she had expected that a sentence like that would put me off she was being very silly indeed. She had become a deep necessity in my life, and, although she sometimes described beautiful women to me, I could not picture them. There were textures to Maria that shone out of her voice and glowed from her body, a sweetness that was like a balm, some rare salve, and I could not imagine any other person in the world ever having such a surrounding aura to her, so her descriptions left me a little cold, and disappointed, that she should think me so shallow, and that she thought that such things were of importance to me.

I had also heard Maryna's description of me, and I had heard and read, in braille, many things, so I had some idea of where I was in the world. It was no longer necessary for them to wipe my backside, and I could bath myself. I had learnt to use an electric shaver, and I knew what things like "encrusted eyes," "snot-nose" and "drool" meant, and how to avoid them. And yet, although my reading and hearing matter was reasonably vetted, a book did slip through that contained a description of a spastic, and I knew I was one, so I was offended that Maria should hold herself cheap, when I was obviously the more severely handicapped of the two of us. Her answer was typical:

"I can see you Daan, and I know everything about you, and I love you. You can't say the same, so don't argue."

There the matter rested. We became a scandal in the village, and people drove by the farm on Sunday afternoons hoping to get a glimpse of us on the porch of the Great House, where we now often sat, with Maria serving us the delicious little things that were cooked up in the kitchen. Mina had taken to the new order of things quite well, considering that her whole way of life had been upset, but I don't think that she really minded. Often she would grumble about being "a blerrie old kaffir that's in the way now," but it wasn't meant unkindly. She was over the age of seventy, and she still came to the house every day, to sit in front of the kitchen fire with her mug of F.G. coffee, and to sample the food, "jus' to make sure that you blerrie kaffirs aren't poisoning my people, you blerrie lot of kommunist bastards," she would say. I think she enjoyed her new way of life, which gave her plenty of sleep, and all the freedom in the world, to bully everybody, and, especially, to terrify the younger servants. Her special pride was the instruction that Maria had issued to the rest of the household: Mina would be referred to as "Nurse Mina" by everybody, including the whites who visited the house from time to time. She had even secured a blank Nurses' Certificate by devious routes, all properly filled out and rubber-stamped, signed by some high dignitary in the nursing world, certifying that Mrs. Mina Long was a registered nurse. Mina had taken the framed certificate and it hung outside her room, nailed to the door, where all the passers-by could see it.

It had been three years since my ear had been repaired, and I was talking and understanding speech to a greater degree every day, even to the extent of realising that nuances existed, far more telling than the actual words. I realised that, among humans, nearly three-quarters of their methods of communication with each other had nothing to do with words, or the actual meaning of words. I became fascinated by the sharpness of the language of tone and timbre, of the ways of silence, and the millions of things that people could say to one another by just keeping quiet. There were lengths of silence, textures of quietness, little thinking hesitations of caution and long moments when things like anguish sent out other vibrations, on other planes of existence, far more subtle than those my ears were able to pick up out of the atmosphere, but my spirit could. I suppose my perception of these things must have been a little more acute than was the case with other people who had all their senses. It is even possible that I was a hyper-sensitive receiver, now that I had become aware of the fact that messages were all around me, directed at me by the trees, the flowers, and all the living things of the world.

I know, for instance, that flowers like being appreciated, and that the fragrant bushes of my frangipani and herb avenue had become attached to me. Whenever I went to them, they had a way of welcoming me, with vibrations so subtle that I was the only person in the world who could feel them, but they were there, and those bushes and plants, shrubs and trees, love me in their way, because I had loved them so much, for so long. That is why I have decided to stay in this place for the rest of my life, and, if I had to go away, I would make sure that it would be for short periods of time only. I really believe that if I went away for months at a time they, the plants, would be very unhappy, and that they would miss me. I feel sure that some of the most sensitive ones would wither and die if I left them alone for too long. That's very conceited of me, but I believe it.

I would wither and die without Maria, and if I ever told Mina to go away, I think she would also die. There are active living things in the world, and they're not just the obviously alive things either. Stones and pieces of wood also have their microwaves, just like the sounds of radio, and they cry out to us with love or anguish all the time. We should not really mess about with things we do not understand, and nature is one of them. I believe that people who change nature have already been damaged to a terrible degree, and that something should be done to cure them. The world should be left as it is now. We must not cut down any more of nature's trees. We may plant our own, and destroy them if we wish, but there has been too much damage done to the ancient world, and we are destroying spirits of which we have no knowledge or comprehension. It is not my place, after my extremely limited life, to indulge in such speculations, but, you know, it seems that people are like that, and I am that way too. We like to think that we have things to say, even if we are inclined to go beyond the limits of our learning, which is what I am doing. I have asked Maria about this, because it worries me very much. She tells me I cannot grasp what "love" means yet, but I think she is the one who needs to learn more, because there can't be more knowledge about love than I possess. If it were to happen, that there was more, then your head would burst open. There can't be more.

My life had been one of painful movement, and I knew by 1973 that I was far from physically normal. In repose, my body appeared to be that of a complete person, but I could move only with great effort. It had become a way of life to me, but, since the introduction of communication to my life, I had become acquainted with matters like running, walking up mountains, the use of the body for an infinite number of pleasurable as well as occupational activities. All of these things were denied me, a world of which I knew nothing.

My own method of locomotion could be best described as an artificially balanced movement of two steps forward, one back, and one sideways, all in one motion, like a walker going into violent spasm. Without support, I would have collapsed frequently, and my control over my way of walking was primitive and of minimum efficiency. I had been told that it had been a proud effort on the part of my father, and that without him I may have died because of sheer hopelessness. A great deal of me had been kept alive, the muscles, nerves, sinews, tendons, circulatory system, as well as the most important of all the factors: my awareness, my own knowledge of my existence, slight though it was, and the ever-increasing efficiency of the machines gave me a life that, although it was as minimal as an existence could be, still none-the-less carried with it the beginnings of self-knowledge, a tiny germ of identity that flowered rapidly and amazingly with the restoration of my auditory faculties.

I became fascinated by my physical condition, exploring my ailment with all the means at my command, both by attempting continuous descriptions of my condition, and trying to note any slight improvements brought about by my new knowledge of the importance of the physiotherapeutic aids at my disposal. Now that I knew that the pain and other distressing discomforts caused by the exercises meant life in a greater degree, I was able to make efforts beyond the normal requirements in order to bring as much life and normality to my movements as possible. It was a despairing gesture though, because there was very little improvement, even after a year, and I went into 1974 with a certain amount of despair, because I had to live with the knowledge that nothing more could be done for me, and that I would be a handsome freak for the rest of my life, which was also running out on me fast.

You can't delay the passing of the days, and I was more conscious, with every year, that there wasn't a lot of time left for me. Fifty of my years had been spent in the tunnel, to be followed by four years of paradise, and I suppose I should have been satisfied with what I had been allowed to experience, but, of course I wanted more. I didn't like the way I was after I'd found out everything about myself. Once I had read of the condition called cerebral palsy, I insisted on Doctor Cloete getting everything for me that had any connection with the subject.

So, through my own studies on the subject, by keeping an up-to-date file on everything concerning my condition and the latest methods of treatment, I came upon the subject of stereotaxic surgery, first performed experimentally on animals, and later, on humans, in about 1960. Those first operations had been performed on the hopelessly insane or those who were in the terminal stages, and they had been dangerous and crude. My own condition was one in which the early damage to my brain had caused a number of distressing symptoms to manifest themselves. The problem with cerebral palsy is the imbalance of muscular control over movements. Instead of the front-and-rear muscles working together in perfect balance, and in combination with the tendons, they work against each other, causing the uncontrolled jerky movements of the spastic. In my case, the individual flexors were overriding the actions of my extensors, which caused me to develop a series of flexor deformities. The continuous physiotherapy to which I had been subjected all my life had prevented the condition from becoming overruled by contractures, so I had reasonably good movement.

In 1972, a certain Doctor Borchard of Johannesburg started performing operations that relieved certain areas of stress in the human personality by means of incredibly delicate surgery, and, as he proved that he was a responsible man, he was given permission by the Medical Council and the Ministry of Health to perform certain types of personality change operations, the only surgeon so trusted and honoured by the profession. By comparison, for instance, his pin-point surgery to remove over-aggressiveness made the usual pre-frontal lobotomy look like a butcher's picnic. A Doctor Hooper in the United States had experimented with the implantation of electrodes in the brain, to relieve spasticity, and both he and Doctor Borchard had worked closely together for a number of years. In Europe Lars Leksell, the doyen of Swedish neurosurgery had, in the meantime perfected a means of introducing a probe into the exact area of the human brain, localising the source of the patient's trouble, and, as early as 1963, the trials and clinical tests had been completed and the first operations were to be performed on spastic patients in Europe and America.

In 1972 Doctor Borchard returned to Johannesburg, but he had to go through a number of years of the usual conservativeness of patients and colleagues alike before his brilliant work took root and produced a number of sensational results. I got to hear of him in 1974, and managed, without telling anyone, to telephone him and to get him to agree to see me.

It was on a wonderful, hopeful morning that Maria drove Doctor Cloete and me to Johannesburg. By his voice, and the lovely music that was playing softly in his reception and consulting rooms, I was immediately impressed with the man. Doctor Cloete, young as he was, and advanced for a country general practitioner, had inherited his father's conservatism, but I had nevertheless insisted that he came along, as it was only polite to include him in decisions that had to be made that day. I must just say, at this stage, that Doctor Cloete had also been working on my case, and he had often visited surgeons in Johannesburg, but his approach had been orthopaedic, and, apart from a number of drastic operations to transplant anterior and posterior tendons to achieve a certain minimal release of tensions, there had been very little of promise from him.

Neurosurgery was also a field in which he had made a certain number of enquiries, but he had, unfortunately, never seen or heard of Doctor Borchard. Doctors are inclined to protect their patients from their bolder colleagues, so it is not surprising that, in my case, the information as to the existence of Doctor Borchard had come about as a result of my obtaining a recording of a speech by the American, Doctor Hooper, to a medical congress of neurosurgeons in California, in which he had referred to his South African colleague.

Doctor Borchard was most kind to Doctor Cloete, treating him with a great deal of respect, especially congratulating him on the excellence with which my body had been exercised under the supervision of his father, and later, by the younger man. He explained that his was a new surgical procedure, not well-known even in the medical world, but certainly no longer experimental.

After examining me and having had X-rays taken of my head from all angles, he kept us waiting for some time, as he went over my case history, which the two Doctors Cloete had kept up to date for all of my life. Then we were asked to go into his consulting room again, and, as we sat down, he asked:

"When can you have the patient at the Edith Cavell Nursing home? I don't see why we should delay matters."

"You mean, you want to operate?" I asked.

"Obviously, Mr. Cilliers," he said, "and the sooner, the better."

"May I ask," said Doctor Cloete, "what do you intend doing, and what chance of success there is?"

"I intend relieving him, as much as possible, of his symptoms. There is every chance of a major improvement in his condition."

"But this is brain surgery, doctor," said Maria. "Surely it is risky; is the patient's life in danger?"

"All patients who undergo major surgery are in danger of their lives, Nurse, you know that as well as I do."

"But this is different?" said Maria. "He has only just, after all those years, learnt to hear. I don't want anything to happen to him now. I'd rather he stayed as he is, than risk . . ."

"Nurse van der Kolff," said Doctor Borchard. "Your behaviour is most unprofessional, but I can't censure you because I see a certain personal element in your attitude. Let me assure all of you: I have considered the case history with great care, and, let me add, with sympathy. I have decided to operate. When can you let me have him? Please, I apologise if I seem abrupt, or theatrical, but these are most dramatic matters. The operation itself is inherently dramatic, and, in these circumstances, the moment is overcharged with emotion. I'm not a cold man, you can't be when you work where I do, deep in the recesses of the human personality. I have all the facts, and I've considered them with due caution, realising that this is not a case that can be taken lightly. No case of neurosurgery is, at any rate. I don't want to delay. When can I have him?"

"Now," I said. "I'm ready, and confident."

"That's what I wanted you to say. Right, Nurse, Doctor, take him over to the Edith Cavell, I'll have my receptionist phone in instructions for preparation, and the operation will probably take place tomorrow afternoon at three p.m. As I've said, it's a highly dramatic procedure, and I don't advise you to be there, but, if you wish, you may both be present in the operating theatre."

"I'd like to be there," said Maria. "And Doctor, will you inform the nursing home that I have many years of experience. I'm an ex-major in the Medical Corps of the Republican Armed Forces, and I would like to carry out all details connected with the patient's preparation and convalescence."

"It will be a pleasure, Major," said Doctor Borchard.

Doctor Cloete made some sort of excuse, that he was needed in the village, and that he would not be able to be present in the operating theatre. We had all expected this, because he wasn't really a surgeon at heart. His father's blood was in his veins as well, and he would remain a country doctor for the rest of his life. Surgery, and things like drills and knives in people's brains, were for other, stronger stomachs. He was a healer in the old tradition, and, although he told me later that he was ashamed of his weakness, he had never liked the atmosphere of the surgical theatres, where living flesh was deliberately cut into, or sawed off, or excised. He did not mind dressing a wound already made, stitching it, or setting a bone, but he could not take up a knife and make a cut himself, without shuddering.

Maria drove me to the modern nursing home, where a private room was awaiting me, and I was made comfortable. My head was shaved under Maria's supervision, and the nursing sisters were properly concerned, as I was a middle-aged man about to undergo perhaps the most dramatic of all surgical procedures. Maria asked about the anaesthetist and his pre-operative examination of the patient, as he had not arrived by six o'clock that evening, but the nurses left it for Doctor Borchard to explain, when he visited my room in the course of his evening rounds.

"No anaesthetist," he said, "this is something the patient and I have to do together. I must be aware of every response of his, so he stays awake. I assure you, there's very little discomfort, about the same as a visit to a dentist."

Many things went through my head that night.

I had learnt so much in the few years that I had been able to hear. It struck me, as I was eating my dinner, that I was actually chewing, something I had learnt only recently, as soon as I had realised what the word "chew" meant, and Maria could explain it to me. I had eaten solid food, and taken a little wine, and I had loved a woman. Surely that was enough? Now, I realised, I was being greedy, and it would serve me right if the whole thing went wrong, and the knife slipped. I still, at that stage, thought that Doctor Borchard would use a knife, in my brain. I was in a state of fear, the adrenaline was assaulting my system, because I was afraid of losing those terribly precious things that I had found.

Maria took my pulse, blood pressure, and temperature. She felt my head, smooth, like an ostrich egg, and the little damp globules of perspiration caused by my cold sweat. She must have given me a sleeping tablet, because, after I had taken a drink of water with some pills, I fell asleep, and did not wake till dawn, when she had a number of other things to do in connection with the preparation. I was not allowed any food or drink that day, and, at three in the afternoon, I was wheeled into the operating theatre, where Doctor Borchard was waiting for me. He was very nice to Maria, and even asked her to help him with certain aspects of the work, although she was not, strictly speaking, a theatre nurse. He explained the whole operation to her, and indirectly, to me, as he was working. There were also microphones hanging above his head, and they were transmitting everything he was saying to a recording apparatus. I was also conscious of a faint whirring sound:

"You will notice the microphones and cameras. They are recording the entire operation, in close-up as well as on a wide-angle lens, for the medical school. So we're on the movies, and we must be on our best behaviour. No dirty words please."

Some other nurses in the room must have brought up the trolley with the instruments. When Doctor Borchard continued, he once again spoke in language I could understand, I think because it was important to him that I knew exactly what he was up to.

"I believe," he said, "that when you have a conscious patient he should be told everything that's going on, especially if it's all going well. Also, there are certain words that I do not use, especially the names of the instruments, as they sound a bit on the gruesome side to the patient, whereas we know that they are just the everyday tools of our trade. The theatre sister and I have a numbered code for the instruments, and I ask by number. Now, I propose to make a lesion in the dentate nucleus, which is the major cerebellar nucleus which controls tone in various muscle groups. A dentotomy does relieve spasticity, and the only practical method of destroying the dentate nucleus is by means of stereotaxic surgery. If we were to open up the brain and start searching we would have no way of finding the dentate nucleus, so, we wouldn't know where we were. Oh, we'd find it all right, but only after damaging an awful lot of brain tissue overlaying it in the process of getting there. So, we use a stereotaxic surgical technique, which is a means of accurately placing a probe into the dentate nucleus, without damaging any of the surrounding brain structures. After we find it, we can use any method we prefer to destroy the trouble-area, like heat with radio frequency waves or freezing by reducing the temperature of the tip of a probe to temperatures of down to minus ninety degrees centigrade. One can even use a crude cutting method with a leucotome, but this is much too primitive, to my thinking. Personally, I use a cryogenic technique with liquid nitrogen as my freezing agent. Now, this gadget that fits around the patient's head, is called the Leksell stereotaxic apparatus, because it was developed by Lars Leksell, Sweden's great neurosurgeon. It is a simple measuring device fitting over the skull and fixed by three pins; one frontal and two parietal. It has fixed markers, being calibrated to give us three-dimensional readings, and we have a corresponding series of fixed markers within the brain. For this particular procedure we will use the fourth ventricle within the brain as the basis of our marker system. We will make the fourth ventricle visible to X-ray by means of the negative contrast caused by air which we introduce into the lateral ventricle through the burr-hole. This is the only stage of the procedure during which the patient experiences discomfort. The plugs in his ears are holding the frame on his head, and they are causing him a certain amount of distress, but it is reasonably bearable, and they will be removed soon. The burr-hole is now made through the scalp and skull, and for this we use a local anaesthetic, so that the patient experiences approximately the same sensation as he would when having a tooth drilled at his dentist. After this, we will make another burr-hole in the posterior fossa, here at the base of the skull through which we will introduce a cryoprobe using the co-ordinates, which we will have determined by our ventriculography to determine the exact position we want.

"The frame is firmly affixed to the skull, and you will notice that I have used a marker mid-line in the sagittal plane to determine the position of the frontal pin and two markers over the infra-orbital margins to give me the Frankfort plane. I have aligned the base of the frame along the Frankfort plane, and the frame is now held by the two ear plugs and the frontal pin, which has been drilled into position. I have determined the correct alignment of the frame by a marker at the base of the frame, by aligning it with the infra-orbital margin. The two parietal pins are now placed in position and the ear plugs are removed. The patient feels no further discomfort, and the frame is now firmly fixed to the skull. You will see that the routine frontal burr-hole is two fingers back from the anterior bar of the frame or there will be no room for the calibrated metal measuring arc which is part of the box-like frame, an essential piece of equipment when you are attempting to find a fixed position in the interior of an egglike shape such as the human head.

"I will now put a brain cannula into the lateral ventricle and introduce twenty cubic centimetres of air. This will adequately fill the anterior horns of both lateral ventricles, the third ventricle aquaduct and the fourth ventricle without giving us too much air on the surface. We don't want that, as it will induce headache and nausea in the patient, and he has quite a lot to put up with as it is.

"The head will now remain in the special head-rest of the Leksell apparatus which enables the frame to fit around the skull without impeding an X-ray beam. And now I apply the optical bench to the frame and I take a lateral X-ray before swinging the X-ray tube round by ninety degrees to get an a.p. view. I will now leave the patient for a while, and we will go to the X-ray room to view the plates. With the various markers and points of reference, as well as the air outlines, I have a series of fixed anatomical markers. I apply a model of the ventricular system and I compare the third and fourth ventricles with a set square, on the X-rays. Now, with the next X-ray, you have measurements in three directions. After applying this information to the guide measuring devices, on the frame with its metal arc, a probe point can be introduced with all the accuracy necessary. It can, in fact, be at one point in the brain only, and you cannot find that point by any other method. We are at the dentate nucleus, where the root of our patient's trouble is situated, into which I will make the lesion that will, I believe, relieve him of much of his spasticity. Now that the brain needle has been withdrawn and the burr-hole closed, a fresh burr-hole is made at the back of the skull, the table is tilted, and we introduce the probe that will carry the liquid nitrogen, our freezing agent, to the target area. This large machine controls the temperature at the point of the probe, which we know, without doubt, to be at the dentate nucleus, in the absolutely correct place in the cerebellum. The lesion is made by freezing, and while I make the lesion I test the patient. I drop the temperature at the probe-point to zero and note the effect on the patient. Here I expect to see some loosening of his movement and, as you can see, he is responding well. If this lesion is satisfactory and produces no ill-effects after sixty seconds, as is the case with this patient, I drop the temperature to minus twenty degrees. Now we can definitely see a loosening of his movements. He is displaying an expected lead-pipe type of rigidity, but there are no side effects or weakness, so let's take the temperature down to minus forty degrees for another sixty seconds. Now you will notice, his rigidity has been almost totally relieved, and this patient is responding to the treatment. If it had not been the case, I would have modified the position of the probe-tip. Now, I will bring the temperature of the probe-tip down to minus seventy degrees, then minus eighty, each for sixty seconds, and now, down to minus ninety degrees for ninety seconds. The probe-tip will then be allowed to warm up gradually. I now have a globular-shaped lesion, one centimetre in diameter, which is all that is needed, because as you can see, the patient's affected leg and arm are normal, completely without rigidity. Now, the probe-tip temperature is thirty-six degrees centigrade and the ice-ball has melted, so it can be withdrawn. I will now close up the burr-hole, remove the frame, and send the patient back to his ward. I have done the worst side first, and he has regained the use of his arm and leg. Three months from now, I will repeat the procedure for the remaining affected leg. When he gets back to his ward he will have to stay there for five days of treatment with antibiotics. We have tried our best to work under sterile conditions, but, because of the great deal of machinery involved: X-ray tubes, the Leksell apparatus and the liquid nitrogen machinery with its controlling equipment, as well as the tape recorders and cameras, it is difficult to be sure, hence the prophylactic antibiotics. Tomorrow the patient will get out of bed, and, immediately, he will commence with intensive physiotherapy, which, I believe will be a continuation in this case. I expect to discharge him after removing his stitches, five days from today."

19

MARYNA

After Daan got the use of his body back to as normal as dammit, because of the brilliant Doctor Borchard and his two operations, we were all very gratified. Our patient was a most handsome person indeed, strong, and filled with enthusiasm for living. He was most devoted to my sister, and would not go anywhere without her, and he would grow moody and depressed if she stayed away too long at the shops, or in the vegetable garden, where she would go with Mina to pick fresh things for the table.

Maria and Mina had become like sisters, and I truly believe that it was an essential relationship for both of them, caused by their closeness to Daan. Both of them knew, without it having to be said, that any enmity between them would have distressed him immensely, so they made determined efforts not to allow their jealousies, or other irritations of any sort, to spoil the happiness in the Great House. Knowing that their sole concern was Daan's happiness, and being determined that he should enjoy as much of his life as remained to him to its fullest, he was treated rather like a spoiled child. His every little wish was treated as a command from royalty, and he luxuriated in the love that was given him.

He had gone through many books in braille, and Maria had read to him, constantly. There were tapes and records by the score, and their home was a riot of flavours, perfumes and sounds. My sister made us all, including Daan, unhappy by her refusal to marry him. She still felt that he did not have the experience of people to make up his own mind, and she told me that marrying him would have made her feel like a thief, so that she could never look even an inoffensive policeman like Sergeant Karner in the face. This was more and more distressing to Daan, as the months went by, but try as I might, I could not budge her an inch.

Both of us had changed, and we never used bad language any more, except in moments of stress or loss of control, which wasn't very often. I had given up my bad language when Dawid had become my lover. After he had died I had resumed my old habits of coarse speech for some years, but, gradually, as my sister's relationship with Daan grew, I respected her wish for a quieter speech-pattern, more gracious than before, and after a while I found that I was enjoying being the perfect lady, as befitted my seniority and degree.

I had long since been released from active duty by the department, although I was still expected to make the occasional report to head office, more as a gesture than as work. I had been writing up my case histories, as well as certain theories that I had formulated in the socio-economic field, and I was respected in the Ministries of Health as well as of Social Welfare, where I often attended discussions on my subject in an advisory capacity.

Dawid's red leather chair had been brought back to my little cottage, and although, in terms of his will, I could have kept the apartment in Pretoria, it was too painful to be there alone, so I told the attorneys to let it go, and to send the furniture to my place in Skeerpoort, where I could look after his things. I would never sit in his chair, but I often felt that he was there, and I would spend at least every Sunday morning in the little farm chapel, with its few acres, that he had bequeathed to me. I could not look at the altar, for many years, without thinking of the day that his coffin had been there, but, with time, the wounds healed, and I felt his spirit again, warm about me.

I had a lot to be grateful for, with my memories of a young as well as a mature love, and my work, that still fascinated me. Approaching sixty, I knew that although the department didn't really need me any more, I still had things to say, and I would have a goodly volume of work for them from time to time. So I continued my researches, and read of all the things that were happening in the world to make it a better place for people to live in.

I lived in a model district, and, like an old hen, I did not allow anything to become slack again. Cracks in walls or broken heaters had to be mended, rusted roofs replaced, and my efforts made whitewash a good selling line at both shops. I visited the Great House often, at least once every weekend and once during the week, when I would stay and have dinner, and Ezekiel, the chauffeur, would drive me home in Daan's lovely old Rolls Royce. This was a vehicle that he had read of once, in one of his books, and he had asked Maria to describe it to him. He had inherited his father's practical mind, and loved to hear about the way things worked. When he had heard what a Rolls was, there was nothing for it but that he had to go into Rosebank, a suburb of Johannesburg, where the agency was, and he had purchased a lovely old 1936 model, with cocktail cabinet, Persian carpeting, cowhide seats, and a smell of polished wood-and-leather. He enjoyed that car as a child would a favourite toy, and often he would run his hands over its polished surfaces, feeling its shapes.

I must say that it was a thrill for me to be picked up and driven to the Great House by Ezekiel, who was a slow, sedate type, perfectly matching the car that he had to care for.

I was forever amazed at the delightful flavours of the edibles in that household. Never have I come across a more masterly kitchen, with its particular flavours, and their ingredients having been passed on for generations of cooks and their assistants.

Daan would never let a day go by without asking Maria to marry him, and I got very angry with her, when she refused him. I didn't care if she looked ugly, there was a lot more to Daan's love than just appearances, and I could not get her to admit it. She was still subservient to her injury, and it depressed me to feel that she would go through her entire life without once knowing that her appearance had, at last, become a zero factor. Her life had been made for Daan. Without her he would never have experienced anything of what living and love was. He put it so well, always, interminably calling his experiences the textures of life that he was going through. He was a most fascinating person in his own right, and there was no longer any reason to pity him in any way.

Maria was an equally fascinating woman, with a deep, wise maturity that fell down when the question of marriage came up. Daan had even threatened not to go through with Doctor Borchard's second operation if she persisted in refusing, but even that bit of blackmail didn't work. She merely made him go, and would not listen to any of his protestations.

"I am not," he would say, "an idiot child, to be humoured. I know my own mind, and I am not going to allow Doctor Borchard to do a thing about my leg before you promise to marry me."

"Yes, yes, yes, all right, now get into the car and let's go, we don't want to keep anybody waiting, and Doctor Borchard isn't patient with rude people."

"So does that mean you'll marry me?"

"But my love, we're already married. I'm your common-law wife, ask any attorney. If you ever try to get away from me and run off with some pretty young floozy, I'll give you the hardest time you've ever had, in court."

"You're humouring me again, Maria," he would say. "Please, admit it, you'll marry me as soon as I can walk up the aisle."

"Let's get the operation done with first, love. Don't throw away your crutches too soon, or you'll fall flat on your bum."

"Maria, I must insist that you stop humouring me."

That was the sort of conversation that went on between them, and it started getting on my nerves. Mina had her own solution to the problem. She told me how she and Adam Long had been tricked into marriage by Bettina many years ago, but I wasn't up to playing that sort of prank on Daan and Maria. There were basics involved here that had to be solved by wisdom, the sort of knowledge that came from the healing processes of the earth and the sun. I wasn't a denizen of that rarefied world, although I suspect that Dawid had been, and that Daan, once he had found himself as a complete being, would also develop the no-nonsense attitudes that were beginning to be a part of his conversation.

His first attempts at using language had been a little self-conscious. He had appeared to enjoy his growing vocabulary. But lately, he had returned to a directness of speech that had a simple charm about it, but also a strength that no amount of verbal ornamentation could match. One day, when Mina and I sat talking in the kitchen, which was one of our habits (because I would often just drop in unexpectedly and have a cup of coffee and a plate of biscuits, which I adored), she asked me a strange question.

"You remember, Nurse Maryna, that time when Baas Daan started listening, when I put my tram sister radio down, and he felt the music like you explained."

"Yes Mina," I said, "that was the miracle day, that opened up the whole thing for him, the whole box of magic."

"Ag man Nurse Maryna man," she answered, "stop that kind of talking now and listen. What about his eyes then?"

"Well, what about his eyes?"

"You remember, when the Oubaas Dawid died, I made him cry, with the big torch?"

"Yes, Mina, I remember now. I think you were just making his eyes burn. Blind people cry, you know."

"Well, I don't know," she said. "I still think it's worth a try."

I couldn't really take her seriously, but I couldn't put it out of my head entirely either. I had a great deal of literature concerning blindness, as it was a big problem in rural Africa, especially among the blacks, who were prone to all sorts of eye diseases. So, for fun, or to pass the time, or perhaps just hoping, I read some of the literature about blindness that had come in my mail.

We had been into the matter locally, but there had been no ophthalmologist who could do anything for Daan, the general opinion being that once eyes had not been used for half a century then regeneration of the long-dead optic nerves would be out of the question. We knew that he had some slight sense of light perception, knowing the difference between a dark room and a sunlit exterior, but the surgeons had expressed regret, and had said that nothing could be done for Daan.

Once again, I had allowed time to go by, without realising that a truth of even a few months ago could now be a lie, and the hopeless case of last year was today's curable patient. In a newsletter from the Pacific University College of Optometry, I.came across a paragraph describing a new series of tests designed to determine the potential for sight of thousands of hitherto incurably blind patients. Called VER, or Visual Evoked Response, it described, for me, a bewildering method of diagnosis and testing by means of electronic amplification and computerised monitoring, which even the technicians concerned admitted was "a very complex procedure." But what interested me most was that it was a report on a postgraduate course and that it had drawn a registration limited to twenty-three optometrists and optometric educators from seven states and two foreign countries.

"Registrands," read the report, "including one from Johannesburg, South Africa, divided their time between lecture sessions and participating laboratory demonstrations, under the tutelage of William Laidlaw, OD."

I wondered, had I found a second Doctor Borchard, a surgeon who was up to date with the very newest techniques in the world? I had to take the chance, even if it proved futile. It was easy for me to get Doctor Laidlaw on the phone, at Pacific University. We have a party line system, and it is virtually impossible to phone anyone at the next village, say Broederstroom, because of the design of the system, unless you are prepared for a delay of some days or hours, depending on your luck, and the outside world of Johannesburg or Pretoria couldn't contact us at all under any circumstances, but a call to California was no problem. The mere thought of the technical problems alone chased the fear of God into the telephonists, and, within minutes, all the lines had been cleared and you were through. Doctor Laidlaw, on hearing that he was being telephoned from South Africa, abandoned a lecture and spoke to me, and I described the case to him as concisely as I could, and he said: "Six months ago I would have said 'no way' but this sounds interesting, certainly worth investigating. Go see your Doctor Teasdale in Johannesburg, tell him you've had a chat with me, and I'd like to hear more about it."

I immediately telephoned Doctor Teasdale and, hearing that I had been recommended by the famous Doctor Laidlaw of California, U.S.A., he was immediately willing to grant me an appointment. There was only one snag, I had to bring the patient along with me, as it would not be possible for the doctor to venture a guess as to diagnosis or prognosis without an actual examination. I did not want to raise Maria and Daan's hopes unduly. The cures that had already been effected had been nothing short of miraculous, but it was that sort of time in the world of surgery, and every facet of medicine seemed to be moving ahead almost faster than most doctors could keep up with it. I did wonder if coveting sight for Daan, as well, wasn't being just a bit on the greedy side. But, on the other hand, if it was possible for him to see then we had to do everything in our power to make it happen. I was not prepared for the reaction from Maria when I drove out and told her what I had done. She was particularly upset, and I felt that I had done something wrong and thoughtless.

"Ryna," she said. "Of course I want Daan to see, more than

anything in the world. But, can't you understand, I can never let him see me?"

"Oh Christ," I exploded, "are you still on that silly theory. It really is time for you to get another, this one has been ridden to the point of being hollow-backed, like a horse that has carried too much weight in its day. You're supposed to be a nurse, and a major at that. Can't you see that there isn't anything you can do to prevent him seeing, if it is possible, and, let me tell you, the possibility is very slight indeed. But whatever your personal feelings might be in the matter, there is nothing you can do about it. Your job is clear, and you must do it."

"You're right," she said. "But I don't like it. Oh hell, Ryna, why wasn't it possible for the doctors to find out these new things about eyes just a few years later? I've had such a short time with him, and now it's all over, in a moment. Just like that. There's a possibility that he will be able to see what I look like, so that ends it. I know what you think, and he agrees with you. But I know what I see in the mirror, and if he ever sees that then I'm afraid it's all over for me. He will be looking at other women in the streets, young and beautiful. I'm not only ugly, but I'm middle-aged as well. My whole life had been mapped out before me. I knew exactly how and why I was alive; because I loved Daan and I wanted to care for him for the rest of my life. And now, this possibility."

"And remember," I said, "before you go panicking too far ahead, it is only a possibility, nobody is at all sure of anything."

"Then, Ryna, the best thing is to take him to the doctor and get him examined."

"Surely," I said, "you must have been expecting something like this. In view of all the other things that suddenly became possible in the seventies, you must have considered the possibility of his eyes also being curable."

"It's a thought that has come up, like the fact that I will die one day. It's one of those things that I pushed to the back of my brain. Well, now it's out in the open. Let's go tell him."

Daan took the possibility with a restrained excitement. He knew that Maria was scared of his first sight of her face, and he handled it very nicely, telling her that he didn't really mind whether he could see or not. We both knew that this wasn't the truth, but it was a nice lie anyway. Mind you, when you come to think of it, he didn't know what sight was. It is one of those concepts that one finds impossible to explain to someone who has never experienced it. Vision can only be a concrete fact, it is not something that can be imagined. Abstract vision can only be indulged in by those who have seen, and who have combined sight with acute perception.

We drove into Johannesburg the next day to interview Doctor Teasdale. He was a young man of about twenty-eight, and his practice was still growing. I was surprised at the length of his hair and his jaunty manner, so far removed from the pompous airs that most specialists display. I was aware, in looking at him, that although he was less than half my age, he was as highly qualified as it would ever be possible for him to be in his chosen field, and, for the first time since Dawid's death, I was aware of my own age.

A lot of water had flowed under the bridge since 1915, when I first saw the light of day. Daan himself had been born only six years after me, and I shudder slightly at the thought of someone seeing, for the first time, at nearly my own age. The problem, as Doctor Teasdale had pointed out to us after he had read through the case history, was whether the optic nerves that transmitted the message of sight to the brain were sufficiently active after all those years of blindness. Once those nerves have atrophied, to put it bluntly, they were out permanently.

What had been discovered were ways of testing even the faintest of reactions, that had in times past been hidden and unknown, with the result that an entire new group of patients with extremely limited visual reactions could now be treated, and a certain percentage of them could be given sight by the new procedures. Doctor Teasdale took Daan through his paces with every possible test available in Johannesburg, and, in the light of his experience at the laboratory at Pacific, he was able to make a comparative diagnosis: That Daan had a chance of regaining his sight.

He had obviously not been blind at birth, but soon after, according to Doctor Cloete's notes, he had suffered an infection which had been transmitted to him by his mother. This infection had resulted in damage to the corneas, and, although it had been adequately treated, the response to the medication had been slow, with the result that it had been impossible to do anything about the infant Daan's blindness. Doctor Teasdale must have known of the nature of the infection, and he tried to keep it from Daan by a description of "certain types of bacteria," but Daan would not be put off. He insisted on the full truth because, he said, he wanted Maria to know. Doctor Teasdale told him that it would be better if young Doctor Cloete, the family physician, explained the matter to him. Daan then surprised all of us by saying:

"I know it was gonorrhoea, so it's unnecessary for you to beat about the bush. One of the first things I did was to read up on the causes of blindness in children born in the early twenties, when the silver nitrate treatment was still not as universal as it is now. When I questioned Doctor Cloete about it, he told me the whole story. It means nothing to me. It's only a fact, and I find a lot of so-called facts boring."

"I'm still not going to say anything to you about it," said Doctor Teasdale. "It's a skeleton in the cupboard, and it's better for it to stay right there. If you have to discuss it, it's better to do so with Doctor Cloete. I doubt if he will be very pleased with me if he found out that I was discussing confidential matters from his late father's files with second-generation patients, in the presence of people who are not members of the family. There are a dozen infections that could have caused your problem, and it's unnecessary for us to discuss them at all. They are, as you say, hardly interesting, and I agree with your assessment. As for Major van der Kolff needing to know, I doubt if she, with her years of experience as an army nurse, will be in the slightest bit interested."

"Only a drip would take gonorrhoea seriously," quipped Maria.

"I still don't think that puns are funny," said Daan. "So, that's all settled, and you can carry on Doctor, sorry about the interruption."

Then Doctor Teasdale got down to Daan's case, and told us that he would attempt corneagraph surgery. There was a chance that the optic nerves and the miniature blood vessels were still alive, capable of sight. He wasn't able to say how much was left. It appeared that one of the eyes had more of a chance than the other, because, by testing as thoroughly as possible, he had been able to determine the possibility of "life" in one eye only; the right one. The left eye appeared to have been damaged in some way quite different from the damage to its counterpart, and he had been unable to detect any life in it at all. It was possible that there was life in it, but Daan would have to go to America, where the measuring instruments were available, for diagnosis and an evaluation before anything more definite could be said. Daan was all for just trying the immediate possibility, "and," he said to Doctor Teasdale, "we'll keep the left one as a spare, just in case."

Once again, as had been the case with Doctor Borchard, the neurosurgeon, Doctor Teasdale was impatient to get going, but corneagraph surgery as well as corneal transplants are involved processes which needed the services of a considerable team specialising in all sorts of tissue matching and related subjects, and, in any case, there was a long waiting list, as donors were few and far between. We were all immediately willing to donate an eye, which, for some silly reason, seemed to make Daan quite emotional, but Doctor Teasdale said that such drastic steps were hardly necessary. The whole thing would be fixed within a few weeks, and he had every hope that Daan would be given some form of sight, no matter how slight.

There were quite fantastic new lenses, as technology in that field had not been idle either, and with the restoration of a little sight, plus a combination of lenses, there was every reason to be optimistic about things. He stressed the eye's proneness to infection, and the risks involved, but Daan was quite willing to go through with the operation. Doctor Teasdale also prepared him for the possibility of failure, as Daan's was an unusual case, perhaps unique. Three days after the operation the bandages would be taken off, and, even if everything had gone off successfully, there would be very little actual vision at that stage. There would be a very gradual improvement during the next three weeks, and, at some stage during that time, he would be able to see quite well. Then it was typical that sight again deteriorated to a stage of near blindness before the final improvement to a fixed norm.

Daan was taken back to the farm and the next month was one of intense excitement for him. He just could not wait to get to the hospital. He spoke of nothing else, and his enthusiasm for the weeks and perhaps months of pain that lay ahead was quite extraordinary. Usually, the sightless, ex-spastic, and there are very few of them, are inclined to lethargy, requiring even specially made equipment to keep their heads in position while their eyes are being tested. Daan was just the opposite, because, as all of us suspected, there was a fount of something more than just everyday wisdom behind his blindness. He was a man of the spirit, and he had found a world within his world that, I at least thought, was a greater world than the one I knew, and I was envious of it.

I was to learn, later, that people who are spastic, especially children, all had this spiritual quality to them, and that, no matter how abnormal their speech or appearance might be, they are never really upsetting, because there is some inner light there, in their eyes or their expressions somewhere that seems to come directly from the soul.

While he exercised his body with new delight at the control over his muscles and his walking, he spoke of little else but the day when he would be able to see Maria and all the things of the world that he had only heard of. This was a prospect that terrified my sister. She had made up her mind that Daan would never see her, and I wasn't able to do or say anything to make her change her mind. She was quite determined about it, and I could see a tragedy developing. I knew that she meant what she said. If Daan could ever see again it would be the end of their relationship, and she had sworn me to secrecy.

So, while Daan was waiting for Doctor Teasdale to call him into the hospital, she was making her own preparations. Her things had been packed, and she was waiting. It must have been a period of anguish for her. She was waiting, as impatiently as Daan, hoping that he would be able to see, because she loved him and wanted everything for him that life had to give, but she knew that, the moment he could see, she would leave. I often wonder if she did not sometimes wish that Daan would not have a successful operation, but that didn't seem likely. She was not that kind of person. No, she must have wanted it for him, although it spelt, for her, the end of her life's happiness.

I don't know if I should have kept quiet about it to Daan. It may have been better if I had broken my promise to her and told him of her intentions. But, knowing him, I believe that he would just have cancelled the arrangements for the operation and left things as they were. He was the last person in the world to cause Maria any distress and, had he known of the pain that she must have gone through whenever he mentioned the operation and all that he wished of it, he would never have spoken of it again, nor would he have gone through with it.

So we were in danger of the classic situation developing in which two people could destroy each other because of love, and

I was right in the middle, having been the cause of the hope in the first place. I thought of telephoning or going to see Doctor Teasdale and telling him of the whole thing. Perhaps he could fix it so that Daan's best vision would be blurred and out of focus, so that the world would look softly lovely to him, and Maria would be beautiful. But I knew, even as I thought of it, that Doctor Teasdale was too much of a gentleman to do such things, he had far too much respect for his work to do a deliberately shoddy job for the sake of emotional considerations. He wasn't interested in the "quality of life" that some of the new doctors advocated; to him sight was life, and the quality of sight was synonymous with the quality of life. And I suppose he would be right in that. A man must believe in the thing to which he devotes his life, or his life isn't worth living. The moment he sells out, he's finished, because of the mirror on the wall when he shaves himself. I often wonder if that is the reason why so many beards are being worn today, but then I remember that their wearers generally comb them into shape with great care. Watch out, I would warn, for a man with an unkempt beard and scruffy hair.

We had this lovely girl, my sister Maria, who was more beautiful than any person I knew, except for my Dawid, and this wonderful emergent personality in Daan. We had a deep and glorious love affair, the envy and scandal of a district stretching thirty miles in all directions. We had modern science doing its best thing, relieving people of their symptoms, making of Daan a modern-day Lazarus risen, but, in spite of all these enormous factors working together at exactly the right time, one more favour from fate would be too much, and the whole structure of happiness and personal fulfilment would collapse like a hut of straw in a small breeze.

Often I would sit in my little personal chapel, and sometimes I even prayed to God for guidance, I who didn't really believe. People thought me pious in my later years, after my sister and I had stopped using bad language, but I never really believed in God, only in Godliness. The Godliness of some of the people I had known, first. Then, later, I saw Godliness in all the things of the earth, all its people and its animals and insects, its rocks, trees and grasses. I became an African, and I felt a kinship with people like Mina and Dawid far beyond the love that I had had for them, in my own way, previously. I am always sorry that it came to me so late in life. I would have liked to be Dawid's real wife, spiritually, while he had lived. So the meaning of the little chapel became known to me very late in life, and I knew why Dawid had given it to me. Sometime, he knew, I would sit in it and understand him, and we would communicate with each other. Although he lay beneath the hooves of his farmyard animals, with Bettina by his side, there was another Dawid, who had been a tree under whose branches I had spent some of the days of my life.

With this realisation I came to understand the strong simplicity of Daan, and I was able to once again kick my sister in the arse (I know that I have stopped using swear-words, and I promise I won't again).

"Maria, you're being very stupid," I told her. "And I have been too. Daan has grown like a tree. He doesn't understand any other kind of growth. And he will look at you as if you are a tree as well. He's not a person, he's an organic growth, and he thinks like one. He's as near to a plant as he is to a person. I like to think that he isn't ever going to be a person, as we know people. He's an ecological being, rooted to the plants that were his brothers when he was a little boy. Those were the family and friends that Bettina created for him, and that Mina could understand with him. Those shapes his father made, and their textures, were not just playthings, they were alive for him, and that's why he is what he is. That sweetness in him isn't just something that he inherited from his father . . . oh, a lot of it was, I admit, but most of it grew as a leaf or a flower grows. For him, you aren't what we generally regard as a human being, you are a tree, a shape and a texture, to which he has responded like a wild thing that grows on the plains. We, as people, can't really understand Daan, but we can love him, as we love the sights and sounds of the world around us. He isn't a retarded throw-back who will settle for anything; he's a man of the future, who has pruned away all the unessentials from his life, so that only the basic, lovely tree remains standing. You've been a little scorched by lightning, and the pruning has been a little rough, but you'll do, as a tree to grow next to."

"Thanks, Ryna," she said. "I'll think about it."

One day, about a week before he went to hospital, Daan spoke to both of us.

"I know," he said, "that Maria is planning something drastic. I know because I can feel it as a grassland knows the drought is threatening. So, I tell you, if you leave me, Maria, I will die, because I need you. We are not divisible. Don't let her do anything silly, Maryna, I trust you to be my eyes until then."

On the day that Daan was taken into hospital for surgery, I stuck very closely to her. We had to wait three days after the operation, and then the bandages were removed. Doctor Teasdale was alone when it was done because he didn't want a lot of "over-emotional bloody women mucking about in the ward while he was busy." He made us wait downstairs, in the foyer of the nursing home, among the old magazines and the smell of disinfectant polish, while he evaluated the results of his work. He came downstairs and took Maria's hand.

"He's going to be fine," he said. "Everything is as planned. In just a month or so he will be able to see you, clear as daylight."

"That was cruel of you, Doctor," said Maria. "You must know how much I dread the thought of it?"

"I couldn't care less about you and your dreads," he said. "You're not my patient. Daniel Cilliers is, and I have his interests at heart. He wants to see you, and that's the only reason why he wants to see. I wonder if you will be cruel enough to deny him the pleasure?"

"You call looking at me a pleasure?" she asked. "Are you bloody blind, doctor?"

"Anything he sees will be beautiful for him. But you must remember, you are going to be his norm. I'm going to be very cruel to you now, but try to think of it in this way, he doesn't know any better, you're his dream of beauty, fixed by his auditory and tactile experiences of you, and those far outweigh the sense of sight. Also, there's a hell of a lot of you that's beautiful. Remember, the face is only about one hundredth of the surface area of the body. Take lips, nose, eyes, take their measurement, and their relation to cheeks, forehead and chin, and you'll find that especially with your lovely eyes, there's very little of you that's ugly, when you consider that the whole of physical prettiness is only about one per cent of beauty. I'll not have you insulting my patient, Major. He's waiting to see you now. You're going to be out of focus for some weeks, in focus for a few days, and out again for about a month after that. As he sees you today, for the first time, softly beautiful, full of pain, trepidation, fear, tenderness and love, he will remember you for the rest of his life. I repeat, I envy him, because he is about to go through one of the great experiences of a man's life."

That day, Maria and I drove back to the farm, and she unpacked her suitcases, and made ready the house for his return.

20

MINA

All of a sudden Baas Daan could see, he could laugh, and run, and there was a new life on the farm. In only a few years, so few that they went by like a dream, he was a whole man. I remember the day of the wedding, when he and Nurse Maria got married. It was the last thing that the Reverend Doctor Webb did at Skeerpoort, before he was found dead in his cottage one morning, when he had not been seen for a day or two. He must have been very happy to marry those two, because he didn't like scandal in the town. He never liked people to talk about the private things that was the business of the people of the Great House only. My own man, Adam Long, also died in the same week that the Reverend George Webb was buried, and I don't know, they say he drank too much, and made his life shorter, but if I had ever told him that he would have given me a clout on the ear. He was a strong man to the end, and we, you know, did it, three days before he went through the road-worthy, as he called dying. I don't know what was wrong with Adam Long. He had just had his gallon, one Sunday, when he said to me: "Hell man, Mina, I feel blerrie crook." Then he lay down on his bed and stopped living.

They say that they are going to make a kind of hospital here, in Skeerpoort, out of the piece of ground with the little farm chapel that belongs to Nurse Maryna, and that all sorts of children will come here to be fixed up, or just taken care of, who were like Baas Daan, when he was young. They call them slap-sticks, or something like that, and I always thought he was jus' paraletic, like Adam Long used to get when he put a whole gallon down in three hours.

Nurse Maryna now sits in the little chapel for a long time, nearly every day. She tells me she knows about what to talk about, and how to shut up, which is a big thing to know about. She also knows about the trees, and the growing things, and she will understand why we, the Balobedu tribe of the Rain Queen, Modjadji, are the keepers of the sacred forest of cycads, that was old before the first man came to the world. The Xhosas have no trees left, nor the Zulus, and their homelands are torn by the wind and rain. We, the Balobedu, know that we are the children of the earth, and that all the things of the earth are our brothers. Nothing belongs to us. We belong to one another. In the Book of the Saints that old Holy . . . Reverend Webb used to read to us, there was a man who was a Balobedu, his name was Francis, and he was a saint.

Now, Baas Daan has taken over the farm, and he is a married man, so all of the old worries are gone. There is to be a hospital in the chapel field, and little children's voices. Baas Daan and his new Missus, Major Maria the nurse, who has a certificate just like mine, are going to pay for the hospital, and the government will give some money too. There will be children getting well on the farm again, and I will be able to tell the people about the old days, when there was just one of those children, and I was his nurse. For many years he was nothing, and I was afraid for him, because to be nothing is not to have the spirit in you, so you will never understand what the wind means, or the clouds. He grew out of the nothing time while he was still a young boy, and he let himself come out into the world. All these years I watched him, as you must watch a yellow-wood tree grow, or a cycad. These pine trees that people plant all over the land of the Xhosas and of the Zulus are not really trees. They grow up in twenty years, and then they are cut down to make planks for cheap furniture and doors. Baas Daan grew the right way, slowly for fifty years, and now he is a beautiful tree, ready to be used by the forest around him, and the little trees and shrubs about his roots, and he shadows the frail, tender shoots, so that they are not scorched. He will allow the long embrace of the twisted lianas around his trunk, and they will grow together, like a weld. He is a holy one of the Balobedu, and while he makes his space in the sacred forest, I will sit at the side of my hut, and move around it with the sun, for the years that are left; and, slowly, as the moments, hours, days, months, seasons and years go by, I will empty my head of all the years of my life, so that there will be no yesterdays to remember with pain, or tomorrows to face with fear and uncertainty. There will only be todays, and the feel of the sun on my face.